HIDDEN GAMES

HALLOWED SAINTS UNIVERSITY

BRANDY SILVER

Copyright © 2024 by Grey Valor Publishing

All rights reserved.

No part of this book may be reproduced in any form or by any electronic or mechanical means, including information storage and retrieval systems, without written permission from the author, except for the use of brief quotations in a book review.

PROLOGUE

The squealing of tires rang in my ears, and the stench of burned rubber was so strong I could taste it. My head jarred as our car rolled over and over on the small road, hurtling toward the Ocoee River. The front windshield shattered, glass spraying all over us. Dad grunted from the driver's seat, and Mom yelped as our car flew off the road and splashed into a deep part of the river, the sound like a large tidal wave rolling to shore.

Wind blew through the front of the car, and my stomach leapt into my throat. The car jerked and stilled.

My brain short-circuited. *What the hell happened? Did we miss the deer?*

An agonized groan from the front seat slammed me back into the moment.

We had to move if we were going to get out of this alive.

"Mom!" I screamed as I shakily attempted to unbuckle my seat belt. The damn thing wouldn't unlatch.

The engine was still humming, but that wouldn't last much

longer. As the car sank, the reality of our situation made my head spin.

I had to get my shit together, or we'd all die.

I broke free from my constraints and climbed between the front seats of our 2018 Honda Accord. I slipped and hit my head on the center console, but the pain never came because of the adrenaline pulsing through me.

Turning to Mom, I pushed the button to roll down the passenger window, knowing that when we were submerged, I wouldn't be able to. At this moment, we were still above the water, but not for long.

"Wake up." I smacked her face. No matter what it took, I had to get them out.

Her head jerked, but that was all I got. Her eyelids didn't even flutter. Blood poured from her head wound, coating her sandy-blonde hair with crimson.

Dad will know what to do. He always told me to take care of my mother, but it wasn't working. I turned toward him...and my world tilted as vomit crept up my throat. A large piece of glass was lodged in his throat.

No.

Dad was gone.

Ignoring the blood, I checked for a pulse. Nothing, not even a wheeze like he was gasping for breath.

My throat dried, and tears burned my eyes, but I didn't have time to lose it.

Not now.

I focused on Mom, unbuckling her seat belt just as the water met the bottom of the window and began trickling into the car.

We had to get out of here fast. I slapped Mom harder, and her eyelids fluttered ever so slightly.

Progress.

"We're sinking. We have to go!" My voice broke, but I held my tears at bay. "Mom." I propelled my hand forward, but she caught my wrist before I could make contact with her skin.

"I awaaake," she slurred, which caused me to worry even more.

She probably had a concussion or worse, but at least she was alive. "Then get moving."

"Yur fathr," she said and turned her head toward him.

"Mom, no." But it was too late.

Her breath caught.

"He's gone. I checked." Somehow, I managed to keep those words intelligible.

"Gedd," she said and started shaking, but she jerked her head as if she were clearing it. "Ot." She gestured to the window.

I wanted to argue and say *you first*, but now the river poured inside, and the car was sinking fast. It might be easier to pull her out after me so she wouldn't have to work too hard.

I half climbed, half swam through the missing windshield frame. The cold water of the Ocoee sent shivers jolting through my body. I turned back to the car, ready to help Mom out.

She moved erratically, not like her usual self. I helped pull her body through the window, but when she finally broke free, she sank underwater.

I dove under, searching for her. I found her only a few feet down, her eyes already closed.

No. I couldn't lose another parent.

I wrapped my arms around her waist and kicked, trying to pull her up, but I wasn't a strong swimmer. We both went under.

The harder I tried, the more oxygen I used. But I refused to give up. I kept tugging at her until my body went slack and my mind grew hazy.

Dad said going rafting would challenge all of us. And boy, he wasn't wrong.

Everything went black.

CHAPTER ONE

Footsteps tapped toward my room, and the annoying beep from the machine monitoring my heartbeat grew faster. For two days, I'd drifted in and out of consciousness, and I wished I could stay asleep. I couldn't even face the handful of friends from the University of Tennessee at Chattanooga who'd come by to check on me.

I didn't want to talk to anyone or have their questioning gazes weighing on me as they wondered but didn't ask what happened.

My reality wasn't worth remembering.

Not anymore.

Moisture burned my eyes, and the back of my throat constricted as I fought to hold tears at bay. This wasn't the time to cry. The beloved Tennessee senator, Patrick McHale, was on his way to my hospital room.

Known for his work on Veteran's Affairs and the US House Committee on Transportation and Infrastructure, the senator had a picture-perfect life with his Stepford-esque wife and cheerleading, charity-focused eighteen-year-old daughter. They were the equivalent of a Hallmark family.

Beautiful.

Powerful.

Everything people aspired to be.

But not me. Not anymore. All I wanted was for Mom and Dad to be alive. To hear their laughter once again, to dance with Mom in the rain and play board games with them while we laughed and accused each other of cheating.

I struggled to accept that they were dead. We'd just finished an incredible day of rafting down the Ocoee and had been heading home, sunburned and smiling.

We couldn't have known it would be our last experience together as a family.

If we'd hit the deer instead of swerving to avoid it, all three of us would be alive.

And if I'd been a stronger swimmer, my mom would be here beside me. Apparently, after I'd lost my grip on her, she'd been sucked away by the strong undercurrent.

I was the sole survivor. I'd failed them both, and all I could do was live with the regret and my memories of them.

If a car hadn't been fairly close behind us and called 911 immediately, I would've died too.

"Is this her room?" a deep, elegant voice asked from outside my door.

"Yes, sir," the nurse who'd been tending to me replied. "We've sent the media away, and we'll be careful to monitor her visitors."

"Good," he said. "Make sure that continues. That girl has been through enough—she doesn't need reporters probing her for details. The best thing for her is to heal and be able to move on with her life, which is why I'm here." He paused. "Please take my card. I'll be paying for any hospital expenses that her insurance doesn't cover."

"Of course, sir," the nurse replied eagerly. "We'll keep the notice to restrict visitation on her records."

"You will do more than that." His voice lowered charmingly. "Do you understand? No one is to talk to her without clearance from me."

My hands turned sweaty, and the beeping of the machine mocked me. In news reports, the senator always seemed nice and charming, but I didn't know what he'd be like in person. Not that I was complaining. A few reporters had barged in yesterday, asking questions that had made me relive the accident over and over again, and I was grateful that wouldn't happen again.

I could still hear the shattering glass and the rush of the water, taste the burned rubber, and feel the chilling wetness. Those things were now ingrained in my mind and would be carried with me forever.

The door to the stark, drab hospital room opened. I ran my fingers through my chestnut-brown hair, trying to tame it. I hadn't brushed my hair since the morning before the accident, and I couldn't make myself look in the mirror, afraid of what I might see.

Pulling the thin white sheet over my faded blue hospital gown, I straightened up, hoping to give the appearance of being somewhat put together.

One of Mom's favorite things to say was, "Fake it till you make it, Evie." She swore that, even when you felt broken inside, if you appeared confident, everyone would be fooled.

I'd never challenged her on it; I always noticed a sadness in her eyes when she told me that. I wanted to know what caused it, but I never asked. I wouldn't make her talk about something that clearly caused her pain, so I'd change the subject and make her laugh instead. She'd had a right to her secrets...the same as I did mine.

The senator stepped into the room, one polished black Oxford at a time, his dark eyes focused on me. He shut the door softly, the skin around his eyes tightening.

The man was even more good-looking in person than he was on television. Most everyone loved him, but Mom and Dad hadn't. I'd asked them several times what they had against a man they'd never met, and they'd laughed it off and said, sometimes, you just knew. Given they thought the best of nearly everyone, their dislike of him told me everything I needed to know.

He stood in front of me, scanning me like I was a biology project and he was trying to decide where to begin dissecting.

My Southern manners took over. "Please, sit down." I gestured to the chair a few feet behind him.

"No, thank you. I won't stay long." He adjusted his black tie and cleared his throat. "I figure it'd be best if I get to the point. I know you're suffering, and I don't want to overwhelm you even more."

"Okay." I bit my bottom lip and picked at my thin covering. I had no idea why he was here. When the nurse had told me that the senator had requested to visit me, my mind had been blown. I'd never had any interaction with this man, and the only plausible reason I could imagine for his interest was the wreck. But why?

He huffed and shook his head. His jet-black hair was so gelled into place that it didn't budge, which almost made me chuckle. I'd never met a man who used more product than I did.

Maybe it was a rich-people thing. Something I couldn't relate to. All our family money had gone toward Mom's chemo. She'd had aggressive breast cancer, and we'd spent every dime on her treatments. It was worth it—she'd been in remission. But that meant nothing now.

"I'm so sorry for your loss." The senator exhaled loudly. "From what I've learned, you don't have any other family. You're all alone. Is that correct?"

If the machine weren't beeping, I would've bet money that my heart stopped. I hadn't known him for a full minute, and he was talking about my harsh new reality. "Yes." I winced as pain seized my chest and my eyes grew heavy.

Sleep. That was what I wanted, but I had this intimidating man hovering over me, so I forced the next words out. "Thank you for your condolences. It means a lot."

"I hope you'll forgive my intrusion, but when I heard about what happened, I felt compelled to come here after I dug a little deeper." His irises darkened, and a sad smile etched his face. "I know that your family home is heavily mortgaged and that you've taken out student loans to cover your costs at UTC."

I stiffened, and a lump formed in my throat. I hadn't known about the house. I'd known finances were tight since my parents had gone into debt due to Mom's cancer, but they hadn't hinted they were that bad off.

"So... I thought I could help you out. Ease your financial burden." He shifted, seeming uneasy, his gaze holding mine.

My stomach churned, and my lungs burned with each breath. "Because of where the wreck was located?" That was all I could think of. Near the place we'd flipped off the road, a part of it had been sunken in, and there'd been press about the highway needing repairs. The state hadn't gotten to it yet. I remembered seeing the senator on the air, talking about infrastructure and how they were going to fix it soon.

"Not fully. The accident wasn't caused by the road, but facts don't matter if the public believes there was more at play."

He hung his head, sincerity flowing off him. "Either way, I...I'm so damn sorry."

For the first time, something stirred inside me. I enjoyed helping others. That was why I wanted to become a psychologist—to help children like me find the home they deserved. Help them find the mental capacity to thrive in their situation, whatever that was. I'd been so lucky that Mom and Dad had adopted me, but so many others hadn't been. I didn't like focusing on myself, preferring to be the one helping other people. And right now, seeing him hurting took me away from my own pain. "It's not your fault. Like you said, it was a deer, not the road. You don't owe me anything." Had he driven two hours south to Chattanooga just because he was worried I might try to change the story and blame the state? I wouldn't do anything like that.

He flinched and then laughed humorlessly. "I wouldn't go that far."

My skin crawled, though I wasn't sure why. He was being nice, but his laugh sounded haunted. "I'm sorry?"

"For what?" His brows quirked.

I hadn't meant it as an apology, though he apparently thought that was the case. "No, I meant, why wouldn't you go that far?"

"Oh." He nodded and waved a hand. "Forgive me. I'm just tired. I had a full day."

He hadn't answered the question, and I didn't want to push. Maybe my concussion was messing with my comprehension. "Of course." I forced a smile, though I wasn't sure it stuck.

An awkward silence descended, and I glanced at my hands and picked at a hangnail on my thumb. I wasn't sure what to say, and he didn't seem ready to leave. Maybe he thought I wanted him to stay?

I opened my mouth to tell him to go just as he said, "I want to run something by you."

I stared at him. Why in the world would a senator ask me *anything*? I scoffed quietly and glanced at him. His expression was dead serious. "Okay."

"I've been wanting to do something for a while now." He strolled to the uncomfortable-looking chair in the room and sat gracefully. "To give back to the community."

I tilted my head but remained quiet, unsure how to respond.

He leaned forward, placing his elbows on his knees. "And *this* horrible situation presented the opportunity."

I bit my bottom lip and wanted to avert my gaze. But I refused. Whatever he had to say, I had to watch him say it. "I'm listening." My heart thundered.

"I would like to offer you an opportunity." He steepled his hands and leaned back. "Something that could help you tremendously for the rest of your life."

My lungs seized as I tried to think through every possibility. I couldn't land on anything I needed except the one thing I knew was impossible—bringing my parents back to life.

What I wouldn't give to hear Mom making fun of Dad for his off-key singing and Dad singing louder in retaliation, causing all of us to erupt in a fit of giggles. Though we'd never had a lot of money, we had so much love for each other. So much so that I was never even tempted to look for my birth parents.

I realized he was studying me, waiting for my answer. "I...I don't understand."

He stood and started pacing, his face growing animated. "I want to pay off your student loans and transfer you to Hallowed Saints University for your senior year of college."

I blinked, trying to replay what he'd just said. It couldn't be what I'd just heard. My concussion *had* to be messing with me, big time. "I'm sor–" I cut myself off. He would think I was apologizing again. "Can you repeat that?"

A blinding smile was his response, and he chuckled. "You heard me, Evie. I want to take care of your student loans and pull some strings to get you into Hallowed Saints University for your senior year. I did some research and Hallowed Saints has one of the top undergrad psychology programs in the country. Studying at HSU will help to get you into an amazing grad school. And with your credits from UTC, you'll be able to graduate on schedule."

The room spun, and my stomach roiled. "That's a nice offer." More than a nice offer. Hallowed Saints was a small, elite private university northeast of Knoxville that many dreamed of attending. Few could actually afford it, and even fewer got accepted. "But one year there would cost more than the debt I've already racked up from student loans at UTC. I truly appreciate the offer, but I'll have to decline."

"Oh dear. In my excitement, I wasn't clear." He walked to the edge of my bed and patted my arm as he continued, "I will pay the tuition for your senior year at HSU. You'll be able to attend whatever graduate program you wish for psychology, and you'll have everyone begging you to intern with them. It'll be the best of both worlds."

None of this made sense. This had to be some sort of dream…no, nightmare…no… I wasn't sure what to consider this. Maybe a blend of the two, but my answer was crystal clear. "I appreciate it, but I can't accept. It's too much."

Yet, a part of me wanted to. If I did, I wouldn't have to go back to the home I'd shared with my parents, where their ghosts would haunt me. The thought of a fresh start somewhere—anywhere—while I healed was so damn appealing.

He winced—slightly, and it disappeared quickly as if I'd imagined it. Hell, I probably had.

"This is something I've been wanting to do, and I've been looking for the perfect candidate. Someone smart and deserving. After what life just threw at you, I want it to be you." He dropped his hands and removed a business card from his pocket. "Think about it. There's no expiration date." He stilled and grimaced. "No, that's not true. There is. We need enough time to rush the paperwork through and have everything in place because classes start in three weeks. So, give me an answer by end of day tomorrow."

I took the thick, fancy, cream business card and rubbed it with my thumb. "Are you even sure they would take me this late?"

"I'm on the board, a huge donor, an alumnus, and I've already informed them of my intent. All I need is your yes and the completed paperwork to make it official."

Never in my wildest dreams would an opportunity like this present itself again. This didn't happen to people like me, yet here I was. There had to be a catch.

His eyes twinkled like he already knew my answer. "Call me, Evie. Say yes. Let me do this for you." He strolled to the door and paused. "I'll be waiting for your answer." Then he left.

I lay back and tried to work through everything. Somehow, saying yes felt like agreeing to something greater…something I didn't comprehend.

Something like hope burgeoned in my bruised chest.

CHAPTER TWO

A loud thump startled me from my sleep. I reached over and snatched my cell phone from the plastic end table I'd bought for this place. I glanced at my phone and groaned. It was three a.m., and my new roommates were giggling loudly upstairs.

I flopped back onto the bed, staring at the unfinished ceiling in my basement room. The heat outside, a signature of August weather in southeast Tennessee, smothered me. Even though Hallow, Tennessee, was at the edge of the Great Smoky Mountains and about fifty miles north of Knoxville, you'd never be able to tell in the summer. The heat was just miserable. Still, the humidity was a little less intense because the town was in a more mountainous area than back home in Chattanooga.

I hadn't initially thought I'd accept the senator's offer. But being in my childhood home had been so difficult. Everywhere I looked had been a constant reminder of Dad and Mom. Every night, I'd sworn I could hear them coming home, hear their laughter from the bedroom.

So, I said yes. When I'd sold the house, I'd texted my

college friends a quick goodbye. Using every penny of my parents' estate, I'd hurried here to secure the basement room in this rental house with two other students who were attending Ridge University on the other side of the city. The place was old and needed some work, but it was better than living on the streets, and splitting the rent with two other students made it something I could more easily afford, though I'd need a job on top of my heavy course load. It was my senior year at a brand-new university, and I couldn't help but wonder if I'd been stupid for taking the senator up on his offer.

I knew what Mom would have said. She'd have scoffed and shaken her head, saying, "Don't look a gift horse in the mouth, Evie."

My vision blurred as unshed tears burned my eyes. It'd been over three weeks since I'd lost them, and the pain wasn't getting any better. Instead, it was worse.

More giggles sounded from upstairs, followed by loud banging. They were going to keep me up all night at this rate, so I swiped my earbuds from the side table and put them in, picked one of my favorite songs that fit the moment—Taylor Swift's "You're On Your Own, Kid"—and tried to go to sleep.

AFTER TOSSING and turning for the next three hours, I finally threw off the covers and put my feet on the laminate floor that didn't come close to passing for wood. I needed to get ready and head over to Hallowed Saints University for a media interview with the senator, buy my books, then search for a job.

Unfortunately, selling my parents' house hadn't left me with much of anything. Between all the time Dad had taken off for Mom's cancer treatments and Mom having to quit her job, our house had been heavily mortgaged. Insurance had refused to cover Mom's treatment, and my parents' retirement savings had been tapped out. Every last cent of the sale had taken care of the mortgage, I had no money to my name.

I flipped on the black lamp on the end table and glanced around the room. It was large, essentially the same size as the ground floor of the house, and I had a small bathroom in the corner all to myself. I'd be able to purchase a cheap desk and could do schoolwork down here, but the basement had its flaws. Mainly, the washer and dryer were down here, I had no closet, and the walls weren't well insulated, which meant I needed to pick up a fan for the summer and a space heater for the winter. Either way, I'd figure out a way to survive for the next year. For that short amount of time, I should be able to handle pretty much anything.

I shuffled to my duffel bag and searched for my best outfit. Senator McHale had mentioned there would be a few reporters on campus to interview us about my attendance and to be prepared. I was quite certain that meant I needed to dress my best since I might be on camera. It was one of the reasons I'd been reluctant to accept his offer—I didn't want to be the face of his charity. But that was just prideful.

Although, when he'd talked about covering my room and board, I'd put my foot down. The tuition was enough.

I found my white button-down shirt, which wasn't too wrinkled, and a black skirt. Simple, conservative, not overstated. This ensemble would help me remain unremarkable, and the reporters might not focus on me. I quickly took a shower, got dressed, fixed my hair and makeup, and slid on my black, strappy sandals. Though my small heels would've been better, I had at least a mile to walk and wanted to be comfortable.

I glanced in the small bathroom mirror. I'd pulled half my hair into a braid at the top of my head and left the back falling down in waves. My steel-blue eyes appeared gray with the light smoky eyeliner and eyeshadow that I used. I darkened my lashes and painted my lips a soft pink, just enough color that I wouldn't look washed out if recorded.

Satisfied, I walked to the door that separated my room from the steps and then tiptoed up the old, creaky wooden stairs. Haven and Leah had finally stopped giggling about an hour ago, not that it had done much good. I'd already been counting down to the alarm by then.

When I reached the top of the stairs, I stepped into the small kitchen. I opened the fridge door to get one of my yogurts, only to find the space filled to the brim with box wine and PBA. No wonder they'd been giggling all night.

After locating my blackberry yogurt, I snatched a spoon and headed across the room to the small square kitchen table right in front of a window.

A low moan came from the living room, and I popped my head over the threshold to find both of them passed out.

Haven's long ash-blonde hair had fanned out around her head, and she was snoring faintly as she slept on the black pleather couch while Leah lay on the floor underneath her. Leah was curled into the fetal position, her copper-brown hair hanging in her face like a blanket. Part of me wanted to wake them up and help them into their own rooms, but another part was afraid to disturb them. They'd both seemed like okay girls at first, but they were clearly partiers.

Instead, I opted to finish my meal, took the throws from the back of the couch, and covered both of them up. Then I turned and left, locking the front door behind me.

My phone dinged. Beth, a college friend, had texted me.

Beth: Good luck. Have a great day! Tell me everything when you get home.

I cringed. I'd definitely not be following through on that.

All it would do was lead to more questions about visits and reminders of my parents.

I noted the time and scowled. I had twenty minutes to walk a mile, which wouldn't be an issue if it weren't for the sweltering heat that already had me sweating. I couldn't be late, so I picked up my pace, hoping to get there before anyone else.

I'D BEEN WORRIED it would be hard to find the school, but that wasn't the case.

I walked a few blocks off the main road to avoid any chance of Senator McHale seeing me as he drove in and wondered what I'd gotten myself into. He'd told me where to park this morning, so he was under the impression I had a car. One that I didn't want him to realize was wrong.

The neighborhood around the rental house was suspect at best, even with the sun out this morning. However, I hadn't found anything else I could afford. It wouldn't be so bad if I had a vehicle, but that was a luxury beyond my means.

The sun rose high in the cloudless sky, mocking me. The sunbeams were already causing sweat to bead on my forehead and neck. I held my phone and watched the map for directions, and soon, a gigantic brick wall appeared on my left, just past the main road—this had to be the Hallowed Saints University campus.

From what I saw in the pictures, the wall surrounded the entire school—wrought iron or a privacy fence wasn't fancy enough, I suppose. From what the website said, the Hallowed Saints campus was one hundred ninety-six acres, which wasn't large by most university standards, but it didn't need to be, given the small, highly exclusive class sizes.

Soon, the gray roofs of the university buildings jutted over the top of the fence. The brick of the buildings blended in with the wall.

I reached the road to the main entrance, which I couldn't have missed even if I'd wanted to, considering the gigantic wrought iron gate ahead with the letters HSU cut into it.

I quickened my pace, eager to get there. I didn't want Senator McHale to see me walking in. Luckily, the gate was open since this was move-in weekend for new and returning students who hadn't stayed on campus over the summer.

I passed the great lawn to the left of the main entrance, and as soon as I saw the area in front of the library to the right, my stomach sank. The road between the great lawn and the library was packed full of media vans, and reporters had congregated on the lawn in front of the library, mics and camera recorders all on hand. I'd thought there might be only a few, but I'd been so wrong. It looked like both local and national news were here.

Worse, already standing in front of the four-story library on the matching brick sidewalk stood Senator McHale, his wife, and his daughter, as well as the most gorgeous guy I'd ever seen. They smiled and waved at the cameras, and as I breezed down the road, the senator's eyes locked on me.

A small frown tugged the corners of his lips. Sweat dripped down my chest and into my bra. Great. Not only had he seen me walking in, but I was going to most definitely stink.

One of the reporters in the back turned, her Caribbean-blue eyes homing in on me. She beamed as she grabbed her cameraman's arm and tugged him toward me.

The world seemed to tilt as more of them turned in my direction. Somehow, I managed to keep my legs propelling me forward. At least, I thought I did because I kept moving closer to the library.

Meeting me halfway, the reporter started, "Hi. This is Michelle with News Channel Ten. Are you Evie Stone, the lucky girl the senator has provided with a full ride to the exclusive Hallowed Saints University?"

My stomach roiled, and I swallowed. I wanted to say no, but I couldn't do that to the senator. Not after everything he'd done for me. "Yes, I am."

More cameras swung in my direction as the reporters in front realized they were missing out on time with me. I could *feel* their cameras zooming in.

I straightened my shoulders, trying not to look overwhelmed. I'd never experienced anything like this, nor had I been prepared for how much chaos surrounded me. I probably should've been; the senator and his family were equivalent to celebrities in Tennessee, between the famous parties they threw and the modeling gig their daughter had finished just last week. Katherine McHale was becoming quite the social media influencer; even I had heard of her.

I tried to walk through the masses, but I stopped moving forward as the reporters piled on me. My heart pounded, and the world seemed to close in, constant questions being thrown my way.

All of a sudden, the sexy guy who'd been standing with the senator's family came plowing through the crowd. His dark-golden-brown hair was slightly messy, though the look seemed intentional, and he wore a white polo shirt with the school's mascot—a gold jaguar standing over HSU in royal purple—on the chest. Even though the shirt wasn't tight, it was clear how lean and muscular he was underneath. That was when it hit me who he was—the other Tennessee senator's son and the school's starting quarterback, Carter Grisham.

"Hey, give her some space," he said sternly, his warm-chocolate-brown eyes darkening as he shoved some reporters back to reach me. When he got to my side, he placed an arm around me, and I could see golden flecks in his irises. They resembled honey. "Are you okay? I know this can be overwhelming."

My throat closed, and it wasn't due to the reporters and the crowd. It had everything to do with my hero beside me.

When I didn't respond, he raised a brow.

Great, they were all going to think something was wrong with me. "I'm fine." I blew out a breath. "Sorry."

"Good." He smiled, and I could've sworn my heart stopped. He edged us forward, helping me navigate the crowd.

I forced myself to look away before I did anything stupid. I focused on the ground in front of me so I didn't have to look at the sea of faces. *One foot in front of the other,* I chanted internally. That was an easy task to focus on.

When we reached the steps to join the senator and his family, Senator McHale himself touched my shoulder and stared into my face. He murmured, "Are you okay? I thought you'd drive and come through the back entrance as we discussed."

"Yeah, sorry." My face burned, and I hoped he thought it was from the heat. "I needed a walk. I thought I would arrive early."

"Reporters always arrive hours ahead of time." He smiled, but it looked jaded. "Next time, we'll plan better."

Next time? My stomach turned.

The senator nodded at Carter, and I noticed he hadn't removed his arm. Carter guided me to one side so that he stood between me and the senator's daughter.

"My dear, sweet wife, Lisa, and I," Senator McHale said, placing an arm around his wife, "along with my esteemed colleague Senator Grisham, who couldn't be here today, have selected this very worthy student of psychology as our personal scholarship recipient to HSU. We are covering her tuition and supporting her promising future. When her personal tragedy was brought to our attention, and we learned she'd not only lost both parents but had already dedicated her studies to becoming a psychologist to work with children coping with loss and changing family circumstances, the three of us knew that this was something we wanted to do together."

Lisa beamed at her husband, her muted coral lipstick making her white teeth pop. Her skin was sun-kissed, making her ash-blonde hair almost appear gray. Regardless, she was beautiful, just like her husband and daughter. "It was the right thing to do." She turned toward me with a plastic smile, her brown eyes cold, chilling me to the bone.

She looked at me like she hated me. Yet the senator had made it sound like both of them wanted to help me.

My gaze swung to Katherine, on the other side of Carter, and I immediately regretted it. She wore a simple but trendy navy skirt with a sky-blue blouse that brought out her cobalt eyes. In every way I looked frumpy; she looked put together. Her espresso-brown hair was pulled into a bun with curled tendrils framing her heart-shaped face. The fact that she'd already started a modeling career made sense. She was even more stunning in person than on her social media.

"Miss?" a tall, middle-aged reporter called out.

Senator McHale came to my other side and placed a hand on my shoulder as he answered the question I hadn't even realized the reporter was asking. "Evie Stone."

"Thank you." The reporter nodded. "Miss Stone, how does it feel being given this amazing opportunity that anyone would covet?"

She might as well have punched me in the gut. Her question was cruel, though I was sure that was unintended. "Well, a little surreal. I didn't expect it. And honestly, I didn't expect to be able to complete my senior year at my previous college since my parents died..." My voice cracked as the agony of losing them slammed into me once again.

"Oh, I—" The reporter's eyes widened. "I'm sorry. I didn't mean to upset you."

"Of course you didn't." Senator McHale patted my arm. "But she's going through a lot. As much as she's told me she appreciates this opportunity, I'm sure she would rather it not have happened. That her parents were still alive, and I understand that. Pain like that will take time to heal."

A tear trickled down my face, and I brushed it away. The last thing I needed was to have a meltdown on camera. "But I am very grateful for Senator and Mrs. McHale's generosity as well as Senator Grisham's support."

"That's so heartbreaking." A reporter who had to be fresh out of college placed a hand on her heart. "And Carter, how do you feel about what your father and the McHales decided to do?"

"I think it's amazing." Carter smiled, making my heart stutter. "Unfortunately, Dad wasn't able to be here, which is why I'm here in his stead. But I hope he's watching so he can hear how proud I am that he helped Senator McHale make this happen for Evie after such a tragedy."

The kindness in both his and the reporter's words, along with the senator's supportive touch, had a sob building in my chest. I hadn't intended to make a scene, but I was becoming overwhelmed.

"I hate to interrupt," Katherine said in a babyish voice, "but I think Eve has already had one heck of a day."

I inhaled. Had she purposely mispronounced my name, or was it a true mistake?

Katherine squeezed between Carter and me and laid her head against his arm. "Why don't Carter and I give her a tour of the library? Then we can show her the bookstore and help her find her books."

My chest expanded, loosening the tight coil inside. I glanced at Senator McHale. Getting away from the spotlight would be amazing, but I didn't want to upset him.

"That sounds like a terrific idea, honey." Lisa mashed her lips into what *might* be a look of concern. "You and Carter help her, and your father and I will meet you there."

Grateful to get away, I smiled and nodded my thanks.

Carter took my arm, and we turned and followed Katherine into the library.

As soon as we stepped inside the older brick building, I took in the elegant off-white walls and the crystal chandelier hanging from the center of the ceiling.

Carter turned to me, still clasping my arm, his forehead lined with worry. "Hey, are you okay? I thought you were going to pass out."

"She's fine, Carter," Katherine bit out and squeezed his other arm. "It was just whatever little act Dad put her up to."

My head snapped back, and my lungs froze. "Act? What are you talking about?"

"Oh, you can cut the bullshit with me." Katherine rolled her eyes and huffed. "And stop touching my boyfriend."

I choked and slipped my arm out of Carter's grasp. For all her beauty, she sure was nasty on the inside. I shouldn't have been surprised my parents had been wary of the family.

"Boyfriend?" Carter's voice hardened, and he stepped away from her. "No. *That* was an act. You aren't anything to me. I'm only here to keep up pretenses for our fathers."

Her bottom lip quivered, and he chuckled bleakly. "That shit won't work with me." He shook his head. "You forget that I know how you work."

Her face smoothed out, but her voice softened. "Carter,

you mean a lot to me. I hope you'll see that we can work things out." She sighed, a sad smile filling her face. "Why don't you go ahead to the bookstore? I have something I want to talk to *Evie* here about before we join you."

Carter studied me, and I prayed he was going to stay so I wouldn't be alone with Katherine, but his phone dinged. He removed it from his back pocket and scowled. Then he shrugged, his nose wrinkling. "Whatever. Good luck, new girl." With that, he headed toward the side door and answered, "I asked you not to call me." His tone turned icy. "No, Mom. I made it—" He strolled out the side door, leaving me behind.

Well, apparently, he wasn't concerned with saving me anymore. I almost wanted to call him back, but the coldness that now radiated from him had me biting my tongue.

As soon as we were alone, Katherine pivoted, a snarl on her face.

And once again, I was clueless about what I'd done to set her off.

CHAPTER THREE

Katherine's nostrils flared. She somehow pulled off the angry look while still appearing put together.

She stabbed a long, crimson fingernail into my chest. "I don't know what your endgame is, but I'm not my father. I won't let some broke gold digger blackmail me."

My chest hurt where her finger dug into me, but I schooled my expression. I refused to give her any additional power. And I had to face facts; she was the one with all the control in this situation. *She* belonged here, while I was the one who'd gotten here because of her father. "I don't know what you're talking about. I'm not blackmailing *anyone*."

She dropped her hand and scoffed. "Please. Daddy wouldn't be doing this without a reason. His poll numbers are *amazing*—he doesn't need some charity case to help him politically, so there's definitely something else going on."

I had to shut this down fast for my own survival and peace of mind. "I *am not* blackmailing him." My lungs seized and I froze. "Wait. Did he tell you I was?" That didn't make any sense, but at the same time, it hadn't made sense for him to offer to pay for me to come here, let alone involve the other senator.

Crossing her arms, Katherine leaned back on her heels. "He didn't. But I know my father. The only logical explanation is that you're holding something over him, and I want to know what it is."

A part of me wanted to nudge her shoulders to see if she'd stumble back because I couldn't fathom how she was able to stand in those stiletto heels. Instead, I inhaled, trying to calm my racing heart. "I don't know why he's doing it either. I've been trying to figure it out. All I can tell you is that he visited me out of the blue in the hospital. I didn't ask him to. Hell, I didn't even realize he knew about the accident until he showed up."

Flipping her hair over her shoulder, Katherine pursed her lips. "That doesn't make sense to me either, but you being here is important to Daddy, so I'll play nice and give you a chance. But we aren't hanging out unless it's in front of the cameras. Got it?"

Some of the tension in my stomach eased. She didn't like me, but she seemed willing to at least not be horrible to me. I'd take it. It wasn't like I expected us to be friends anyway, but acquaintances would be nice. "Understood."

"Good. After five minutes, follow me." She whipped around and marched toward the door on the side of the library that Carter had gone through.

When she stepped out, I realized I had no idea where the bookstore even was. I felt stupid... which was silly. I'd never been here, and I had a perfect GPA from my previous college. But something about Katherine made me feel insecure.

I hated it.

My parents had told me that people's imaginations played tricks on them and that things were never as bad as they feared.

Once again, I reached for my phone, ready to call them. To tell them what was happening and that they'd been *so* wrong. But as I held my phone in my hand, I realized I couldn't call. They wouldn't answer.

Tears burned my eyes, and I blinked furiously to hold them back. I was already a sweaty, smelly mess—I didn't need to add mascara streaks to the ever-worsening picture.

I glanced out the library's front doors and saw that the senator and his wife were still talking to the media. Luckily, the doors were tinted, and no one had seen my confrontation with Katherine.

A figure walked toward me from the interior of the library. My vision was still blurry, so all I could make out was a tall, muscular build.

"Hey, are you okay?" the person asked and hurried to me.

I laughed and fanned my hands before my eyes. My mind raced, and my head throbbed. I didn't know how to explain this. "Yeah, sorry. Just a little lost."

"Oh, hey. Happens to the best of us."

Finally, my vision cleared and revealed another gorgeous guy. He wore a casual, short-sleeved navy-blue shirt, and part of a tattoo peeked out from under one sleeve. He also carried an HSU royal-purple backpack.

My hand itched to lift the sleeve so I could see the rest of the tattoo, but I didn't want to make this encounter even more awkward.

I realized that I was blocking his way out of the library. "Oh, I'm sorry," I stuttered, moving out of the way. He probably felt like he had to talk to me since he needed to pass me.

"Why are you sorry?" He ran a hand through his dark-brown hair, his brows furrowing.

I gestured to the spot where I'd just been standing. "I was in your way."

"No, you weren't." He chuckled, his light-brown eyes warming. "I saw you talking to the senator's daughter, and it didn't seem to be going so well. I wanted to check on you, and now I've learned you're lost. Where do you need to go?"

If I'd been smart, I would've studied a map before coming here, but I'd been so focused on finding a place to live and selling the house that I hadn't thought about the campus yet. "The bookstore."

"You're in luck." He winked. "Because I have absolutely no clue."

The corners of my mouth tipped upward. "And how does that make me lucky?"

"Because we can search for it together. I actually planned on finding it this morning too." He glanced outside, where the media was, then gently clasped my arm and led me toward a side door. "There's only one thing better than being lost alone."

"Oh, really." For the first time in weeks, my pain receded, and I truly smiled. "And what would that be?"

He nudged my arm with his shoulder. "Being lost with someone else. That way, you can hang out while you're both desperately trying to figure out which way to go. Besides, I know the basic campus layout, and I bet we'll find the bookstore in the commons." He held the door open for me. "We can go around the back of the auditorium and the lake to prevent the media from seeing us and head there."

I breezed through the door. "So you *do* know your way around? You seem like you're older than a freshman anyway."

"Hey, so do you." He scrunched his nose and thrust his hands in his pockets as we took a right toward another large building. "I'm not a freshman. I'm a junior. I transferred from another university when I was offered a football scholarship."

"Great." My stomach sank. That meant that he knew

Carter Grisham and might wind up not wanting to be friends with me—something I could use right now.

"That didn't sound too sincere." He faked a gasp and placed a hand on his chest. "I promise I'm not some dumb jock."

I laughed, though it was a little forced. It was time to rip the bandage off so he could go ahead and disregard me. "I'm a senior. Senator McHale and Senator Grisham pulled some strings and got me in."

"Ah, we have a lot in common." He chuckled. "Senator Grisham was the one who got me a scholarship with McHale's backing and helped me transfer here."

So, helping me *wasn't* off-brand for the senators. Why was Katherine acting like it was unheard of and accusing me of blackmail?

We walked past a large building with a sign that said Hallow Auditorium and a sparkling lake lay about a quarter mile ahead. A few students walked past us, dressed in designer clothes that probably cost more than my monthly rent.

I looked at the handsome stranger beside me. He had at least six inches on me, and I was a decent height for a girl at five-eight. I wanted to get to know him better, so I forced myself to say something. "To be admitted here, you can't be dumb. But are you any good at football?"

"Actually, I am." He smiled. "And my old college tried everything to get me to stay, but my education is more important to me. Besides, a few of the alumni have been recruiting from other places over the last couple of years, and several strong players transferred over the summer. We're hoping to go to the championships this year. With Carter Grisham as the QB, we have a good chance."

"Are you hoping to be drafted by the NFL?" The college

championships were a huge deal, and if they did have a strong team, there'd be a lot of eyes on them.

He shrugged. "Not my goal. Even though you can make a lot of money, a career in the NFL doesn't last nearly as long as one you can enjoy until your midsixties or longer. I figured, NFL draft or just a great education, this was the best place for me. Eventually, I'll be living the American dream like almost everyone else."

I remembered something I'd heard on the news. "And the few NFL players who make a ton of money when they're young often go bankrupt before they're middle-aged."

"You know what that means?" He waggled his brows.

I paused and turned toward him. "What?"

"That won't be me. Because I decided to go to the school at the top of the education pyramid that also happens to have a kick-ass football team. Either way, I'll be prepared for whatever comes next."

"Have you started training with the team?"

"Yeah, over the summer." He chewed his bottom lip. "I don't know what I was expecting, but the people here are a little…"

"Entitled?" I should have shut up, but after the hellish morning, I couldn't lock it down. "Manipulative?"

His warm eyes sparkled. "Tell me how you really feel."

"I'm sorry." The last thing I needed was word getting out that I'd bad-mouthed HSU students. I'd already started my time here with a bang. If I wasn't careful, I would learn how much worse everything could get. "I was teasing."

"No, you're right." He rubbed the back of his neck, his arm muscles bulging. "I was going to say snobby, but your adjectives work too."

We reached the lake. The breeze rippled the dark, murky water, and my gut clenched. I averted my gaze. A few oak trees were growing around the lake, giving it a natural feel despite it being manmade on a college campus.

"Mom says—" I cut myself off, my heart breaking. She didn't say *anything* anymore. "I mean...my mom *used* to say that the old saying 'If you don't have anything nice to say, don't say anything at all' should be a golden rule for everyone."

"Well, I disagree." He shrugged. "I think if we were all more straightforward and not as politically correct, the world would be a better place."

I snorted. "You don't want to be PC, yet you came to the very school where most politicians send their children."

"I can endure anything for two years."

"I said something eerily similar just a little while ago." I wrapped my arms around my waist, needing something to hold on to.

Silence descended, but it wasn't awkward at all—maybe we could become friends.

As we walked across a lawn, he asked, "So...what's your name?"

"Evie." I tucked a piece of hair that had fallen out of my braid behind my ear. "What about yours?"

"Grayson."

We didn't talk as we continued our trek behind more buildings, and soon, we approached a larger one.

Katherine, Carter, and some other guy stood outside it. The other guy had beautiful bronze skin and a strong jawline. His short, dark hair was perfectly cut, and his face was clean-shaven.

All three of them could've been a picture from a campus brochure. But when they zeroed in on us, my heart skipped a beat.

"At least someone helped her," Carter said, his tense jaw

making his sculpted face even more rugged. Out of the three guys around me, he was the most handsome by far.

"Yeah, I found her at the library and learned we both need books for class tomorrow." Grayson smiled lazily and moved closer to me.

Carter placed his hands in his pockets and nodded. "Thanks, man. She can hang with us while you get your things. Senator McHale is on his way."

Katherine glowered at me. A lump formed in my throat.

Grayson must have noticed because he shook his head. "I'll wait with you all. I want to thank the senator for getting me in here."

The guy I didn't know chuckled. "Damn, Katherine. Your dad has been busy."

"Yes, Samuel. He has." Katherine rolled her eyes.

"Look, two reporters are heading this way to talk to us." Carter nodded at Katherine and me, then gestured at Grayson. "You head in there with Samuel, and we'll meet you inside."

Grayson fidgeted, and his gaze settled on me.

Carter shifted, looking agitated. He rasped, "I wasn't asking, scholarship boy. Now bounce."

My teeth ached from how hard I was clenching them. I'd thought Carter was a good guy, but now he was acting just as bad as Katherine.

Widening his stance, Grayson narrowed his eyes. "I promised Evie I'd take her to the bookstore."

These two alpha males were staring each other down, and the senator was on his way. Maybe coming to school here hadn't been smart after all.

CHAPTER FOUR

Carter and Grayson glared at one another. Somehow, I'd become the center of this standoff, and I didn't like the attention. It was going to be hard enough trying to survive this year, especially with Katherine putting a target on my back. Any additional attention I received would only make her more determined to get rid of me.

"Again, I want to thank the senator since he got me in here," Grayson said, and he shuffled closer to me.

A vein bulged in Carter's neck. "You can tell him another time...or even when we come into the bookstore. Right now, you and Samuel need to get the fuck out of here."

His voice was authoritative, sounding much older than his years.

Grayson glanced at me again, turmoil in his eyes. He was a good guy, a saint compared to Carter and Katherine, and I could tell he didn't want to leave me with them, but at the same time, Carter was his quarterback, and he was probably used to following his lead.

As if hearing my thoughts, Carter gritted out, "I'll make you pay at practice if you don't get out of here."

"You wouldn't." Grayson sneered. "I'm left tackle. If you hurt me, you won't have protection during the game."

Samuel huffed. "Come on, guys. Let's all just go inside."

Carter rolled his eyes. "We have a backup who was just fine last year. We don't need a guy like you who's here to further his own gain by association."

Tilting his head back, Grayson clenched his jaw. "Are you saying I'm just here to hang around people like you? Might I remind you that *your father* recruited me from my old university? Not the other way around."

"And yet, you and she"—Carter pointed at me—"jumped at the first opportunity to come here. I'm not my dad, and I won't let someone ride my coattails, so you need to get in line."

My chest ached. Carter had seemed so nice at first. Now, he was acting like a different person. What had changed between meeting him and now?

Coming here had been a horrible decision, but I couldn't take it back. I hated that Katherine and Carter clearly thought I'd blackmailed my way in so I could use their connections. That was the last thing I'd ever do, but they weren't going to listen. Well, I wouldn't cower. That would only make them attack me more. Instead, I'd try to save Grayson from making a permanent enemy of Carter.

Glancing sideways, I saw the senator and his wife heading in our direction with two reporters. I was running out of time.

Inhaling, I turned to Grayson and forced a smile. "Hey, it's okay. If you're staying for me, I'm fine. The senator is almost here."

Grayson held my gaze, then nodded. "Fine. I'll head into the bookstore."

"Okay," I said a little too brightly, but damn, I wanted this altercation to end.

He kept his gaze on me a moment longer before turning his attention back to Carter. He adjusted his backpack and smirked, then winked at me and headed to the door.

When I looked back at Katherine, Carter, and Samuel, I found Carter's piercing eyes homed in on me. My pulse spiked, and my stomach somersaulted. There was something unnerving about having his undivided attention, and as much as it thrilled me, it also petrified me because I was certain that stare wasn't one of interest. I was also certain he was pissed off at me, but I had no idea why.

"Come on." Samuel smacked Grayson's back. "Let's get out of here before Carter kicks your ass in front of the cameras."

Grayson looked at me one more time before he spun and marched toward the thick cherrywood doors leading inside, Samuel following.

"Carter, I know you don't want any animosity between players on the field." Katherine watched the two of them disappear. "But be careful of him. He doesn't like you being in charge."

My entire body tensed into one big knot. These people assumed everyone wanted what they perceived as theirs. Their status, their money, their college... The ego was extraordinary.

I had no interest in being part of their clique. All I wanted to do was keep my head down and do my work so I could go to a great grad school and earn my PhD; then make a difference in kids' lives. That was my only goal. I didn't want to buddy up with Katherine and cruise on her sailboat—or whatever the heck rich people did.

Just then, the senator arrived, beaming. "I'm so glad you three got some alone time together. I was just telling Bob and

Michelle that I can count on the two of you to show Evie around the campus and help her get settled."

The male reporter, who had to be Bob, held out his mic to us. "From what I know, Miss McHale and Mr. Grisham are the two best students to show you around here. Miss McHale, I heard you might have landed a cameo on *Law and Order*."

Katherine giggled and blushed, proving she could do the latter on command. She glanced at the concrete sidewalk and ducked her chin. "I cannot confirm or deny."

She had the innocent act down, and it made me resent her more. At least own the type of person you were.

I winced internally. My attitude was hypocritical since I had lied about why I'd walked here. I wasn't owning who I was, but I didn't want the senator to attempt to spend more money on me. He'd done more than enough...more than anyone else ever had besides my parents.

"I think that speaks for itself." Bob chuckled.

"And Mr. Grisham." Michelle leaned forward, and I noticed how much makeup she had on her face. I'd heard people on screen had to wear thick makeup, so maybe that was the reason. She held out her mic to Carter. "We hear there's been a shake-up on the football team this year with some player transfers. How do you feel about that, and do you think you can win the championship?"

Carter's charismatic side shone through again. He smiled, and unlike Katherine, it seemed genuine and not calculated. "Well, we did win a bowl game last year, and the new recruits feel like they've always been part of the team. I can't predict the future, but with guys like them on the field, nothing's off the table."

Now, both reporters turned toward me, and my chest tightened. I chanted internally, *Please don't ask me anything. Please.*

"Miss Stone." Michelle pressed her lips together. "What are your plans for this year?"

I almost laughed. I doubted the real answer—surviving—would be taken well. "To work hard and make sure that I don't let Senator McHale, Senator Grisham, or their families down… not when they've done so much to get me here."

Senator McHale burst out laughing. "Oh, Evie. You don't need to worry. You had a perfect GPA at Tennessee State University—I'm sure you'll do just fine here."

My stomach clenched. Yet another thing he knew about me, but of course he'd know that. He'd needed my transcripts to get me accepted here.

Not wanting to be outdone, Bob moved forward. "What about extracurricular activities? What do you plan to do?"

I froze. I wasn't sure how to answer that. I wouldn't have time to commit to a permanent activity—I was going to have to get a job to pay for rent, food, and all the other random expenses that I'd have while attending here. I didn't want to lie—what if they followed up?

Carter stepped forward, placing a hand on my lower back. "Evie just got here, and she's still trying to get acclimated. She's just been dealt a mind-blowing loss. I doubt she's had time to think about extracurriculars yet, but she'll figure it out. I'm sure of it."

And just like that, he'd become a nice guy once again. Man, I was getting whiplash because it was like the two sides of him were at war over which would come out. No doubt, the camera had everything to do with this show of support.

"What's your major, Evie?" Michelle asked.

That one didn't require much thought. "Psychology. I want to get a job with the state to help children in foster care and help evaluate potential parents to ensure they're a good fit."

Carter's breath caught, and his brows furrowed. His hand dropped from my back.

His reaction indicated surprise, but I didn't know why that would be. He must have known what I was studying, given his father had also supported my acceptance here.

"What a great life goal." Michelle placed a hand over her heart as a sad smile spread across her lips. "That's an important job that will make a huge impact. What inspired you to decide on that major?"

"I was adopted." I bit my lip but held my head high. "And I never felt like I was because I had amazing parents. They treated me like I was their own, and no one realized I wasn't their biological child unless one of us told them. I was lucky, but so many kids aren't. I want to give every child a chance to feel safe and loved, and this is one of the best ways I know how to achieve it."

Beaming, Bob patted Senator McHale's arm and said, "No wonder you chose to sponsor her. With a lofty goal like that, she'll have a very bright future. I bet there aren't many students as qualified either."

My face flamed, and I stared at the concrete.

"Yes, she is quite worthy," Mrs. McHale said, but I heard a hint of tension in her tone. "But don't worry. We'll make sure we give her everything she needs to be independent from us and stand on her own." She cut her gaze at me.

Message received. Mrs. McHale didn't like having me around any more than Katherine did.

Bob turned to Carter. "I can see why your father also wanted to support this young lady, given your work behind getting the foundation Touchdown 4 Kids off the ground."

I startled. Carter volunteered to help underprivileged kids? My jaw dropped as he replied, "Touchdown 4 Kids is a great organization doing their best to give children access to learning sports no matter their personal circumstances. I have been honored to help them gather the necessary paperwork to get the organization structured to ensure that it's nonprofit and can accept donations easily."

"And will you be funding the organization—" Bob started.

"Well, I hate to cut this short..." Carter said as he walked over and wrapped an arm around Katherine's waist.

My heart panged. It had to be the stress and the heat of the day. However...it didn't help that I found Carter extremely attractive, especially now that I knew he wanted to help kids too.

"Katherine and I should take Evie to the bookstore and help her find her books before they're picked over," Carter continued, and he reached over and gently gripped my arm.

My skin prickled at his touch. The sensation was strange and disconcerting. However, I didn't want to make a scene, so I didn't jerk away.

"Of course." Senator McHale chuckled. "It's hot out here anyway. Head on in while Lisa and I finish up with Michelle and Bob. We won't be long."

Katherine stepped out of Carter's grip and kissed her father's cheek before turning around and looping her arm through mine like we were already friends.

This time, I wasn't fooled. She'd already shown her true colors, and I swallowed hard, trying to keep bile from inching up my throat. After today, things would be better. The senator wouldn't be here, and the media wouldn't be around. I could come and go on campus, and no one would notice me. This would be the hardest day that I had.

The three of us strolled to the door with me in the middle, forcing one foot in front of the other. Carter still held my arm, and the tingles were surging through my entire body. Katherine gripped my other arm tightly. Maybe she thought I might try to run away.

I moved faster, wanting to get away from the cameras and free of both of them touching me.

"Slow down," Katherine hissed. "The last thing we need is for the reporters to think we're running off, and besides, I can't run in heels."

I inhaled and slowed my pace. When we reached the door, Carter quickly opened it and waved Katherine and me in.

I walked into a large room with purple walls and gray tiled flooring, with at least two hundred rectangular tables spaced around it, each table seating eight. On the other side of the space, an open cafeteria gleamed, ready for students to arrive, with Hallowed Saints Café written across the awning. That space was decorated in a lighter shade of purple than the room with the tables.

We continued toward the other end of the building, where the entrance to the bookstore was. When we got far enough away from the doors, Katherine released her hold on me with a frown.

I waited for a barrage of insults, but she didn't say anything; she just continued to march toward the bookstore.

Carter eyed me. I nearly flinched, but I refused to give him any sort of reaction. I didn't need to make myself more of a target.

"You did good out there," he said.

My body warmed at his praise, and I looked directly at him and immediately regretted it. Those eyes were dark, the kindness gone, and worst of all, calculating, as if he were trying to see straight into my soul.

"She did decently." Katherine spun on her heels. "The last thing you need to do is compliment her. We still don't know why she's here."

I rolled my eyes. "How is your father helping me any different than getting Grayson and other football players to transfer here?"

"It's not." Carter grimaced. "Those assholes shouldn't be here. Our team would be fine without them."

"That may be true." Katherine shrugged. "But it helps that your dad recruited strong players who were already being scouted. It ensures scouts will come here and gives you a better chance of being drafted."

She had a point, but the way she presented it made it seem like the cameras were still rolling.

"We'd do just as well if they weren't here." Carter scowled. "I've worked my ass off, and if I get drafted, it won't be because of them."

I didn't want to listen to this conversation. The disgust rolling off Carter strengthened my urge to leave. Plus, the longer I stayed here, the less time I would have to find a job.

I breezed past Katherine into the bookstore, glad that they continued talking. That would give me a few minutes' reprieve.

A flyer on top of all the older ones on a pinboard at the entrance caught my eye.

Summer Internships in Spain for Psychology and Business Students.

Wow. A trip like that would be amazing, but I couldn't afford my next meal, let alone hope to be chosen for something like that. I'd been taking Spanish because there was a large Hispanic population near Chattanooga and I wanted to help those kids too, and studying in Spain would help me with that goal.

Pushing that dream away, I walked toward the bookshelves, reading signs to find my class texts. Grayson appeared at my side.

Not wanting him to ask any questions, I pulled my

schedule from my back pocket and unfolded it so I could see what books I needed. "Here's what I'm looking for." I read the list off to him.

The two of us went to work, searching for it all.

The bookstore was a lot nicer than the one at my former college. The carpet was thick and dark purple, and the walls were muted gold, the decor the shade of the school colors.

Luckily, the place was hyperorganized, and I was able to find a used copy of every book I needed. The new ones were already gone, the opposite of how things had worked at TSU. But I'd rather have used books with former students' highlights and notes.

I found everything on my list except the camera needed for my photography class. That was something that they'd loan us in the classroom.

"Well, that's it." Grayson glanced at his own pile of books and then mine. "Unfortunately, that means that it's time to deal with…" He trailed off, a smirk on his lips.

I turned around to find Katherine right behind me. She glanced over her shoulder just as Senator and Mrs. McHale entered the store.

She moved toward me and said, "Here comes Daddy. You're going to play nice with me, right?"

I hated that she had such control over me because I didn't truly have a choice. It was either play along or have a rough senior year being stuck with her. "Of course."

Lifting an eyebrow, she looked me over, trying to gauge my sincerity. She was afraid I was going to rat her out to her daddy. Part of me wanted to do just that.

CHAPTER FIVE

The senator and his wife were now only twenty or so feet away. The senator's attention was locked on Katherine, Grayson, and me while his wife glanced in the direction of the exit. I was pretty sure she'd rather be anywhere but here.

On television, they came across as the picture-perfect family, but seeing them in person exposed some cracks in Lisa's and Katherine's facades. There was a coldness to them that made them hard to relate to, whereas the senator was even more charismatic in person, commanding the room, much like Carter.

"I'm serious. Let's be friendly, okay? And we can just ignore each other on campus when he's not here." She bit her bottom lip, but her eyes didn't hold any warmth.

Grayson chuckled and leaned toward me while he murmured, "Does she think that will actually make you play along with her? Even Carter isn't this bad. He's just an arrogant prick."

Like he'd been summoned, Carter stepped around the closest rack of HSU T-shirts. My breath caught as we locked gazes. He had a slight scowl on his face, which made me fear that he'd heard Grayson.

"Listen here." Katherine tossed her hair over her shoulders like she had earlier. "You can't talk about my boyfriend—"

"*Not* your boyfriend, Katherine," Carter gritted out as he stepped beside me. "We broke up last semester, and there's no going back."

Katherine's entire body recoiled. "Right. Sorry. I'm still getting used to us not being together." She wrapped her arms around herself just as the senator strode up in front of us.

"And that's a damn shame." Senator McHale patted Carter on the back and continued, "Your father and I were ecstatic that the two of you were dating. We had visions of you getting married someday, but there's still time. Maybe you'll work things out." He smiled hopefully at Carter.

Pressing his lips together, Carter stayed silent. His expression said it all—they weren't getting back together.

Our group descended into an uncomfortable silence. Mrs. McHale strolled up to us, hiding a yawn behind one hand.

"Sir." Grayson shifted his books into one arm and extended his hand. "I'm not sure if you remember me, but I transferred from Ohio State University. You and Senator Grisham came there to meet me and some of the other football players."

Senator McHale beamed and clasped Grayson's hand, shaking it enthusiastically. "Of course I do. You're one of the best left tackles out there. I was ecstatic that we were able to bring you here."

"It's an honor to be here." Grayson beamed before releasing the senator's hand. "And I wanted to thank you for making it possible. Cole, Damien, Alex, and I are thrilled to be part of the HSU team."

With five books in my hands plus the binders I'd picked up, my arms ached from the weight. It was yet another reminder that I was weaker than I should be. My heart clenched at the memory of my mother in the car with the water rushing through the windows, dragging the vehicle down. If I'd been more stringent about exercising instead of spending all my time studying, maybe she would still be here.... My pulse grew a little ragged, and suddenly, the weight disappeared.

I came back to the present to find my books in Carter's hands and him, Grayson, and the senator staring at me with concerned expressions. Katherine and Lisa were scowling as if I'd blanked out on purpose to get attention.

"Are you okay?" Senator McHale asked kindly.

That was a question I despised, but his concern seemed genuine. "Yeah, sorry. I just spaced. Today has been kind of a blur."

Katherine placed a hand over her heart and batted her eyes. "When you aren't used to the media, I imagine it's daunting." Her words were condescending.

There were so many ways I could have replied, but none of them were appropriate. Not with the senator in our presence.

"Well then, let's get your books taken care of, and you can head back to your apartment and relax." The senator placed an arm around my shoulders and guided me toward the front of the bookstore. "Tomorrow will be a big day, so you'll need to rest up to be prepared."

Rest sounded nice, but if last night was any indication of what life would be like with my roommates, I doubted I'd be getting much of it. Still, I forced a smile, eager to get away from this group. Between my weird, conflicting emotions toward Carter and Katherine's hatred, I was looking forward to not running into either of them anytime soon.

Awareness crept across my body, and the hairs on the nape of my neck rose. I knew that Carter was following us. I'd never been so hyperaware of another person before, and of course, it would be *him*—an enigma I didn't understand who also happened to be the obsession of a girl who clearly hated my guts for being here. But then I realized *why* he was behind us— he had my books.

I paused and spun around, and Carter damn near collided with me.

His eyes narrowed. "What are you doing? Are you trying to get hurt?" I heard clear accusation in his tone, and alarm bells rang in my head.

I scoffed. "What? No! Why would I do that?"

His face turned to stone. "Oh, people usually have their reasons."

There was a hidden meaning there—the future psychologist inside me sensed it—but I had no clue what it was. "I promise. I just realized you were carrying my books, and I didn't want to burden you."

His stern expression slipped as he examined every inch of my face.

A chill ran down my back. He was searching for something, and I had no idea what it might be.

"It was an accident, Carter." The senator took the books from him. "Nothing more. Don't read into it."

I started seeing black spots and realized I'd forgotten to breathe. Carter's eyes were still searching my face, and the scrutiny had me losing my mind.

Then he shrugged and took a step back. "Well, if you don't need me anymore, I'm going to run and talk to Coach Prichard."

"Thank you for being here." Senator McHale nodded. "And I'd appreciate it if you could make sure Evie, Grayson, and the other new team members find their way around. Nothing like having the captain of the football team to help other students get oriented."

"Yes, sir." Carter's gaze shifted back to me. "It was nice meeting you."

"Same." I moved to turn back around but then paused. He'd already started walking away. "Carter," I called out, liking the way his name rolled off my tongue.

He stiffened and turned toward me, his face in a neutral expression. "Yeah?"

"Thanks for your help today." I wrapped my arms around my waist, hating how awkward I felt around him. "With the media...twice...and my books just now. I appreciate it."

He nodded and spun back around, then marched toward the door. When he passed Grayson, he clapped him on the back, acting more friendly than I expected.

Whatever conflict they'd had was apparently settled. Must have been a guy thing.

When I turned back around, Senator McHale was staring at me. He smiled as he placed my things on the checkout counter, and the few remaining reporters snapped pictures of us together. My skin crawled as they shifted their perspective to include the cashier ringing up all my stuff in a photo.

"Don't worry about Carter." Senator McHale smiled sadly. "He's a great man. I wouldn't want my daughter to be with him if he weren't. He's just got some personal issues to work out."

A bitter laugh stuck in my throat, but I swallowed it whole. I wanted to say, "Well, don't we all," but the senator probably wouldn't get it. He seemed happy and full of life...everything that I wasn't anymore.

But that was why I was here. To focus on my future and forge a career that would make a difference. Maybe if I got all that sorted, I could wind up happy, like him.

I'd been hanging out near the lake, away from everyone, for two hours. I was afraid to leave because the senator hadn't left yet, and I didn't want him or the reporters to catch me walking back to my rental house with my books.

It wasn't that I was ashamed. A lot of people struggled with money, but the senator had just paid my way into this school and for all my books. I feared he'd want to try to fix *this* as well, and I needed him to stop.

I would've been stupid to turn down this opportunity, and I'd been desperate to get away from the ghosts that haunted me in my hometown. I felt guilty about that. Like I was trying to forget my parents. Though I couldn't, even if I had wanted to. Their essences were infused into my identity, and the sacrifices they'd made for me...even some biological parents wouldn't have done that. It had been an honor and a privilege to know them, and I'd gotten even more than that.... I'd gotten to call them mine.

For the hundredth time today, my vision blurred. Thoughts of them were never far away, and being in this ridiculous situation where I couldn't even leave without making a scene made me feel trapped.

I breathed slowly, attempting to stop the anxiety attack creeping up on me. I focused on the lapping water below me and leaned against the trunk of a tree, closing my eyes.

"Uh...Evie?" a voice called from behind me.

Shit. This was *not* making things better.

Maybe if I didn't respond, they would think they were mistaken? But then I heard the shuffling of feet hitting the mulch where the concrete ended.

The person was coming toward me.

"Hey. Are you okay?" This time, I recognized the voice.

Grayson.

My stomach dropped, but my muscles relaxed. The combination was strange, like hoping it was someone else, but also relieved it wasn't them. I wiped my eyes and inhaled slowly. "Yeah, I'm fine."

I glanced over my shoulder and saw Grayson, now wearing black shorts and a gray sleeveless workout shirt. I saw the tribal tattoo that took up his entire upper arm. It was even more intricate and detailed than I'd imagined and looked damn good on him.

His warm eyes filled with concern, and he pointed at the bags around me. "I'm going to be honest here and tell you I'm having a hard time believing you." He came a little closer, ducking under a tree limb, and squatted beside me.

Gritting my teeth, I forced myself not to cringe. I could lie, but he'd call me out on it. "I don't see why you'd say that."

"Well, it's hot as hell out here. You're drenched in sweat, and your book bags are surrounding you like a fort protecting the princess." He scanned the ground like he was looking for a threat.

I licked my lips. "I might have seen some fire ants, and though I know they can technically still get me, it still provides them an obstacle course and not direct access."

He laughed. "Fire ants? You're scared of them?"

"Let's say I had an incident when I was six." Memories of that day washed over me. "Dad and I were playing tag, and I decided to dash up to the soft sand because he ran slower there. And..."

"You stepped on a fire anthill," he finished for me.

"I know that twist was hard to guess, but yes." I shivered at the memory. "My foot felt like it was on..." I trailed off and pointed at him.

He raised a hand. "Let me guess! Fire."

"No wonder you got a scholarship to this bougie school,

Grayson." I leaned back, feeling lighthearted once more. "You, my friend, are a genius."

"Well, then, let me be the one to officially rescue said damsel in distress and get you out of this horrible, life-threatening situation." He stood and extended his hand to me.

A part of me was more than ready to take it. He was funny and handsome, and he already felt like a friend. But if I stood and left, I'd be out there with my books, and what if the senator saw me? "I..."

"I'm not leaving without you." He picked up a sack of books while keeping his other hand extended. "So...this is going to get really uncomfortable if you make us stay like this for too much longer."

Shrugging, I tried to appear nonchalant, though my lips were fighting to tilt upward. "I don't know. It might be good for you to stand uncomfortably for a prolonged period of time. It could help you with endurance, which you need for football, right?"

"My endurance is just fine." He winked. "Maybe I could show you sometime."

Face flaming, I averted my gaze. Had he just propositioned me? "And here I was impressed that you hadn't resorted to pickup lines."

A large hand engulfed mine, tugging me to my feet. He said, "Evie, you perv. That wasn't a pickup line. That was me hinting I wanted you to come to one of my games."

And that made me want to disappear. I'd just made a complete ass of myself.

He scanned my face, smirking. He leaned down and whispered in my ear. "Did those fire ants attack your cheeks after all this time?"

A shiver ran through me, but I forced myself to glare at him. "No. An arrogant scoundrel is to blame for that."

"Aw." He winked and ducked under the branch once more. "I'm only teasing. I'm not saying I'm above hitting on you, but when it happens, it'll be totally classier."

I froze. My heart hammered. He was handsome, funny, and sweet, but I was broken. I didn't have the space for anything like that...not now.

When he stepped from under the tree, he turned toward me with a concerned expression. "Hey, did I do something wrong?"

"It's just... My parents just died, and I'm at this new, strange school." I stumbled from my spot, moving closer to him, wringing my hands. My heart dropped. Just when I thought I might be gaining a friend, I lost him in the next instant. "I..."

He hung his head and closed his eyes.

This was it. This was when he'd tell me to move along. I didn't want to hear it, so instead, I reached for the bags. "Look, I've got to go." I had no clue where—anywhere but here. When he let me have them, it confirmed what I'd already known.

As I took a hurried step away, he reached out and gently grabbed my wrist.

"Evie, wait."

CHAPTER SIX

"Hey," Grayson said as he turned me slowly toward him. "Don't rush away like that."

Exhaling, I focused on the sidewalk. I hated being weak; this wasn't like me. But losing my parents was impacting me more every day. From what I'd read, being injured myself had delayed my reaction, and the longer I went without seeing or hearing them, the more real the loss became.

Grayson took the bags back from my hands and set them on the ground. He sighed. "Evie, please. Will you look at me?"

Inhaling, I straightened my shoulders and lifted my head.

His sympathetic expression caught me off guard. Kindness emanated from his eyes.

"I'm sorry if I upset you." He rubbed the back of his neck, his arm muscles bulging, making his tattoo dance. "I can only imagine what it's like to lose a parent—it has to be hard as *fuck*. Losing both at the same time... I don't even want to think about it. And then to come here and have all the cameras on you and that nasty bitch spitting fire at you for just being here, well...

that's a lot to handle. You don't need some douchebag hitting on you on top of it all."

I needed to lighten the mood. "No, I don't." I scanned the area exaggeratedly. "Do you see one coming to do that?"

He rolled his eyes. "No. At least, I hope not. That would make the situation even more awkward than it already is."

I chuckled, some of the heaviness ebbing from my body.

"But seriously." He dropped his hand back to his side. "I'm the douchebag, and I'm sorry. I was just having a good time with you, and I find you attractive and funny—it just kind of slipped out."

Unsure how to respond, I shrugged. I should probably say thank you, but I wanted to move on from this conversation. "It's fine. You weren't being a douche. In fact, you're a super-nice guy."

He frowned. "Nice? That's not the adjective you want a girl to use to describe you."

"Remember, don't want to date right now." I crossed my arms, determined to keep the conversation light. "But who knows what I'll think when that changes." I didn't want to lead him on. That wouldn't be fair to either of us. Besides, he was a football player, and I'd bet the cheerleaders would be all over him soon—if they weren't already.

He laughed and picked up the bags again. "I guess we'll have to wait and see. So where are we off to?"

I bit my bottom lip and tapped my legs.

"Let's add super nice and stalker to my running list of appealing attributes." He groaned. "This keeps getting better and better."

Great, I was taking us right back to awkward again. "No, it's not that. It's just..."

He tilted his head, waiting for me to continue. When I didn't, he prompted, "Just?"

There was no point in trying to hide it from him. Besides, out of everyone I'd met, he would be the one most likely to understand. "I don't live on campus, and I don't have a car."

His brows furrowed. "You aren't staying in one of the dorms?"

I placed a hand on my hip. "Do you need me to repeat what I just said?"

"Lovely." He sighed. "Let's add *stupid* to the ever-growing list of my winning qualities." He blew out a breath. "I'm just surprised. The senator paid for your tuition and books—I assumed it was a full ride."

"That's the thing." That had to be why the media outlet was all crazy—because of the generosity of the McHales. "It's not a scholarship. He paid out of his own pocket to bring me here. He offered to cover a dorm, but I didn't accept it. He's already doing too much as it is. So, I'll find a job, buy a cheap car, and voilà, no problem."

Grayson glanced at the main entrance to the school and pursed his lips. "So, the senator hasn't left yet, and you don't want him to see you walking home."

"Hey!" I beamed and pointed at him. "You've got deductive skills, so there's that."

"With low expectations like that, there's only one way I can go." He gestured to the sky. "Up. So I'll take it, ma'am. And I can do one even better."

I leaned back and crossed my arms. "Oh, really? What's that? Punch Katherine in the face for me?"

He laughed, the sound so free. "The request is justified, but no. I won't hit a girl." He waggled his brows. "We can jump into my Jeep, and I can drop you off at your place. The senator won't see you walking, your books will be safe in their bags and won't need to be carried, *and* my car has AC."

My heart thudded against my rib cage. I wasn't sure if

allowing him to drop me off was smart. The more people who knew stuff about me, the greater the chance Katherine or Senator McHale would hear about it. But taking the ride *would* beat sitting around in the heat and being hungry, and this entire morning had already cut into my job-hunting time. "Okay, but I need to hear you say you won't tell anyone where I live."

"I promise. Your secret is safe with me, and I'll even add that I won't tell the senator about your lack of a vehicle."

I examined him and then motioned for him to pass me. I was desperate to get out of the sun. "Then lead the way."

I GUIDED him through the streets toward the house. He had the air conditioning blasting, and I aimed the vents on the passenger side right on my face. I was so thankful that his older hunter-green Jeep Wrangler didn't have leather seats because, with the temperature today, I would've been dripping with sweat, and I was already beyond glowing. Instead, the vehicle had the dark-gray cloth that I favored despite the clip-on top being a light tan.

We pulled up in front of the white house with red shutters that I called home for now, and I reached for the door handle just as Grayson turned off the Jeep.

I froze. "You don't have to come in."

My roommates' beat-up red Honda Civic and gray Mazda 3 were parked in the driveway, which meant that they were here. The last thing I wanted was to have Grayson walk inside to find them passed out drunk in the living room.

"Uh... First off, rude." He side-eyed me and then lifted two fingers. "And second, I want to help you carry your stuff in. Those books are pretty heavy, and who knows..." He leaned over the dashboard, placing a hand over his mouth as he whispered, "Fire ants could be waiting for you nearby. You'll need someone to distract them."

I should've never told him that story. In fact, I'm not even sure why I did. I'd go with heat stroke. "That was a made-up story. I was just pulling your leg to see if you were gullible. Unfortunately for you, that's another negative on that ever-growing list you're so keen on adding to."

He opened his door and scoffed. "Lies! The fear in your eyes couldn't have been faked." He then opened the back driver's side door and snatched my three bags from the back seat.

I heaved a sigh. "Let me check on my roommates and make sure they're decent first."

He was determined to come inside, and trying to talk him out of it would only make him more determined to know why. I hurried to the house.

There were two windows on either side of the door, and I tried looking through the window on the right to see if Leah and Haven were still passed out, but the blinds were closed. I could hear the murmur of the television, and I hoped that was a good sign.

I unlocked the front door and walked into the living room. Both girls were sitting on the couch, clearly still hungover. They had dark circles under their eyes, and they each held a small plate with a piece of toast and a mug of coffee in their hands.

Haven looked up and smiled. "You're home!" Then she winced and clutched her head with her free hand. "Damn. That was too loud even for me."

Leah spilled some coffee and grimaced. "No shit. Now I have a third-degree burn."

I hurried to the kitchen and grabbed some paper towels. While I was in there, Haven asked in a quieter voice, "Where have you been? When we got up, we hollered down at you, but then we realized you were already gone."

They'd looked for me? "Oh, sorry. I had to go buy my books for school."

"What?" Leah groaned. "I thought registration was tomorrow. I swear, Haven, if you fu—"

"I didn't." Haven frowned. "Remember, she goes to HSU."

Leah's head tilted back. "Oh, that's ri—"

When I stepped back into the living room, I understood why Leah had stopped speaking. Grayson had opened the door, and he stood on the threshold, surveying the room.

Both girls gawked like they'd never seen a man before.

"Grayson," I exclaimed like I hadn't expected him to come in. What the *hell* was wrong with me? I handed the paper towels to Leah just as Grayson held up my bags in his hands.

"Uh...sorry?" He strolled the rest of the way in and shut the front door.

Lovely.

He put the bags on the cheap laminate floor and shoved his hands into his gym shorts. "You were in here longer than a second, and I was just standing at the front door when a gust of wind blew it open."

Ugh. No wonder I hadn't heard him come in. I hadn't shut the door to begin with. I was way too flustered for my own good. "Oh, yeah. Sorry. Leah spilled something, and I got distracted."

The two girls glanced at each other and then burrowed deeper into the couch.

Now I wished they were still passed out. This was way more awkward.

"So...um." He cleared his throat. "Where do you want the bags?"

"I can take them." I didn't want to be rude, but I was uncomfortable. I didn't know him well, and I didn't know these girls yet, and they were hungover. "Thank you for the ride. I really appreciate it."

He opened the front door and pulled out his phone. "Let me give you my number. If you ever get into a situation where you need a ride again, text me."

I relaxed. I'd feared he would try to fix my predicament, but he didn't. Just offered to help me if I decided I needed it. "Okay." The word slipped out before I even realized I'd agreed. I didn't want to give him mixed signals and lead him on. "I mean—"

"It's only if you need me, Evie." He smiled, friendly. "This isn't committing to dating me. Hell, you never even have to use it. Just keep it so, if you find yourself in a bad situation, you have someone to call."

No expectations. I could get behind that. I rattled off my number, and he typed it in and then sent me a text. "There, now I'll know it's you and I won't ignore you." Then he left.

The girls *woo*ed behind me, making my face burn. I hadn't had close friends growing up, and the few that I'd hung out with wouldn't have acted that way. They would've been too embarrassed.

I hurried after him, shutting the door a little too hard behind me.

"Grayson," I called.

He stopped at the bottom of the two red stairs that led to our door and turned toward me. He didn't say anything, just stared.

"Thanks for everything." I wrung my hands. "Seriously, and I'm sorry if I came off rude. I just met those two yesterday, and they got drunk within an hour of that."

"Hey, it's okay." He put a hand on my shoulder and continued, "It's been a day...for both of us. If you wanna meet up on campus tomorrow, just text me or give me a call."

I bit my lower lip. "Yeah, I may do that." Having a friend on campus would be nice. Hell, having a friend at all would be great. And for some reason, I felt comfortable in his presence.

"Yeah?" He grinned. "Then I'll make sure to have my phone on."

"Bye." Hovering out here any longer would be weird, and I didn't want to lead him on. Sure, he was attractive, kind, and funny, but I seriously couldn't even fathom starting a relationship now. I had to take care of myself.

I spun and went back inside, only to find the TV paused and both girls staring at me. Now, I wished I'd made things awkward outside.

"You're going to Hallowed Saints University?" Leah's mouth hung open.

"Uhh...yeah. I told you I was a student." I didn't like the look they were giving me.

Haven gestured at the front door. "And you found a sexy-ass man like him on your first day there?"

I didn't know how to respond to that. "Is this a problem?"

"*No*," Haven exclaimed and then winced again, clutching her head.

Leah didn't flinch. "If you're going there, then why are you living here? You must have money."

"Senator McHale is paying my tuition but not for housing, transportation, or food." I tried to make the explanation simple. "And my family isn't rich—quite the opposite. I'm about to go look for an evening job."

"What kind?" Leah tilted her head.

That was a weird question. "Any kind as long as it makes good money."

"My brother owns a bar about a mile from here." Leah took

a bite of her toast. "He needs some waitresses. I can get you on, and we could work together if you want."

This sounded way too good to be true. "What's the pay and hours?"

"Minimum wage, but you keep all your tips." Leah lifted her chin. "It's good money because a lot of people from HSU go there since it's so close to the university."

Ahh...that was why she was watching me. She wanted to see if that would bother me. Little did she know all that did was entice me further. They had money to tip. "I'm in."

"Sweet." She removed her cell phone from her pocket. "I'll let him know that you and I will be there tomorrow night from four to midnight."

"Good choice." Haven saluted me. "Way better money than the coffee shop I work at in the evenings, but I get off by nine, unlike you suckers, which makes it worth it."

That was the thing. I'd rather make more money than get off early. I needed it. Everything at this school was expensive.

Now that I'd found a job and spent half the day outside on very little sleep, I was exhausted, so I headed downstairs to the basement and got my stuff ready for tomorrow. Then I crawled into bed.

For the first time since I got out of the hospital, life didn't seem so dire.

All I had to do was avoid Katherine and Carter, and I'd be fine.

CHAPTER SEVEN

On Tuesday morning, the first day of school, I rolled onto campus at nine thirty and searched for the university gym. I'd studied the map the night before and knew exactly where I needed to go, but for a school with such small class sizes, the campus was still quite large.

I hurried past the student center and toward the sports complex across from the stadium. My ten o'clock class was weight training, a subject I was determined to take to become strong. If I'd done it sooner, then maybe Mom would be alive.

I walked past a basketball court and down a long hallway with purple walls and smooth golden floors till I reached a huge room with double glass doors containing various weight-lifting and body-toning machines. A large selection of free weights and a purple mat floor sat to the right.

I walked in and froze. Grayson, Carter, Samuel, and at least twenty other guys turned and stared at me. I wanted to disappear. The entire football team was here, right where my class was to begin.

This had to be wrong.

I was about to turn and walk away, but Carter's gaze met mine, keeping me in place.

My heartbeat quickened as I took in his rugged face and gorgeous eyes. There was something about him that tugged at me.

A guy I hadn't seen before was talking to him, but Carter wasn't listening. He moved toward me, and the guy who'd been talking to him frowned.

I straightened my shoulders, ready to stand my ground.

With every step Carter took, my stomach fluttered more. He stalked toward me like a man on a mission, his eyes seeming to pierce something inside me, stirring up emotions in places that felt dead. He glided to a stop in my personal space, and his cinnamon-lavender scent hit my nose. I was damn close to salivating.

"What are you doing here?" His deep, sexy voice sounded like music.

I stared at him, immediately forgetting he'd asked me a question. He was shirtless, and despite being lean, he was *ripped*. His shoulders were broad, and he had a six-pack that did all kinds of inappropriate things to me...like give me the urge to trace every curve to the small trail of hair that led down into the waistband of his shorts.

"Take a picture. It'll last longer," he snapped, his eyes darkening.

That snapped me back into the present. I lifted my chin. "No picture needed. I just can't believe that you go around shirtless on campus." The words were out before I thought about what I was saying, and I could have died. That was the worst excuse. It would've been better to own up to checking him out, but no. I had to deny it and then *obviously* lie about it, making myself seem even more pathetic.

My face grew hot, and I had to press on before my blush

became explosive. I could feel the heat rising with every passing second.

He grinned, momentarily making my brain stop working. "Well, if you can pull your gaze away from me, you'll see that many of the other guys in the room are shirtless too." He crossed his arms, making his already delicious body somehow even more... Hell, there wasn't a word to describe *that*.

Move the conversation along, Evie. "I'm here for weight training. There's supposed to be a class. I'm not being a creeper or stalking the football team."

His smile fell, and then he scanned me, taking in my black leggings and my royal-purple crop top. Now I wished that I'd worn a shirt that covered my entire body, but all that Target had was either sweatshirt-like workout shirts or these damn things, so I'd chosen the style that would keep me cool, knowing that my ass would be kicked since I hadn't worked out in forever.

"Only the football team signs up for this class. There isn't an instructor because the coaches provide our weekly program." He glanced over his shoulder.

Was he freaking calling me a liar? I dropped my olive-green backpack and removed my schedule from the front pocket. I smacked it on his chest, and my hand stung from hitting his muscles.

How was that even possible? It was like his chest was made of bricks instead of flesh.

Unfazed, he snatched the schedule from my hand and scowled. "What the *hell*? This isn't supposed to be an open class for any student to take."

"Let me tell you." I placed my hands on my hips and glared, hoping I was shooting at least half the daggers Katherine had managed his way. "Had I known the football team *was* this class, I wouldn't have taken it." I'd hoped there'd be a girl I could team up with to figure out how to use all this stuff, and now I was stuck with the freaking football team. Yeah, I'd much rather *pass*.

Carter's face turned stony as he snarled, "Yeah, right. I believe that. Situations like this aren't a coincidence when it comes to girls like you."

I jerked back as if he'd slapped me. It was clear that was intended as an insult. "What the *hell* does that mean?"

He narrowed his eyes.

Getting stronger wasn't worth this abuse. I'd drop it and sign up for Jazzercise or something. That would still help me build up my endurance. "Forget it. I'll switch classes."

I spun around, but then a callused, muscular hand clasped my upper arm. The roughness shot a thrill right through me, catching me even more off guard.

"Don't." He sighed, turning me back toward him. "Stay. The last thing I need is Dad finding out I sent you packing. I'd never hear the end of it."

"He won't find out." The last thing I wanted was to get even more on the bad side of Carter, Katherine, and their posse. Though I didn't understand the hostility, I did get that I was encroaching on his territory. "I won't say a word to anyone."

"You won't have to. Admissions or whatever will. They'll assume someone on the team caused you to change classes, and then I'd never hear the end of it."

"But—" I didn't want to work out with the football team, but I didn't want to cause him grief either, even if it technically was warranted.

He held out my schedule. "Just…come in. You can work out on the equipment we aren't using. It won't be a big deal if we don't make it one."

I snorted. "I wasn't the one who made it a big deal." I took my schedule back and stuffed it into my bag.

"Yeah, okay." He shrugged. "I deserved that. Sorry for being a jerk."

His easy apology shocked me. Once again, it was like I'd just talked to two different people housed in the same body.

I didn't want to push it any further. "I'll keep to myself. Seriously, had I known that you all were in here, I would've run. Working out with you guys is the last thing I want to do."

The corners of his eyes tightened as he examined me. It was the same look as the one from yesterday. Like he wasn't sure what to make of me. At least the struggle to figure each other out wasn't one-sided.

Done arguing, I picked up my bag and walked around him, then strolled past the group of gawking football players.

"Hey, Evie." Grayson beamed and came over to me. He scanned me from head to toe. "Are you in here with us?"

I shrugged. "Yeah, apparently, I somehow got into this class by accident, but don't worry. I won't distract you all. Go do your big, burly football guy stuff."

I walked to the far corner of the room, where the free weights were. Lovely. I didn't know the first thing about them, but this was the farthest spot from the guys. I tossed my bag down and stared at the weights. And then, I picked some up and started to experiment, taking my time.

Tonight, I'd have to look up how to weight train.

My heart stopped as I stared at the piece of paper I'd drawn from my photography teacher's bowl of random slips.

The class was small, with only fifteen students, and we were all seated at an oblong wooden table. One end didn't have a chair since the whiteboard was there, and the usual royal-purple walls were starting to feel claustrophobic.

Professor Garcia handed out gently used Fuji GFX 50S IIs that we were to call ours for the semester.

Each one of us had randomly picked one of fifteen subjects to take pictures of during the semester—plays, musicals, concerts, school social events that were organized by organizations, big events like homecoming that were organized by the school, and sports, which were divided into softball, girls basketball, girls tennis, girls soccer, girls volleyball, baseball, boys basketball, boys tennis, boys soccer, and football.

I blinked several times, wishing that I was reading my assignment wrong.

Football.

This had to be a joke. Out of *everything,* this was assigned to *me?* A one-in-fifteen chance, and yet, here I was. No matter how many times I blinked, the piece of paper that I'd drawn still showed the neat, tight font with that stupid word staring right back at me.

Professor Garcia strolled up and chuckled. "I bet every person in here wishes they'd gotten that one."

Butterflies took flight in my stomach. "Then I can switch with someone."

She leaned over, her blonde hair falling over her shoulder and her hazel eyes bright with amusement. "Nope, you were the lucky one to pick it. All selections are final, but thank you for being considerate of your classmates." She put her pad on the table and wrote *football* next to my name.

The flutters in my stomach dropped and settled hard.

Professor Garcia stood and smoothed her black, frilly shirt over her black skirt, then moved to the girl beside me.

"I got swimming." The girl wrinkled her nose and flipped her long, voluminous warm-brown hair over her shoulder. She had natural highlights that complemented her milk-chocolate-brown eyes, reminding me of Selena Gomez. "Which is great. I was on the swim team in high school, so I at least know where to stand to take pictures. Besides, I'd pick anything over football." She shivered.

"Aw, Sadie." Professor Garcia chuckled. "Your father would be so upset if he knew you said that, but don't worry; I won't tell him."

My brows furrowed.

Sadie rolled her eyes. "My dad is the school's football coach, and all we do is live and breathe Jaguar football. Any excuse to be away from that, I'm all for."

I forced a smile, certain it looked more like I was passing gas. "Well, don't worry. I'll take extra photos for you."

She laughed. "If you do, make sure some are of that new guy Grayson's ass." She bit her bottom lip and waggled her brows. "That is the one thing that makes being forced to go to every single game worth it."

My brows arched. She had a thing for Grayson, and it was his first semester here too, so how did she already know him? But then I remembered him mentioning he'd been here all summer for training. "Well, I could put in a good word for you." That would probably make things easier between Grayson and me after our disastrous flirting nonflirting.

Her mouth dropped open, and she leaned into me. "You know him?"

"Yeah, I met him yesterday." I nodded as I put my camera back in its case. The last thing I needed was to break it and owe the school a couple thousand for it. "He's a good guy. He helped me find the bookstore, and then I ran into him later at the pond, and he helped me get my things home."

"Oh." Her face fell a little. "I ran into him after he left the bookstore, and he said he was going to the gym."

Shit. She seemed upset. I was trying to encourage her

interest but had most likely made the situation worse. "Oh, he was, but I was having an issue, and he offered to help."

She smiled, but it didn't seem as bright as before. "Yeah, he's a good guy like that." She shrugged. "Well, if you need any pointers about how to handle the guys, I'm your gal. Dad goes on about each player like they're his own sons."

"I might take you up on it." I blew out a breath. "I don't even like sports."

"Me neither, but at least the guys are nice to look at." She smirked and glanced at her phone.

"All right, that's it for the day." Professor Garcia clapped and gestured to the door. "I'll see you on Thursday. Just remember to get the camera out and mess around with it. Get comfortable with it and see what you can figure out on your own. We'll go over aperture, shutter speed, ISO, and all the basics next class."

Eager to get home and get situated since I'd be working late tonight, I packed my bag and slung it and the camera carry case onto my shoulders. I strolled out of the classroom and down the hallway painted in the school colors. I suspected I'd hate purple and gold by the end of the school year; they seemed to be everywhere, a constant reminder of where we were.

As I hit the double doors and made my way outside, Sadie caught up to me.

"Hey, uh..." She paused and glanced at me.

I was a little taken aback that she wanted to talk. She hadn't seemed super thrilled with me inside after I told her about Grayson helping me. "Evie."

"Evie." She adjusted her bag on her shoulders, and I noticed that she wore casual jeans and a comfortable cotton T-shirt, unlike most of the other students here, who seemed to be putting on a fashion show. She continued, "Sorry if I was a little off in there. Just... the whole school year is sorta overwhelming, and most people are only nice to me because they know I'm the football coach's daughter."

"It's fine." I waved off her concern. "I get it. What year are you?"

"Junior." She bit her bottom lip. "But each year is more intense than the last."

I knew how she felt. I loved studying psychology and genuinely enjoyed the classes and learning about all the ways our brains worked. It was like a puzzle, and trying to piece it all together had me fascinated. But the subject was intense, and with my scholarship situation, I felt more pressure than ever to succeed. "Well, I'm sure you'll do great."

We were walking by the student center, and, of course, Carter, Samuel, Grayson, and a few other football players I didn't know were standing out front. Some of them were tossing a football back and forth. They couldn't even go a second without playing.

I knew the moment Carter saw me because the hair on the nape of my neck rose.

Why was I so attuned to him and whatever he was doing?

"Evie," Grayson called and jogged across the sidewalk to us. "No need to text, I'm here." He patted his chest, grinning, and then his attention slid to the person beside me. "Sadie."

"Hey," she said a little too brightly.

"I'm done with classes today." Grayson's attention landed back on me. "Are you?"

I nodded, but before I could elaborate, Sadie interjected, "Me too."

It was almost like she hadn't spoken because Grayson's focus remained on me. "Wanna get some lunch? My treat."

Sadie's happiness deflated faster than a balloon.

Whatever was going on between them, I did *not* want to be

a part of it. "I would, but I need to head home and get ready for work."

He tilted his head back. "You already found a job?"

A guy with olive skin and dark-brown hair with dark-auburn highlights elbowed Carter. He chuckled hatefully, his gray eyes bright. "Oh, I bet Senator McHale has her tied down all right."

A few of the other guys laughed, but Carter's face remained a mask of indifference. His eyes were locked on me. "You need better jokes," he said as if he was bored.

I had no clue what they were hinting at, but I was certain I didn't want to figure it out, especially since the senator had been thrown into the mix. Instead, I chose to get out of this situation. "Yeah, I did. So I need to get moving, but you and Sadie could do lunch."

"Yeah, I could do that." Sadie then winced before she shrugged, trying to play coy. "I mean...if you wanna."

Grayson frowned. "Yeah, sure. I hope next time you're free, Evie."

"We'll see." I chose my words carefully. I didn't want to hurt Grayson's feelings, but I also didn't want Sadie to think I liked Grayson as more than a friend. Sadie was the only person today who'd made an effort to talk to me. "See you guys later."

I took off across the lawn, wanting to get away from the university. This place had me on edge, and I clearly didn't belong here.

The entire way, Carter watched me.

Some foolish part inside me wished he'd just talk to me, and another hoped desperately that he wouldn't.

But when I heard footsteps behind me, my feet slowed down regardless.

CHAPTER EIGHT

The way my body tingled, I had no doubt Carter was the one behind me. That was just how over-the-top super aware I was of him. I'd never been so strongly attracted to a man before, and of course, it would be *him*, of all people.

"Hey," he rasped, and his rough hand gripped my arm again, tugging me to a stop.

I inhaled, and his scent made me dizzy. Slowly, I turned toward him and glared into his eyes, trying not to notice the cut of his jawline or his faint scruff, which somehow added to his sexiness.

Yeah, there went not noticing anything about him, but hell, even his eyes were captivating. *Focus, Evie, and not on his looks.* I cleared my throat.

He smirked but didn't remove his hand. "You shouldn't have done that."

"Done what?" All I'd done was walk past him.

"Pushed Grayson to eat with Sadie." He moved closer, crowding me. "That's Coach Prichard's daughter."

Was this a riddle? If so, it was a damn good one. "She told

me that, and he's a football player. And they know each other. She seems sweet, so I doubt she'll try to break his arm or leg or anything."

He blinked and bit that tantalizing full bottom lip.

I wondered what it would taste like. Not that I personally wanted to experience it, just out of curiosity. This close, I could see that his hair was still slightly damp, and he smelled like soapy cinnamon lavender.

"Are you that clueless?" He dropped his hand and frowned.

And I hated that he was making me feel dumb. I knew I wasn't, and I wasn't about to be that girl who found her worth in some random, spoiled rich guy. "Apparently, I am. So why don't you fill me in?"

"We aren't supposed to hang out with her. She's off-limits." He nodded toward the student center, where they were walking in together. "If Coach thinks they're dating, he could bench Grayson to teach him a lesson."

I cringed. Now that I thought about it, if those two did date and Grayson broke Sadie's heart, I'm sure their coach wouldn't be thrilled. "I'm sorry." I hung my head. "I didn't mean anything by it."

"Yeah, I'm sure you didn't." He rolled his eyes, the coldness back on his face. "Don't do it again. Got it?"

I despised how he was talking to me. He wasn't my boss, but he was the son of one of my benefactors. I couldn't be completely rude, but I lifted my chin and refused to look away. "It was an accident. The last thing I want to do is cause problems for either one of *them*. So, for *them*, I'll make sure not to do that again. But it has *nothing* to do with you. *Got it?*"

His gaze warmed, causing the golden flecks in his eyes to shimmer as he smirked. "You're full of surprises."

"And you're full of arrogance." I adjusted the bag on my shoulders. "Is that all?"

"Yeah." He nodded, the warmth disappearing once again.

"Hey, Car."

When I heard that fake babyish voice, I understood the change.

Katherine bounced by me. She wore ripped jeans shorts and a purple, puffy-sleeved crop top. "I was looking for you. I need to talk to you about something." She looped her arm through his.

I hoped he wouldn't tell her what I'd done. She was looking for any reason to dislike me more than she already did. Worse, seeing her touch him made my heart sink.

He removed her hand and flicked it away. "What the fuck are you doing?"

The corners of my mouth inched up, but thankfully, I caught it before I broke into a smile.

Chuckles sounded from the football players still standing in front of the student center.

Katherine stiffened. Placing her hands on her hips, she said, "Touching my—"

"Don't finish that sentence." Carter's neck corded. "You ruined that last spring break when you fucked the pool boy. Maybe you don't remember, but I do...since I walked in on you two in your room."

Okay, I *really* didn't need to be here for this, but at least I now knew there was one person Carter liked even less than me —Katherine.

She huffed. "I was going to say *friend*. However, since we're on the subject, how many times do I have to tell you it was a mistake?"

"Yeah, you're right." His nostrils flared. "We *were* friends, but that's changed now."

That was my cue to leave, though I did rather enjoy seeing Carter put Katherine in her place. I turned and hurried away.

I needed distance from this school. Everywhere I turned around, I was stepping in something I was unprepared for. But most importantly, I needed space from *him*.

THE NEXT WEEK and a half flew by. I kept my distance from Carter and the other football guys despite having weight training with them. I'd walk in and talk to Grayson for a second before splitting off and keeping to myself the whole time. Carter kept an eye on me, but we didn't talk; we just stared each other down any time we passed one another.

I focused on my psychology class, knowing I needed to ace it if I wanted to get into Stanford for grad school. I was contemplating applying just for the summer internship in Spain to get in more volunteer hours since I was pretty much slammed with school and work.

Avoiding Carter also meant I didn't run into Katherine, which was a win. Things were calm on campus, and Sadie and I were even becoming friendly despite Carter ruining the almost lunch date she'd had with Grayson. In fact, we were planning to meet on Sunday at the school library to do some work together.

I reached the all-brick front of the bar where I officially worked. This was my tenth night, and Joe, Leah's brother, had told me to plan on working Tuesday through Saturday from here on out. He got a little disgruntled when I'd informed him that, depending on the football games, I would need some Saturdays off, but once he saw that I was a hard worker, he decided the hassle was worth it.

The place was nicer than I'd expected, with clean cement floors, ten booths along the side of one wall, three U-shaped tables in the center of the room with eight chairs on each side, and four pool tables and five dart boards. The long bar was built on the wall across from the U-shaped tables, but there wasn't any seating there. It was just for the help to pick up the food and drinks when they were ready.

The walls were simple wood, and the ceiling was simple tile, but the pendant lights hanging throughout the room gave it a more elegant vibe. This wasn't the type of college bar I'd been expecting, but with its name, Hallow's Bar, it actually seemed fitting.

My one complaint was that it reeked of smoke like most bars do.

My first few nights, I'd worried that Carter and his friends would show up, but so far, no one I recognized had stepped foot inside. Plus, I'd been manning the dishwasher, which meant I hadn't had to interact much with anyone other than my coworkers. So tonight, I wasn't extremely worried.

When I walked in at five, the place was almost full.

Leah strode past me with two trays of drinks, somehow balancing them despite moving so quickly. That was a skill I'd yet to master.

I went to the bar where Joe was making a green-colored drink. I stepped behind the end of the counter and opened the drawer where we kept our personal items during shifts, just as he nodded to me.

"Dishwasher again?" Though I didn't get tips for washing dishes, the hourly wage was higher, and I got to stay away from people. It was a win-win.

"Nope." He shook his head. "Tonight's busier than it has been, so I need you to help Leah and Cindy. You're on waitress duty."

Well, there went my plan to put in my earbuds and listen to the new Taylor Swift album while I washed the grime away. I forced a smile. Hopefully, I'd make more money in tips. "Where do you need me?"

"Ask Leah." He picked up a beer glass and began pouring a draft IPA. "Take a pad and a pen, and get your ass to work."

I snatched an apron from the hanger on the wall and tied it around my waist. I was wearing a thin black tank top and jeans, having seen the stains from food and drink Leah came home with on her shirts. Then I grabbed the pad and pen and rushed off to see where they needed help.

Every pool table and dart board was occupied, and man, these people were *thirsty*. The first hour was the roughest, but I started getting the hang of being a waitress. In fact, Leah and Cindy had given me exactly a third of the area, and I was constantly moving.

A group at my U-shaped table got up and left, and another group immediately took half the spots. I finished dropping off a Jack and Coke and a Long Island Iced Tea to two college girls who were on their way to getting completely plastered and then grabbed a damp towel to clean off the table.

When I reached the table, I went into the center, facing the new occupants, and focused on stacking the dirty glasses and wiping down the table. I didn't even glance up. "Hey, my name is Evie. I'll be your waitress tonight. What can I get you all?"

"Oh, I know," a guy said and chuckled. "A body shot that I drink off you. I don't care what the liquor is as long as it's on your body."

I froze as my heart thudded. Leah had warned me there would be creepers, but I'd hoped she was exaggerating. Clearly, that was wishful thinking.

More large guys strolled over, and my pulse thundered in my ears as a shiver ran down my spine. One of warning.

"Ah, at a loss for words," another guy cooed while his buddies chuckled.

I lifted my gaze from the table to him, wanting to put a face to the jackass. With his attitude, I expected ugly, but he wasn't even close.

He was thick and built like a football player with buzzed blond hair and crystal-blue eyes that might have been mesmerizing if he wasn't such a douche. Four other guys with similar builds sat to his right, watching the show, shit-eating grins on their faces.

The one next to Buzz Cut elbowed his friend. His jade eyes sparkled. "Dude. You left her speechless. I bet if you ask her to strip down to her bra and panties for us, she will."

They thought I was flattered. I grimaced and laughed. "Nope, no stripping, no body shots. You want a shot in a glass that I serve you on the table, fine. What kind?"

"Aw, come on." Buzz Cut pouted. "I'll tip you real good."

"She said no, asshole," a familiar deep, sexy voice said from behind me. "You should be used to hearing it by now."

Of course. Tonight, of all nights, Carter was here. When I was waitressing for the first time with a customer trying to bribe me to take my clothes off. That sounded about right.

Buzz Cut's smile fell. "This is none of your concern, *preppy*. Find someplace else to sit."

Even though I did *not* want to face Carter, I didn't want to deal with this guy anymore. He and his buddies were being rude. If I let them keep it up, they'd continue to harass me. Taking a deep breath, I turned to him.

He was even more spectacular than usual, and I almost wouldn't have recognized him in jeans and a casual white polo shirt. He wore an Atlanta Braves baseball hat with his bangs hanging in his eyes. His hair color looked a little darker than usual, as if it was wet, and that clean, soapy, cinnamon-lavender scent hit my nose again. He must have bathed recently.

Samuel flanked Carter on one side while the other guy, who'd been mouthy earlier, stood on the other.

"What can I get you guys?" I pulled out my pad, somehow knowing they wouldn't be obnoxious... at least, not in the same way as the guys behind me.

"I want a whiskey, neat," the mouthy guy said, his gray eyes keen with interest. He leaned forward. His hair looked damp, like he'd just showered as well. "And a double bacon burger, medium well, with double fries." He rubbed his stomach. "Coach killed us at practice tonight, and I'm fucking starving. But when we beat those douchebags behind you, it'll totally be worth it."

"You beat us for the first time last year," Buzz Cut shot back. "Don't worry. That won't happen again. We'll send you entitled preppies crying back to your parents like every other year."

Rival football players. Great. Just what I needed. They must attend Ridge University, the other college in town. It was only a few miles from Hallowed Saints and way more affordable, with four times the number of students. Most students who came to the bar went there.

Samuel rolled his eyes but didn't say anything. He was dressed in slacks and a button-down, maintaining his usual campus look, unlike Mouthy and Carter.

Carter was looking only at me. It was unsettling, like he didn't see anything else around us. "I'd like Yuengling, draft, with a burger. Please."

Then Samuel said he wanted the same as Carter, so I turned to walk off.

"Hey," Buzz Cut hollered after me. "What about us?"

I pivoted on my heel, placing a hand on my hip. "If you can act respectfully, then I'll take your order. But one more pervy comment, I'll make sure Joe escorts you out the door." I knew he would—I'd seen him do it for Cindy and Leah a couple of times. He had a no-harassment policy, but some guys liked to see what they could get away with.

"And Joe won't be the only person you'll have to deal with," Carter warned, sending goose bumps all over my body.

It was the heroic version of him all over again.

"Fine." Buzz Cut sighed, and then he and his friends gave me their orders.

I hurried off to put them in. Luckily, I was so busy that I could only deliver their food and check on their table every now and then. Surprisingly, Carter, Samuel, and the mouthy guy, whom I learned was named Jack, were pleasant. They weren't demanding; they waited until Buzz Cut and his friends were gone before they left, and all three of them left generous tips.

I was so damn busy that I couldn't keep glancing at Carter. The night flew by, and when the last people left and Joe locked the doors, my feet were numb.

Leah and Cindy had taken off already since they'd been here before me. Joe cleaned the bar while I wiped down the tables.

When I finished, I headed to the bar just as Joe moved in the direction of the kitchen.

"Need me to do anything else?" I asked while yawning.

"Nah, you've been running around all night. Go on home. It's late. I'm going to help the kitchen crew clean up." He strolled into the opening that led to the kitchen and then paused. "Good job tonight, by the way."

"Thanks." I smiled. Waitressing hadn't been horrible, and I'd made more than I had washing dishes, thanks to my tips. I couldn't complain about that. "See you tomorrow."

I headed out the front and glanced at the time. It was one in the morning, and I had to walk. I dug into my bag and removed my pepper spray—better safe than sorry—then began walking quickly toward home.

As soon as I stepped onto the sidewalk, an engine started in the parking lot. Headlights lit up on a black Escalade.

Not thinking much of it, I continued my trek until I noticed that the vehicle had turned and was driving slowly behind me. My heart thudded, and I picked up the pace, running across the road into the parking lot of a Taco Bell that still had its lights on. I needed to get somewhere with other people.

The SUV turned into the parking lot and pulled up beside me. I gripped the pepper spray, and as soon as the window rolled down, I spun around and sprayed it into the driver's eyes before I recognized them.

My heart dropped into my stomach, and I dropped my pepper spray on the pavement. The loud *clank* could barely be heard over my pounding heart.

Carter slammed on the brakes as he growled, "What the *fuck*, Evie?"

CHAPTER NINE

The words "I'm sorry" lodged in my throat, but then I realized he didn't deserve them. The heat of anger rushed through my veins.

I laughed, the sound foreign to my ears, full of misery and hurt; all my angst from my parents' death was finally catching up to me. In this moment. With *him*. "Are you serious right now? I should be asking you what the *fuck*, not the other way around!"

Carter rammed the car into Park right there near the sidewalk. Luckily, it was late, and there weren't a lot of people around—the whole issue to begin with.

"I was trying to make sure that jackass didn't wait around to harass you," he gritted out, tears streaming down his face as he rubbed his eyes frantically. "So, yeah, my question is valid, and an apology would be nice."

Oh, he wanted an apology? He'd get one all right. "Oh, I'm so *sorry* that I protected myself when a vehicle started following me from a parking lot in the middle of the night and then proceeded to pursue me like some stalky-ass creeper!"

Grumbling, he kept rubbing his eyes. "I swear, this is worse than being sacked during a game."

My anger fizzled as I watched him suffer. His eyes were clamped shut, and so many tears were running down his face that he seemed to be sobbing. Worse, he wouldn't be able to drive himself home...which meant this fell on me to handle. "Where's your phone? I'll call one of your friends to come get you."

"Fuck no." He banged a hand on the steering wheel. "I don't want them to know about this."

My heart ached. I had a sinking suspicion he didn't mean the pepper spray but that he'd stayed to watch over me. Was he embarrassed? My own heart now seemed to have two separate personalities because it imploded and then leapt with excitement in the next second.

He'd stayed to watch over me. Why would he do that? Maybe, despite all appearances, he didn't hate me after all...and my heart sank all over again. He still wanted people to *think* he couldn't stand me. I would *not* be the girl who got all giggly over that.

"Fine." I reached inside the vehicle and unlocked his door. "Move to the passenger seat, and I'll drive you there."

"So you can walk home even later by yourself?" He shook his head, somehow acting authoritative despite his state. "Fuck no. That's not happening either."

Taking him home with me wasn't an option. Between my roommates and him finding out where I lived, I'd rather run off and leave him here in the parking lot. "You have two choices. Let me call someone for you, or let me drive you home. If we flush out your eyes, you'll be better in about an hour, if not less. But the more you rub them, the worse it's going to be."

He huffed and got out of the car. "The address is in the navigation system under HSU home."

My mouth dropped open. I hadn't actually expected him to agree to let me drive him. I took his arm and led him around to the passenger side, my skin hypersensitive where the two of us touched, but I told my heart to settle down. This attraction to him had to stop. It would only complicate matters. "You don't live on campus?"

"Hell *no*." Carter wrinkled his nose. "I like my own space. Freshman year was bad enough."

He was a bit of a control freak, so I shouldn't be surprised.

After he got settled, I climbed into the driver's seat. My body sank into the comfortable cushions, still warm from his body. My stomach did that weird flip again. I moved the seat forward, taking in the sleek, dark interior of the vehicle.

With all the bells and whistles, it might be worth more than my old house. Instantly, I regretted offering to drive him home. What if I crashed it? I was already up to my eyeballs in debt; I didn't need to add this car to my ever-growing list.

"Are you sure you don't want me to call Samuel, Jack, Grayson, or even..." My throat tightened, but I forced the next name off my lips. "Katherine?"

"I'm sure you'd love to call Grayson," he sneered, looking intimidating even in his current situation. "But, no, *Evie*. You did this to me; you get to clean up the mess."

I jabbed my finger into the navigation screen, trying to figure out how his GPS worked, taking my frustration out on the display. I sort of wanted to do that to his eyes instead, but I knew that when I calmed down, I would be ashamed of myself...especially if I caused permanent damage, so I forced myself to relax.

Finally, I locked in the address and followed the instructions. When the GPS had me turn farther away from where I lived, I sighed. It was going to be a long night, but at least it was only a five-minute drive. It wouldn't add too much time to my walk...or, worst case, I'd suck it up and Uber.

The houses became nicer as we drove, which wasn't shocking. I expected no less from him.

His head lay on the headrest and tears were still streaming. A little bit of guilt settled into my chest as the adrenaline was wearing off. I probably should have checked who was trying to talk to me instead of just shooting him with the spray. But I never expected it would be *him*.

This was why I stopped myself from poking him in the eye earlier.

The GPS had just alerted me that we were a quarter mile from our destination when a large new townhouse complex came into view on the right. It was a three-story dark-gray building with a white roof and trim. When it told me to turn right and rattled off the house number, I noticed that the driveway led downward into a garage.

"Do you want me to pull into the garage?" I glanced around, searching for the opener.

"Nah." He unfastened his seat belt. "I'll deal with it later."

That was fine with me. I turned off the vehicle and darted to his side just as he was climbing out. He hung his head but reached into his pocket, removing his keys. "The house key is here," he said.

I took his arm and led him to some stone stairs with a black iron railing and helped him up. When we reached the solid cherrywood door, I unlocked it and pushed it open. We stepped into a living room with all-white walls that opened into a huge, gorgeous kitchen. I led him behind a white couch decorated with a variety of gray pillows and two comfy-looking chairs on either side. The couch sat across from a dark-charcoal fireplace with white trim around it. Above it, the wall was a white shiplap with a gorgeous picture of a sunset over a river.

My heart clenched, and I jerked my gaze away from the image to the two seats on either side of the couch, one a dark gray that matched the fireplace tile and the other a light gray. Right next to the fireplace was a television with white cabinets underneath it and more river pictures above.

"Let's get you to the sink." I gripped Carter's wrist and led him across the maple hardwood floor into the spotless kitchen. The bronze sink was in the center of a large island with a striking white countertop that matched the walls and cabinets. I led him past the bar with its four dark wood barstools.

The place was immaculate, which I found a little unsettling for a twenty-two-year-old college man. I'd expected it to at least be messy, but it was a lot like Carter's outward appearance—clean, precise, and put together.

I turned on the water, planning to let it warm to at least room temperature, when Carter nudged me out of the way and stuck his face under the water. He tilted his head, letting the stream pour into his eyes. He hissed. "This is not making it feel better."

Water poured all over his face, even into his hair, somehow making him even more gorgeous. Who knew him being a hot mess would have my hormones even more frazzled?

I shook my head, trying to focus on what he needed. "Well, you have your eyes closed. You need to open them."

"Easier said than done when you aren't the one in the situation," he muttered. His jaw clenched as he opened his eyes. "*Fuck.* That hurts."

Unsure what to do, I grabbed some paper towels from the wire rack next to the sink. "It should get better soon." Or, at least, I hoped it would. I swallowed and rubbed my fingers over the smooth, cool countertop. "At least you don't have a game tomorrow."

He grumbled, "Not helping."

I rubbed my hands on my jeans, trying to calm the shaking. I didn't know why I always got nervous around him, but it was even worse tonight.

A loud ring nearly startled me out of my skin. I figured it was Carter's phone, but then my back pocket vibrated. I put the paper towels next to the sink, yanked out my phone, and saw Leah's name roll across the screen. "Here's some paper towels when you need them. I gotta take this."

"Yeah, I'll just be *here*."

I mashed my lips together to prevent a laugh from escaping. I was pretty sure that he hadn't meant to be funny.

I put the phone to my ear as I walked back into the living room. "Hello?"

"Evie! Where the hell are you?" Leah yelled over loud music.

My stomach dropped. Of course they were having a party. They'd had one last weekend, too, and I'd stayed down in my room, waiting for the loud noise to end. "I got tied up." There was no way in hell I'd tell her where I was. They still hadn't let me live down bringing Grayson home.

"Oh..." She sounded intrigued. "Please tell me it's the fun, kinky kind."

I frowned. "Afraid not."

"Well, you need to get here quick." She moved the phone closer, causing her words to blur. "Your boy is here."

"My...boy?" I had no clue what she was even referring to. The only guys we knew in common were the people we worked with and...Grayson. What was he doing there?

"Yeah, tall, sexy, and delicious." She giggled. "He's here. I told him you should be home any second, but I started getting worried. You told me you'd Uber, or I would've stayed."

I hadn't wanted to put her out by making her wait for me and didn't want to use money when work was only a fifteen-minute walk from the house. "A friend picked me up, and we're hanging out for a minute. I'll get there as soon as I can."

"That's fine." She giggled. "I'll keep your boy entertained, so the other girls here back off."

Girls? As in plural. "How many people are there?"

"Just twenty or *so*." She said, her words hinting at a slur. "See you soon. And be safe." She hung up without waiting for me to say bye.

I put the phone back into my pocket and stared at the painting above the fireplace.

Car rolling. World spinning. Metal crunching.

The walls closed in on me, and my breathing turned ragged. I remembered the rush of the water flooding the car and the blood covering Dad's face. Mom's rasping. My desperate attempts to unbuckle.

My legs gave out, and I landed on something hard as I relived my parents' deaths all over again.

Something hard wrapped around my waist, and I kicked, trying to get away. I had to break free and save my parents! But the harder I tried to yank away, the more securely I was held.

"Evie." Carter's deep voice grated in my ear, and then I was picked up.

The memory slipped away, and the room I was in came back into view.

My head sagged against something warm and firm, and then the sound of a steady heartbeat pounded in my ear as my body tingled.

Awareness trickled back to me.

I was in Carter's arms, in his house. My face flamed, and I stiffened and inched away from his chest. I couldn't believe I'd had a panic attack in front of him. Until now, I'd only had nightmares of that day.

"Are you okay?" he asked, his arms still gripping me like a lifeline.

I cleared my throat, trying to ignore the embarrassment crawling down my spine. "Yeah, sorry. I zoned out."

"Clearly. Are you okay to stand?"

There he was, being a nice guy all over again. "I'm fine."

He put me gently on my feet, and I wanted to run out the front door instead of facing him. But I needed to check on him since I had pepper sprayed him. I braced myself and looked him in the eye.

The kindness there was the last thing I expected. There was no judgment or revulsion. It was as if he understood what had just happened.

Something brimmed between us. I wanted to take a step toward him and press myself to his chest all over again. His gaze zeroed in on my mouth, and he licked his bottom lip slowly.

His head lowered, and my legs moved closer to him of their own accord. I placed my hands on his chest, feeling the curves of the muscles and the warmth of his skin through his shirt. But when I noticed the wet neckline of his shirt, I stilled, remembering why I was here and who I was with.

Using every ounce of willpower I had, I took a quick step back and dropped my hands. "Are your eyes better now?" If so, I needed to get out of here.

Jerking his head back, he blinked and straightened. "They still burn a little, but yeah. They're a lot better."

"Good." I forced a smile, though my heart was still beating wildly. We'd come so close to kissing, and usually, he couldn't stand me. "Then I'll leave you to do whatever it is that you do. Thanks for checking up on me." I doubted he'd ever do it again.

I turned to head out the door, but he pivoted around me, blocking me from leaving.

He arched a brow, his eyes tightening as he said hoarsely, "Are you in a rush to meet someone?"

He towered over me, jaw clenched and nostrils flared. He glared at me expectantly, waiting for my answer.

For that reason alone, I wanted to clamp my mouth shut and not say anything. But I was quite certain he wouldn't let me leave until I answered him.

Trying to calm the anger heating my body, I lifted my chin. "It's late. I'm tired. I've been on my feet, serving people for eight hours, and they are killing me."

"Not answering my question." He crossed his arms, his biceps bulging underneath his polo. Even with his reddened eyes, he could be a model. A stoned model...but a model nonetheless.

"I *did*." Crossing my arms, mimicking him, I rocked on my heels. "The only thing I'm rushing to is my bed." With loud music blaring overhead, but at least it would be *my* bed and away from him. He had my stomach twisted so tight that I didn't know if I was feeling flutters or nausea.

His neck corded. "And who's going to be in that bed with you?"

CHAPTER TEN

I huffed and stared into his eyes. He was acting...strange. "And why would that matter to you?"

"We wouldn't want the senator to think you were sleeping with other people—like Grayson—*would we?*"

And there was the asshole I knew. I'd been waiting for him to make his appearance. It was about time. The insinuation was clear, and he might as well have kicked me in the gut with how much it hurt. "Is that what you think of me? That I'm sleeping with a *married* man old enough to be my *father?*"

"Well, he did pay your way into HSU." His face softened slightly. "It makes sense."

"Yes, Carter." I lifted a shaky finger, wishing like hell it was steady, but still too angry to care that it wasn't. "I'm sleeping with him, so he'll give me a full ride, yet I'm working at a bar five days a week in order to pay rent, pay off my parents' debts, and be able to eat. Makes *so* much sense."

Something passed over his face, and he dropped both arms. "Is your car in the shop? Is that why you're walking?"

I laughed. "Nope. No car. Just walking."

"What about an Uber?" He arched a brow.

"Adds up." I ran a hand down my face. "And right now, I need every dollar. But please, don't tell the senators any of that."

"Why? You'd have it easier if I did. They'd handle all your problems for you because they brought you here. Women have done worse to get what they want."

All the fight left me. Maybe I should've just said yes, the senator is waiting for me in my steamy hot basement of a bedroom, naked in my bed. But for some reason, I didn't want Carter to think poorly of me. I was tired of everyone thinking the worst of me, so I bared my soul to him. "He tried to pay for a dorm, and I said no. He's already doing too much by sending me here for a year."

"You told him no, knowing you'd have to work like this?" All traces of anger were replaced by furrowed brows and blinking. "Why?"

I raised both arms to my sides, palms up. "I didn't want to take advantage. I can work for the rest. He can do something for someone else in need with that money."

Carter scratched the back of his neck and examined me as if he was seeing someone else standing in front of him. "You're not shitting me?"

"If you don't believe me, fine." I shrugged. I had enough things to work through, and convincing him to believe me wasn't one of them. "I don't have anything to prove to you." His accusation slammed through me again. "Why would you think I was sleeping with the senator?" Oh god. My chest constricted, and I couldn't breathe. "Has he done that before?" Did *everybody* think I was sleeping with him? I stumbled back a few steps, dropping onto the couch. I sank my head into my hands, wanting to hide from the entire world.

"No, he hasn't, but him sponsoring you was just so out of

the blue and unexpected," Carter said as the couch dipped beside me, and his leg brushed mine as he sat. "Katherine said—"

"*Katherine?*" I lifted my head and gritted my teeth. "Well, if she said it, it must be true. After all, she cheated on you—her moral compass is high."

He winced. "That's fair. Neither this nor dating her were the best decisions I've ever made in my life. But still, I've known women to use leverage over people like him."

"Even so. Why would you even believe that, knowing her?" He wasn't going to get off by being less growly and assholey.

His face slipped back into a mask of indifference. "It made sense from my personal experience. So tell me the real reason he did it then?"

"You know. As *fun* as this was, let's never do it again." I wasn't going to sit here and be questioned repeatedly on *why* I was at HSU. I didn't have any better answer than he did, and he *knew* the senator. "Seriously."

I stood, ready to get home. I'd rather deal with blaring music and drunken shenanigans than *this*.

"Fine," he bit out and then collected the keys I'd left on the island. "I'll drive you home."

"No." I gestured to his eyes. "You said they're still bothering you. I'll be fine."

I marched to the door, but his footsteps pounded behind me. When I reached out to grab the door handle, hands wrapped around my waist and spun me toward him.

Before I could catch my balance, he squatted and threw me over his shoulder. My front side hung down his back while his arms wrapped securely around my bottom. In what had to be one fluid movement, he had the door open and was carrying me outside.

"Put me down," I yelped and smacked his ass. Just like his chest, I ended up hitting pure muscle.

"Not happening," he said and continued down the steps toward his Escalade. "You're not walking home."

His words were like ice water to the face. I didn't want him to see where I lived and what I was walking into. "I'll call an Uber." I'd spend ten dollars just to get him to head back into the house.

When we reached his vehicle, he opened the passenger door and tossed me inside. He slammed the door and jogged to the driver's side.

I clenched my hands, letting my fingernails dig into my palms. I wanted to get out and walk back, but all he would do was follow me. At the end of the day, it would take longer and still result in him learning where I lived.

Sliding into the car, he grinned. "No getting out and trying to run away."

At this point, I was beginning to believe he was a mind reader. "I thought about it but figured you'd just follow me home like a crazed stalker."

"Stalker?" He scrunched his face. "Don't flatter yourself."

"You were the one waiting in a black vehicle for me to leave work." I fastened my seat belt while tilting my head. "So…I'm going with stalker."

He laughed, and my body nearly stopped functioning. I'd never heard a sound like that from him. It was genuine and carefree…deep and sexy. In other words, dangerous because I already found him *way* too tempting.

"Eh, I guess I deserve that." He backed out of the driveway and turned in the direction of the university.

I shook my head, trying to remove the stupor and start my brain functioning again. "How do you know where I live?"

"Let's call it a good guess." He blinked and rubbed his eyes. "You were walking in this direction when you left the bar."

Oh. Right. That was what got me into this mess, to begin with.

As we got closer to HSU, I noticed his knuckles blanching on the steering wheel. He was either stressed or upset about something.

With each street we turned down, his demeanor darkened. It had changed from relaxed to concerned to annoyed, and now his jaw was clenched and his body rigid. In other words, his whole asshole persona was on display.

Lovely.

I heard loud music thumping, and when the house came into view, I sighed and dropped my head. "She said it was a *small gathering*."

His head jerked in my direction. "Yours is the house with cars lined up and down the driveway and road with shit music playing?"

There were at least twenty cars parked out front, and our house was small. I sighed. "Yup. My roommates like to, uh...drink?" I hadn't meant for it to come out like a question, yet here we were. *A lot of things happened tonight that shouldn't have... so let's just keep piling it on!* That was my motto lately, one I didn't approve of.

Several people stood in the front yard, including Grayson and another guy I'd seen in the weight room, who had to be on the football team. Three more guys were talking to them, and girls stood on either side of the guys and another in front of Grayson, giggling.

"Fuck this," Carter rumbled. He eased his vehicle into the small opening between the driveway and Grayson's Jeep, which was parked on the street, and drove across the yard straight at the people standing in front of the porch.

My heart thudded as we hit a spot in the grass that jerked the wheels, and when he stopped the car a few feet shy of the others, who'd yelped and backed up, I let out a shaky breath. I didn't know what that was about, but I knew he was full-on asshole Carter once more.

All eyes were locked on us, the conversation dead in the water. Grayson's gaze flicked between Carter and me, and his forehead creased.

"Uh...thanks for the ride." I reached for the car door just as Carter turned off the vehicle like he wasn't leaving.

I froze and swallowed, and those damn tingles sprouted and shot down my spine.

"Is that all I get?" he asked curtly.

My head spun like all the oxygen had suddenly left the air. I had *no clue* what he was asking, and I was quite certain that if I didn't answer appropriately, he'd get even more angry. I leaned forward, pulled some cash out of my back pocket, and started counting one-dollar bills. "Will twenty do?" An Uber would've been cheaper, but he had a huge-ass car. This should cover the gas.

"Are you fucking with me right now?" he snarled.

I glanced at him and froze.

His cheeks were flushed, and his nostrils flared.

I leaned my head back. "Carter, I'm tired. I don't even know how to answer that question. Gas money is the only thing I can think of that you might expect."

He practically growled at me. "Let's get you to your room." He opened his car door and climbed out.

My heart galloped, and trepidation pooled in my stomach, the usual combination when it came to him. I sat in the car, trying to get my bearings.

Grayson watched Carter's entire performance, and I

dreaded being alone with him in the future. No doubt, he'd ask me hundreds of questions.

When Carter continued to my door, I didn't know what he was doing...until he reached for the door handle.

Whoa. Cold, Dark, and Broody was opening my door for me. It made this look like a date. My stomach fluttered, and I flinched. It was sad that I needed to remind myself that this most definitely was *not* a date. Besides, I didn't want a boyfriend...right?

Right.

Most definitely right.

He opened the door and took my hand, tugging me out of the seat. My body hummed, and heat spread through my belly.

When my feet touched the ground, he released me, and I immediately missed his touch.

"Carter," Grayson said formally, and then his attention landed on me. "Evie."

"Hey." I scanned the group.

"Grayson," Carter mimicked, placing his hand at the small of my back and leading me toward the others. "Cole."

"Hey, Cap." The other guy on the football team saluted, his ocean-blue eyes twinkling. His sandy-blond hair was messy, and longish bangs hung over his forehead. He was a couple of inches shorter than Carter and Grayson, around six feet. "Gotta say, I'm surprised to see you here. I didn't realize you two were..."

I didn't know how to respond. Thankfully, he wasn't talking to me.

"Don't start shit." Carter arched an eyebrow, but his hand stayed firmly on my back. "I just picked up Evie from work and wanted to make sure she got home safely."

The sultry redhead on the right side of Grayson laughed

loudly. "Oh, so you're Leah and Haven's roommate. They're inside, you know."

"Regina," the raven-haired girl in front of Grayson hissed. "Not subtle."

No, she was not subtle at all, but that was more than fine with me. I just wanted to run downstairs and hide in my room... from *everyone*. I forced a smile and glanced at Carter. "Thanks for the ride. I'm good now."

"Yeah, no problem." He shrugged. "I figured I might stay for a little while."

He wasn't leaving? His entire body was tense. Why was he staying?

Whatever.

It wasn't my problem.

"Great." I stepped away, causing his hand to drop from my back. "Well, I'm sure you, Grayson, and Cole will have a lovely time." I pretended to tip my hat at the girls, who clearly wanted me gone so they could regain the guys' attention and then headed to the side door, which led straight into the kitchen.

As soon as I opened the door, the music blared even louder in my ears. They were going to get the cops called on us. Truthfully, I wasn't sure how they hadn't been already. Both Leah and Haven were in the kitchen, and Leah was attempting to pour Malibu rum into two red Solo cups, but she kept missing and splashing it on the table.

I hurried over, taking the bottle from her. "Please tell me that's not for the two of you."

"Evie! You're home." Haven beamed and moved to hug me and almost fell over instead. Luckily, she caught the table and held herself up.

"It's about damn time," Leah grumbled, swaying offbeat to the music. "And yeah, those are ours. Grab another cup, and make one of your own."

Dealing with drunk people was easy. "Sure will." I pretended to pour more liquor into the cups while they slurred about Grayson and Cole being here. Then, I filled each of our cups entirely with Coke. I handed one to each of them and lifted a brow. "I hope I didn't make those too strong for you."

"Bish, please." Leah snatched hers from my hand and took a huge gulp. Then she coughed, her eyes bulging. "Oh my god. You're going to have to tell me how much liquor you put in it. It's the strongest drink I've ever had while still tasting the Coke. It's phenomenal."

I mashed my lips together, trying desperately not to laugh. "A true mixologist never reveals their secrets." I winked at her.

Haven took a sip. "You're right. This is amazing."

"You're welcome. Now go in there and host while I clean up this mess." I waved them off, ready to sneak away and be alone.

"Fine. But you better come join us." Leah lifted her drink, and the two of them stumbled into the living room.

I quickly cleaned off the table, picked up my own Coke, and then snatched a yogurt from the fridge, and headed downstairs.

The humidity had been sweltering upstairs, and there wasn't much of a reprieve in the basement. Worse, I had no AC. I turned on my fan and hurried into the bathroom to take a quick shower and cool off.

When I was finished and dressed in my pajamas, I unlocked the door and headed back into my room, only to smack into a solid wall—er, I meant chest.

CHAPTER ELEVEN

The wind was knocked out of me on impact, and I struggled for air. It wasn't from the pain of running into someone; every ounce was due to the fact that someone was in my room.

I stumbled back, my heart constricting. When I realized it was Carter, I was finally able to inhale...until I saw the anger on his face.

I thought I'd seen Carter angry. But, boy, I'd been wrong.

His neck was corded, and his bangs hung over his forehead, giving him a messy look. I could hear his teeth grinding.

I swallowed and moved to walk around him, but he looped his arm around my waist and pulled me against his chest. My body trembled, and I relaxed into him. That was until he spoke.

"What the *fuck* is this?" he rasped, a dangerous edge to each word.

"You're going to have to be a little more specific." I lifted my head, knowing that cowering would make him feel even more in control. This was *my* room. He didn't get to come in here and insult it.

"I don't think I can be. This whole evening has been one giant shit show."

I pushed a finger into his chest. "Then *leave*. You weren't invited down here in the first place!"

"That's half of this huge fucking problem."

Uh...what? I pulled back, and my mouth dropped open. "You wanted me to invite you into my room? You, Carter Grisham, are not lacking any sort of confidence."

He dropped his arms, and a vein bulged between his eyes. "Do you think this is funny?"

I ran a hand through my wet hair and slowly walked across the room to my bed. I was so damn tired; all I wanted to do was *sleep*. Not party, not argue, and definitely not deal with the grumpy, broody quarterback who all of a sudden was dominating my night. "Any way I answer that will only piss you off more."

"Well, at least you're aware of *something*." His jaw worked, the muscle flexing underneath. "Do you know that *anybody* could come down here while you were showering or while you're sleeping? There isn't a lock on the door."

I blinked, trying to process our ever-evolving... Hell, I didn't even know what to call it. It definitely wasn't a friendship, but *relationship* didn't work either. The best I could come up with was "dysfunctionship," but that wasn't a real word...until *now*. "I locked the bathroom door and took my clothes in there." I waved at my hot pink yoga pants and the cheesy black T-shirt Mom had bought me for my birthday in June that said, "Just let me sleep."

"Okay, what about when you're sleeping?" He crossed his arms, making his stupid sexy muscles bulge.

"Light sleeper." I tapped my head. "If someone tries to draw a mustache on my face with a permanent marker, I'll catch them red-handed."

"Is this some kind of joke to you?"

"You already asked me if I thought this was funny." He reminded me of one of those standardized tests that asks the same questions multiple ways to see if you answer differently. "No, I do not find this funny or think it's some sort of joke. I'm tired and want to go to sleep." I pointed at my shirt to emphasize the point.

He laughed humorlessly. "How can you sleep down here? It feels like a humid death swamp even with the fan on."

I shrugged and flopped onto my bed. "What do you want me to say? I can barely afford *this*. Believe me, it's not ideal, but it's only for a year."

"A *year*." He shook his head. "Hell no. I'm calling Senator McHale now." He pulled out his phone.

And just like that, I was wide awake. I jumped off the bed and raced toward him, snatching the phone from his hands.

He blinked several times. "Hand me my phone."

I put it behind my back like I was a little girl, but I didn't care. "You can't call him."

"Give me one good reason why not."

I inhaled, which wasn't smart. Because of how close he was, I drew in his scent, and it made my mind fuzzy. I had to focus. The last thing I wanted him to do was to call the senator. So, I said the first thing that popped into my mind. "Because it shouldn't matter to you. This isn't *your* problem. It's mine, and I can handle things fine on my own."

Something flickered in his eyes like he was deciding something. He must have made a decision because a cocky grin spread across his face. "Not a good reason."

He snaked a hand around me, going for his phone; I twisted and got away. Sadly, my victory was momentary because he grabbed me by the waist and hoisted me up. I wiggled against him, trying to break free, and he tossed me onto my bed.

I landed on my stomach in the center of the bed, clutching the phone under my breasts. He crawled after me and flipped me onto my back so we were facing one another.

Bucking underneath him, I tried to squirm free, but he straddled my waist and gripped my hands, then pinned them over my head.

"Now, are you going to behave?" he asked.

My chest heaved, but with his body all over me, it was impossible to catch my breath. Each time my lungs filled, my breasts brushed against his chest. Lungs screaming, I couldn't even suck in enough oxygen to answer.

Something shifted between us, and warmth flooded back into his irises. His gaze landed on my lips, and this time, I was the one who licked them. I smelled a hint of mint. I wondered if he tasted like it too.

His forehead wrinkled. "You shouldn't have this effect on me."

My stomach somersaulted, and my heart pounded against my rib cage. I was thankful that I wasn't alone in feeling...whatever *this* was. I opened my mouth to say something, but he lowered his head.

The kiss wasn't sweet; it was urgent. His soft, firm lips pressed against mine, and his tongue swept in, claiming my mouth. I tried to move my hand to fist his shirt and bring him closer, but his grip tightened, holding my hands in place.

He was completely in charge of the kiss.

Every stroke of his tongue had my body warming even more for him. I'd never been kissed like this before, and worse, I was certain I never would be again.

The loud music faded. He tilted his head and deepened our kiss, and a flash of white-hot need curled in my stomach, so intense that I wrapped my legs around him, drawing him closer.

He groaned and pulled his mouth away from mine, then kissed his way down my neck. My eyes closed, lids heavy with desire, focusing on the soft caresses of his lips. His tongue rolled across the base of my neck, and a soft moan escaped me.

"You're going to make me do the very thing I promised I'd never do," he whispered against my neck.

"And what's that?" I wanted him to tell me—but also to keep kissing me. I didn't care if it was my lips or my neck as long as his mouth was somewhere on me.

"Not listen to my head," he murmured as he moved so that one of his hands gripped both my wrists. He ran his free hand through my hair and then down my side until it rested at the bottom of my shirt.

A shudder tore through me, and something clenched inside me. I should've probably been offended by what he'd said...but I couldn't be. I understood it. Doing this with him right now was beyond stupid. Nothing could ever truly happen between us, but for once, I didn't want to be practical. I just wanted to feel something other than the gripping loss of my parents and home. He did things to me that I'd never thought possible, and each one of his touches ignited something that burned deep within my soul.

Just as his fingers slid under my shirt and I arched my back on a gasp, the door that led down to the basement opened.

"Evie?" Grayson called. "Are you decent? I heard the water stop."

Carter stilled and whispered in my ear, "Pretend you aren't here." His hand hitched higher, grazing the bottom of my breast.

Goose bumps spread throughout my body, and my chest hitched. This was moving way too fast, and though I didn't want it to end, Grayson's presence brought reality washing over me.

Footsteps clomped down the steps. "Evie? Are you okay?"

My heart thudded. He was coming down, and Carter was still on top of me. I dropped my legs back onto the bed and tried to get out of his arms again, but his grip was like a freaking vise.

"Please, get off me," I hissed, not wanting Grayson to walk in on us like this.

Carter smirked and released me while slowly getting up and snatching his phone back.

Just as Grayson took the final step behind the wall to my room, Carter stood completely, and I yanked down my shirt.

"Oh," Grayson said as he paused at the entry to the basement. "I didn't realize..." He took me in, his face pale.

I ran a hand through my hair and realized my wet locks were clumped together. Not only that, but Carter's lips were swollen, which meant that mine must be too, and there was a noticeable bulge in Carter's pants.

There was no doubt what we'd been doing, and the way Carter grinned made me want to smack that look off his face. He *wanted* Grayson to know what we'd been up to.

"Uh... should I go back upstairs?" Grayson winced.

"Yes," Carter said at the same time I replied, "No."

Carter arched a brow, daring me to...I didn't know what.

"He was just leaving." I stood, fighting the urge to yank on my shirt again. I could feel where it was raised in the back, and the memory of Carter's rough hand against my skin had me aching for him to touch me all over again.

"Not leaving." Carter sat on the edge of my bed then leaned back with his hands folded underneath his head.

I knew he wasn't joking. He was dead serious.

"Dude, she wants you to leave." Grayson gestured to the stairway. "In case you didn't get the hint."

"Don't care." Carter pointed at the ceiling. "Not with a

party like that going on upstairs. Anyone could come down here while she's sleeping."

The thing was, he was right. I needed to put a lock on the door. "This is my home, and Leah and Haven wouldn't let someone do that."

"Two guys are down here now." Carter pointed at himself and then Grayson. "And they didn't say a thing."

I sighed in annoyance. "They know we're all friends."

"Friends?" The corner of Carter's mouth twitched. "Is that *so*?"

Swallowing, I blinked a few times. I wasn't sure what he was getting at. Was he upset that I'd called him a friend? "Well, Carter, you're the one down here, refusing to leave, concerned with my safety. What do you call *that*?"

Both of them wore similar expressions—foreheads lined and deep frowns.

The entire day crashed over me. "Guys, I'm tired. I just want to go to bed." I yawned, not even needing to pretend.

"Fine." Something passed through Carter's expression, and then he stood and marched past Grayson and up the stairs. Every stomp up the stairs sounded full of authority...just like him.

My heart ached as I watched him disappear.

Grayson placed his hands in the pockets of his jeans. "Evie, I hope you know what you're getting into with him. He's a senator's son, and–"

"I got it." I already knew that I wasn't good enough for him, but hearing Grayson say so hurt. "And there's nothing going on between us. I told you I don't want to date."

"Well, sleeping with Carter isn't a better decision." Grayson sat on the edge of the bed. "He's a good team captain and a great quarterback, but–"

"Please. Don't. I get it. I'm not sleeping with him. I promise."

All of a sudden, the music stopped, and then Carter's voice boomed out, "Party's over. Get out."

"What the *hell*?" a guy moaned.

"Fine, if you still wanna be here when the cops arrive, be my guest. I was just trying to do you a solid."

The scurrying that followed was chaotic as everyone suddenly decided they needed to be anywhere else.

There was a bang on the door that led downstairs as Carter yelled, "Grayson, let's go. She wants to sleep."

I *almost* wanted to kiss him again.

Grayson rolled his eyes. "I'd better go." He smiled sadly.

"Let's have lunch Monday after class," I offered, hating that I'd hurt his feelings. "I don't work that day, so I won't have to be in such a rush."

The warmth in his eyes returned. "Yeah, I'd like that."

Another bang rattled the door, and Grayson stood. "Guess that's my cue. We have practice tomorrow morning. Good night, Evie."

"Night."

Before I even heard the two of them leave, I'd fallen asleep.

"What the hell was that, Evie?" Leah complained from her spot on the couch. She was slouching with a bottle of Pepto Bismol propped on her stomach. "I mean, the guy is hot, but he totally ruined the party."

I took a bite of my granola bar and propped myself against the doorframe that divided the kitchen from the living room. I chuckled. "It was, like, three in the morning, and you have to work in three hours. You should be thanking him."

Haven sat on the other end of the couch with a wet washcloth on the back of her neck. She was pale and clearly hungover. "Yeah, I'm with her. We need to slow down on the partying. This is the second weekend I've felt like complete shit."

"Hey." Leah stuck out her tongue and then groaned. "We're only young once."

"And you have only one liver." I lifted my yogurt cup, saluting her.

"Ha ha." Leah took another swig of the medicine. "I'll be fine for work."

"I hope so. I don't want to be there alone if it's busy like last night."

A rumbling sound reached us from our driveway, and then the engine cut off.

"You two expecting anyone?" I asked as I headed to the front door. I knew they wouldn't be getting up to answer it in their current state.

"Nope." Leah placed a hand on her head. "But please open the door before they ring the doorbell."

I shouldn't. I should have let whoever it was ring the doorbell, but I didn't have it in me. When I opened the door, the world seemed to tilt.

"What are you doing here?" I gasped and stepped outside, not letting him in.

There stood Carter Grisham, a smug smile on his face and a bag in each hand.

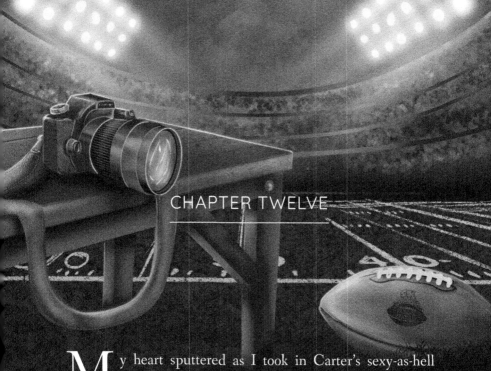

CHAPTER TWELVE

My heart sputtered as I took in Carter's sexy-as-hell appearance. His hair was messy, bangs hanging into eyes that were dark with determination, while a little bit of scruff made him even more manly. Need from last night clenched in my stomach, taking me by surprise.

He scanned me, and I realized that I was still wearing my sleep shirt with no bra and my yoga pants. He smirked and lifted his hands. "I brought biscuits, a door lock, and there's an AC unit in the car."

My mouth dropped open, and my eyes widened. He was taking care of me, but I couldn't allow that. This was my mess, and I wouldn't take advantage of him. "Thank you, but I'm fine. It's not needed." I crossed my arms, trying to look firm.

Rocking back on his heels, he grinned. "That's okay. I'll just come by every night and make sure your roommates aren't throwing a party. But if you want to see me so bad, wouldn't it be better to just invite me over instead of forcing me to come to protect your virtue?"

"That's not why I don't want the lock." My face burned,

and the next words slipped out before I could stop them. "And my virtue is more at risk with you around than not."

He chuckled cockily. "Then I guess you better let me install the lock, but it's cool if you don't. We can have a repeat of last night."

My lungs froze, and he leaned down, crowding my space. His lips hovered inches above mine, his minty breath blowing across my face with his cinnamon-lavender scent mixed in. He smelled intoxicating, and I wanted to feel him all over me once again.

That was enough to wake me up.

Falling for him would be dangerous. My heart couldn't take it when he broke it... I was barely holding myself together as it was. "Fine." I lifted my chin, trying to appear unaffected. "The lock and food, but not the AC unit. Just tell me how much I owe you."

"We can handle that later," he murmured, and his lips landed on mine.

My mouth parted, welcoming him and forgetting why I hadn't just done that to begin with. When his tongue slid inside, I whimpered, already wanting to climb him.

"Who is it?" Haven called from inside the house, bringing reality crashing all over me.

He groaned but didn't move an inch. "They're pains in the ass. You know that?"

I laughed and grabbed the door handle behind me, opening the door and stepping back. "It's Carter."

As the two of us stepped in, Haven removed the wet washcloth from around her neck and ran her fingers through her hair. She smiled, probably trying to appear normal, but she was clammy and pale from her night of drinking. "Oh, hey."

"Don't 'oh, hey' him." Leah wrinkled her nose. "He ruined

the party and had us freaking out that cops were going to show up any second."

Carter breezed in like he owned the place and shut the door behind him. "Well, it was almost four in the morning, Evie was tired, and the noise down there was even louder than it was upstairs. She doesn't have a lock on the door, so any pervert could've snuck downstairs and messed with her. So, yeah, I handled it because she asked me to leave."

"Wait." Leah's brows furrowed. "It's loud down there?"

"It's fine." I wanted to disappear. Not because I didn't want to stand up for myself; it was just because I couldn't afford to live anywhere else. At least, not right now. "I can buy earplugs."

"Yeah, so you won't hear the pervert until he's right on top of you. That makes it all better," Carter said dryly and lifted a brow. "If she wants to deal with earplugs, whatever. But I'm going to put a dead bolt on that motherfucking door."

Haven placed a hand on her chest. "I'm sorry, Evie. I didn't think about the door situation. I mean, granted, our friends aren't like that..."

"And you personally knew everyone at the house last night?" Carter countered, his jaw flexing as his eyes darkened.

"Well...no." She bit her bottom lip. "But I'm sure—"

"*Sure* won't cut it." He strolled into the kitchen and placed the brown bag on the table. "Here's some biscuits. I figured you all might need some after the night you had."

I couldn't help but watch every move he made. His muscles rippled under his polo shirt, and his jeans molded to his ass. Even if I wasn't in weight lifting with him, I'd know he worked out. He might not be as bulky as some of the players, but he was lean and muscular...the very type I liked. The kind I could wrap my legs around and hold on to for dear life.

Leah took another swig of her medicine. "My stomach is

yelling no, but I'm pretty sure it'll make me feel better." She groaned and sat upright.

Haven beamed, her attention locked on me.

Great. She must've seen me checking out Carter. I had to get whatever attraction was brewing between us shut down and quickly. Somehow, between last night and today, that spark between us had intensified into a wildfire.

"I'll get you one." I spun on my heel and hurried into the kitchen. All the way, I could feel Haven's drilling gaze on my back.

Carter dropped the other bag by the door to the basement stairs. "I gotta go get my tools and the AC unit. I'll be right back."

As he brushed past me, I clutched his arm. "I'll concede on the lock but not the unit. I don't have the money to pay you back for that."

The area around his eyes tightened as he paused. "I don't expect you to pay me back. It's not humane how you're living down there. Hell, even with the unit, I'm still not thrilled with this situation."

I sighed. "Why do you care? And don't give me the bullshit reason that it's solely because of the senator. You could have pretended not to notice."

"I don't know. I shouldn't care; you're right. But I couldn't sleep last night, knowing about this, and you asked me not to tell the senator, which I still don't understand. So, this was what I settled on. If you don't accept this, I'll be calling him."

The world tilted, and I wasn't sure if it was because he'd just threatened me or told me he cared. "Fine, but I want the receipts. I'll pay you back...even if it's in installments." I refused to become one of those women who expected others to handle their problems. I needed to rely on myself.

He rolled his eyes and nodded at the bag. "Fine. Whatever. We'll continue the charade. The receipt's in the bag."

My hands clenched at my sides as he huffed into the living room. It was like he didn't believe that I would pay him back.

I marched to the bag and pulled out the receipt. My heart dropped hard in my stomach. The dead bolt was about twenty dollars, which was fine. However, he must have picked out the most expensive AC unit because the five-hundred-dollar price tag had my stomach roiling. I might not have the cash to pay all of it back even after a month, but I didn't care if I had to eat ramen noodles for the rest of my life. I'd give him every dime I got.

"Evie," Leah whined from the living room.

Clutching the receipt, I huffed. "Sorry! I was looking at the lock he bought." I hurried to the bag and found ten breakfast biscuit sandwiches in there. "Uh, what kind do you want? There are four sausage, bacon, and egg, three sausage and egg, and three bacon and egg." I rattled off her options, shocked at how much food he'd brought.

"Bacon and egg, please," she whimpered. "God, I don't know why I do this every weekend."

"'Cause you're a glutton for punishment." Haven snorted but then groaned. "I'll take a sausage and egg."

I picked out the ones they wanted, and when I went into the living room, Carter reentered with the standing unit and drill.

As he passed me, I tossed their food at them and said, "You *both* are gluttons. Every weekend, you wake up hungover both Saturday and Sunday. Neither one of you learns."

"How are you so sober after the strong drink you made all of us last night?" Leah opened her wrapper and took a big bite.

Somehow, I managed to swallow my laugh. I didn't want them to know what I'd done last night, or they'd never let me make them my *strong* drink again. "I only had one and must have a higher tolerance than you two."

Carter arched a brow before disappearing into the kitchen, and I followed him, not wanting to hear them continue complaining. He set the unit in front of the stove and pulled out the stuff for the dead bolt before whispering, "You didn't drink anything last night. I didn't taste it."

I shuffled over to him and winked, my body warming from the memory of our kiss. "I know. The drink I made them was all Coke. They thought I put rum in it, but I didn't."

His face turned stony. "I see." Then he turned and went to work.

Down in my room, the AC was running and the room was much cooler, which only made me angrier. Carter was now upstairs in the living room, and I had no idea why. He'd been acting like a jackass and ignoring me since I'd told him about the Cokes.

What the hell was his deal?

When he'd come down here to set up the AC unit, I'd tried to talk to him, but I might as well have been talking to air. He'd just grunted, and that was it.

I put on jeans and a black V-neck shirt and got ready to leave for work. I needed distance from Carter, and for some reason, he was still here. I was beyond flustered because it seemed like he'd rather be anywhere else, and I had to deal with his charming personality.

In the bathroom, I brushed my hair, pulled it into a low ponytail, and then put on a little bit of makeup. Just enough to hide the bags under my eyes, along with some mascara and lipstick. As soon as I slid my sneakers on, I headed upstairs. I needed to leave now to walk to work.

Not wanting to see Carter again, I slipped out the side door of the kitchen and marched toward the sidewalk.

As soon as I walked past the house, the front door opened, and Carter came barreling out. He had a breakfast biscuit in one hand and his keys in the other, and his cold stare landed right on me.

"Where the fuck are you going?" he barked.

"Oh, *now* we're talking?" I spun toward him and placed my hands on my hips as my heart thundered. "When *you* want to know something? How about this—fuck off." I pivoted on my heels and continued toward the sidewalk. Hurried footsteps pounded behind me.

Once again, a large arm wrapped around my waist and lifted me off the ground, forcing the air from my lungs. Carter carried me toward his Escalade while taking another bite of his biscuit.

Something was *seriously* wrong with him. "Put me down!"

"I'm assuming you're heading to work, so I'm driving you there." He walked around the back of his vehicle to the passenger door.

"You've done enough for me today," I said and tried to jerk out of his arms, but it was like ramming into a freaking brick wall. "I can walk."

"Stop it. If I drop my biscuit, I'm going to be pissed."

I laughed so hard my throat hurt. "Like that's not your constant. All you ever do is growl, frown, or look like you're trying to figure out a complex math problem."

He put me down, and his brows furrowed. "Complex math problem?"

"Yeah, like that." I pointed at his pained expression. "Like you're not confused; you're just existing and trying to suffer through it." Didn't everyone feel that way about math? Or was it just me?

"Or we could just go with boredom." The corners of his mouth tilted upward.

Okay, he had a point. Maybe that would be better, but his laughing at me set me off more. "Whatever. My point is, you've been ignoring me for the past three hours, and now you manhandle me to get me into your vehicle? That's *not* how this works."

"I just spent three hours putting a dead bolt on your door and getting your AC unit set up. I came here to do that and take you to work, but I wasn't sure what time you went in, so I stayed." He opened the door and pointed at the passenger seat. "The least you can do is let me take you. It's not safe for you to walk."

"And then what?" I crossed my arms, but his concern was easing some of my anger. "You're going to pick me up when I get off tonight?" He had to see how ridiculous he was being, and once again, I was baffled why he even cared. Sure, we had some sort of attraction thing between us, but clearly, that was all it was...not that I wanted more.

"Yeah, I am. What time do you get off?"

Wait. I must have misunderstood him. My head tilted back. "Carter, I don't expect you to do that."

"Doesn't matter." He gestured around the neighborhood. "This isn't a nice area. If you aren't going to take care of yourself, I will."

I shook my head. None of this made sense. "But *why?*"

"It doesn't matter." He pointed at the seat again. "Get in the car, or I'll do it for you."

I believed he would, and though I wanted to know what his deal was, I had to get to work. "Fine." I wanted to keep at least some sort of dignity.

The entire ride to the bar was completely silent. And when he pulled up to let me out, he asked again, "What time do you get off?"

I almost didn't tell him, but I suspected he'd just camp out here if so, and I didn't want that. "About the same time as last night."

"Okay, I'll get here a little early, just in case." He didn't look at me, just stared out the windshield.

"Yeah, thanks." I quickly climbed out and slammed the door a little too hard, then marched into the bar.

Luckily, it was already busy, so I dropped off my things, grabbed a pad and pen, and immersed myself in work.

I didn't know what Carter's game was, but I'd be damned if I'd play.

THE NIGHT FLEW BY, and about two hours before closing, I went toward a newly arrived group to take their order, only to find Grayson, Cole, and two other guys I recognized from weight lifting as their fellow football scholarship teammates, Alex and Damien, in the booth.

"Hey, you." Grayson smiled. "I was hoping we would luck out and be in your section."

Cole scanned the bar from his spot next to Grayson. "Is Carter going to make an appearance anytime soon?"

My face burned, and my mouth dried. I cleared my throat. "Not that I know of." With him, there was no telling.

"Well, then, we better rush formal introductions." Alex extended his hand, his ebony eyes twinkling. "I'm Alex." His white shirt molded to his muscular frame and put his gorgeous bronze skin on display. He was lean, like any good running back.

"Evie."

"Oh, we know." Damien chuckled, his massive, muscular chest shaking. He sat on the end opposite Grayson, almost half of him falling out the side. He was the team's offensive center lineman. His mocha eyes scanned me as he ran a hand through his dark-brown hair. "I must say, you're the only person I've ever seen who has that much of an effect on Carter."

My heart thundered. I didn't want to hear that. "Well, I'm pretty sure it's because my mere existence pisses him off."

Alex ran a hand over his bald head. "Maybe, but I don't know."

I wanted this conversation over pronto. "What can I get you all?"

They gave me their orders, and I smiled and excused myself. Grayson stood and chased after me.

I paused and lifted a brow. "Did you forget something?"

"Nah, I was wondering if you wanted a ride home." He scratched the back of his neck. "But it's cool if you don't."

The fact that he'd asked made me more than willing to take him up on the offer. Of course, it helped that I could tell grumpy Carter not to worry about me and thus halt whatever strangeness was going on between us. I beamed, "I'd like that. Thank you."

"Sounds great. We'll just hang out till you're off. I'll be at the booth with the guys." He winked, retreating to his friends.

"Hey, wait." I realized I didn't have Carter's number. "Uh... Carter told me he was taking me home, and I don't have his number to tell him not to bother—"

"Don't worry." He removed his phone from his back pocket. "I'll handle it."

My stomach lurched. Carter seemed to have a problem with me hanging out with Grayson. I opened my mouth to tell

Grayson I'd find another way home when he lowered his phone.

He winked. "There. It's done."

Shit. I had a feeling that Carter wouldn't be thrilled, but the damage was done.

An hour later, Joe told me I could head home. I made my way out to the parking lot, where Grayson told me he'd be waiting once we kicked all the customers out to clean up, and found him pulled up next to the sidewalk with the engine running.

I hurried to climb in and leaned my head against his headrest. My feet were throbbing. "I'm so freaking exhausted."

Grayson put the car into drive and pulled out. "I'm sure that party last night didn't help. It was loud and packed."

"You're telling me." I turned in his direction. "Carter came by earlier and put a dead bolt on my door, so even if there is one tonight, I'll be safe in my room."

"About that. What's going on with you and him?" Grayson's hands clutched the wheel tightly, his knuckles blanching.

That was a fair question. "I don't know. I'm not even sure we're friends. He just…shows up and sort of takes charge."

"He's like that on the field too." Grayson bit his bottom lip. "But, I mean, are you two dating?"

"Lord, no." I shook my head, my breath catching. "Like I've told you, I'm not interested in dating. He showed up last night when I got off work and took me home." I left out the details about him getting pissed about me walking and about blasting him with pepper. "That was it."

He exhaled and grimaced. "When I walked downstairs last night, it looked like there was something going on. You two really aren't…?" He trailed off.

We might have been if he hadn't come downstairs, but

luckily, he had and stopped a potentially disastrous mistake. "He and I... I don't know what we are. I think he's watching out for me because his father helped Senator McHale sponsor my acceptance here, so Carter thinks that he has to help too." I shrugged. That was the only thing that made sense. "I don't know. But I will tell you one thing. I *do* consider you a friend."

"A friend." His smile faltered. "Yup, that's me." He pulled up in front of my house. "And it looks like there's no party tonight."

"Thank goodness." I opened the door but then paused and leaned over the center console to give him a hug. "Thank you. And we're still on for lunch Monday, right?"

"Wouldn't miss it for the world." He gave me a small salute, but his focus lingered on my lips.

I cleared my throat, a little uneasy. I hoped I hadn't made him think I was up for kissing any guy who brought me home.

"Good night." I jumped out of the car and hurried to the side door, giving him another wave before going in for the night.

THAT SAME DAMN nightmare haunted me. I woke up in tears with a shattered heart, panicking. Somehow, I'd missed my alarm and overslept, and now I was running late for class, which was lovely since it was hot as balls outside.

I threw on jeans, a teal shirt, and my sneakers and then snatched up my backpack and raced out the side door...only to find Carter parked in front of the house.

I stopped in my tracks and blinked. But each time I opened my eyes, he was still there.

The window rolled down, revealing his perfect, messy hair and strong jawline. "Evie, get in the car. We're going to be late."

Not thinking twice, I jogged over and climbed in.

As I buckled the seat belt, I took a deep breath, drawing in his scent. It was intoxicating, and my head spun.

I looked at Carter and smiled but froze when I saw the *bored* expression on his face. He wasn't happy, and I had no doubt as to why.

Grayson.

Maybe I should just walk. Getting hot and sweaty before class would be better than whatever was going to happen here.

I clutched the door handle, ready to open it, when he gunned the gas and the car lurched forward. He growled, "Don't even fucking think about it."

CHAPTER THIRTEEN

I kept my grip on the door handle for appearances. I wasn't dumb enough to jump out of a moving vehicle. "What is your problem?" I already knew, but I needed to hear him say it.

"Maybe *Grayson* should text me and ask me that question. Oh, wait. I'm the one who's here, taking you to school. Not *him*," he said curtly as he stared at the road.

My blood heated and I glared. "Neither *you* nor *he* is responsible for being my chauffeur, and you *didn't* have to pick me up." Now, I wished I hadn't gotten into the car.

He didn't respond. The only sign he'd heard me was the tic in his jaw.

A smart person would have let it drop, but between the dream and Carter treating me like crap, I didn't have the capacity to guard my emotions. My heart throbbed, and tears burned my eyes.

No. I refused to let some man break me. "If you were going to be an asshole about picking me up, why even bother?"

"Because I don't want something to happen to you!" he bit out. "It wouldn't be good for either senator's reputation if the student they sponsored to attend HSU got mugged walking to and from her dumpy-ass rental."

So that *was* the reason. Hearing him confirm it hurt. I didn't know what I'd been expecting, but I was being foolish. "And mauling me in my bedroom helps protect me *how?*" I regretted the words as soon as they left my mouth, but they were already out there.

This time, his gaze landed on me, his irises dark. "I'm a guy. I have needs. I'm sure Grayson got the same thanks when he took you home Saturday night. I hope the dead bolt I *paid* for and *installed* helped give you privacy and that the AC that *I paid* for kept you two cool while you *mauled* each other."

There was asshole Carter right back in rare form. Luckily, I hadn't run by the bank the last few days with my work scheduled and had cash. I unzipped the front flap of my bag and pulled out the three hundred dollars I'd earned the past two nights of work. I tossed the money at him. "There's three hundred. I'll give you the remaining two fifty when I get it."

The money scattered, the AC blowing it all over the vehicle. It was mostly ones, so it looked like a lot of cash.

Some dropped into his lap, the center console, and in the back seat.

His frozen expression cracked, and he raised his brows before he slipped his mask back into place. "So that makes it okay for you to mess around with both me and a teammate?"

I rolled my eyes and crossed my arms. "Unlike *you*, Grayson doesn't have to barge into the house and into my room. He's invited." I was being a bitch, but dammit, he didn't get to act this way without me swiping back. Besides, if he stopped picking me up and spending time with me, it would make ignoring this inconvenient attraction between us a whole lot easier.

His body turned rigid, and his nostrils flared. "Are you fucking serious? Did you *sleep* with him?"

His accusation was like a punch to the gut. "Well, he wouldn't take cash ..." I trailed off, letting him think what he wanted. In fairness, I hadn't lied once, and what he thought of me was shining through.

Chest heaving, he kept his stony expression in place, and our ride was completed in silence.

When he pulled up in front of the building where my psychology classes were held, he slammed on the brakes.

I inhaled sharply. "How did you know?"

He jerked a hand through his hair and yanked his bangs over his forehead. "I finish class an hour after you, so I need you to hang out somewhere until I'm done."

I leapt out of the car and tossed my bag over my shoulder. He was so strange! He was clearly pissed but still offered to take me home. "You don't have—"

"Fine, then I won't," he snapped, his jaw twitching.

I didn't have time to deal with his mood swings. He was the one being a jackass, I just hadn't corrected his assumptions. I spun on my heel and slammed his door and stalked off to class.

AFTER CLASSES, I entered the student center and went straight to the cafeteria. I hadn't eaten here yet, mainly because of the prices, but I'd promised Grayson I'd meet him for lunch. If I bailed on him again, I was certain it wouldn't go over well.

I still couldn't believe the various options. It was nothing like the cafeteria at TSU; everything here was made from scratch. There was a section of leafy green salads and toppings, gluten-free foods, authentic Italian foods, and—thankfully—hamburgers. That was what I'd get.

Standing in line to ask for a made-to-order burger, I found myself behind Sadie. She had earbuds in, tuning out the world.

Leaning forward, I said loudly, "Hey!"

She startled but when she recognized me, she grinned and removed a bud from one of her ears. "Hey! How was your weekend?"

"A little insane." I rolled my shoulders. "The place where I work was extremely busy both Friday and Saturday. Yesterday, I slept most of the day and then finally did some homework."

"That's so nice." Her eyes sparkled. "I got to help Dad with football training. He had me running after the guys, bringing them water and towels all weekend. You would've thought they'd get to take yesterday off, but he still had them training. He's stressed about the game on Saturday."

Right. Saturday. It was the first football game of the season, which meant I had to attend to take photos. Yay, me. I'd gotten the camera out yesterday and gone outside to snap some pictures. I was surprised how much I'd enjoyed it, but taking photos of static trees and flowers was different than capturing moving guys in tight, fitted uniforms bending over...especially when *one* certain domineering guy would be involved. "At least it's a nice view."

She bit her bottom lip and blushed. "Yeah, it definitely is."

I laughed, which helped unravel some of the turmoil from this morning. Between the nightmare and Carter's attitude, my insides had been all twisted. Something about Sadie was relaxing. "You eating with anyone?"

"No, are you?" She averted her gaze to her phone.

"Just meeting Grayson."

When the edges of her mouth tipped downward, I added, "Wanna join us?"

She tucked a piece of her hair behind her ear. "I'm sure he wouldn't like that."

"It's not a date," I assured her. But then I began to worry. I hoped that he didn't think it was. And if he did, then I *needed* her to join us. "I promise. I'm not interested in dating anyone while I'm here."

"Really?" Her mouth dropped open. "Not even a football player?"

My traitorous mind went to Carter as if he was even an option. "Nope. I need to focus, find a good psychology graduate program to apply to, and graduate. Those are my three goals for this year."

"If Dad heard you say that, he'd be telling me you have a good head on your shoulders." She pulled the other earbud from her ear. "And yeah, if you don't think he'd mind, I'd love to do lunch."

"Then it's a done deal."

The two of us ordered our food, grabbed it, and checked out. As we were walking toward the seats, Grayson breezed into the room, an easy grin spreading across his face.

"Hey." He strolled over to me and nodded at Sadie. He asked, "I'm going to get some pasta. Where do you plan on sitting?"

I pointed over to an open booth across the room. "Sadie and I will be over there."

His smile faltered a little bit. "Oh, yeah. Sadie too. Cool. I'll be there in a second."

"See ya." I headed to the booth I'd pointed at.

Sadie sighed. "I should sit by myself. He didn't seem happy about me joining you two."

"No, it's fine." I didn't want to lead Grayson on. If there was a chance he thought this was a date, I needed to make it clear that it wasn't. There was no better way than to make sure another girl joined us. "I'm telling you. It's not a date."

"Okay, fine." She shrugged and scooted into the booth.

I sat on the same side as her but on the end. I'd picked this booth so I could see into the breezeway in case Carter showed up. I could jump up and leave without Grayson knowing I was avoiding his captain. I didn't want anyone on campus to witness any drama with Carter, especially not Katherine. She already hated my guts.

"Are you going to be at the game on Saturday?" I took a bite of my cheeseburger.

She bit into a fry. "Yeah. I don't help Dad during the games, but I'll be in the stands with Mom and my brother."

"Oh, how old's your brother?"

"He's eighteen. He'll be attending here next year and, of course, will be on the football team." She rolled her eyes and popped in another bite. "I might be Daddy's little girl, but Will is his golden child. The star quarterback he always wanted."

I wrinkled my nose. "That kind of sucks." Since I didn't have siblings, I didn't truly understand, but it sounded like it wouldn't be fun.

"Nah, it's fine. I mean, Will and I are close. He's a typical arrogant athlete but a good brother." Sadie took a sip of her drink. "So I can't complain."

Grayson appeared and sat across from us. He had a large plate of lasagna and fettuccine.

"Hungry much?" I teased as I pointed to his food with a fry.

"Yup. Coach has been working us extra hard." He rubbed his stomach.

Sadie nodded. "He has been, and you've been doing amazing." Her cheeks flushed.

"Thanks." He stabbed a noodle with his fork and turned his gaze on me. "I went to the bar on Sunday after practice, but it was closed."

That was one of the things I liked best about working there.

"Yes, it's closed every Sunday. It's like Chick-fil-A in that regard."

"Did your roommates wind up having a party Sunday night? Your house was unusually quiet Saturday when I dropped you off." He took a bite, his eyes twinkling.

Sadie stiffened.

"Nope." I glanced at her, wanting to include her. "My roommates have a tendency to party."

"Yeah, I showed up Friday at her house, and the place was crawling with students and loud music." Grayson shook his head. "I couldn't get over it."

"Well, you and Cole seemed to be having a great time when Carter and I got there." I don't know why I added the last part. Whether it was to make a point to Grayson or Sadie, the words hung between us for a second.

"Wait. You were with *Carter* Friday night?" Sadie's eyebrows lifted.

"Yeah, some guy gave me a hard time at work Friday night, and Carter, Samuel, and Jack were there when it happened. Carter stuck around to give me a ride home." Now, I wished I hadn't said anything. I wanted to stay low-key about whatever had been going on between us. My heart twinged at *had been*, but it was for the best. Carter obviously thought poorly of me. I waved a hand, wanting to change the conversation. "So, what's everyone saying about the game Saturday?"

And that was enough for us to move to a safe topic —football.

We talked for a while, and then, all of a sudden, the prickling sensation on the back of my neck sparked to life. I glanced toward the entrance to find Carter strolling directly toward us. Samuel and Jack flanked him, talking, but Carter's eyes were locked on me.

When Carter continued straight instead of turning to the

right to head into the cafeteria, Jack's brows furrowed.

Shit. Why was he coming over here? We'd said all we needed to this morning. "Guys, I gotta go." I picked up my tray, my stomach churning.

Sadie asked, "Is everything okay?"

Grayson already had his attention locked on Carter, who was now grabbing a chair from a nearby table and pulling it up to the end of our booth, blocking me in.

"No need to rush," Carter said sternly and smirked. "We can hang out here a little while before I take you back to your house."

What was he *doing*? He'd told me he wasn't taking me home. My body stiffened, and I wanted to run out the door.

A huff came from across the table, and I regretted stealing a glance at Grayson as soon as I saw his horrible scowl.

"You want anything, man?" Jack asked as he strolled up to us.

"Bring me a salad with my usual toppings." Carter didn't bother taking his eyes off me as he answered. There was something dark in them, like this morning.

Jack snickered. "All right, well, I expect a big ol' tip."

"Here's a tip. Stop being a jackass." Carter glanced over his shoulder at his friends.

"Like that will actually happen," Samuel countered while shoving Jack in the shoulder.

My heart thudded. Other students were staring in our direction, and I didn't like it one bit. "Carter, you should go."

His irises darkened. "Yeah? You ready to go?" He reached over and took my tray. He stood. "Jack, never mind. I'm heading out."

I slouched in my seat and wished he'd stop talking so loudly. The table that hadn't been paying attention was now staring. I wanted to crawl under our table and hide. My whole goal had been to be invisible and get through this year, and this was the opposite of that. Carter demanded attention.

"Whatever." Jack continued toward the cafeteria, not bothering to say goodbye.

"Jackass." Carter snorted as he stood and put his chair back at the vacant table. He then pointed at me. "Come on, let's go."

Grayson scooted to the edge of the booth. "She said you should go. Not that *she* wanted to."

Ugh. They were going to have another pissing match, which would draw even *more* attention. Eager to get the hell out of here, I stood. "I'll see you guys later. I have some studying to do for my psychology class."

"Studying, huh?" Sadie mashed her lips together and arched a brow. "Okay."

Grayson didn't laugh. Instead, his face reddened.

I gritted my teeth, aggravated at myself for not moving quicker. I could've prevented this entire scene.

"Yeah, okay, I'll see you all later." I moved, not bothering to attempt to get my tray back from Carter. As I left the student center, I turned my head to the side so some of my hair fell over my face...like that would prevent people from finding out who I was.

"Evie?" Carter called out. "What the hell is your problem? You're not the victim here." He jogged up to me and caught my arm. "I deal with enough victim mentality from someone else without you adding to it."

Luckily, we were now out of view of the student center, so I pivoted toward him. "Of course not, I'm the *villain*, right?" I threw a hand out at the student center. "What was *that* in there?"

"What?" He shrugged. "You said this was where you were going to be. What's the big deal? Did I interrupt your lunch date with Grayson?" He scowled.

"*No.* That's not it. You said—"

"So it was a *date*?" His tone dropped low on the last word.

I dropped my bag on the walkway and glared at him, the hot sun beating down on us. I didn't even try to hold back my sarcasm. "Yes, most dates I go on, I make sure there's another woman there. I like the competition."

Ever since my parents had died, I'd felt like a shell of myself. But every time he came around, he brought me back to life—just not always in good ways. If I wanted to survive here, I needed to hold my tongue, but that was becoming increasingly impossible...at least around him.

"Please." He scoffed. "As if you have any competition, and don't pretend you don't know it. You're fucking hot, which is part of the problem."

My body tingled, and it physically hurt me to not step toward him. Did he really just call me hot? And why did it even matter? I rasped, "Yes, *I'm* the problem. Not you and all your assumptions."

"How are they assumptions when you didn't deny anything?" He moved closer, his face turning red. "If they aren't true, what sort of mind game are you playing?"

My lungs stopped working. "If you think I'm playing mind games, then why do you fucking care?" I needed asshole Carter to bring me back down to reality.

He swallowed, and heat flooded his eyes as his gaze homed in on my lips. "You know why."

My throat seemed to close. That response wasn't what I'd been expecting. I thought he'd accuse me of more ridiculous things and curse me more. I had to push him. "I need you to tell me."

"Because—" he started.

"What's going on out here? Is there a problem?" a babyish voice said from behind me.

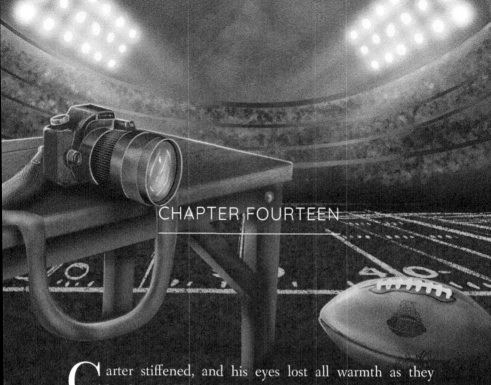

CHAPTER FOURTEEN

Carter stiffened, and his eyes lost all warmth as they hardened. He stared directly over my head at our newcomer—Katherine. "Nope. No problem. You can continue to pass us without stopping."

She huffed, and her heels *click-clacked* on the sidewalk as she moved to my side. Her nose wrinkled.

I didn't feel beneath them, just uncomfortable around these types of people. My parents and I always struggled with money, and I didn't understand the entitled behavior and self-righteous attitude of the rich. I didn't want to become more of a target for Katherine and people like her—being around them made me feel dirty, like part of their personality might rub off on me. I'd rather be broke and happy while working my ass off than deal with people like them.

"This seems like a lot of drama for two people who barely know each other. I just wanted to make sure everything's all right with Evie...you know, for our daddies? This sort of looks like a lovers' quarrel." Katherine lifted her chin and looked down her perfect-sized nose at me.

My stomach lurched. I didn't need to give her any more ammunition.

"Who I *date* is none of your concern." Carter edged between Katherine and me and continued, "Once again, I don't owe you anything. Least of all, any sort of explanation."

A zing coursed through me, followed by dread. He hadn't denied we were involved to Katherine, but that had to be to make a point.

She scoffed. "We're supposed to be pretending we're together in front of the cameras for our parents' sake."

I wanted to laugh but swallowed the sound. I wasn't sure how their being together helped their parents other than a little extra publicity. It wasn't going to make a difference for either senator's reelection.

"There aren't any cameras here, Katherine."

Her cheeks flushed as she huffed. "I refuse to allow you to make a fool of me."

"Oh, *Kat*," he said in that cold, distant manner. "I'm not the one who makes you look foolish. You do that all by yourself. I just refuse to allow you to drag me along. The past summer was truly eye-opening."

Her head jerked back.

Damn. I bit the inside of my cheek to prevent a smile. She deserved every word. There were definitely good qualities to Carter. I'd seen them in fleeting moments ever since I first met him.

Katherine had yet to do anything other than make my skin crawl.

"Now, why don't you run along," he said as he moved to my side. I could now see his face, including his evil grin. "I'm sure the other cheerleaders would *love* to hear about this encounter." He stopped and tapped a finger to his lips. "Unless you haven't told them that we broke up and that's the real reason you're bothering me. But *Kat,* that can't be it."

Katherine fisted her hands at her sides. "Stop calling me that. You know I hate that nickname."

He spun on his heels. "Come on, Evie. Let's go."

That sounded perfect to me. I moved to follow him, but a small hand grasped my arm. Nails dug into my skin, causing a sharp pain to blast up my arm.

A shiver ran down my spine at the veiled threat. Normally, I wouldn't cower, but she was the daughter of the very man who'd paid for me to come here. I had to be careful.

"Katherine, I'm not dating anyone." I turned toward her, needing her to see that I wasn't lying. "I'm not even messing around with anyone. I'm not that type of girl."

Her hold on my arm relaxed. "Not even Grayson? I hoped when I heard he was hanging around you that the two of you were a thing. You haven't even kissed?"

She was prying, and I could see Carter stiffen from the corner of my eye. I blew out a breath because I didn't want rumors to start, and I had no doubt she'd spread them. "Not even a kiss with Grayson. All he did was take me home one time."

A forced smile spread across her face, but something like disappointment flashed in her eyes. She cleared her throat and said, "Well, good. Football players are best considered off-limits, especially when you need to focus on not letting my daddy and Senator Grisham down. You should focus on your *studies.*"

"Katherine," Carter warned. "We can talk later."

"Yeah." She dropped her hand and beamed at him. "When? Tomorrow night, we're attending the sorority party together."

"I'll stop by your dorm later." He nodded toward the parking lot. "When practice is over."

Bile inched up my throat. He'd actually given in to her.

Twirling a piece of her hair around her finger, she winked. "Well, you know where to find me." Then she spun around and bounded toward the student center.

Both of them were awful. Her fake concern and niceness, and him going along with it.

He sighed and examined my arm, which now showed four red nail marks. "I'm sorry that just happened. This is my fault."

"Not all of it." I shook my head and took a step back, needing distance. "But your little performance played a clear part."

"Maybe if you'd told me that nothing happened with Grayson, this wouldn't have happened." Lips pressed into a firm line, he spun around and waved me to follow him.

I hated to oblige him, but I didn't want anyone else to see us together, so I swallowed my pride and followed him. "You *assumed* and were being an *ass*. I didn't see the need to clear the air."

"Well, I thought you making plans with me and then having someone else cancel them was rude." He glanced at me from the corner of his eye as we walked to his vehicle. "And worse to hear it from Grayson."

That was fair. He'd gone out of his way to help me, although he hadn't had any issues pointing that out earlier. However, this version of Carter made me want to settle things between us. He wasn't being a complete douche. "I wasn't trying to be rude—I didn't have your number. It's just that you keep doing stuff for me, and I hate feeling like a burden."

"You didn't ask me to do any of it," he said as we reached his vehicle. "In fact, you've been fighting me on it. This is all on me, so take that into account."

He had a point there, but it didn't make me feel better.

We slid into his car, and neither of us spoke. We'd said enough to last the entire way.

When we pulled up at my place, I expected him to turn off his car and walk me in, but he kept the vehicle running. He removed his phone. "We should've done this before now, but what's your number? I'll send you a text so you have mine. That way, I can let you know if something comes up and I won't be able to pick you up."

His demeanor was softer, more like the controlled expression he wanted others to see. At least he wasn't being an asshole. I rattled off my number and opened my door. I kept hoping that he'd follow me, but as soon as I opened the house door, he pulled away.

All of a sudden, I felt incredibly alone...and I didn't have my parents to turn to. Pain seared through me, filling every bone, and I rushed into the empty house and went downstairs, trying to keep from losing it.

For the rest of the week, Carter kept his distance. When he couldn't drive me, he had Jack pick me up and take me home from school, which turned out not to be so bad, other than the sad fact that I missed Carter. Jack was actually loud and funny, not the entitled snob I'd worried he might be.

Jack even started eating lunch with Grayson, Sadie, and me at the student center before dropping me off at home, but Carter never joined us. It was almost like he didn't exist until I saw him in weight training class or he came to chauffeur me to and from work, barely acknowledging me in the car. I kept hoping something would change, but it didn't, and the charged silence was becoming painful. Luckily, Friday night, Leah and

I worked the same shift, so I was able to text him that she was my ride to and from work.

I got no response, but I knew he got the message because he didn't show up.

Now, I was getting ready for a football game I didn't want to attend. I'd have to be on the field, taking pictures of the team and the *cheerleaders*, which meant I'd have to watch Carter from afar. I had no clue why I was so hung up on a guy I'd known for such a short amount of time. When he was near, he was all I could think about—he consumed me.

Unfortunately, I had no ride to the football game. Grayson was the only one on the team who knew I would be there because Sadie and I had been talking about it at lunch when it was only the three of us. I didn't know why, but I'd asked him not to tell anyone. He'd looked at me funny but hadn't said anything. That was one of the things I was growing to appreciate with Grayson—he never pushed. He just let me be.

Carter had texted and asked if Leah was taking me to work today, and I'd promptly responded that I was off and had something to do for class. He didn't follow up, but he had to be relieved.

I pulled out some ripped denim shorts, a cute royal-purple shirt I'd found online for cheap, and a pair of socks. I got dressed, braided my hair, and put on some natural makeup, wanting to look nice. I refused to investigate why, but I didn't really need to. *He*'d be there, and I already paled in comparison to Katherine, who'd be wearing her cute cheerleader uniform and makeup that looked professional.

After slipping on my shoes, I glanced at the time. Nearly six. The game started at seven, but people would already be there. I might as well head over and get shots of the guys warming up. Better than being here alone and spinning my wheels.

For the first time in a week, I found myself walking to school. The sun was setting, but the humidity nearly smothered me. This was the worst part about living in the South; the air was so thick at times I felt like I was living in a fishbowl.

It wasn't long before I strolled up to the gates. Every available parking spot on campus had been taken, including the open spots around the greenways. Parking was nearly filled up across the street from the stadium, where several parking lots had been constructed by the school for this very reason. I followed a line of cars toward the back left of the campus, heading to the stadium. I hadn't been inside yet, but it was so gigantic I could see it from the student center. The oval building was all white with an open top. The parking lot surrounding the stadium, where people had been parked probably since this morning, was packed.

Each garbage can I passed was full of beer cans, confirming that students had been tailgating. Everyone was pumped about the first game of the season against our neighboring SEC school —the University of Tennessee at Knoxville.

Apparently, this game was a huge deal because it counted toward the national championship. I strolled up to the closest entrance, studying the large letters proclaiming it Jaguar Stadium. There was already a line of people waiting to go through security and enter, so I headed to the shorter line for people authorized to get in immediately. As I strolled up to the man, I lifted my camera, removed my student worker pass, and showed it to the guard. I hadn't brought a purse, and they nodded, allowing me inside.

I pulled out my phone and texted Sadie that I was here. She'd told me to let her know and she'd help me get onto the field. As I stepped into the large cement area inside the stadium, I found all types of vendors selling popcorn and hot dogs, hamburgers, nachos, and a variety of other things.

The walls crept in, and the voices around me grew louder as people jostled me. Between having to be here and knowing I'd see Carter, I felt like the world was closing in on me.

Sweat pooled in my armpits, and I kept inching away from everyone until my back was against a wall and I couldn't move any farther. Still, people kept coming, and I grew dizzy like I wasn't getting oxygen.

This was a panic attack. That was all. I wasn't actually dying. However, that didn't ease the panic swirling within.

"Evie!" Sadie's voice called out to my right. I turned my head, desperate to get on the field where people wouldn't be right on top of me.

I saw her, but a massive group of people was between us. She waved me to her.

Great. This was going to be *fun*. I breathed through my mouth and put my phone back into my pocket, gripped my camera, and scurried across to her.

When I reached her, my lungs worked a little easier. "This is insane." TSU had a decent football program, but this stadium made that one look like a baby.

"Well, it seats over one hundred thousand, and UTK is close by, so a lot of their fans are coming, and our team is expected to kick ass this year." Sadie stopped at a door with two guards in front of it. "It's going to be full, so yeah."

This place was almost ten times the size of TSU's. No wonder it was so overwhelming.

As soon as the guards saw Sadie, they opened the door, revealing a wide staircase that led downstairs. This had to be the area for the home team and cheerleaders to access the field.

When the door shut, the loud noise was cut in half, along with the scent of salty buttered popcorn and body odor. I inhaled deeply, trying to calm down.

"Are you okay?" Sadie's brows furrowed.

"Yeah, sorry." I wiped my forehead with the back of my hand. "Not great with crowds."

"Well, it'll be better on the field. There'll be a lot of people, but not like up there."

At the bottom of the stairs was a huge, open hall mirroring the one above but with hardly any people. Along the side of the hallway that connected to the main stadium and not the field, there were four doors, and I assumed they led to the locker rooms and offices. Straight ahead was a tunnel that led directly to the football field.

Both teams and the cheerleaders were out there warming up. The team on my left was all decked out in Jaguar royal purple and on the right in volunteer orange. I hated that, even from this far away, my eyes immediately found Carter. I would recognize his commanding presence anywhere.

"Thanks for bringing me here. I would've gotten lost." I tried to smile, but it fell flat. This place was huge, but our professor had said one of the professional photographers on-site would be happy to help me. The assignment was about students getting experience.

"No problem." She gestured to the door closest to us on the left. "Going forward, you should come in the same way as the players and cheerleaders. You won't have to deal with that mess, and this door will bring you right here. After the game, I'll meet you here and show you where to go outside. I'm sorry I didn't think to tell you earlier."

"I should be okay. One of my friends already promised to take me home. I can figure it out from here."

Sadie bumped shoulders with me and said, "Yeah. Okay. Now, go out there and get some great shots."

Tensing my shoulders, I stepped out onto the field. Spotting a man holding a huge camera and sticking close to the Jaguars, I picked up my pace, heading to him.

He snapped a few pictures and then looked at the screen on his camera, observing his work, then looked up as I reached him.

"Hi. I'm Evie, and I'm here to take pictures for the school and my photography class. Professor Garcia said that you'd be expecting me?" At least, I hoped I'd approached the right bald, middle-aged guy dressed in a Jaguar HSU shirt. There were actually several out here, but he was the only one with a camera.

"Yes," he said loudly, a smile on his face. "I'm glad you got here early. Most students don't their first time. It's actually simple. The first game isn't usually as big as this one but just do your best. Follow the team on the sidelines and get shots without getting in the way. Also, be sure to take some shots of the cheerleaders and the band, especially at halftime. That's your goal today."

That sounded easy enough. "Got it."

A shiver ran down my spine. Carter knew I was here.

"It's best to start shooting while they're warming up to get your bearings." He nodded toward the team. "Go ahead and start. I'm going to grab some water."

I looked at the team, immediately locating Carter, number twelve. He'd been so distant lately that I didn't want to be near him, but I had a job to do. I pushed aside the sensation and moved closer to the team.

All of a sudden, a player ran toward me and pulled me into his arms, then twirled me around. When I saw Grayson's kind eyes through his football helmet, I couldn't help but grin.

"You're here. We all thought you'd be working tonight." He beamed.

I rolled my eyes, trying to sound annoyed. "Of *course* I'm here. Football is my photography assignment."

He dropped me back to my feet but leaned closer to me. "You're here to see me. I know it."

Before I could tell him no, another player sauntered over and said, "Back off, G-dawg."

By the walk alone, I knew exactly who it was.

Jack wrapped an arm around me, pulling me into his side. "Evie's really here for me. She and I came up with the stupid excuse of pictures for her to be nearby and appreciate my level of awesomeness." He leaned down so his helmet touched my head and cooed, "Now remember, my right side is my best side, so I need you to capitalize on that shit for me. Got it?"

"You're wearing a helmet." I smacked the top of his head and chuckled. "There are no good sides."

"No good sides?" He scoffed and grimaced. "Baby, every angle is good. Even my bad side is better than any of these assholes on one of their *good* days."

The hair rose on the nape of my neck just a second before Carter's voice boomed, "What the fuck is going on here? We're supposed to be warming up."

Jack smirked. "Dude, I'm just flirting with my girl. She and I have gotten *close*."

If looks could kill, Jack and I would be dead.

"You sitting with us at lunch and telling us about all the girls you screw is *not* close." Grayson snorted. "I don't want to hear that shit, let alone Evie."

Carter's face flushed, and I wasn't sure why.

"Don't worry, Evie." Grayson snorted. "I'll take you home tonight so you don't have to suffer through Jack's monologue."

"You two, go. *Now*." Carter commanded. "Coach is going to notice we aren't warming up." He glanced at me with a scowl. "I thought you said you were working on a school assignment."

I blew out a breath. I hadn't wanted him or Jack to feel

obligated to pick me up, but I could tell he was upset despite ignoring me this week. Instead, I lifted my camera. "I am. Taking pictures of the game." Not wanting to continue talking to him after being ignored all week, I turned around and gave both Jack and Grayson hugs. "Break a leg, and I'll make sure to get pictures of you both."

"So you can put them on your spank wall?" Jack waggled his brows.

"You think I'm going to use your picture to mastur–" I couldn't even finish the word with all the guys staring at me. My face flamed, and I stuttered, "*No!* For the school website."

"Dude, just no." Grayson flung an arm around Jack's shoulders and tugged him away. "Why you gotta embarrass her like that?"

"It's fun. She's so damn cute when she blushes."

Carter growled, which had me glancing his way just in time to watch him hurry after Jack and shove him in the back a little too hard.

"What the *fuck?*" Jack gritted, spinning around to face Carter.

Without thought, I marched after them, fisting my hands, but before I could reach them, a man stepped in.

I recognized him immediately. Sadie's father, Coach Prichard.

Coach Prichard removed his royal-purple visor, his green eyes narrowed. "What the hell is going on here? You know what? I don't care. Just get your asses together, we have an important game to win." He then pointed to the opening to the left of the field. "Everyone in the locker room *now*."

The guys removed their helmets, but Carter hadn't stopped glaring at Jack and Grayson.

Katherine bounded over and threw her arms around Carter's neck. He stilled but didn't remove them.

My heart somehow shattered.

Not wanting to watch any longer, I focused on getting a few pictures of the team leaving the field.

After twenty snaps, not that I was counting, Carter strode past, heading to the locker room.

He paused, turning to me. "Hey."

This time, I ignored him. He could be on the receiving end of the strained silence.

I could tell he didn't like it. He jogged a few steps toward me. "Evie," he said and touched my arm gently.

I lifted my chin, my eyes narrowing. "I'm done playing whatever your game is. Go talk to Katherine." With every ounce of strength I possessed, I turned and strode down the sideline toward midfield, the direction that got me away from him.

But I left a small piece of my happiness behind with him.

CHAPTER FIFTEEN

A part of me wished that Carter would chase after me and tell me I'd misread the situation, but that was pathetic and unrealistic. He'd pawned me off on Jack, and the few times Carter had wound up driving me, he'd barely said a word. And he hadn't talked to me anymore since Katherine had seen the two of us together and thrown a fit.

I had to stop being unrealistic and naive. Even though being around Carter distracted me from my grief, he caused even more chaos. I needed to work to be more independent *for myself*.

Putting the drama behind me, I focused on my school assignment.

To avoid watching the cheerleaders, I kept my gaze on the center of the field and walked to the fifty-yard line. The photographer who'd helped me was back now.

I'd nearly reached him when something hard slammed into my side. I stumbled but managed to keep myself upright and not fall in front of a hundred-thousand-plus people. My camera slipped from my hands, but luckily, it had a neck strap I'd used, so it wound up just hitting my breastbone.

Head snapping back, I turned to find Katherine standing there with a smug grin.

She batted her lashes and pulled me in for a hug, most likely to appear as if she was apologizing. But as she clutched me, she dug her fingers into my shoulders and gritted out, "Remember what I said about Carter." She leaned back, her eyes tightening. "Look, I know he's all deep and broody with glimpses of a kind, considerate guy. It's easy to fall for him. I've seen it hundreds of times. But though I made a horrible mistake and he's bitter, he'll get over it, and we'll get back together. I don't want to see you get hurt. I mean, with the car wreck and losing your parents... Let's not even talk about you being adopted."

My heart clenched. Though her tone sounded kind, her words were the slap in the face she intended them to be. But it wasn't like I could call her out. That would only make her like me less. Besides, I'd already decided to avoid Carter, so it wasn't like I was bowing out because of her threat.

"You have nothing to worry about. Carter was just helping me because of your dads." I hated giving her the satisfaction, but I had to remember that my goal was to survive and get through this year. Clinging to Carter and making even more of an enemy of Katherine was the opposite of that.

"Good. I'm glad you realize that." Katherine smiled her fake smile that, once upon a time, I thought was sincere. "Just remember that...for your own sake."

It sounded like a veiled threat, so I merely nodded.

Luckily, the photographer walked up to us, ending the conversation. "Hey, how's it going? Did you get any good shots yet?"

Katherine flipped her hair over her shoulder and kissed my

cheek before saying, "I gotta get back before the cheer coach yells at me. Make sure you get some good pictures of me. I know *Dad* will appreciate that."

The insinuation was clear—she'd mention to her dad *I* was the one taking pictures.

I wanted to raise my middle finger, but I kept the bird locked in its cage. Too many witnesses around.

"We sure will." The photographer beamed then turned to me. "Let's see what you have."

I pulled up the pictures I'd taken so far and showed him.

He nodded. "You've got raw talent. Those are better than some juniors majoring in photography. Are you sure you're a newbie?" He held out his hand. "I'm Theo, by the way."

"Evie." I glowered. "Which you already know. Sorry. But not a complete newbie. I took a few classes before my mom got sick. I never picked it up again until I took this class."

"No worries. I should've introduced myself earlier. I'm glad you're back at it." He nodded to the end of the field. "How about we both head down there and take pictures of the team running in?"

I forced a smile, hoping I managed to come off as sincere. "Sure. Let's do this."

In silence, we walked toward the end zone as we both messed with our cameras, trying to get the settings right while losing light.

Almost as soon as we got into position, the cheerleaders ran by and lined up to welcome the team to the field. I begrudgingly took pictures of them, making sure I got some of Katherine, and then the announcer came over the intercom and the audience went wild.

My ears rang, and I didn't believe it could get any louder. Yet, as soon as the football team was introduced, the whole stadium went up another two decibels. When the football team flooded the field by breaking through a royal-purple-and-gold Jaguars banner, everyone jumped to their feet, stomping and cheering.

Of course, Carter, Jack, and Samuel were in front, leading the team in, but the crowd never lost their enthusiasm until the entire team made it to the sidelines, ready to get onto the field.

The energy was contagious. I snapped dozens of photos of the team and the fans cheering for them.

Soon, the game started, and everyone, including me, was enthralled. Carter completed pass after pass. By halftime, HSU was up seven points, and the energy of both teams was invigorating.

When the players went back to the locker room at halftime, Carter ran to the edge of the field, almost brushing past me, and when his eyes locked with mine, something squeezed in my chest.

No. I wasn't going to keep doing this. I forced myself to look away, at a complete loss as to what was going on between us, which meant I had to keep busy.

During halftime, I took pictures of the marching band and the cheerleaders, and all too soon, the football players came running back onto the field.

Despite wanting to not pay attention to Carter, it was hard when he was the star quarterback. No matter how many other people I took photos of, it always came back to him.

By the last two minutes, the game was tied. HSU had the ball, and Carter, Grayson, Alex, Jack, and the others rushed to the field to take their spots. Carter set up, calling the play to everyone. When the ball was snapped, Carter took several steps back as Grayson tackled a UTK player coming straight for Carter. Alex raced toward the end of the field and turned toward Carter, waiting for the ball.

Carter launched it, the football sailing in a perfect spiral across the field, and Alex didn't even need to jump. It just flew into his arms. He pivoted and dashed the last five yards into the end zone.

The announcer yelled, "Touchdown!"

The crowd went wild. Our team had won their first game and a very important one.

And I got pictures of it all, lost in the moment, capturing the Jaguars' triumph and camaraderie and enjoying the way taking pictures provided a high all over again.

As the team danced off the field, I continued to take shots. The cheerleaders ran after the football players, and the stadium began clearing out.

Theo walked over to me and patted my back. "Good job! I can't wait to see what you submit to your professor."

I nodded. "Thanks for your help. I guess I'll see you next week."

He winked. "You got it."

With nothing else to do but wait, I walked off the field and hung out by the door Sadie had pointed to that the players used to come and go. As I waited for Grayson, I flipped through my pictures, checking to see what sort of shots I'd gotten.

Surprisingly, I really enjoyed taking them. It was exciting and, in a way, relaxing. I wouldn't say I was a great photographer by any means, but I had done pretty well.

The door opened, and a few of the players I didn't know trickled out. I'd been hoping that Grayson would be one of the first out or that he'd at least beat Carter.

Voices from the next room grew loud, and when I heard a babyish voice that could only belong to Katherine, I knew I had to get out of here. If she saw me waiting by the door, she would assume I was here for Carter. And I didn't want to get higher on her shit list.

I darted down the long hallway. I could hide on the field if needed. I managed to dart behind a large column that marked the entrance to the field just as the door opened.

"Don't worry, ladies." Katherine chuckled as I hid at the large cement frame entrance. She continued, "The guys can't resist a party, especially one thrown by *me*. We can use the three dorm rooms. It's not like the RA will break it up with my father being a major donor here and all."

I rolled my eyes. She was so entitled. Hell, Carter was too. And I hated that I was cowering, hiding. If she knew, her ego would inflate even more.

I hoped my parents weren't up there, watching me now.

One of the girls giggled. "I need you to help get Jack to notice me."

"Just wear something low-cut and tight," one of the other girls said. "That's how I got him to sleep with me last year."

That sounded about right. Jack liked to sleep around. He'd made that clear during the first ride he gave me to school when Carter didn't show up. He'd asked me for a blow job on the drive to the school, and my mouth had dropped open. That was when he'd winked and said, "I see you're ready." When I'd blushed profusely, he laughed and told me he was kidding... unless I truly was willing. And somehow—I wasn't sure why or how—we became friends despite everything.

When the door opened and shut and the girls' voices grew quieter, I straightened but chose a new spot to wait at the end of the hallway in case one of them needed to come back in.

Trying to calm my nerves, I searched through my camera's photos once again, and not too long after that, Grayson, Jack, Cole, Alex, and Carter walked out of the locker room together.

Of course, Carter was with them. It was almost like he meant to infuriate me tonight.

Refusing to give him more power, I lifted my head high, walked toward them, and smiled. "You guys killed it!"

"Fuck yeah, we did. When I'm playing, losing isn't an option." Jack jogged over to me and hugged me. "Did you doubt me, my little tomato?"

And just like that, my face flamed once again, proving his nickname fit me too well. I shoved him, trying to push him off me, but he barely budged.

He waggled his brows. "Weight class is not doing great things for you. Maybe we need to try working out my preferred—"

Carter's jaw clenched, and Grayson snorted and pushed Jack off me.

"Stop being a jackass," Grayson said and chuckled. "I don't know how she and Sadie put up with you and that mouth all the time."

"Because it can do wicked things to them if they're willing." He waggled his eyebrows at me.

I'd realized a while ago he was so over the top with me because he knew I wasn't interested.

"Dude, stop being an idiot." Cole crossed his arms.

Alex looked at Cole. "You know that's not possible. It's his constant. Even the coach can't get him to quit."

"Oh, please." Jack waved a hand. "Evie and I are friends. That's all. She's not my type. She's smart, confident, and has her shit together."

My chest warmed. "Oh, I think that's the sweetest thing you've ever said to me."

Carter crossed his arms, remaining silent with his gaze sternly on me. Something unreadable once again crossed over his expression.

"Hey, there's a party on campus." Grayson ran a hand through his hair. "You wanna go?"

There was no way in hell I'd be going to that party, but I didn't want to sound rude. "I'm tired. You guys made it hard to keep up so I could get pictures. I don't want to hold you up, especially with the awful traffic outside. You go, and I'll call an Uber." I snatched my phone from my back pocket, trying to keep up the charade. If Carter realized I had no intention of calling one, he wouldn't let me leave without Jack or Grayson taking me home.

Jack pulled out his keys. "I can drop her off. I won't miss anything because the party won't start until I walk in."

I laughed, which surprised me. That was what I liked most about Jack; he had that effect on me. "You quoting Ke$ha now?"

"Yeah. She's a badass." He patted his chest. "She's number one on my list of girls I'm determined to fuck."

"No, man." Carter shook his head, the commanding tone present once again. "You already promised the cheerleaders you'd go straight there. I'm not going, so I can drop her off on my way home."

My traitorous heart thundered, which made me livid. I'd just vowed to avoid him. "Then head home. No need for a detour. I'll take an Uber." I turned toward the other guys. "Go. Have fun. I'll see you all on Monday."

"Nope." Grayson touched my arm. "I'm taking you home. I already said I would. We can watch a movie at your house or something."

The idea of not being alone sounded way too appealing. With my nightmares plaguing me, and since Carter stopped coming around, I'd been dwelling on memories of my parents. The moment I was about to tell him I'd like that, Carter interjected, "You want to go to the party, and I can take her home. There's no reason for any of us to make it more difficult. Besides, Grayson, I need you to keep Jack and Cole in line. We have practice tomorrow, so they don't need to get shit-faced. Out of this group, you're the one I trust most."

"Hey!" Alex pouted.

Just then, Coach Prichard stuck his head out of the team door. His expression smoothed over and he looked relieved. "Grayson, I thought I heard you out here. A reporter just requested an interview with you about your transfer. Come talk to him before you head out."

"See, you can't do it anyway," Carter said and patted him on the shoulder. "Don't worry, man. I'll get her home."

There was no way I was going to get out of this. Grayson glanced at me, and I forced a smile, hoping it came off sincere.

When Grayson went back into the locker room, Jack bounded over and kissed my cheek and then whispered in my ear, "Give Carter a chance." Then he opened the door and waved Cole and Alex through while stating, "Lookee there, Alex. You got your wish. You get to babysit me and Cole."

When they headed out, Carter and I remained alone, staring awkwardly at one another.

"Look, I seriously can—"

"I want to talk. I think we need to clear the air between us." He bit his bottom lip as if he feared I might say no.

Maybe talking would give us both closure and end this thing lingering between us. "Fine."

He opened the door for me, and I walked past him, making sure I didn't touch him. I didn't need my hormones clouding my thoughts. In silence, we walked to the closest parking lot where he'd parked his car. Soon, we were pulling out of the university, the tension intensifying and swirling between us.

However, when he pulled up to the light where he was supposed to turn right to my house, he wound up turning left. "Carter, you're going the wrong way."

"I thought we agreed to talk." He pressed the gas, driving farther away. "There won't be any interruptions at my house."

I gritted my teeth. This wasn't what we agreed to. He told

me he was taking me home before he went to his own house. He'd been ignoring me, and now he wanted to talk, and of course, it had to be on his terms. He decided things for me all the time —he spent time with me when he wanted, he ignored me when he wanted, we talked when he wanted, and now he even decided, without telling me, that we were doing it at his house.

I was so damn sick and tired of not having a say. This was ending now.

He slowed down for the next light, so I did the only thing I could.

When he came to a stop, I unlocked the door and jumped out.

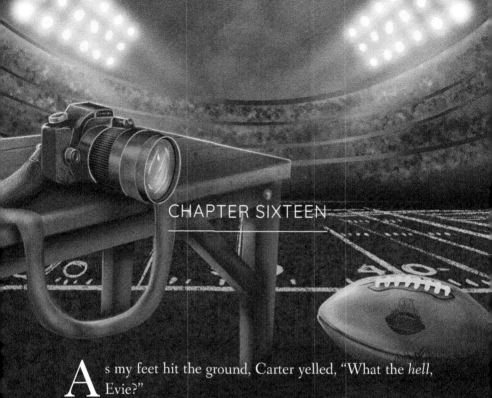

CHAPTER SIXTEEN

As my feet hit the ground, Carter yelled, "What the *hell*, Evie?"

I didn't pause. I slammed the door and ran to the sidewalk and into the parking lot of a steak house heading in the direction of my home.

I glanced behind me. Carter was still stuck in traffic from the game, and I hoped I had enough time to get far enough away before he found a place to turn around.

My heart pounded as I picked up my pace. I was tired of this entire situation. Sure, Carter made my pain momentarily go away, but it was because I was either annoyed with him or kissing him, neither of which was a helpful solution. In fact, it was downright unhealthy, especially since I'd been learning all about it in my psychology courses. One thing was certain—I was tired of him trying to control me. I might not be ready to take on Katherine, but dammit, he had the power to break me if we kept doing this.

My camera thumped against my chest. I'd had fun taking

pictures, but now it was in my way, and I couldn't afford to break it. I cradled it against me and took off at a fast jog.

Cutting through the middle of another parking lot, I barreled toward a street that would lead me to my neighborhood. As I reached the next road I needed to cross, tires squealed from behind me.

Dammit.

The light for the street I wanted to cross turned red, and as soon as the vehicles stopped, I took off in a sprint.

My side cramped, reminding me just how out of shape I was. But I wasn't giving up, so I ignored the increasing discomfort. When I passed the first house, I didn't stop. The fact that Carter hadn't appeared yet gave me hope that it would take him more than a minute to catch up.

By the time I passed the second house, pain pierced my side, and my vision blurred. Sweat coated my body. I had to stop and bend over to take some deep breaths, trying to clear my head.

A car turned down the road behind me.

I froze. Carter had found me.

Soon, his black Escalade pulled up beside me, and I forced myself to keep walking. He matched my speed and rolled down the window.

His face was flushed, and his nostrils flared. "What the *fuck*, Evie. Get in the damn car."

I shook my head, not bothering to say anything.

He growled, "Get in the car. I'm not going to ask you again."

I lifted my hand, saluting him with my middle finger.

Pounding his fist against the steering wheel, he snarled. "I'm going to stop the car, pick you up, and throw you in."

The pure rage and determination on his face made me laugh. "Leave me alone, Carter. You've ignored me all week. I was willing to talk at my place, but of course, you decided to change plans without consulting me. So, please, go away."

"You're not walking home—"

Every time, he used the same damn excuse. "Unlike what you think, you actually don't have the right to dictate what I will or will not do. You don't get to ignore me and then change your mind and decide we should actually talk. And you *definitely* don't have the right to take me somewhere I didn't agree to go. I'm tired of allowing you to disrespect me. So, I'm telling you now, I'll be fine walking home on my *own*. Please leave."

I picked up my pace to make my point further and get home quicker. I had another ten minutes of walking to do, and sweat was trickling between my boobs. I expected him to drive away, deciding I was more of a problem than I was worth.

"Why do you have to be so fucking impossible?"

I snorted, the bitterness taking me by surprise. "I'm trying to live my own life and make it through this year without Katherine killing me. You're the one who keeps barging into my life, demanding that I *not* work out with you in a workout class yet insisting that either you or Jack drive me around everywhere. I'm fine on my own. If you leave me alone, I'll leave you alone, and everything will be *calm*." My heart sank, but I ignored it.

"Evie, I can't drive away." He sighed.

I couldn't look at him, or I risked taking back everything I'd just said, so instead, I trudged forward. "Carter, you're off the hook. Your dad and Senator McHale will never find out. We can pretend you were unaware of my situation. Just let this go."

"I don't *want* to be off the hook," he snapped, causing me to turn toward him.

What I saw shocked me. His expression wasn't angry anymore but creased with worry.

"If I promise to take you home, will you get in the car?"

The pain in my side hadn't fully receded, and sweat was soaking my shirt. I hated to give in, but air conditioning did sound nice, and he wasn't being an asshole. However, I shook my head. "Can't risk it. You told me you were going to take me home last time."

"I swear. Evie, please," he begged. "I'll drive directly to your house. If I'm lying, I'll never bug you again."

My feet stopped, and I turned to look at him. He was turned toward me with a hand on his chest, appearing sincere.

"Fine." I took a deep breath and climbed back into the car.

As soon as I sat down, he turned the air conditioning on full blast and pressed the gas pedal. We rode the entire way to my house in silence. He pulled up to the curb of the house but left the vehicle running.

As expected, neither of my roommates was there. Leah was working and didn't get off until about midnight, and Haven had plans with some friends.

I had unbuckled and grabbed the door handle when he asked, "Can we talk? Or did I ruin that by trying to take you to my house?" He bit his bottom lip and ran his hand along the steering wheel.

He'd actually asked. He hadn't demanded it, and even though I wished my roommates were home, this could give me closure. "Sure, I guess. As long as you don't get demanding."

"I promise to try. I have a feeling if I get that way, you'll tell me to leave."

"Yes, I will."

He turned the car off, and I went to the front door so we could sit in the living room. I wasn't about to risk going downstairs. The last time we were in my bedroom, things went in a direction I hadn't planned, which wouldn't be the case tonight.

I got out my key and unlocked the door, and the two of us went inside. When I sat on the couch, he arched an eyebrow.

"We're not going to your room?"

I shook my head. "There's no party, and my roommates aren't home. We might as well hang out here."

"Okay, that's fair." He nodded. But instead of sitting down, he stood in the middle of the room and paced.

Determined for him to speak first, I leaned back and waited.

He licked his lips and shoved his hands into his jeans pockets. "I know that I've been ignoring you. But I swear there's a good reason."

Tilting my head, I crossed my arms. "And what's that?"

"Katherine." He opened his mouth to continue, but I burst out in bitter laughter.

The sound was so harsh that it jarred me, and I gasped.

He scowled, stopping in his tracks. "What's so funny?"

"That you think that's a *good* reason." I wiped tears away before they could roll down my face. "And that you think I'm stupid enough not to already know that. I mean, you shut down after she confronted us outside the student center, and you've been escorting her to school events."

His chest expanded. "You underestimate her."

I jerked my head back as something heavy settled in my chest. "Are you saying you're afraid of her?" I called bullshit. I'd seen the way he put her in line several times without batting an eye.

"I'm not. But *you* should be. She was dying to get a hold of you the first day you came here, but she held off because her father asked her to behave. So when she saw the two of us together, just like that, she planned to destroy you."

Now, he was being dramatic. I rolled my eyes. "Destroy? Come on. Maybe make my life hell, but I think you're giving her too much credit."

"No, I'm not." He rolled his shoulders. "She's a good

actress. Pretends to be nice, but she's utterly vicious. She won't mess with me because of who my father is, but you, with no family...you'd be easy for her to break."

The seriousness on his face had fear rolling through me again. I hadn't been fighting back against Katherine, mainly because of her dad, but there *was* something sort of unhinged about her.

"Look, there's a reason she showed up outside the student center when she did." He clenched his jaw. "Someone must have told her about me sitting with you, Grayson, and Sadie. Though she hasn't been harassing you for the past few weeks, don't think for a second you aren't being watched by her friends."

Now he was making it sound like I had a stalker. Lovely. Might as well continue to load on the problems.

He took a step toward me and lifted both hands. "That's why I've been ignoring you. I had to stay away so she'd lose that desire to cause problems. That's it. I was doing it to *protect* you."

I lifted my chin. "I've seen the posts of you two at several events. So you're dating again?" My heart pounded. The answer shouldn't have been important, but it was.

"God *no*. I agreed to go with her to several things over the summer when she asked in front of our parents, before you even came into the picture. I've just got to get through the last few, and I'll never have to go anywhere with her ever again." His face scrunched in horror. "That ship sailed, and to be honest, even when we were together, neither one of us was happy. It was really for our parents' sake and appearances."

I suddenly felt lighter. I'd been so certain he'd gone running back to her.

He stared at the cheap vinyl floor and scuffed one of his feet across it. "What I'm trying to say is... I'm sorry. I should've told you what was going on instead of ghosting you like that. But I didn't want you to worry. That's one reason Jack was taking you to and from school—so he could keep an eye out for any of her shit and so she'd think you were taken with him." He wrinkled his nose at the last part. "I swear, I only set that up to protect *you*."

I swallowed, and my traitorous heart thumped wildly. So much for cutting ties because I believed him and, worse, understood what he was saying. I'd seen how she looked at me, but for some reason, I couldn't let this go. "What happened when you went to her place after you dropped me off that day?"

"I dropped by and told her to retract her claws. That it was a complete misunderstanding and that she'd misread the entire situation. That Dad had asked me to make sure you were settling in all right, which is true. He asked me to check in on you that morning, though I'd already been doing it. But that's why I had to give us space—because I know what she's like. What she would do."

I leaned back in my seat and crossed my arms. "You told me you were only watching out for me for your father and Senator McHale. Was that not true?" I tried to appear relaxed, but my blood was rushing through my veins.

"I lied. I didn't want to admit it then, but there's something about you." His eyes warmed, causing the gold flecks to stand out. "I felt it that first day when the reporters swarmed you. I wanted to believe what Katherine was saying because it made sense. But the more I'm around you, the more I can tell that you're different from anyone I've ever met. Hell, even Jack sees it and likes you, which is rare. I didn't expect it."

The first part of what he said replayed in my mind and tugged at me. "What do you mean you wanted to believe what Katherine said?"

"People have a tendency to use me. You know, for status,

money, or the combination." He began pacing once more. "Ever since birth, I've run into users, and I've had my share of more than I ever wanted to encounter. I don't like getting close to people because of that. Senator McHale decided to pay your tuition out of the blue, and he got my dad to support it. There had to be a reason. That's why I thought you got here by blackmailing the senator. But the more time I spend with you, the more you don't ask for things, and the more you try to help or not take me for granted, the more I realize that that *isn't* you. It can't be. You aren't pretending."

He chuckled awkwardly and ran a hand through his drying hair, causing a few pieces to fall into his face just the way I liked, and continued, "You threw me off guard, and every time I'm with you, I'm more intrigued."

Heart jolting, I placed my hands on the couch to help prop myself up. He'd just complimented who I was as a person.

"I get that I fucked up and need to earn back your trust." He glanced at the floor and then at me. "So, can we start over? Can we be friends?"

"How will that work with Katherine involved?" That was the whole reason he ghosted me. "And why change your mind about needing distance now?"

"We'd need to be extra careful about not being alone together in front of her, but you're friends with Jack and some of the football team now, so us being in close proximity to one another makes sense. That's the thing. I don't want to stop being around you. So...I think we have to settle on being friends...if you're open to it."

He rubbed the back of his neck. "Seeing you tonight joking around with Jack and Grayson...I was jealous. I've missed you, and I know I want you in my life. It's been a little bleak without you."

This was a lot for him to ask of me, especially considering

how I felt about him. But he'd just laid his heart on the line, and he was giving me the power. "Only if you promise not to be an asshole again, and if you need to ignore me, you talk to me first and don't just vanish."

"I can do that." He placed a hand on his chest.

This was a bad idea, and I should tell him to leave. But I didn't want him to.

I nodded toward the kitchen. "I've got some popcorn and ramen calling my name. You wanna stay, eat crap food, and watch something?"

He grinned. "That sounds perfect. I'm starving."

I stood and stepped toward him, forcing myself not to rub my body against his. I quipped, "Are you trying to say that you'd rather stay here than go home or to a party?"

Shrugging, he winked. "Parties are loud, and my teammates get stupid. Besides, if I want to go pro, I can't treat my body like shit. Not only that, but I gotta get up early to meet with a man about a program he's starting, so partying is the last thing I want to do."

In other words, he was driven. I'd sensed that the first day I met him. Maybe that was part of his problem.

"If I'm starving, you must be too." I grabbed his arm and tugged him to the kitchen, ready to relax and wind down with him.

Within minutes, we were sitting on opposite ends of the couch with food and watching *The Walking Dead*.

A few episodes later, Carter yawned and stood. "I hate to do this, but I need to head home. I'm exhausted."

My chest constricted, and I realized that I didn't want him to leave. But I wasn't going to force him to stay. "You going to be okay driving home?"

He winked. "Yeah, but I need to head out now before I'm

not able to. I've got to get some rest for practice. What are your plans tomorrow?"

"I'm going to study in the library." I needed to get some work done. It was hard to study here with how loud my roommates could be.

"Library, huh." He pursed his lips. "You want some company? I could stand to spend some time there for a couple of hours before practice."

I arched a brow. "You said we can't be alone in case Katherine sees us on campus. And besides, you're the star quarterback. Aren't good grades just handed to you?"

He stuck out his tongue. "First of all, there's no risk of Katherine seeing us. She's afraid of the library. And second, I only wish they handed out good grades. Senior year of my international business degree is kicking my ass."

It felt so natural to joke around with him; it was almost scary. "Okay. Then I'm in."

"Good." He stepped closer and gave me an awkward hug. "I'll be here at eleven to pick you up."

Warmth spread through my body, and I had to fight the urge to kiss him. "See you soon."

I watched him walk out the door to his vehicle, and I knew, without a doubt, that I wouldn't be getting any sleep.

CHAPTER SEVENTEEN

When my alarm buzzed, I jumped out of bed and pulled on a pair of shorts and a lavender shirt before getting ready. Whatever happened between Carter and me today would define how this new agreement would go. I both anticipated and dreaded seeing him. My nerves were getting the best of me, which was sort of silly. We were only friends after all. That was what we'd agreed on last night.

One of the bedroom doors opened on the other side of the house, and from the way it squeaked, I knew who it was.

Haven.

She strolled into the kitchen with an oversized gray sleep shirt on. She yawned, but when she saw me, her eyes widened. "Wow. You're dressed and ready for the day early. You heading somewhere? It's Sunday."

"It's almost eleven." I chuckled. "Most people don't call that early."

"Girl, we're in college and in our twenties." She placed a hand on her hip. "On a Sunday, eleven is the butt crack of dawn."

I gestured at her and tossed my yogurt in the trash can. "You're up too, so what does that say about you?"

She scoffed. "Please, I'm not fully awake yet. For all I know, this is still a dream." She shuffled to the Keurig and fumbled around like she could still be asleep. "Hey, I was thinking the three of us could watch a movie and chill today. We're always so busy running in different directions or partying it'd be a nice change of pace."

"Later today? I'm actually about to head to the library to do some work."

She tilted her head, observing me. "You look awfully nice for such a late night and heading to the library. I'm assuming a certain man is involved." She finally got the pod in the Keurig, hit Brew, and then arched her brow. "A certain *man* who's been ignoring you, which Leah and I had to hear about for the past few days."

My face burned. "I wasn't *that* bad."

"Yes, you were, but it seems like the two of you made up." She shook her head. "I never imagined when I got back at midnight, I would find you two sitting next to each other, sharing a bowl of popcorn with zombie blood everywhere. It must be lust if you allowed him to talk you into watching *that*."

I chuckled. "That was actually me. I forced him to watch it." Lately, I couldn't watch anything realistic, whether it be happy or sad. Either way, it reminded me of my parents, the loss of them or missing their faces and voices. At least *The Walking Dead* was about zombies. Even though there was tons of death, it wasn't even close to real.

She rolled her eyes. "Sometimes I wonder about you. But Evie, please tell me you made him explain why he ghosted you. He just left you hanging, and it hurt your feelings. I don't want to see him get to you like that again."

I cringed. "We've only known each other for three weeks. I

promise I won't let my guard down so easily again." Being with Carter made me feel happier than I had in a long time, and I didn't want to lose any opportunity to enjoy that. There was something about him that soothed my pain. When I was with him, I was able to breathe easier.

Grayson, Sadie, and Jack were great and funny, but they didn't tug at me the same way.

"But he *did* have a good excuse, and he knows that if he ever pulls something like that again, I won't forgive him. We agreed to be friends."

Haven surveyed me again. "Friends, huh? I don't think you'd wake up and get ready like that if it was us heading to the library."

I tensed. She did have me there, and with the glare she was giving me, she knew it as well.

Luckily, the sound of a vehicle pulling up in front of our house rumbled to our ears, which meant it was most likely Carter. "Hey, that's him. I gotta go, but please don't worry. I'll be back later, and we can have girl time. I promise."

"Just be careful—and I'm holding you to it," she said as she followed me into the living room. "When Leah and I were searching for a roommate, we didn't plan on finding someone we'd like. But we got lucky when you came here, and even in this short amount of time, we've become friends. We just want to look out for you."

Warmth spread through me. I had a few friends from back home, but when Mom got so sick, I pulled away from almost everyone. And then, I was focused on studying and working to help pay the bills. This was the first time I'd made time for people in years. It was nice. "I won't be stupid."

She nodded. "All right, text me if you need anything. I'm hanging around here today so I can pick you up. We know how Carter doesn't like you walking," she teased.

I stuck out my tongue at her as I picked up my backpack then gave her a side hug before bounding out the front door.

When I stepped outside, Carter was getting out of the car. He wore black gym shorts that showed off his muscular legs and hard ass and a white shirt that hugged his lean figure. His hair hung in his face in the messy style that I liked most on him. And when his gaze landed on me, I got the feeling he could see into my very soul. His eyes were like windows into his own, and right now, they shone with happiness to see me.

He hurried over to open the passenger door, which he'd never done before.

As I walked up, he shook his head. He said, "You know, I hate to admit this, but *The Walking Dead* was entertaining. A little depressing, but it was a good story." He took my bag from me and set it in the back seat as I climbed in and buckled up. After shutting my door, he walked around the front of the vehicle and was in the driver's seat within seconds.

He started the car and smiled, stealing my breath as he asked, "Are we going to watch some more tonight? I was thinking maybe you could come to my house."

My heart thudded. It wasn't because I didn't like his house. It was way nicer than mine...but we'd be alone. And if we were alone, I might lose my head, which I couldn't risk with how attracted I was to him. "I promised my roommates that I would hang out with them. Why don't you join us? We're going to find something to watch here."

He frowned before smoothing out his expression. "Are you sure they'd be okay having me over?"

"They won't mind at all." In fact, they'd probably prefer it so they could grill him. They didn't know him well, which was part of the problem. "And I'd like you to be there." I focused out the window, not wanting to see his reaction. He'd opened up by inviting me over, and I wanted to do the same thing.

"If that's what you want, then that's what we'll do." He nodded and put the car in drive.

When I glanced at him, he was smiling...and it seemed sincere, like maybe me inviting him over was the very thing he needed.

On the way, he told me about the meeting he'd had that morning with a guy named Kyle, the man working to expand the nonprofit organization Touchdown 4 Kids that the reporters had mentioned the day I'd met Carter. The goal was to give underprivileged kids who showed promise in football a chance to be coached by people who would help further their abilities and create their own team.

"I'm going to talk with my dad next time he's here about using some of my trust fund to help Kyle get it going." The way Carter's eyes lit with excitement confirmed what I'd always suspected. He was a good man but guarded. For a moment, his guard was completely down.

All too soon, we were pulling into a spot next to the library. A few cars were there, but not many, which wasn't surprising.

When we walked in, I took in the massiveness of the library. The floor was marble throughout, which I found obnoxious, but other than that, it looked like any normal library I'd seen before, with rows and rows of books and about twenty rectangular tables for people to use.

As I scanned the tables, my gaze halted on Cole and someone across from him. The other guy was hunched over, a bottle of Pepto Bismol on the table next to him. He wore a baseball cap pulled low, but instead of looking at the book underneath him, he was cradling his head in his hands.

The guy must have felt me staring because he somehow managed to lift his head from his hands and stare back.

My heart stuttered. It was Grayson.

"Hey, what's wrong with him?" I asked, glancing at Carter.

His brows furrowed until his attention landed on that same table. "Uh...I don't know. I didn't hear anything."

"Maybe we should join them?" For appearance's sake but also because I was worried about Grayson. Maybe he needed to see a doctor.

Carter frowned but nodded. "Yeah, we probably should."

The two of us headed over, and I sat next to Grayson. Carter pressed his lips together but didn't say anything as he sat directly across from me.

"Hey, you," Grayson croaked, and he smiled before his expression crumpled. He looked even worse close up, with dark circles under his eyes and his face pale. His royal-purple HSU shirt made him appear almost ghostly.

"Are you okay?" I placed the back of my hand on his forehead. He felt cold and clammy, not feverish.

Cole snorted. "It's called drinking yourself into oblivion."

"Seriously?" Grayson glared. "You're just going to rat me out like that?"

"She's concerned, so yeah." Cole lifted his chin. "She shouldn't be concerned because of your dumbassery."

"What the *fuck*? You were supposed to be keeping an eye on Jack," Carter gritted and rubbed his temples.

I winced. Getting wasted didn't sound like Grayson, but what did I know? I'd known him for only a few weeks.

"Don't worry, man," Cole said and punched Carter in the arm. "He didn't get stupid at the party. He waited until we dropped a drunk and sexually satiated Jack off before heading back to our dorm room and drinking his own ass into oblivion. I bet Jack is worse off."

"You guys weren't supposed to let him drink like that." Carter then pointed at Grayson and continued, "*None* of you were supposed to drink that much."

Grayson grabbed his Pepto Bismol and took a big swig.

"Well, you can thank Katherine for Jack's situation. She kept his cup filled, and then he disappeared with her friend."

Katherine. Always Katherine. It was like that witch was haunting the entire football team. I had a sinking suspicion I knew which friend had her way with Jack. I remembered her voice vividly.

Rubbing the back of his neck, Carter tensed. "I tried calling him and Samuel this morning. Neither picked up."

"Don't worry about Samuel. He had one beer and was done." Cole tapped his pencil on his book. "But someone might have to pull Jack out of bed."

I grimaced. Football practice wasn't going to be fun for Jack or Grayson. Maybe that would teach them a lesson.

"Of course they will." Carter shook his head and then glanced apologetically at me. "I hate to do this, but I gotta go check on Jack. He's going to give Samuel hell, so it'll probably take two of us to get him up. If the full team doesn't show up for practice, it's not just them; it's all of our asses."

Disappointment knotted hard in my stomach, but I needed to study anyway. It wasn't like we were going to be talking about personal stuff or anything, so I forced a smile. "No problem." I stood, ready for him to take me back home.

"Do you have a lot of work to get caught up on?" Carter picked up his bag, throwing it over his shoulder.

"Yeah, but it's fine. I'll figure out a way to get the stuff done at home."

"Why not stay here?" He gestured to the library. "I can take you home after practice. We should be done by three."

I glanced at my phone. That was a little over three hours, and I'd brought plenty of stuff to work on. "Okay." And that would give us a little more time together. Besides, he planned on watching TV with me and my roommates anyway.

Carter strolled around the table. As he passed me, he ran

his hand along my upper arm before using it to smack Grayson in the back of the head.

"What the—" Grayson groaned and hung his head. "Dude, my head is killing me as it is."

"Good. Don't be an idiot again," Carter retorted as he strolled toward the doors.

I turned my head, enjoying the view of him walking away. With each step, his shorts hugged his body in a delicious way. I knew from experience his ass was as hard as it looked and enjoyed—whoa.

I had to stop.

He and I had agreed to be friends, and the last thing I needed was to admire his ass, his muscular chest, and his strong jawline.

Yup. Going to stop thinking about it riiight now.

Grayson reached for the Pepto Bismol again, and I caught his hand.

"Have you eaten anything yet?" I tilted my head, already knowing the answer.

"Nope! He hasn't," Cole chimed in. "Been trying to get him to do that all morning, but he's determined to drink his *shake*."

"Medicine isn't a shake." I arched a brow and snatched the bottle away. "Why did you even come here like this?"

He cradled his head once again. "Because I have an exam tomorrow that I need to study for, and I'll be exhausted after practice."

"Well, you're not gonna get much studying done like this." I stood and touched his arm. "Why don't we get something to eat? I'm hungry, and if you eat something, you'll start feeling better and might be able to at least handle practice?" Though I didn't have the cash to spare, Grayson would be more likely to come with me if he thought I needed food as well.

Leaning back, he groaned. "Fine. You're right. I'll get something to eat with you."

Cole laughed humorlessly. "Of course. When she suggests it, you listen, but when I say the same thing, you tell me to shut the fuck up."

"She's cute." Grayson shrugged. "You're not."

My face grew hot, but I tried to play it off. "You coming too, Cole?"

"Nah." Cole arched a brow at his friend. "I ate earlier, and I need to study. But you can leave your stuff here if you want. I'll keep an eye on it."

At least I wouldn't have to lug the backpack around. "Sweet. Thanks." I dropped my bag on the floor and hurried to the library doors.

I waited there for Grayson, who was walking slower than normal, and soon enough, we were trekking toward the student center.

Sweat beaded on his face, making his complexion worse.

Now I felt bad for making him come with me. Maybe he should've just waited inside. "Do you want to head back and let me go grab you something?" I asked.

He placed a hand on his stomach. "Not sure what I can handle. I want to see what they have on hand."

A few students were on campus, but not nearly as many as during a school day. It was sticky, early September, Southeast Tennessee hot, and a ton of people were probably hungover.

Sweat glistened on my skin, and I could only imagine how hard football practice would be in this heat.

Grayson cleared his throat. "So, are you and Carter doing whatever it is you two do again?"

I tensed. "I have no idea what you're talking about." This was definitely a conversation I didn't want to have, especially with him.

His gaze settled on me. "Do you think I'm stupid?" He raised a finger. "Wait. Don't answer that."

"I don't blame you." I laughed, hoping that right there changed the topic of conversation.

"What I'm getting at is, when I walked into your room that night, you two were fooling around."

I opened my mouth to object, but the words died. I didn't want to lie. "We didn't have sex. I mean, we only kissed." No matter what I said, it was just getting worse.

He huffed. "Well, that happened, and then he sort of disappeared, but then he demanded to take you home last night." He scratched the scruff on his face. "Are you guys seeing each other again?"

"We weren't seeing each other to begin with." Yup, I needed to shut my mouth. My heart sputtered. *Just answer his question.* "He wanted to talk to me about the craziness of the first two weeks, so we talked. He and I are just friends. We agreed to that last night after he apologized."

"Okay, good." Grayson's face smoothed. "That's really good. I tried calling you when I got home last night to check on you, and you didn't answer, so I—"

I froze and turned toward him. "Grayson, I'll admit we got carried away that night, but we sorted everything out. We're friends. Nothing more."

"Hey, you two. I was hoping I'd find Evie." Katherine's babyish voice reached my ears like an unwelcome screech just outside the student center.

I hadn't even noticed her.

My heart sank, but I was determined not to be aggravated by her.

That was until Katherine grabbed my arm and tugged me toward her. "Let's have a little chat over here."

CHAPTER EIGHTEEN

I clenched my hands, removing my arm from her grasp.

Out of *all* the people to run into here, she'd be the one. Today of all days. The day after Carter and I decided to be friends and keep our relationship hidden from *her*.

Reluctant to deal with her, I continued, not slowing down, as if I didn't see her at all. Fortunately, Grayson followed suit and played along.

She scoffed and then pivoted so she was in front of me again but, this time, blocking my way. She placed her hands on her hips. "There's no need to be rude. We're among friends, right?"

"You made it clear we aren't friends." I lifted a brow.

Rolling her eyes, she blew out a breath. "Don't be so melodramatic. I just want to talk for a second. It won't take long."

She wasn't going to leave me alone, and I had no doubt she'd love to rat me out to her father. "Fine. Just a minute. Grayson and I are getting something quick to eat before he has practice."

He arched a brow, and I could hear the question he was asking without him saying it. *Have you lost your mind?*

The answer was probably yes, but it would be best if I didn't confirm it...at least not verbally, so I nodded. "I won't be long."

Not budging, Katherine rubbed her hands together. "You heard her. She wants to talk."

His face strained as he glared at her. I suspected if he hadn't been feeling so poorly, he'd have a few choice words for her, but instead, he sighed. "I'll be in there, waiting for you, trying to figure out what I can eat." Grayson winced in distaste. "Text me if you need me."

"Aw, you two make such a cute couple." Katherine placed a hand on her heart and batted her eyes. "I love it when two underprivileged people are given a chance and they find love with someone similar along the way. It's always a good story. Too bad she wasn't there last night when you were knocking back those drinks. Maybe her presence would've helped you not overindulge."

He flinched, causing my heart to drop into my stomach.

Please don't let his current condition have anything to do with me. The last thing I wanted was for things to get weird between us. She was going to make this all worse if he didn't just go on in. "I'll text you if I'll be longer than expected."

"Okay," Grayson replied, avoiding my gaze as he walked away.

Katherine and I watched Grayson go into the student center, leaving the two of us alone outside.

As soon as he went through the double doors, she turned toward me.

Twirling a piece of her hair around her fingers, Katherine smacked her gum. "Something funny happened last night."

My blood ran cold. She waited for me to say something, but

I kept my mouth closed. I didn't want to help her by feeding into whatever game she was trying to play with me.

Finally, she continued, though some of her smile had slipped. "Carter didn't show up at the party like everyone expected, and neither did *you*. He was supposed to be my date."

This time, I smiled, and I hated how my heart fluttered at learning that he'd chosen me over her, especially when I hadn't asked him to. "I didn't know you were expecting me. If I'd known, then I still wouldn't have come."

She laughed, but the sound was off. "You're always invited to our parties, Evie. After all, my family sponsored you. But I was worried when both you *and* Carter didn't show up. Is everything okay? Did something happen?"

I shrugged, trying to choose my words carefully. She was attempting to figure out if I was the reason Carter stood her up. "Well, I was tired and went home to get some rest. I can't speak for Carter, but maybe he didn't feel like a party. Or maybe he was there, but you didn't see him. It sounds like it was large. Your best bet is to ask him." I was not getting between those two. There was no fucking way.

Her eyes narrowed. "I'll do that. But let me make this clear. Stay away from him. Keep your focus on Grayson—that will end better for you."

A shiver ran down my spine. This sounded like a peace offering, but I wasn't sure if it was sincere or just a way to keep me from being more of an obstacle. If she was offering a truce, I should take it. Carter himself would advise me to. "Katherine, all I want to do is get through this year. I promise. Getting on your short list is not part of my plan. I'm going to focus on school until I graduate. Honestly, that's been my goal all along."

She inspected me, making me feel like a cell under a microscope.

"Good." She nodded. "That's an amazing goal. Let me know if there's any way I can help keep you focused." Then she turned and walked away, leaving me alone.

I hadn't expected the conversation to end so easily, but I wasn't going to complain. Taking a deep breath and trying to calm the buzzing in my body, I went inside.

She'd given up too easily as if she wanted me to believe that she'd bought my story. Things with her couldn't be that cut and dried, so I pulled out my phone and shot Carter a message, telling him everything that happened and that I was going to get Haven to pick me up and take me home.

He responded immediately, agreeing with my takeaway and saying that he'd be over later.

Then I sent off a message to Haven, asking her to pick me up in two hours.

With everything settled, I hurried to the cafeteria, where Grayson was glaring at all the options. He looked like he wanted to barf. I chuckled internally. At least he was learning a lesson.

I headed over to help him find something, my conversation with Katherine repeating in my head.

The next few weeks passed in a blur. We were already halfway through September, and Carter chauffeured me to and from school, dropping me off in a parking lot instead of pulling up to my buildings. Then, in the evenings, he was never late taking me to and from work.

With the time he spent taking care of me, I was becoming dependent on him. There were even times when I texted him for rides just to see him. This petrified me, but I couldn't stop, so I asked Joe if he could make sure there were a couple of nights that Leah and I worked the same schedule so we could ride together, which he had no problem doing. I wasn't quite sure why I hadn't thought to ask him for that earlier.

On nights when Leah wasn't able to take me home, Carter, Grayson, Jack, Cole, and Samuel would come visit me while I worked. Overall, things were going great.

The past four days, it'd been raining constantly, so when Friday night came around, the bar was even more packed than usual. My skin crawled as people bumped into me, and I had to remember to take deep breaths.

Carter was taking Katherine to some sort of dinner with the heads of the school. Yet another date he'd promised to escort her on, and I couldn't get the idea of him with her out of my head despite us being just friends.

Pushing the thought away, I marched to my new table, where people had just sat down in the corner of the room. It was Grayson and Cole.

I arched a brow and pulled out my pad and pen. "Why are you two here? You have a noon game tomorrow. Carter said you all were going to bed early."

Cole snorted. "I know this might be surprising, but even though Carter is our captain, he isn't our boss."

"He'd disagree." I chuckled. The thing was, Carter truly cared for their well-being and wanted everyone to kick ass tomorrow at the game.

"That's true, he would." Grayson rolled his eyes. "But don't worry; we'll be just fine. The night before a game, Cole and I struggle with sleep. Going out is kinda tradition."

I wasn't so sure about that. It was a game between HSU and the other university in town, Ridge U, and they were huge rivals. "What can I get for you?"

They rattled off their orders, and I scurried away to turn

them in. Though they weren't worried, I was going to expedite their order.

As Joe filled their drinks, I checked my phone to see if Carter had texted anything. I saw I had one message.

I didn't find a message from Carter telling me he'd gotten home. He'd always texted me good night, and I glanced at the clock and realized how late it was. My stomach dropped. Was he still with Katherine? If so, this was a lot later than just a dinner with the heads of the school.

Instead, there was a group text between Haven, Leah, and me.

Haven: Hey, I've got a party going tonight. Get your hot asses home ASAP so we can hang out.

Great. Another party. I truly loved those two, but had I known how much partying they liked to do, I would've at least *tried* to find an alternate living situation. Especially considering how hard it was raining—everyone would be crammed inside the house.

"Evie!" Joe called from the bar.

When I looked at him, he nodded toward the Coke and Dr Pepper he'd poured for Grayson and Cole.

We were too busy for me to lose focus, but I couldn't push Carter out of my head. Where was he, and what was he doing with Katherine?

THANKFULLY, the night stayed busy, so I couldn't spend too long worrying about Carter. However, I kept checking my phone for a text from him.

Despite my protesting, Grayson and Cole left just a few minutes before closing at one in the morning. I kept telling them they were going to be tired, but they both claimed to be restless and unable to sleep. They'd tried before coming here.

I couldn't blame them. If I had a game the next day against my biggest rival, I think I'd be too amped up for sleep as well.

Carter didn't seem to let anything faze him...like he was comfortable in his own skin. A confidence I wished I had, especially after not hearing from him.

About thirty minutes after closing, Leah and I had finished our tasks and were in her Mazda, heading home.

She turned onto the road and blew a raspberry. "You know I'm always down for parties. But, girl, I'm exhausted."

"Same." I pursed my lips. "But that's never stopped either of you, so this is the norm for me."

She stuck out her tongue as she turned on our road. "I know as soon as I get a few drinks in me, I'll be ready to go. But maybe we need to find other jobs, so we're not working this late. That way, we'll have energy straight out of the gate to keep up with Haven."

I chuckled. "That won't happen. We enjoy where we work." Even though we didn't make an exorbitant amount of money, it kept us busy, and it was better than working at a fast-food restaurant.

"Yeah, you're right." She yawned. "But don't tell my brother that."

When we reached the house, the party was in full swing despite the rain. I'd been expecting the university to call off tomorrow's game, but Carter told me that wouldn't happen. The staff was taking care of the fields, and games were rarely canceled, even when it rained like this.

Leah and I dashed from the car into the house, trying not to get soaked. As soon as we stepped inside, Haven stumbled to us. "You guys! Go get a drink. I bought spiced rum and pineapple juice, so we're fully stocked."

"That's exactly what I need." Leah beamed, already raring to go.

That happened quicker than I expected.

"I'll make you one too, Evie," she offered as the two of us strolled into the kitchen.

I shook my head, though, for the first time, I was tempted. I'd love to find a way to get Carter out of my head. "I'm good. I'm heading down to get some rest. I have to wake up by eight for the noon game so I can take those pictures and then work tomorrow night."

"Ugh, don't remind me. Everyone is going to that game." Leah pushed through a group of people surrounding the table that held the drinks.

She was already in her own world, so I swerved around the few bodies hanging out in front of the stove and opened the door to the basement. As soon as it closed, I locked it, once again thankful that Carter had installed the dead bolt.

I turned on the lights and clomped down the stairs, eager for bed. I wasn't even going to take a shower. I was just going to pass out.

However, when I stepped off the last step, my foot sank into water. My sock and shoe became instantly wet. I turned the corner and glanced around.

My chest constricted. There was at least a foot of water covering the entire basement, which meant every piece of furniture was going to be ruined.

Worse, my duffel bag, which still held several outfits of mine because I had no space, was on the floor, submerged in the flood.

Tears spilled down my face. I didn't know what to do. This was everything I had. And I couldn't go to sleep anywhere else in the house. The party was raging.

I wrapped my arms around my body, trying to anchor

myself. I removed my phone from my back pocket, ready to call Carter, but stopped short. I always called him when I needed something, and I hadn't heard from him tonight. He must still be with *her*. I refused to call and come off as even more needy if she was with him.

I pulled up Grayson's contact instead. He and Cole had been at the bar not too long ago, so there was a decent chance he was still awake.

Grayson answered on the first ring. "Hey, Evie. Is everything okay?"

I never called him this late, so it made sense that he was concerned. A sob broke through as I said, "My room's flooded."

He paused. "What do you mean it's flooded? Are there people in your room? I can hear the music, so your roommates must be having a party."

"There's at least a foot of water covering the floor. I don't know what to do. Haven and Leah are drinking, and I don't want to take their cars, but I can't stay here."

He cleared his throat. "I'm on my way. I'll come get you so you can stay with me and Cole tonight."

"Wait. In your dorm?" I grimaced. I didn't want to stay with them, especially on campus, but my options were limited. They each had their own room, so there was that.

"It'll be fine. The RAs are asleep and frankly don't give a shit. Guys have their girls sleeping over. Just get your stuff together and be ready. Bring everything you can so nothing else gets ruined."

"I'm not sure you want me to. All my clothes are soaked." Hell, I had nothing to sleep in other than what I had on my body.

"It'll be fine. We can wash them here. Just grab what you can. I'm heading out now and will be there in ten minutes."

Easier said than done. I inhaled deeply, trying to calm my

nerves and focus on the next task. Tasks made things easier for me.

I sloshed through the water, gathering everything I could. I salvaged my toiletries and soaking-wet duffel bag. Luckily, my backpack and camera were on top of the desk, so at least my school supplies hadn't been ruined, and my clothes could be washed.

Scanning the room, I tried not to focus on the muddy water that was now knee-deep. That was when I noticed the source of the problem. Around the small windows at the top of the room, right above where the ground ended, water funneled through the sides like the frames weren't sealed.

Lovely.

Not wanting to spend any more time in this nasty sludge, I waded to the stairs, heading back to the kitchen.

The duffel bag was heavy, thanks to the water, and I gritted my teeth, taking the stairs one at a time. With each step, the bag hit my side, further soaking my right hip. I tried to keep my backpack and camera as far away as possible.

Each stair was another battle.

When I reached the top, I marched through the kitchen. Luckily, there were fewer people in here, and they were so drunk they didn't notice me.

As soon as I was outside, I had to hover close to the side of the house where a small section of the roof jutted out, trying to keep my backpack and camera dry.

Then the wind shifted, and the rain slanted toward me.

No matter what I did, I couldn't win. And I was truly petrified. I wasn't sure there was a way for me to recover from this, at least financially, while attending HSU.

Grayson's Jeep pulled up, and I saw his door open.

I knew I should walk toward him. I needed to hurry. But for some reason, I couldn't move from this spot. I needed Carter.

CHAPTER NINETEEN

His door slammed, and he darted around the back of his Jeep as he jogged across the yard toward the front door.

I needed to stop him since I was at the side door and it was pouring. If he went to the front, he'd get Haven and Leah involved, but I was frozen.

Tears spilled down my face as I stood there, powerless.

I'd thought I was getting a little better despite the recurring dream of my parents' deaths replaying over and over, but in this moment, having lost everything and having no family to turn to, I felt more than broken. The constant void inside me had grown, sucking the life out of me like a black hole.

Destroying.

Obliterating.

As he reached the porch, I managed to shout, "Grayson, I'm over here."

He stopped and turned in my direction. His eyes widened as he took me in while I tried desperately to huddle under the small overhang.

"Evie, why are you waiting out here?" He darted toward

me, his shoes splashing on the wet, soggy grass. The rain pelted his body, causing his gray shirt to cling to his chest.

When he reached me, his forehead creased. "Did something happen?"

I shook my head and wiped the tears from my face, but more just continued to come.

"I'm—" I started, but a sob stopped me. I took a moment and tried again. "Fi—" But another sob racked my body. I couldn't speak *or* stutter.

He wrapped his arms around me, pulling me tight against him. I cradled my camera, protecting it, but buried my face in his soaking-wet chest. The tears came harder, and I wasn't sure if I was ever going to stop crying.

After a moment, he leaned back and cupped my face as he lowered his forehead to mine. He vowed, "It's going to be okay. We'll figure this out tomorrow. Right now, we need to go."

My throat was so tight I wouldn't bother trying to speak again, so I nodded.

He reached for my duffel bag, leaving me with my camera and backpack. "Have you told Haven and Leah where you're going?"

I shook my head. I should've told them, but I wasn't in the right frame of mind. I needed to escape and get away from all the people and noise. Even out here, the thumping could still be heard.

He wrapped his arm around my shoulders and said, "We'll text them when we get to my place."

The two of us walked to his Jeep. My feet were soaked, and each step seemed heavier.

When we reached the trunk, he removed two empty trash bags, and I placed my backpack and camera in the back as he put my duffel bag in one of the bags, and then he handed me the other.

"We can put your pants and shoes in this one when you're ready to take them off," he explained.

Thankfully, he didn't try to talk to me on the way to his dorm. All he did was turn on the seat warmer, which puzzled me until I noticed that my entire body was shaking.

But it wasn't from the cold.

My emotions had taken control of me, and another sob escaped, causing me to quiver even harder. I'd worked so hard to be independent, but after one flood, I was completely at everyone's mercy.

We passed through the university gates, and I clasped my hands, trying to get myself together because we'd be walking into his dorm soon. I couldn't go inside a sobbing mess.

He turned left and parked in the dorm lot across the road from the student center. Then he jogged to the back, pulled out my stuff, and led me into the ten-story brick building.

The inside was gigantic, with leather couches and numerous wooden tables surrounded by four seats each. TVs hung in every corner, but all of them were turned off at the moment.

The place was vacant except for four guys playing a board game in a back corner.

Grayson didn't pause as he walked straight to the elevators. Within a few minutes, we were on the fifth floor and at his door.

Inside, Cole was placing a pillow and blankets on a leather couch. There was a black futon kitty-corner to it, both the couch and futon positioned strategically near the TV and PlayStation.

A small kitchen held a stove, a microwave, and a mini-fridge. A round table with four chairs sat across from it.

This place was close to the same size as the house I shared

with Leah and Haven. It wasn't upscale like Carter's duplex, but it was still nicer than what I'd rented.

"I'll sleep here." Grayson pointed at the couch. "You can take my room."

"No," I said forcefully, my voice deeper than normal. "I'll sleep here. I've already put you out enough."

Cole smiled sadly. "If you want, you can take a shower. I put one of my shirts and boxers in there so you have something to change into." He grimaced. "I hope that's okay. When Grayson said your place was flooded, I figured you might need something to wear."

Both of them were being so kind. "Thank you, but—" I glanced down and noticed water puddling underneath me from my shoes and clothes. I sighed. "I'm unfortunately going to need to take you up on that offer."

"It's fine." He winked at me. "You're one of the few I'm willing to offer that to."

He was trying to make a joke and be kind, but it fell flat.

"Take a shower and toss your clothes outside the door." Grayson dropped my backpack and camera on the kitchen table. "I'll take them and your bag downstairs and start a load of laundry."

Once again, I was putting them out, but I wasn't sure what else to do. "Thank you. Just let me know how much I owe you." My throat constricted. Money. It always came back to the one thing I didn't have enough of.

"It's the door at the end of the hall. There's already a towel in there too." Cole gestured to the hall on the right. "Grayson's room is on the left, and my room is on the right."

Not wanting to stand there dripping any longer, I removed my shoes and waddled down to the shower. I turned the water on and stripped, tossing my clothes in the hall like Grayson asked.

When I stepped into the shower, tears began all over again. I enjoyed the feel of the hot water as I took my time getting clean, knowing that, at least in here, no one could see me fall apart. I cried about not having Carter with me and because everything I'd worked toward was gone.

I'd run out of tears by the time I turned the water off. Slipping on Cole's clothes felt strange, but sleeping in my sweat-and-rain-soaked shirt from work wasn't an option, especially since my jeans had been taken to the laundry.

When I stepped out, I noticed that my water mess had already been wiped up. In the living room, I found Grayson sitting on the couch and Cole nowhere around.

"Are you sure you don't want my room?" Grayson asked as he stood.

"You've got a game tomorrow...or today, rather. You need good sleep, especially with how little you're going to get now because of me. And I'm going to pass out. I'm pretty sure I could sleep in the soggy grass outside without issue." After the long, hard cry, I was exhausted.

He frowned. "Not funny, but okay. When I get up in the morning, I'll put your clothes in the dryer. And before I leave for warm-ups, I'll bring them up to you. It'd be better if you stayed in the room even though the RAs don't care. I don't want to start any rumors."

Ugh. I hadn't even thought about that, but he was right. "Thank you."

Looking me over, his frown deepened. "Are you sure you're okay?"

There was no telling how I looked. I'd avoided looking in the mirror before coming out here, but my eyes burned, which meant they had to be red and swollen. "I'll be okay. Promise."

He sighed. "Okay. If you need some water, we have cold bottles in the fridge."

"Got it." I tapped my head, trying to lighten the situation.

Chuckling, he hugged me again and then kissed my forehead before disappearing down the hall into his room.

A part of me wished that I felt something other than platonic about him.

Not wanting to think anymore, I lay down on the couch and glanced at my phone. Still no text from Carter.

Sleep came almost instantly, temporarily relieving me of my heartache.

I STARTLED AWAKE. Someone was pounding on the door. I sat up quickly on the couch, the room spinning. For a second, I lost my bearings, feeling dizzy and confused.

But when Cole came running down the hall, reality crashed back over me. I wasn't hungover from drinking but crying.

"Little pig, little pig, let me in," Jack's voice called from the other side of the door. "Because I can hear footsteps on the other side of the door, and someone is going to be late if they don't get their ass out here."

Okay, maybe I was dreaming because that was weird, even for him.

Cole stumbled to the door in his pajamas. His hair stood on end, and he wiped a hand down his face. "Where's Grayson? He was supposed to wake me up."

I bit my lip, but now a memory of him telling me he was heading down to get my clothes filtered back into my head. "I think he's downstairs in the laundry room."

Wanting to get out of the room before he opened the door, I pushed the covers off me and stood. "Wait–"

But he'd already opened it before I could finish.

"You dumbasses better be glad…" Jack started but trailed off when he saw me. He pointed at me and asked, "Why the hell is she here, wearing *your* clothes?" He rushed into the room, slamming the door. "You know this isn't gonna go over well."

Cole grimaced. "I know, and we didn't want anyone to find out for that reason. It's not what it seems."

I blinked and pulled the boxers up since they were about to fall down. "Are you two speaking English? I have no idea what you're talking about. Grayson said the RAs wouldn't care."

"Great. Grayson is involved too." Jack ran his fingers through his hair. "No one tells him until after the game."

"Tells who *what*?" I placed my hands on my hips and squared my shoulders.

"Damn." Jack shook his head, glancing at me. "I'm just glad I wasn't the dumbass this time. Usually, it's me. It'll be nice to see Carter pissed at someone else."

"Carter?" My stomach dropped. "What's wrong? Is he okay?" Was that why he hadn't texted me last night?

Arching a brow, Jack shook his head. "Is she really that clueless?"

"Yup." Cole nodded. "And you know it too. You've been around her as much as I have."

"*She* is here." I patted my chest. "And *she*—er, *I*—want answers."

Jack came over and ruffled my hair, winking. "Don't worry, E. You'll find out soon enough." He nodded at the door. "Come on, man. Carter's going to eat us for breakfast if we're late. Where's Grayson?"

"He'll be a little behind us." Cole grimaced. "Tell Grayson we headed to the stadium?"

"Sure." It wasn't like they were going to answer more questions anyway. Dread pooled in my stomach. What did Carter have to tell me? Did it have something to do with Katherine?

Cole stepped into the hallway, and Jack snorted before stepping out and shutting the door behind himself.

My eyes burned, and my brain was foggy, especially since I didn't understand a damn thing that had just been said.

Glancing at the time, I noted the game started in two hours. I was also running short on time, especially since I needed to get there with my camera to set up.

In the bathroom, I found the towel I'd used the night before. I started the water in the shower just as the front door opened. I popped my head into the hallway. Grayson jogged into sight and dropped my dry and clean duffel bag on the floor. He was already dressed in his workout tank top and shorts. "Here's your clothes. I gotta go. I'm running late."

"See you soon," I called as he ran out the door.

I went to my bag and unzipped it. Grayson had folded everything neatly, and I smiled gratefully even though he couldn't see me. I took out a royal-purple shirt and shorts.

Hurrying back to the shower, I quickly got ready and ate in the room. Then I grabbed my camera, put my rain jacket hood up to keep my face hidden, and hurried out the back entrance of the dorm.

The rain wasn't coming down as hard, but it was a pretty steady drizzle. Despite that, the stadium was already packed with people, and more stood in lines to get in.

As I walked to the stadium, my stomach roiled. If Carter and Katherine had gotten back together, I'd have to see them the entire game. I didn't know if my heart could handle it, but I didn't have a choice. This was for a grade.

This time, I went in through the players' entrance, showed my badge, and got onto the field to set up for the game. The horrible night before faded away as I focused on taking the perfect shot, even in the rain.

Time flew by, and I enjoyed the game, taking picture after picture. I managed to get a shot of Grayson's amazing block and several gorgeous passes as the ball left Carter's fingers. I even begrudgingly took some of Katherine and the cheerleaders but purposely didn't watch them whenever Carter made a good play or came off the field because I knew that Katherine would be trying to get into his arms, especially if they were back together.

It was silly for that to bother me, but it did. He and I were friends, but she was a smug and self-centered person.

When the game was over, I had nowhere to go, especially since Sadie had come down with a cold and hadn't attended the game. I couldn't get into Grayson's and Cole's dorm without them, so I was forced to wait. Luckily, the cheerleaders left as soon as the game was over, probably uncomfortable and cold in the rain.

I leaned against the wall next to the door, heart pounding, and pulled out my phone to see if there were any updates from Haven and Leah. Unfortunately, there were. They'd called the landlord, but he hadn't returned their call.

Of course he hadn't. Apparently, he wasn't responsive unless we were late with the rent. This was going to be a huge mess, and I didn't have my own money to take care of it. This was what rental insurance was for, but the landlord hadn't required proof, and none of us got any since my property wasn't worth much to others, just me.

Pressure built between my eyes. Great. I had a headache forming, and I had to work at the bar tonight. It would be busy, and I was already exhausted. Worse, I might be forced to face Carter if Grayson didn't hurry his ass up.

The door to the locker room opened, but I didn't glance up. Normally, Grayson was one of the last to leave.

I sensed a huge form hovering over me, and I looked up into

my favorite pair of eyes. The gold flecks weren't visible, which meant he was upset.

I studied his expression, taking in the clenched jaw.

What the hell reason did *he* have to be pissed?

"Carter?" I whispered. "What's wrong?" He was standing here, scowling at me after he'd just won a game. I'd even gotten a picture of him and his dad together when he came off the field, and he'd looked ecstatic.

"Don't pretend you don't know." The skin around his eyes tightened. "Did you sleep with Cole?"

I gasped, which clearly was the wrong thing to do. My blood ran hot, and I tried to control my anger. "Are you being serious right now? You're asking me that after spending the entire night with *Katherine*?"

His face twisted into disgust. "Don't try that manipulative shit on me. You know I wasn't with her, so from that deflection, I'll take your answer as a yes." He spun around, ready to march back into the locker room.

The pain around my heart eased, and then I grimaced. "No, I didn't sleep with him."

He paused but then didn't turn around.

"Last night, my room flooded, including all my clothes. I slept on Grayson and Cole's couch; Cole loaned me a set of his clothes while Grayson washed mine."

"Why didn't you call *me*?" Carter pivoted back toward me, his expression not as cold but still strained. "I would've helped you."

My throat thickened. "Because you never texted me to tell me you were home and good night, and I didn't want to bother you if..." I couldn't finish the sentence. "You know. But you were the first person I wanted to call. I had your name pulled up."

He removed his phone from his pocket. "Fuck!" He

groaned. "I didn't press send." He came back and showed me the screen where I saw his good night message typed out. Then something shifted in his face, and he growled. "I'm tired of fighting this." He wrapped an arm around my waist and pulled me to his chest.

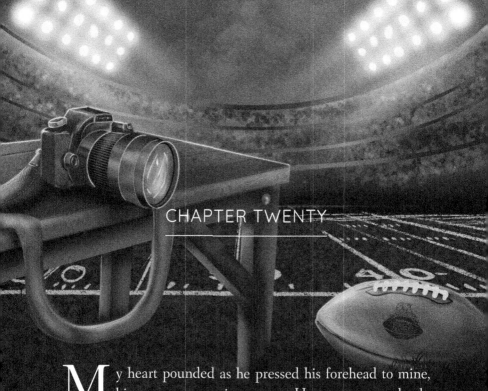

CHAPTER TWENTY

My heart pounded as he pressed his forehead to mine, his arms warming me. He was completely surrounding me, and I willingly gave myself over, dizzy from his scent.

Time ceased to exist. It was just him and me in our own little world—until footsteps from the locker room pulled me out of the temporary reprieve from my own personal hell.

The noise was the equivalent of a cold shower, and I took a step back, detangling myself from him.

The locker room door opened, and Grayson, Cole, and Jack strolled outside.

"Dammit." Jack's eyes flicked between Carter and me as he continued, "Did I already miss the fight?"

"There wasn't a fight, dumbass." Carter's eyes darkened to almost black. "You failed to mention that she was staying on their couch because her room got flooded."

"Oh." Jack tilted his head back. "They didn't tell me that."

Cole arched a brow and crossed his arms, causing the already formfitting, royal-purple athletic wear tank top to mold to his muscles even more. "I tried, but you wouldn't shut up about how much trouble I was going to be in."

"She was wearing your clothes," Jack protested, gesturing to me.

Carter stiffened, and his jaw clenched again.

"Because all my clothes were soaked from the flood!" I lifted both arms. "And the clothes I wore to work smelled like cigarettes, so I wasn't too keen on sleeping in those either."

Grayson stepped over and threw an arm around me. "I washed her clothes at our place and dried them this morning before I came here. That's why I was a little late."

"And no one thought of telling *me*?" Carter pounded his chest. "She's *my*—" He stopped abruptly.

I wanted to laugh because I understood why he'd fumbled. We'd said we were friends, and we were. But sometimes, like today, it felt like more, especially since he'd even admitted he had a hard time fighting *this*.

"Your *what*?" Jack waggled his eyebrow. "Buddy? Pal? Chum? Hobnobber?"

"Man, what the *hell*?" Cole huffed. "Now you can come up with words, but *I* had to do our chemistry paper because words aren't your strong point?"

I almost had the urge to kiss Cole for the distraction despite it not being intentional. "We all wanted you to focus. Your dad flew in this morning for the game." That was when I glanced around, searching for the man in question. "Where is he?"

"He left." Carter ran a hand through his hair, and it fell into his face in that way I loved. "He came in last night for our dinner with the school heads, but he had to leave after the game to head back to DC."

I waved a hand. "Even better that I didn't call and get you involved." Here he was, complaining about me when his dad had been in town. If I could go back in time, I would cherish every moment of quality time I had with my parents.

"He would've been all right at my house for twenty minutes while I helped you," Carter insisted. "All we did was argue anyway. He won't—" Carter made a strangled noise, and I remembered he'd planned to talk with his dad about the organization he wanted to fund, Touchdown 4 Kids. My heart sank. Clearly, it hadn't gone well.

Carter was glaring at Grayson's arm, which still rested over my shoulders. I resisted the urge to shrug off Grayson. Sad as I felt for him, Carter would have to accept that I had other friends, including guy friends.

I wanted to change the topic again before Jack tried to bring it back to whatever Carter and I were calling ourselves. "As much as I'm enjoying this riveting back-and-forth, I need to eat something and head to work." And figure out where the hell I'd go after that.

Leah and Haven had been texting me, saying I could room with one of them until the basement was fixed, but they both had a full-size bed, and their sleep schedules were completely different from mine.

"Then let's go grab your stuff so we can get you settled," Carter said as he gently took my wrist.

"All her stuff is washed, so she's good there," Grayson said as he kept hold of my shoulder. He looked at me. "I can take you and pick you up from work, and you can crash on the couch or in my room."

"Told ya this wasn't gonna go well," Jack snickered and moved to the side of the door, leaning against the wall.

I should've known he wouldn't stay quiet.

"Why would she..." Carter trailed off and looked at me. He sighed. "Can we talk for a second?"

Okay, I hadn't expected that. "Sure." I glanced at Grayson and smiled. "Give us a moment?"

Carter tugged me about ten feet from the others as more football players came out of the locker room and started talking to Grayson, Jack, and Cole.

Carter blocked my view of the others and licked his lips. "You should stay with me."

My jaw slackened. I hadn't expected that. "At your house? That's too much. I can just sleep on the couch at the house or something."

"Where your roommates will keep you up all night or wind up having a party?" He arched a brow. "It's Saturday night—you know how they are. And since we won, the other team will be drowning their sorrows. Why not stay with me? We're friends, and I have an extra bedroom."

Heart fluttering, I tried to keep my head on straight. Staying with him wouldn't be smart, but out of every alternative, it made the most sense. He had an extra bedroom and at least two bathrooms.

The only other true alternative was to rent a cheap-ass hotel room, but I didn't have the cash to do that. "Grayson said I could stay with them." However, that couch hadn't been comfortable, and I wouldn't kick Grayson out of his room and force him to sleep on it.

Carter arched his brow. "First off, you say you want to stay under the radar. Living in a guys' dorm is *not* the way. And second, you'd rather crash on their couch than stay at my house where there's a spare bedroom and bathroom you can have all to yourself?"

"But being at your place would still give me a reputation." I tilted my head, staring into his eyes.

"Evie, I live in a duplex. There are no other students around me." He blew out a breath. "Why don't you want to come home with me? I'll take you to and from school and work. It makes sense for you to stay with me. Just temporarily until your room is fixed."

He had me there. He usually did those things anyway, and I would have my own space.

A lump formed in my throat. The problem was I'd be near him all the time.

His nostrils flared in frustration. "I'm trying to be good here. What I really want to do is scoop you up and throw you in the SUV to take you home, but I know you'd hate that." His jaw worked. "The room is almost as big as the one you had in the basement, and it would be all yours. There's a full bathroom attached to it. You won't have to share any space with me except the kitchen and living room."

"I don't want to be more of a burden." That was the other thing—I didn't want him to see me that way.

"You aren't a burden," he said sternly, reaching out and cupping my face. "I wouldn't offer this to anyone else but you. Aren't we friends? That's what friends do. Why are you okay staying with Grayson and Cole when they have a much worse setup than I do?" Hurt flashed in his eyes, making my stomach roil.

A sour taste filled my mouth, and I hated that I'd caused him pain. "Because I feel more for you than I do them, and that makes it dangerous to stay there," I whispered.

"*That's* the reason?" he rasped.

I nodded and looked down, worried about what I would see on his face.

"Then let's go get your things." He took my hand and tugged me toward the others. "Because that's the same reason I can't stand the thought of you staying anywhere else."

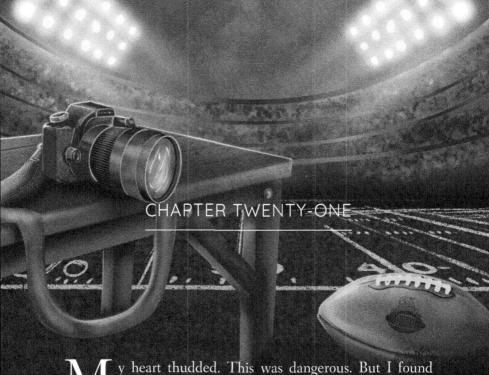

CHAPTER TWENTY-ONE

My heart thudded. This was dangerous. But I found myself nodding, and his body relaxed.

We'd both just admitted to feeling more than friendship for each other. This could get messy fast.

The two of us went back to the others, and Carter nodded at Jack. "Why don't you take Evie to my place while I grab her stuff from Cole and Grayson's room?"

"In other words, so Katherine and her spies don't notice anything amiss." Jack waggled his brows. "Okay, I'm down. But we'll need keys."

Carter pulled out a key and tossed it to me. "That'll get you in the front door."

"Hey, why does she get a key and not me?" Jack pouted.

"Because I trust her," Carter said and pointed at Jack. "I don't trust you. You'll make a copy. And the next thing I know, you'll be having sex with somebody on my couch...again."

Jack snickered. "Hey, that only happened once!"

"And I changed the locks and bought a new couch because of it," Carter countered.

"Only because you were jealous I used it first," Jack retorted and threw his arm over my shoulders. "Come on, Evie. Let's get the hell out of here... Just *you* and *me*." He waggled his brows, which had me giggling.

"Not funny, man." Carter smacked Jack on the back of the head. He then gently grasped my wrist. "Do not, under any circumstances, give him that key. He'll have it copied before the night's over."

Jack pouted. "Man, not cool. I'm your bro. Bros before—"

I whipped my head in his direction, arching an eyebrow.

"Delightful friends." He beamed a little too blindingly.

"Good correction." I poked him in the chest, trying not to laugh. For once, I felt a little lighthearted. I looked at Carter. "Don't worry. I won't take my eyes off the key. I don't want to walk in on him and whatever girl he gets underneath him for the night and then have the couch be a constant reminder."

"I'm not always on top. Sometimes, they're on top. I like variety." He winked.

My face burned, and I knew my cheeks had to be reddening, considering the huge-ass smirk on his face.

So, of course, he leaned closer to me and said, "But if you prefer, I could change it up and use your bed."

"Not funny," Carter growled.

Jack lifted both hands. "Not with her. With somebody else." He then pursed his lips. "Though I'm not saying I wouldn't be down for a threesome."

"Ew." I closed my eyes, trying to wipe the mental image from my mind. "Stop. Not happening."

"I agree," Carter muttered as he shoved Jack in the back. "Not funny, man."

Grayson and Cole glanced at each other, and Grayson cleared his throat.

"Evie, you can stay in our dorm. It's seriously fine,"

Grayson said and nodded at Cole. "The two of us talked about it. You'd be on campus, so it could make things easier for you to get to class."

I understood what he was doing. He was a good friend and worried about me staying with Carter alone, especially after how badly Carter had hurt me not too long ago. I got it, but sleeping on their couch or taking over one of their beds wasn't right either. "It could take more than a couple of days to get my room fixed. Besides, I doubt the RA would be thrilled with a girl staying in your place for many consecutive nights." I didn't want to hurt his feelings, but Carter's place really was the best option.

"Well, if you change your mind..." Grayson cleared his throat. "You know you can call me."

"Oh, she's clearly aware," Carter deadpanned. "You were the one she called last night."

Obviously, I had hurt his feelings too, though I hadn't meant to. But Carter was going to have to get over it. I hadn't done anything wrong. I'd been trying to be considerate of *him* and his choices.

Cole shook his head. "Man, we had just left her work not even an hour before she called us. She knew we were awake and struggling to sleep. Let it go."

"Aaand...listen to that." Jack cupped his ear. "The rain is coming down harder."

Jack was right. The faint drizzle had grown steadier again. It would be raining hard soon.

"Come on, Evie. Let's go." Jack slung an arm around my shoulders and dragged me to the player exit just as more people came out of the locker room.

When we got a few steps ahead, he murmured in my ear, "The longer we stay, the more those two are just going to repeat the same thing. I don't know about you, but I'm sick of it."

I rolled my eyes but remained quiet. Unfortunately, I did feel like a point of contention between Grayson and Carter. I glanced over my shoulder and saw the three of them following us. Carter's gaze locked on me, sending a shiver down my spine.

Jack held open the door for me, and the two of us sprinted to his black BMW M5, the rain hitting us. He opened my door as the downpour began, and I slid into the comfortable leather seat.

As Jack jogged to his side, I watched Carter, Grayson, and Cole climb into Carter's Escalade.

Rain pelted the windshield, and within seconds, Jack was in the driver's seat and easing the car into drive. But instead of cranking up the music like he usually did, he began to drive in silence.

His face creased as if he was concerned. He drove through the university campus, and when I'd almost had enough of the silence, he said, "You really did hurt him, and he's trying to let it go, but he can't."

There was no point acting like I didn't know who he was talking about. "I don't understand how." I laid my head against the seat. "Carter was out with Katherine and never texted, so I wasn't sure what was going on. And also, he needed a good night's rest so he could be entirely focused on the game. He needed to do well, and I didn't want to mess that up for him. For your team."

"I'm not saying you're wrong." Jack glanced at me. "In fact, I think you did the right thing, but that doesn't take away the fact that he feels vulnerable, and he hates that."

I shivered, paying attention as we inched toward the entrance to the school. There was so much traffic. "Grayson's my friend too. Or I could've just as easily called *you*."

I could feel Jack's gaze on me as he turned on the heat.

"Even if you'd called me, he would've been hurt...just not quite as bad because he knows I'm not a threat. Don't pretend that you and Carter aren't more than just friends, even if you haven't defined it yet."

My heart fluttered, and I wasn't sure how to respond. For Jack to say that, Carter must be struggling the same as I was. Maybe that was the real reason Katherine had gotten upset the other day... But none of that mattered. Carter had made it clear that we couldn't be together, and I agreed. Having my heart broken wouldn't be wise, especially when I was still grieving for my parents.

"I'm glad he gave you a chance to explain, though I'm surprised by that." Jack smiled sadly.

That was an odd thing to say. "What do you mean?"

"It's not my story to tell," Jack replied and turned the music up. He switched it to an oldies station that was playing "Girls Just Wanna Have Fun" and sang at the top of his lungs...just like he had always done. The Jack persona was back in place.

And that was exactly what it was.

A persona.

He was serious and observant. I'd just seen proof of it.

He and Carter being friends finally made sense.

I closed my eyes, trying to ignore his awful voice, and thought about the discussion we'd just had.

If there was any truth to Carter feeling the same way about me as I did him, then maybe staying with him wasn't the smartest idea...but it was too late now.

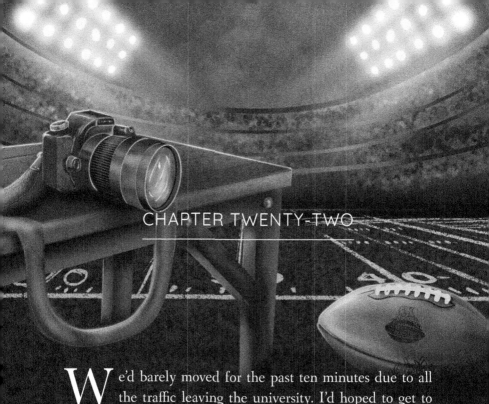

CHAPTER TWENTY-TWO

We'd barely moved for the past ten minutes due to all the traffic leaving the university. I'd hoped to get to Carter's duplex and at least run a brush through my hair and put my camera down before I headed off to work, but that wasn't going to be possible.

You wouldn't think we were sitting in standstill traffic, considering Jack was still belting out music. I truly believed that he'd picked the station with the most annoying songs to see how long it would take to break me.

I blew out a flustered breath and thumped back in my seat with crossed arms.

That caught his attention. He looked at me and pursed his lips as he turned down the music. "What's your deal, pickle?"

"First off, really?" I arched a brow. "Because ew. I don't even know how you get laid."

His jaw dropped. "Hey, it's part of my charm." He winked, undeterred. "And girls love it. Hell, they love anything I do. I could fart the alphabet, and they'd still get wet for me."

"Again, *ew*. None of that would ever work on me." And I

was officially ready to move this conversation along. "And I could walk faster than this." I lifted my hand toward the huge line in front of us. "I'm supposed to be at work in fifteen minutes."

Placing his hands on the wheel, he cut his eyes toward me. "I'll address the most pressing comment first. I don't do it for you 'cause you're jonesing for another man." He glanced forward once more. "And I can't help it that our football is awesome and everyone came from all across the world to see us play."

He meant Carter's dad, but I wasn't going to humor him by pretending I believed him. "Can you take me straight to work? Or, better yet, maybe I should just get out and walk. It would be a lot faster than this, and I'd rather deal with the rain than be late."

As I reached for the door handle to get out, Jack locked the doors and put the child locks on. "Not happening. Carter would eat my ass. And even though I'm open to *all* dirty things, he is not my type. Besides, you don't have a change of clothes, so you'd look *wet*."

I rolled my eyes. "Seriously. Is everything that comes out of your mouth required to be sexual in nature?"

He beamed and lifted his chin, proud. "Most definitely. I pride myself on my ability to wittily twist everything into a weird combo." He wagged his brows. "Get it. Weird combo. Like stretches."

"Just stop." I lifted my hand, wondering if I could somehow manage to get out the back. "Just unlock the door and let me out."

"Dude, I don't even know if I'm taking you straight to work. Let me call him." He pushed buttons on his steering wheel, getting ready to make a Bluetooth call.

"Focus on driving." I removed my phone from my pocket. "I'll send him a text and inform him of our plans."

I sent Carter the text as we finally got to the front where the traffic light was, but of course, it turned red, stopping us once again.

My foot tapped as I grew more antsy.

However, my phone dinged right away.

Carter: Makes sense. Traffic is awful. Be careful, and I'll be by later.

My heart skipped a beat. I'd be seeing him tonight and many others for the foreseeable future. He would have driven me to work and school regardless, but knowing that I'd be staying with him in his home...it caused my body to warm.

I had to shut that sensation down.

He and I were just friends.

The light changed to green, and I said, "Go straight."

"I take it the boss said okay." Jack glanced at me.

"It doesn't matter what the boss said." I arched an eyebrow. "I make the decisions in regard to myself, but yes, he's now aware."

"Fine. I'm assuming, since he's not calling me, he's good with it, so I'll take you straight there." He turned the music back up, and I was kind of relieved to end the discussion.

There were so many emotions swirling through me; I wasn't sure which one to home in on.

Thankfully, I didn't have to worry about that or Jack's singing for very long because we finally arrived at work, and somehow, I was only ten minutes late.

I jumped out of the car. "Thanks!"

Before I could shut the door, Jack said, "Wait."

"I'm late for work." I bounced on my feet. "What?"

He grinned. "I need the key to Carter's house. You know... to check things out for you."

"Nice try. Now bye." I shook my head, slammed the door, and jogged into work.

The place was already busy with people wearing colors from both universities.

Ridge University pouted into their drinks while HSU fans were giggling and laughing after the football team's win.

I hurried to the bar and put my stuff into the cubby while Joe rubbed a hand down his face.

"What's wrong?" I asked.

He went back to mixing a drink. "Stay alert for anyone hostile. We need to prevent a fight from breaking out, especially with the way these kids are already drinking."

I glanced up and saw different groups glaring at one another. A few already had multiple drinks drained, so he was probably right, which was sad since it was over a football game. "Sorry I was late. I got stuck in traffic."

"It's fine. I knew you were required to take pictures of the game anyway, and Leah reminded me."

My head tilted back. "She's already here?" I knew she'd gone to the game, and I was a little shocked that she'd beaten me here, given Jack had special parking.

He nodded. "She left the game early and got here about an hour ago."

Leah breezed out of the kitchen and hugged me. "Hey, are you coming back home tonight? You can sleep in my room. There's another party, but my room will be off-limits."

And that was one reason I'd agreed to stay with Carter. The last thing I wanted to do was try to sleep right next to the living room, where all the sound was coming from.

"Thanks, but I'm going to stay at a friend's house tonight." I purposely left off which friend that might be.

"Oh, okay. We're gonna call the landlord again on Monday.

He hasn't returned our call yet, but it's the weekend." She grabbed her pad from her back pocket.

I bit my tongue and didn't say anything. Besides, it was still raining, and no doubt, water continued to pour into the room. I doubted anyone could do anything until the weather improved.

All of us went to work, and the hours flew by. The place kept getting more packed as more people arrived, and the drinks needed constant refilling.

"Hey!" someone shouted, and I turned around to see what they needed.

But then I stopped short.

It was the guy who'd hit on me the first night I waitressed.

He winked. "Hey there, gorgeous." His voice was slurred.

Yeah, I wasn't handling this. I'd get Joe involved.

I turned to walk away when he grabbed my arm, forcing me back around.

"Hey. I said hi," he snapped.

"Hi." I tried jerking out of his hold.

His grip on me tightened, his fingers digging into my skin. "Just because you go to HSU doesn't mean you're better than me. In fact, maybe I should teach you a thing or two, so you understand we're on the same playing field." The threat rang in his voice. "Aren't you that quarterback's plaything from the other night?"

A lump formed in my throat. "No."

"Wait." He blinked a few more times as if he was trying to see just one of me. "You *are* the football team's slut, right? You were on the field, taking pictures of them."

A familiar, deep voice came from my side. "If you're in the mood to harass the quarterback, here he is. Leave *her* alone. *Now*."

I turned to see Carter there with Grayson, Jack, and Cole behind him.

Every time I was around, Grayson and Carter didn't get along well, but they always seemed to be together lately.

"And let me say, I've been *itching* for a fight." Jack beamed and wrapped an arm around my shoulders. "Especially when one of you messes with our girl."

The guy stiffened and looked around. The friends who'd been with him last time were across the room playing pool. He had no backup.

Finally, he huffed. "Just get me another drink."

I shook my head and ignored my racing heart. "You've had plenty. You don't need any more."

"It wasn't a request. It was an order." His jaw ticced.

Dropping his arm, Jack tensed while Carter moved and placed his hand on the small of my back. He stepped closer to me so there was no space between us, effectively claiming me.

A shiver of pleasure ran down my spine.

"She said you've had enough," Carter rasped. "If I hear you harass her again, I'll be the one who deals with you. Got it?"

Grayson, Cole, and Jack inched closer, flanking us. It was clear we were united.

The guy's jaw twitched as he stumbled despite standing still. "Whatever," he mumbled and then staggered back to his friends.

The crisis was averted, at least temporarily, and I turned into Carter, our chests brushing, and smiled. "Thank you."

"Anytime." He grinned, making my heart skip a beat.

"Uh, you're welcome," Jack said loudly, his chin propped on Carter's shoulder.

I rolled my eyes. "And thanks to the rest of you." I purposely avoided Jack's gaze and looked at Cole and Grayson. "If you hadn't stood behind Carter, that guy might've been stupid enough to fight him."

"Hey!" Jack pivoted around Carter and snapped his fingers.

"I'm right here too, you know. I was the one who truly instilled fear in that jackass."

"Hmm." Carter angled his head. "Why am I not surprised that the common term *jackass* has Jack's name in it?"

Cole tilted his head back and rubbed his chin. "It's so fitting. Everything makes sense now."

Grayson snorted and shook his head but didn't say anything.

"Wait!" Jack frowned. "No. That's not—" He paused.

"I think you guys broke him." I laughed, my body feeling lighter.

"Hey!" Joe called from the bar. "Evie, I'm glad your friends are here, but people are waiting." He gestured to the booths along the wall.

Right. Work. The last thing I needed was to lose my job, especially when I had lost so much of my stuff. "What do you guys want to eat and drink?"

I quickly jotted down their order and moved to the next booth waiting for me, then focused on keeping up with orders and refills, praying nothing more would happen.

Carter and I pulled into his garage after one in the morning.

I opened my door just as he yawned and walked around the hood.

"I'm sorry I kept you out late." He'd had a huge game, and then he'd hung out at the bar for a couple of hours. I'd hijacked his evening, though I hadn't meant to.

He opened the door that led into his basement and waved me in. "I wanted to be there, so you don't have anything to apologize for."

Warmth enveloped me because I knew he wasn't just

saying that. Carter didn't do things unless he wanted to, and I had no clue how I'd become someone he was willing to go out of his way for.

"Nonetheless." I entered the basement, taking in the light-gray walls and the wide-open space with a pool table and dartboard. The floors were the same hardwood as the living room, and there was a bar in the corner stocked with liquor and wine.

He didn't have to come to a crowded bar to hang out; he had everything he needed here.

"Come on, let's get you upstairs so you can shower and get some rest," he said and took my hand, leading me to the stairs. We walked up to the first floor of the house, where the living room and kitchen were, but he circled around to another flight of stairs.

At the top, he opened a door right across the hall and waved me through. "This is all you."

I entered the room, which was the size of Grayson's and Cole's entire dorm room. A king bed sat to the left against the wall. A huge white wooden dresser with a large flat-screen TV sitting on top of it was positioned next to the door to the bathroom. Matching nightstands stood on either side of the bed, which was neatly covered in lavender sheets and a matching comforter. The room smelled like lemons.

Rubbing a hand over the comforter, I tilted my head. "Did you clean the room?"

He placed his hands in his pockets and nodded. "Yeah. I didn't want you to sleep on musty sheets, and purple felt like a color you might appreciate."

I smiled. "I do."

He rolled his shoulders and cracked his neck. "I put your clothes in the closet that's connected to the bathroom, and your toiletries are in the shower and by the sink. Is there anything else you need?"

Without thinking, I launched myself into his arms. He'd taken care of everything for me. Something no one else would ever do. Not anymore...not since my parents died.

Immediately, he returned my embrace, pulling me tightly into his arms.

I drew in his delicious scent and fought back tears. "Thank you so much."

"Hey." He loosened his hold and placed a finger under my chin, tipping my head up so we were looking at each other. Tenderness was etched on his face, and the golden flecks warmed in his eyes. He traced his fingertips across my face. "Anything for you."

I grew light-headed. For some reason, I believed him despite our rough start.

He exhaled and lowered his head to mine. Our lips were millimeters away, but it might as well have been miles. Everything inside me yearned for him to kiss me...to touch me.

When his hands tightened around my waist, I had no doubt he felt the same tug.

But then he sighed and pulled away. "Go take a shower and get some rest. You've had a long twenty-four hours."

I wanted to pout, but I nodded.

"Good night," I whispered then stood on my tiptoes and kissed his cheek.

He groaned as his hands snaked around my waist again. "Evie, you're killing me. I'm trying to do right by you, and you're making this so damn hard."

His words rushed through me, and I brushed another kiss at the corner of his lips.

"Get some sleep." He leaned back. "You've had a rough day, and you're not thinking clearly."

But that was the thing. I knew exactly what I wanted. "Carter—"

"No decisions tonight." He leaned back. "You need a good night's rest. We have all day together tomorrow."

My heart pounded. "You don't have practice?"

"Nope. Between the win and the rain, Coach gave us the day off."

"Sounds like a *Walking Dead* kind of day."

He chuckled. "That sounds perfect." He leaned down and pressed his lips against mine before pulling back. "Good night, Evie. I'm right across the hall if you need anything." And then he walked out of the room, leaving me alone.

My lips tingled, and even though I felt the ache of his absence, something warm was swirling inside me.

I hurried into the bathroom, taking in the marble countertops and shower, and found the large walk-in closet to the left. I pulled out a pair of shorts and a soft shirt, grabbing a towel in the corner. And then I stepped into the most luxurious shower I'd ever experienced.

After a quick shower, I got ready for bed. Within minutes, I'd crawled into the softest bed in the entire world. I smiled. I hadn't felt this happy since before my parents died.

Guilt blanketed me, weighing my body down as I drifted off to sleep. I tried pushing the sensation away and focusing on Carter's face, and finally, sleep came.

THE CAR GROANED, and suddenly, we were rolling off the road. The river crept up, and I could see the backs of my parents' heads. I knew exactly what was going to happen, but the memory was going to play out the same way it always did.

Soon, I was rolling down the window, frantic to save both Mom and myself.

And once again, I wasn't strong enough to save her.

"No! Mom!" I screamed like I did every damn time. "No." Tears streamed down my face.

The crippling realization that I wasn't going to be able to save her without drowning myself slammed into me. The deep heartbreak sliced my insides, and I couldn't breathe as I was submerged in the water.

I whimpered and reached desperately for Mom.

Something encircled me, holding me back.

This was different. This wasn't how it went, but I knew one thing: I was going to drown. Maybe if I died, I would finally find peace.

My body shook, and I knew that this was it. This was my end. Then I heard a faint voice.

"Evie."

The word was muffled, but that made sense. I was underwater.

"Evie, wake up," a deep, familiar voice said louder.

I shook even harder.

"Evie, please. You're scaring me."

Carter.

My eyes flew open, and I found myself cradled in Carter's arms. His scent, warmth, and concern enveloped me, and I sobbed.

"Baby, what's wrong?" he asked, leaning back. When he saw that my eyes were open, his forehead creased even more.

"My parents—" I broke off, tears pouring down my face. "I was there again."

He cupped my cheek and placed his forehead against mine. He said, "No. Babe. You're here. You're here with me. I won't let anything bad happen to you."

I'd never known I needed to hear those words until this moment when something snapped inside me. I needed him, and I was tired of fighting it.

Wiping the tears from my face, I wrapped my arms around him and kissed him.

He stiffened. "Dammit, Evie. We can't do this. You're upset. It's not right."

"I'm sure. I swear." I cupped his cheek. "I need you. *Please.* Especially tonight."

His jaw twitched, but his eyes darkened with desire.

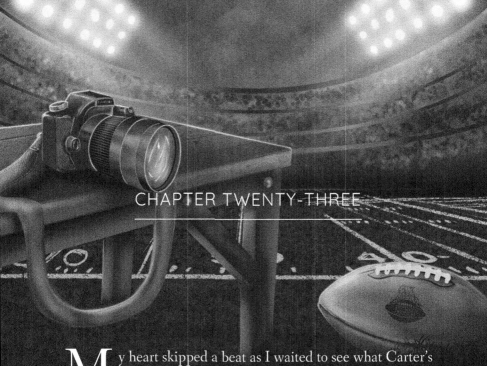

CHAPTER TWENTY-THREE

My heart skipped a beat as I waited to see what Carter's next move would be. I would respect his decision. I wouldn't force him to kiss me or touch me if he didn't want to.

He huffed and lowered his lips to mine. Within seconds, he deepened the kiss with fervent need, and my body warmed even more.

This kiss was different.

Urgent.

Full of desire.

I opened my mouth, allowing his tongue entry. He didn't hold back, devouring every inch of me, and I slid my hands around his neck and into his hair.

Tangling my fingers into his shaggy mane, I gently pulled, and a deep groan vibrated in his chest.

He pulled my body harder against his, and I could feel every muscle underneath his shirt.

As our bodies pressed together, my nipples hardened and I tore my mouth from his to bite into his bottom lip.

"Fuck," he hissed, and I snaked my hands under his shirt

and traced each curve of muscle. He quivered under my touch and reached down to grip my hips, pressing me against him.

When his hardness rubbed my core, a shock of pleasure shot through me despite both of us still being clothed.

His hands slipped under my shirt, his palms running up my sides. He left a trail of goose bumps in his wake, and my skin prickled from his touch.

His mouth crashed back onto mine, and his fingertips grazed the skin under my breasts. My heart stopped, and I desperately wanted him to continue. He paused, and my desire surged so strongly it was torturous, but I didn't complain because his mouth was still on mine, making me dizzy.

After a few beats, one palm cupped my breast, and I dug my fingers into his skin. When I didn't protest, he rolled his thumb over my nipple and need clenched my stomach.

I'd never felt desire like this. I wanted to rip his clothes off so he could fill me.

Head fuzzy, I yanked his shirt upward, breaking contact. "Off," I commanded. I needed to feel his skin on mine with no barriers.

He chuckled sexily and removed his shirt, and I did the same. His gaze landed back on me, and his breathing quickened as he ogled my top half. I'd never felt so desirable. Not that I'd had sex with many men; I'd done it only a handful of times during my senior year of high school.

"Evie," he whispered as he pulled me close. "You're so damn beautiful."

"Show me," I whimpered, needing his hands on me. I kissed him, and he rolled us, so he hovered over me. I wrapped my legs around his waist, pulling him closer as he brushed my core.

"You're gonna kill me," he growled, and then he kissed down my face to my neck.

I chuckled. "At least it's a death worth having."

He gently sucked on my neck, which had me rocking against him. Then he continued south, kissing his way down my chest until his lips hit one nipple. He lightly licked it, making me arch against him. I rolled my head back, and he took it into his mouth.

I'd never felt like this with anyone before, and I was quite certain I never would again.

All of a sudden, he started to roll off me, but I tightened my legs, trying to keep him firmly in place. He laughed, his late-night scruff scraping my nipple, and then he gripped my legs and removed them from his body.

"Hey," I complained, about to grab him again when he slipped his hand into the waistband of my shorts.

I froze, and he stilled.

"I want to touch you, Evie." He kissed my breast. "Can I?" He then slipped my other nipple into his mouth.

"Oh yes. Please." I was begging, but I didn't give a damn as long as he followed through.

He nipped my breast lightly as he slipped his hand between my thighs. I was pretty sure I was about to combust right then and there.

His tongue flicked my nipple, and his fingers circled between my lower lips.

Pressure coiled inside me, and heat churned through my body.

Wanting to touch him, I slipped my hands into his waistband and paused like he had, silently asking permission.

He trembled at my touch, and I took that as permission as I moved my hand under his briefs and wrapped my fingers around his hardness.

A deep, throaty groan left him, giving me more courage. I

stroked him, enjoying how he felt in my hand. But when he slipped his fingers inside me, my vision grew hazy.

Our breaths became hoarse, but he didn't stop sucking on my breasts. He quickened the pace of his hand, and I matched his speed, wanting to make him feel just as good as he was me.

Need built within me as he drove me closer to the edge. I knew I did the same to him because his hips swiveled, increasing our rhythm.

He moved his fingers quicker and pressed a little harder. My free hand caught his. It wouldn't be long till he pushed me over the edge.

"I need you," I moaned. I tried removing his hand, but he shook his head. I added, to make sure I was clear, "Make love to me, please."

Pulling his mouth from my nipple, he whispered, "Not tonight. Not like this."

I moaned. "But I need more."

He winked. "Don't worry. I'll give it to you." And then he devoured my breasts once again. This time, his fingers grew a little rougher, the exact pressure I needed.

"Carter," I gasped, sounding needy as fuck, but I didn't care. I stroked him, his body beginning to shake just as an orgasm exploded within me.

My breath caught as pleasure flooded me. He released my nipple and groaned. He pulsed in my hand as he found his own release.

We lay together, panting.

I rolled to face him, and our eyes locked.

Wrinkling my nose, I stuck out my tongue. "That wasn't exactly what I wanted."

"Really now? That's not what it felt like." He chuckled as he rolled out of the bed.

I almost pouted until he removed his pants and briefs. "Let

me tell you. Coming in my pants like a teenager was more fun with you than it's ever been."

He dropped them on the floor, and I greedily took in every inch of him as he stood before me, completely naked for the first time.

And just like that, my body was ready to go again. "Carter..."

He grinned. "You like what you see?"

I nodded. "Definitely."

He jumped onto the bed, making me giggle as he threw the covers off me. He gripped the edges of my shorts, pulling them down and off.

"If you get to see, so do I." He waggled his brows.

"No complaints here." I smiled so wide my cheeks hurt.

He kissed my lips and said, "Not tonight."

I was ready to argue when he gave me a wicked grin and lowered his head between my legs.

WARMTH SURROUNDED ME, and strong arms anchored me to something comforting. Cinnamon and lavender filled my nose, tugging at something deep within me. The scent was familiar, one of my favorites ever. A steady drum was beating in my ear, the sound reassuring.

I felt safe for the first time in a long time.

If this was a dream, I wouldn't mind never waking up. It was a lot better than the nightmares that plagued me.

My parents.

The night before crashed back into my mind, and I opened my eyes to find that I was splayed over Carter's bare chest. The same chest I'd bitten and clawed mere hours ago. The memories had need clenching deep within my stomach, wanting more of him.

I couldn't believe he'd fallen asleep with me and that we'd had a night full of touches, kisses, and getting intimate with each other's bodies.

Cold fear burrowed in my chest. What would happen when he woke up? Would he regret everything that we'd done?

Escape echoed in my mind, and I leaned my head back, ready to creep out of bed. Maybe it'd be better if I wasn't cuddled up next to him when he woke.

However, as my gaze traveled over his face, I found warm, gold-flecked eyes locked on me, surrounded by thick eyelashes. His hair was pushed to the side, messy and sexy. Heat washed over me.

"Good morning," he murmured, grinning.

I was pretty certain my heart stopped working along with my lungs. He had that effect on me.

"Hey." I bit my bottom lip, my face growing hot.

He was grinning at me.

He kissed me and said, "Let's cook some breakfast. I'm starving."

My stomach gurgled, and he laughed.

"I take it you're in agreement."

I buried my face in his chest, completely off balance after last night and how he was acting now.

He smacked my ass gently. "Come on. I need your help. No more bashfulness, though it is cute."

Untangling himself from me, he climbed out of bed. I glanced up to find him still naked, every glorious inch of him on display. He was even more attractive today than last night, even with the room lit.

Not wanting him to drag me out of bed, I jumped out on the

other side, realizing I was just as naked as he was. We had been so impatient for each other that we hadn't stopped touching each other until we both were so sleepy we couldn't move.

I searched the floor and found my shorts and shirt wadded up next to the corner of the bed. I grabbed them and dressed quickly, and when I glanced up, he was standing there, watching me.

"You're gorgeous," he murmured. "The prettiest girl I've ever seen."

My heart fluttered, and I eyed him. "You're not so bad yourself." He'd only put on his flannel pajama bottoms, every curve of his torso and arms easy to see. His body was just as I'd imagined, chiseled, perfect.

He held out his hand, and I walked around the bottom of the bed and took it. He laced our fingers as we walked downstairs.

As soon as we entered the kitchen, I glanced at the clock and froze. It was two in the afternoon. "Breakfast? We need to have dinner at this point. We almost slept the day away."

"Well, we did have a long night of exercise." He winked and removed a pan from underneath the stove.

I blushed and found the floor interesting. Even though he sounded happy, I didn't want to check to see if there was regret anywhere on his face.

"Hey, there's no reason to be shy with me."

"I know... It's just that I feel kind of bad." I shrugged, wanting to be honest. "You made it clear that we were friends and you couldn't do *this*. I feel like maybe I ruined that."

He put down the pan and crossed over to me, placed a finger under my chin, and gently forced my head up. His eyes warmed to liquid gold as he stared into my soul. He said, "If I didn't want to do that, I wouldn't have. And fuck what I said before. You should know that I'm not one who falls for manipulation."

"Not manipulation, but maybe a sense of obligation to a friend who needed comfort." In fairness, I hadn't tried to manipulate him. I'd just needed *him*, especially at that moment. "This complicates our relationship."

Arching a brow, he asked, "It does?"

Though I wasn't certain what he meant, I didn't like the sound of that. "I'm not a friends-with-benefits type of girl if that's what you're thinking." I wrapped my arms around myself. "So it does matter."

"You know I'm not the type of person who shares." He chuckled tenderly.

"I'm not either."

He leaned his forehead against mine and removed my arms from my waist to replace them with his, pulling me against him.

Keeping my head tilted up, he asked, "If it had been Grayson, Jack, or Cole, would you have done with them what you did with me last night?"

I shook my head. "No. Of course not. I don't feel the way about them that I do for you."

"Good." He blew out a breath. "Then why can't we be more than friends?"

There was no doubt I'd misunderstood him, or this was a dream. Those were the only two options. "You were the one who told me that we can't be together because of Katherine. Remember? That's why you ignored me for so long. And you still have to go on some dates with her, right?"

Sighing, he nodded. "She's still a factor, Evie. We don't want her to focus on you. She's cruel. But...what she doesn't know can't hurt her, right?"

"Date in secret?" A part of me liked the sound of that. Something that was for only the two of us.

"More than date. Be with one another exclusively. We're already friends, so it's not like we can't be friendly at school. Just no touching there. She'll have to deal with us being *friends*. Either way, we're together. You and me." This time, he was the one who looked away.

Though I hated to hide our relationship from Katherine, not having to worry about her would be nice, but I couldn't get completely on board with that. "I'm sorry. I can't."

His head snapped back, his attention lasered in on me. He rasped, "Why not? Did you not enjoy our night together and spending time with me?"

"I did..." I sighed and took a step back, needing to clear my head. "And I *do*, but that's the problem."

When he tried to pull me against him again, I placed my hands on his chest. If he kept touching me, he'd break me, and I refused to compromise my morals. "I need to go back to my house."

He ran a hand through his hair. "What the *hell* just happened? You seemed on board, and then you shut down."

"I can't be with you like *this* and then go to a game and watch Katherine put her hands all over you, standing by while you go on dates with her."

His eyebrows shot up. "I don't respond to her. I ignore her, and on our dates, we barely touch. I make sure of it."

"But you don't *not* respond either. You let her touch you, and it already made me so jealous when we were *just* friends. I can't be more and then watch that and know that you're out with her." It hurt too much, and I already had too much pain to deal with. "How would you like it if I was around someone who was all over me like that?"

His eyes narrowed. "Does the name Grayson ring a bell?"

I rolled my eyes. "Grayson doesn't hug me. He doesn't try

to kiss me. And he *definitely* doesn't keep telling people that we're getting together—it's just a matter of time."

His jaw twitched. "No, it's worse. He's playing the friend angle, and it works for him. You called him instead of me the other night."

And here we went again. "This was a mistake. I shouldn't have come here. I'm going to text Leah or Haven to come get me."

I spun around to look for my phone, but he caught my hand and turned me back toward him.

"How about this? We promise to be exclusive and together, but we keep it secret, and we can see where we are at the end of the year."

"Didn't we *just* go through this?" Maybe I'd lost some brain cells from the orgasm.

He snickered. "Let me finish." He kissed my cheek and continued, "Listen, the next outing with Katherine is my last, and I'll make it short. It's a fundraiser our parents asked us to attend, so I can easily separate from her and stay for an hour, then leave. Then I'll end any pretense of a relationship with her, and you ensure that you and Grayson remain friends. But if something bad happens, you call me first. No matter what."

I canted my head, observing him. "I don't want to cause problems between you and your family."

He tugged me against him again. "My dad already knows what she did to me, and he understands why I don't want to be with her. It won't be a problem. Not with me and my dad. Senator McHale can fuck himself."

Laughter bubbled out of me unexpectedly. "All right. We're together, but let's take this one day at a time."

Waggling his brows, he kissed me and leaned back slightly. "Which means you'll be staying right here with me until your house is fixed."

I tried to hide my smile, but I couldn't. "Yes, I'll stay. Even if I wanted to, I can't walk away. At least, not right now. I mean, you're going to make me breakfast."

He snorted. "Touché. So, I better get on that before you try to run away."

I watched him swagger back to the pan to make breakfast. And I couldn't help but wonder if I'd made a mistake even though it felt right in this moment.

CHAPTER TWENTY-FOUR

The entire day with Carter was amazing. He made us a delicious breakfast of sausage and cheese omelets with hash browns, which I devoured. I hadn't even realized how hungry I was until I took the first bite.

He then took my hand, and I'd hoped he'd take me back to the bedroom upstairs, but he surprised me. He led me straight to the couch, declaring it was a day for the two of us to watch *The Walking Dead* together.

I sulked, not even attempting to hide my disappointment. After all, I wanted to consummate our relationship, but he just chuckled, saying that we had time for that later. That he wanted to cuddle and spend time with me.

How could I argue with that?

We got comfortable on his couch. I lay on his lap and one of his arms draped over me while the other one played with the ends of my hair as I turned on the show.

If it hadn't been for the pictures of the rivers hanging everywhere in the living room, it would've been perfect. But each time I glanced at one of the images, my parents' accident removed any sense of peace and joy. A constant reminder of what I'd done...how I failed them.

"What's wrong?" he asked, taking the remote from my hand and pausing the episode. "You wanna watch something else?"

If only that was the problem. I sat up and glanced at the time. It was only seven in the evening. "No, sorry. I'm just having a hard time concentrating." In fact, I wanted to do something that would take my mind off my parents completely.

He winked. "Why's that?"

My body warmed. Now, *that* was a good way of getting my mind off the past. I moved so I straddled him, leaned into his ear, and whispered, "Well, I told you earlier, but you said we had to spend time together like a non–sex-crazed couple."

His hands grasped my waist. "I most definitely did *not* say that. I want us sex-crazed but also want to spend time with you as a person. That's something my mom had no interest in with my dad, and that's exactly the type of relationship I'm not looking to have. Worse, my dad married another cold woman who doesn't want anything to do with him, and my half sister shuts everyone out. I want us to enjoy each other for more than our bodies." His hand slid up my shirt, cupping my breast. "And I really like hearing you call us a couple."

"I like saying it." I rocked against him.

Our eyes were locked onto each other's.

Inching up my shirt, his gaze traveled to my breasts. "I'm good with being sex-crazed right now if you are."

I nodded, unable to talk.

"Good." He lowered me to the couch, his mouth on my breast.

Moaning, I dug my nails into his already shirtless back as I arched my head back, but then my attention strayed to a picture of the river once again.

My body tensed.

He released my breast and rose, staring into my eyes. "What's wrong?" His brows furrowed. "Did I do something wrong?"

A hard knot settled in my stomach. "No. Of course not." I moved to kiss him, wanting to end the awkward moment, but he pulled back.

He shook his head. "Babe, something's up. It has been ever since we came down here to eat breakfast. Do you not want to be here?"

This was something I definitely didn't want to talk about. "I do. There's no place I'd rather be."

Arching a brow, he tugged my shirt down and sat upright. "Don't bullshit me. I would never do that to you."

"No, seriously." I sat and took his hand in mine. "I want to be with you."

"Then what's the problem?" His hands tensed and jaw clenched. "I don't like feeling like you're keeping something from me."

This reminded me of the Carter that I first met. The one who turned into an asshole. "It's the pictures."

His forehead lined. "The pictures?" He glanced at the ones around the room. "Of the river?"

"Yeah." I scooted to the other end of the couch, feeling weird, and tucked a piece of hair behind my ear. "It..." I blew out a breath. "They remind me of the accident."

He froze. "What do you mean?"

"Our car rolled into a river." The dreams of the night before resurfaced, and my vision blurred.

"Fuck. I didn't even think—"

"That's what I was dreaming about last night when you heard me." I wiped away a tear that had trailed down my cheek. "I was trying to save Mom again."

"Your mom? They were both dead."

Now that I started, I couldn't stop. The guilt had been hanging over me for so long. "Dad was. Mom wasn't. She was barely conscious, but she was alive."

"What happened, Evie?" Concern laced his words as he took both my hands in his, anchoring me.

"I...I couldn't save her."

"Of course you couldn't. It was a horrible accident," he murmured, pulling me into his chest. "There was nothing you could've done."

More tears streamed down my face. "There was." I looked up, staring into his eyes. I needed to see the moment he saw me for what I really was—a weak coward. "I could've saved her, but I wasn't strong enough."

"What do you mean you weren't strong enough?"

"I couldn't swim and carry h-her." My voice cracked as my heart constricted. This had to be what a heart attack felt like. "I failed her. If I'd been strong enough, I could've saved her. I wouldn't be alone."

His indigo irises turned midnight, and his body stiffened.

And my heart shattered. He wasn't going to see me the same way anymore. He'd see me for what I was.

A horrible person.

"I killed her," I whimpered. I hadn't saved her when I could have.

"Oh, baby." Carter placed his finger under my chin, tilting it upward. He continued with a thick voice. "Is that why you're in weight training?"

I nodded. "If I ever find myself in a situation like that again, I don't want to let someone else down..." I sobbed. "I don't want to let them down like I did Mom."

He groaned. "I'm a fucking asshole."

When I expected him to recoil, he leaned over, cupping my

face. He whispered, "Her death isn't your fault. You did the best you could. If you kept trying to save her, you would've died."

Scooting closer, he kissed me. "You *both* would've died."

"That's what the police said and why I haven't told anyone. But Carter, I'm responsible. If I was strong enough...I could've saved her." I glanced at one of the photos of the river, the memories of the waves thumping against the car and the water dripping in consuming me. "If I'd been in better shape, exercised or something... Things would be different."

He pulled me into his chest. "It wasn't your fault. None of it was your fault. Fuck, Evie. The current would've taken you with that added weight. There are so many variables, but at the end of the day, you did the best you could. And you're sure as *hell* not responsible. Did you drive the car off the road?"

I didn't know why, but for some reason, I needed to hear someone push back. "No."

"Then you shouldn't be holding *any* accountability." He kissed my forehead and then stood. "None at all." He marched over to the picture on the left and took it down from the wall.

"What are you doing?" I blinked, trying to get the dam that tore loose inside back in place.

He gestured to the other pictures. "Removing these."

"What?" My jaw slackened. "No. This is your home. This—"

"I love kayaking down the river, but there are other things I love too." He removed another one, placing it face down on the fireplace. "And I know an amazing photographer who can go with me on a hike so we can take pictures of trees and mountain ranges. And those pictures I'll treasure even more because not only will they be taken with her, but we get to spend non-sex-crazed time together to get them."

I laughed, unable to tamp down my joy. "What is it with these non–sex-crazed times you're wanting?"

He frowned. "Watching TV, talking, cuddling. Those types of things. You know, all the things that prove you're in this relationship for me and not what I can give you."

I gasped. "What do you mean? Of course I'm in it for you."

Shrugging, he took another picture down. "That's not always been the case."

A hardness settled in my stomach. I didn't like how that sounded. "Are you trying to say somebody used you for money and connections?" The thought of him having sex with someone else already bothered me, but that was his past. One that wasn't fair of me to judge, but to think someone tried to use it as some sort of weapon? Well, that was downright sick.

His face softened. "Not me, but somebody else. And it got nasty." His shoulders tensed. "And kids always take the brunt of it, which is unfair to them. So I just want to make sure that I never get into a relationship with someone who doesn't enjoy my actual company, which probably sounds stupid for a twenty-two-year-old man."

My heart constricted. "Carter, I'm so sorry." No wonder he'd been suspicious of me showing up here and Senator McHale paying for everything.

"You have nothing to apologize for." He removed the last picture on the left side of the room and added it to the pile on top of the fireplace next to his PlayStation. "There. All the pictures are down."

He was changing topics, and I didn't want him to, but I wouldn't push it. That wasn't right, and he had opened up to me just now. He'd tell me everything when he was ready. "Do you want to talk about it?"

"Not really." He sighed and strolled over to me to take my

hand. "I know you just opened up to me, and I'm not fully reciprocating. But it's hard for me. It's baggage I've had my entire life. And it's always stuck with me that there are people out there willing to do anything to have leverage over someone else."

His entire life. Now, I was certain he meant his mother, and I wanted to hunt her down and ask her what the hell was wrong with her. Carter was an amazing man, and she'd hurt him as a little boy. What kind of person did that?

"Well then." I forced a smile, wiping the tears from my face. If he'd kept asking questions when I'd asked him not to, I'd have been upset, so I wouldn't do that to him. "You really didn't have to take down your pictures. This is your home."

He pulled me to my feet, tucked a lock of hair behind my ear, and whispered, "I want to take care of you. I want to do things right for you. I fucked it up in the beginning, and I'm so damn sorry. But now I have an excuse to bring you somewhere to take pictures where I can actually watch you. Believe me, that's a win."

I stood on my tiptoes and pressed my lips to his. "You don't have to change anything for me. If you love the river, you should cherish it, not remove it because of some bad memories I have."

"Don't worry. I have my own memories." His body relaxed as he pulled me close. "And you don't need to change either. Your determination and heart were what drew me to you in the first place." He deepened our kiss.

I pulled away. "I'm not trying to ruin the moment, but we should probably talk." I decided to be blunt and get it over with. "How many people have you been with?" I didn't want to know the answer, but if we were moving forward sexually, we needed to be honest with one another.

"Believe it or not, I don't sleep around. I've been with five women, and I'm negative. We're tested for football physicals. You?"

That number was a lot lower than I expected, but after what he'd told me, it made sense. With his baggage, he wouldn't risk sleeping with just anyone. "One guy, senior year of high school. We dated that year, and it just sort of happened."

"I want to kill him," he growled, his hands tugging me toward him. His mouth claimed mine, branding me.

But I didn't want to push something physical with him, not after what he'd confided. I pulled back, placing my hands on his chest, and asked, "Now that the pictures are down, you wanna watch more *Walking Dead* or game on your PlayStation?"

He captured my lips. "Not in the least." He grabbed my ass, lifted me up, and headed toward the stairs. Our tongues twined together as he took each step one by one. I should've been afraid that he'd trip and fall, but I trusted him.

Completely.

At the top of the stairs, he walked straight through the doorframe to my guest room, and I moved down, kissing his neck. He groaned as I grazed my teeth over his skin, and he lowered me to the bed.

His mouth met mine as his hands swept under my shirt, cupping my breasts once again. As he toyed with my nipples, I wrapped my legs around his waist, rubbing myself against him.

"You're going to kill me," he hissed and bit my bottom lip.

I laughed. "That's my goal."

He kissed his way down my neck while his hands lowered to the hem of my shirt then stripped it off.

Unable to restrain myself, I leaned forward, brushing my hands down his chest, slowly tracing each curve of his muscles.

He shuddered and leaned forward once more, taking one breast into his mouth. He flicked his tongue over my nipple, and his free hand took hold of my shorts and yanked them off like he was just as desperate for me as I was for him.

I reached for him, wanting to touch him, but he caught my hand. He murmured, not removing his mouth, "Not yet."

Rolling to his side, he slipped his hand between my legs and rubbed my core. His fingers slid inside me as his thumb hit the sensitive spot, almost sending me over the edge already.

"Carter, please," I panted. I didn't want to end without him. I was so damn close.

Then he removed his hand.

I moaned. "What do you think you're doing? I'm not done yet."

He chuckled. "Being a tease."

I opened my mouth, ready to inform him that I could finish myself, when he stood and removed his bottoms.

Every inch of him was on display, all hard and ready...and delicious.

Reaching out to touch him, I eyed him as he moved to the nightstand, opened the drawer, and pulled out a condom. He slipped it on, and I was jealous that he was doing it instead of me. I wanted to feel him any way I could at that moment.

"Are you sure you want to do this?" I asked. He hadn't wanted to last night, and I didn't want him to think I was pressuring him now. "We can do other things like we did last night."

He moved back toward me, positioning himself between my legs. "I didn't want to do this last night because you were upset. I didn't want you to make a rash decision and regret it. But if you still want to, I'm definitely more than game."

"Uh, yeah." Need soared inside me.

Leaning over me, he chuckled and kissed me again. "Thank fuck." He eased me higher onto the bed so my body was completely off the floor and followed me. When we were in position, he brushed his hardness against my core.

I whimpered, not above begging for him.

"You sure?" he asked, positioning himself against me.

Instead of saying anything, I pushed against him. His tip entered me.

"Damn, baby," he groaned as he slowly continued.

Kissing me, he slid all the way in and paused.

I'd never felt so full before, and it was a little uncomfortable. He slid one hand from my neck down to my breasts and stomach as if soothing me, and after a few seconds, my body adjusted to him.

I moved my hips, and he followed my lead. We took it slowly, each thrust better than the last.

A deep noise vibrated in his chest, making me feel even more desired.

I rocked against him and leaned up to devour his mouth. A crazy yearning built inside me, and I sucked on his tongue hard, wanting him to know I needed more.

He was still going easy, so I pushed him onto his back and rolled on top of him.

The gold flecks warmed his eyes, desire filling them and me. He eagerly scooted up against the headboard, and I grasped it to help anchor myself.

As I rode him, he watched me, breathing fast. "You're so beautiful, Evie."

His hands gripped my hips, increasing my pace as he thrust along with me.

That was when my own body reached the edge, so I slowed, wanting to drag out the moment.

"Don't stop," he gritted out, his fingers digging into my skin.

"I'm almost done." I whimpered, wanting the release but not wanting this moment to end.

He quivered underneath me as he rasped, "Let go. I am too."

Those tremors took me right over the edge. We climaxed together, riding out our pleasure. And when we stilled, I crumpled into his arms. He tugged me onto my side and spooned me, and we lay like that until we were ready to go again.

Unfortunately, Monday came, which meant our time alone had come to an end, at least temporarily.

We'd gotten up and eaten breakfast together, and now we were on our way to school. Carter's hand was in mine, but the foreboding feeling of not being able to touch one another at HSU had me on edge.

Carter pulled into his normal spot, the rain still drizzling.

"Here, let me get you the umbrella," he said, reaching behind my seat.

"Thanks." I smiled and prepared myself for not only the rain but to play the part of his friend.

When I reached for my door, he took my free hand into his. He said, "One little kiss. It's raining, and we're in my car. I need something to last me until we're away from here."

It probably wasn't smart. We were at school. But...everyone was rushing to get out of the rain; no one would be paying attention to us.

"I guess," I teased and rolled my eyes. "But only cause you're so hard up."

"Oh, I am." He leaned down, kissing me.

And it wasn't a quick kiss. His tongue slid into my mouth, and I lost all sense of anything outside of his feel and taste.

The moment was broken by pounding on the windshield.

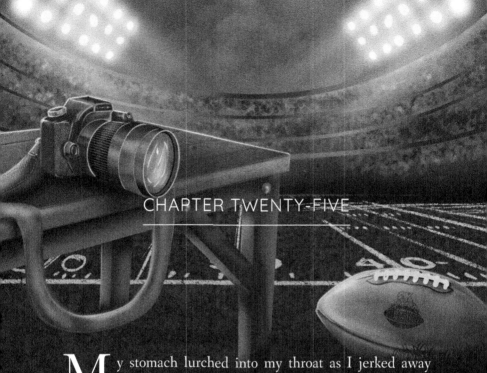

CHAPTER TWENTY-FIVE

My stomach lurched into my throat as I jerked away from Carter. His head snapped toward the windshield.

I wanted to hide while he was ready to fight. That sounded about right in our relationship. Granted, this was Carter's vehicle, so it would be pointless for him to pretend he wasn't inside.

"I'm going to *kill* that jackass," Carter spat, and I followed his gaze.

Even with the deluge, I could tell it was Jack standing in front of the driver's side, wearing a wide smile on his face, a huge purple rain jacket covering him from head to toe. He waggled his eyebrows and gestured between Carter and me.

Great. Out of everyone, Jack would be the one to catch us. Carter and I might as well track Katherine down and tell her ourselves. I groaned as my heart took my stomach's place. Now, two organs were in the wrong spot.

Our relationship was over even before it had begun. Our secret was out, and there was no going back to fix it.

"He's a fucking dumbass." Carter rolled his eyes, not seeming angry. Not like I was.

Then Jack proceeded to hump the air in front of the vehicle, not seeming to care that a Civic had parked on the other side of him.

Carter flipped him off. Jack burst out laughing, and then he formed a circle with one hand and stuck the finger of his other through the hole.

And now we were back in elementary school. "He really is a dumbass." And going to ruin everything for us.

When Jack's gaze landed on me, he frowned and hurried to my side.

"Uh. What is he doing?" I scooted away from the door and closer to Carter.

Before Carter could answer, Jack opened the door. He smiled so wide his teeth showed. "Well, hello there. What are *you two* doing?" He snickered. "I'm in international law with Carter this morning and know, for a fact, he doesn't have chemistry first thing."

"Man, just no." Carter shook his head. "That's not even funny."

"Oh, come on." Jack leaned his head back a little. "That was hilarious."

"Not at all." I didn't know what to say, so I decided to say, "Please don't tell Katherine."

"He won't," Carter murmured, taking my hand.

However, Jack placed his hands on his chest. "I'm offended, E. I'm not a snitch."

"Don't you have a class to go to?" Carter flicked his eyes to the library. "Like, *now?*"

Lifting a finger, Jack leaned his weight to one side. "First off, library's not class. Even though I do like to get my schooling in there—behind the bookshelves, if you know what I mean."

Unfortunately, I knew exactly what that meant. Jack had two common topics he liked to discuss: sex and himself.

"Remember you were just talking about international law, which we have together?"

The rain came down harder, hitting Jack's raincoat and splashing my legs, but you wouldn't know it. He stood there like he didn't have a care in the world, his backpack protected underneath his raincoat.

"But..." Jack pointed at me. "Evie's here."

"Go, man. I need to talk to her for a minute," Carter's voice lowered, indicating he was getting annoyed. "We have less than ten minutes now."

"Talk. Yeah." He nodded with an approving grin. "I hear ya. I'll make sure to take notes for you."

I rolled my eyes. "I have my own class to get to." I reached over, trying to shut the door despite him blocking it.

"Hey." He snapped his fingers. "I'm standing right here. It can't shut."

Tilting my head, I glared. "It will if I close it hard enough."

"Wow. E has a 'tude." Jack bobbed his head. "I like this side of her. I need to catch you like that more often."

I tensed, and Carter placed a hand on my wrist. He growled, "Leave."

"All right." He lifted both hands. "I'll let you get back to studying." He did air quotes. "While I go get my learning on and cover Carter's ass."

Carter blew out a breath. "Thank you."

Jack moved away but then paused. He winked at me and asked, "How come every time I gave you a ride here, I didn't get a thanks like that?"

All humor vanished off Carter's face, and his nostrils flared. "Get the hell out of here *now*."

"Fine." He dropped his hands and grabbed the door handle.

"You might want to be more careful if you don't want Katherine to find out." He shut the door and headed to the sidewalk that led around the library.

I watched his retreating figure, wishing I'd just told Carter no to the kiss. "How soon until she finds out?"

Carter shook his head. "He won't say a word. He's loyal and trustworthy, just a pain in the ass." We both watched his retreating figure.

"Are you sure? He's got the biggest mouth I've ever seen, and that includes everyone I've known since birth."

He laughed. "That's true, but I trust him implicitly. I promise he won't say anything. He's my best friend, and he likes you. That's hard to accomplish, so he won't do anything that would hurt either one of us."

My heart warmed, and finally, my stomach and heart found their normal locations. I remembered how serious Jack got with me when he was talking about Carter. If Carter trusted him, then I would as well—at least until he gave me a reason not to.

I leaned to kiss him one more time and stopped myself. One person had already caught us. We didn't need to tempt fate twice.

Brushing his hand with mine, I scooted to the door and hiked my bag over my shoulder before accepting the umbrella. "I'll see you later. Text me when I need to meet you back here."

"It should be around two," he called out.

I jumped out of the car before I had second thoughts and tried to kiss him again, heading straight to class.

THE NEXT DAY, Carter and I got to school earlier than normal, so we had time to make it appear like we hadn't ridden in together since we had weight lifting where Katherine liked to stalk—er, walk by from time to time.

Since the parking lot was empty behind the stadium, Carter wound his arm around my waist, pulling me over the center console. His lips were on mine before I could protest, and as soon as his tongue grazed my lips, begging for entry, I forgot why this was a bad idea.

Last night had been amazing. We'd come home, ordered pizza, and binged several episodes of *The Walking Dead* before retiring to the room I was staying in for several rounds of foreplay and sex. Each time we connected, it was better than the last, to the point where I was concerned that I could truly become sex-crazed.

Carter tasted like delicious mint, and I eagerly reciprocated each stroke of his tongue. My body was warm, buzzing from his touch. I moved to feel more of him when he caught my hand.

"School," he rasped. "Remember?"

"Damn education," I said as I tried to slide my hands into his pants once again.

Chuckling, he pulled away. "Don't worry. We'll have time for that when we get home before I take you to work."

Heat flared inside me. "But why wait?"

He booped my nose. "Because you don't deserve a romp in the parking lot outside of school where people can see us. I don't want you to get a reputation."

"Romp?" I wrinkled my nose. "*Really?*"

He wrinkled his nose back at me, making me laugh. I never dreamed we could be like this together, but being with him felt right.

I huffed. "Since you denied me, I better head on in before I try to become an evil temptress."

Leaning down, he kissed me once again. "That would be wise."

I hurried out of the vehicle, the rain hitting me as I jogged toward the weight room. Apparently, there was more rain than average this year, which meant it would take a while to fix the basement. A part of me was relieved because I got to spend more time with Carter, but another part warned me this was too good to last and that I needed my own space for the inevitable.

But at this moment, I didn't have a choice.

In the weight room, I threw my duffel bag in the corner like usual. Then, I went to the free weight section, trying to figure out which exercises I wanted to do today.

I'd googled and learned some basics, but nothing impressive. I was afraid to do anything too complicated in case I didn't have the form down and wound up hurting myself. I couldn't injure myself and not be able to work.

A little while later, the glass door opened, and I heard several guys enter. It was time for the football team to arrive, and then I heard Jack's cackle.

Of course, he'd laugh first thing in the morning. He couldn't be human. I continued with my bicep curls, trying to focus on my task. However, I kind of wanted to time things so that I needed a break when I could see Carter working out.

The usual clanking of the bars filled the room, but then I heard footsteps coming my way. Jack appeared and saluted me. "Want some help today?"

I blinked a few times. "I'm not supposed to train with you guys." Carter had made that crystal clear on my first day, and even though we were dating now, I didn't expect that to change. Especially since we were trying to hide *us* from Katherine.

He winked. "Don't worry. I have it on good authority that he won't care."

Putting down my ten-pound weight, I arched a brow. "Oh, really now?"

"There might be a chance he suggested it." He shrugged. "But either way, I'm the one wanting to help you. Not him. So, what do you say, E?"

The football team was full of experts in weight lifting. If I truly wanted to get stronger, I could use their help, and I had no doubt, after what I'd shared with him, that Carter was the one behind this offer. But I'd play along and stroke Jack's ego. "I guess."

Grayson strolled up, his forehead creased. "What's going on here? Everything okay?"

"Nothin' to worry your tiny little head over." Jack wrapped an arm around my shoulders. "I'm just gonna help little E with her workout."

"All of a sudden, we're *allowed* to do that? I thought we didn't need 'distractions' that might mess up our weight-lifting routine." Grayson crossed his arms.

Now, *that* sounded just like the Carter of a few weeks ago.

"If you're scared of our captain, then it's best you heed his advice." Jack waved him along. "But for me, E is worth the risk." He took hold of my hand and guided me toward the bar setups where all the guys worked out. However, he took me to the corner farthest from the door and put me on the last bar at the wall, then took the vacant spot next to me.

Grayson followed and took the spot across from me.

Jack came over to my setup and said, "You're gonna do what I do. But you know... not as heavy because"—he flexed his muscles and kissed his biceps—"you're not me."

"Thank fuck." Grayson snorted.

"He's just jealous." Jack scoffed. "Pretend he's not there." Then he lifted one of the bars and handed it to me before retrieving one like it for himself and adding fifty pounds to each end.

Glancing at his and then my own, I said, "Hey, you're forgetting something. What should I put on mine?"

"Nothing." He lifted the bar behind his head and rested it on the backs of his shoulders. "At least, not yet. Let's see how you do with that first."

I pouted. The whole point of weight training was to get strong, and he wanted me to use a measly bar.

He grinned. "Don't worry, you'll thank me later." He then proceeded to show me how he wanted me to squat.

Thankful to have guidance, I gripped the bar and followed his movements.

I SLID INTO PHOTOGRAPHY CLASS, still dripping with sweat. I'd never worked out so hard before, and we hadn't even done any cardio. Worse. Because of the torture Jack was inflicting on me, I'd lost track of time and hadn't gotten a peek at Carter doing his training.

Luckily, I had deodorant stored in my bag, so I was able to change and reapply, but my hair was still damp and stuck to my face.

I slid into my usual seat next to Sadie, who glanced at me with a scowl on her face.

"Are you okay?" Something was off. I knew she'd had a cold, but now that I thought about it, she hadn't sent me a text all weekend like she usually did, not even on the morning of the game. I hadn't noticed because of the whole flooded-room debacle and then what had happened between Carter and me.

Since I was running down to the minute, I removed my camera from my bag and turned it on. We were going outside to take random shots of whatever Professor Garcia assigned us because she said experience and learning from our mistakes were the best ways to learn.

"Nothing," Sadie said shortly before turning her back to me.

Uh...there was *definitely* something wrong. I didn't know what to do. I didn't want to push her; that wasn't my style. But when she turned to the girl on her other side, who usually annoyed her and acted like her normal self, I knew she was upset with *me*.

And the worst part was I was *clueless* as to why.

When the professor released us to take pictures on the grassy knoll outside the classroom, Sadie didn't wait for me. She speed walked out of the room so fast that I was quite certain she had superhero capabilities.

I hurried after her. "Sadie, wait up."

She slowed down, but not much. Damn near panting because my legs felt like jelly after Jack's abuse, I finally caught up to her.

Her frown deepened, and she continued to stare straight ahead, avoiding my gaze.

"I don't know what I did, but I'm pretty sure I've upset you."

"Nope," she said forcibly. "We're fine."

Fine.

She used that word, and I shrugged my shoulders.

That was when she sprinted across the greenway and started taking photos of a bird flying overhead.

Out of everyone at school, she'd been the nicest to me. I had to make things right, so against my better judgment, I caught up to her again. "Okay, then why are you giving me the cold shoulder?"

"I'm not." She turned her back on me and took pictures of the literal grass on the ground.

No matter which direction I moved, she turned the other way to take a picture of something.

Fine. I could take a hint. "I'll leave you to it. Are you going to eat lunch with us today?" I figured she'd say yes, especially since she had a crush on Grayson. That would be my chance to corner her and make her talk before he got there.

"Nah, I got homework to catch up on." She turned around, her eyes darkening. "Besides, you two probably don't want me there anymore since you've been sleeping over."

I flinched, which probably seemed extremely guilty. Somehow, she'd heard that I'd stayed in Grayson's room. That must have been why she hadn't texted me. Of course, she hung around with the players, with her dad being the coach and all. "Sadie, it's not like that. The other night—"

"No, it's *great*. You two are perfect for each other." She took a few steps backward, gaining distance. "Look, I really gotta take this seriously. I'll talk to you later."

Before I could respond, she trotted away, leaving me behind.

I TRIED TALKING to Sadie again after class, but she ran off. I wanted her to understand that she had the wrong impression, but she didn't give me a damn chance. I wound up being later than Grayson into the cafeteria and found him in our usual spot.

As I sat down across the table from him, Grayson arched a brow. "I think you're missing a shadow."

"Nope." I frowned and grabbed my plastic fork to mix up my chicken fettuccine. "She's not coming. She found out that I slept over at your place this past weekend."

He stilled, holding his burger an inch from his mouth. "Why does that matter?"

I tilted my head. "Are you serious right now?"

Taking a large bite, he nodded and talked around his mouthful of food. "Why would she care?"

"Because she thinks we're dating."

"But we're not." He frowned and then smirked. "But we could change that."

Carter's words from earlier replayed in my head. I'd thought Grayson had gotten over his crush, but maybe he hadn't. "Please, I'd eat you for supper. And she's into you, so thinking we're with each other is upsetting her." I watched his expression.

His mouth tensed. "She and I will never happen. She's the coach's kid."

A tray landed in the spot next to me, and Jack slid into the booth. He asked, "Are we talking about Sadie?"

"You're still gonna sit with us, man?" Grayson's brows furrowed. "I didn't think you were the one bringing her and dropping her off."

"Fuck yeah, I'm sitting with E." He scoffed. "She and I are official workout buddies." He waggled his brows. "I make her sweat and groan."

I snatched a piece of chicken from the top of my pasta and tossed it at him. "Keep dreaming, sicko."

He leaned forward, tucking a piece of hair behind my ear while murmuring. "Give me a chance, and I can teach you things—"

I heard a click and the sound of a babyish voice coming from a table over. "Now, *this* is interesting."

My blood ran cold. I didn't have to turn around to recognize the voice.

CHAPTER TWENTY-SIX

Katherine sashayed over to our table, her gaze moving from me to Jack. "Hey, I haven't been able to talk to Carter today. Can you pass along that he needs to pick me up at six for our date?"

I gritted my teeth, having forgotten that their final "date" was tonight.

Unlike me, Jack's carefree persona didn't falter. He leaned back, placing an arm around my shoulders, and flashed her a huge smile. "Sure. I can remind him to report for his community service hours at six tonight. Should he wear the orange jumpsuit as well?"

Her grin dulled slightly. "Not funny, and if you don't want Gina to get the wrong idea, maybe you shouldn't have your arm around another girl."

Jack chuckled. "We aren't exclusive. She knew the rules. To get me between your legs, you have to agree to no strings. If she gets hurt, that's on her. Not me."

"Dammit, Jack," Katherine hissed, all pretenses gone

"She's my *friend*, and you're Carter's friend. You can't do that shit this time."

"If you had higher expectations, then that's your own damn fault," Jack shot back, pulling me closer to him. "But let me say, if I were going to settle down, it wouldn't be with *Gina*." He winked at me. "E is pretty chill *and* hot."

"*Her*? Out of *everyone*?" Katherine blinked, and her pretend smile slid into place. "Surely, you could find someone who's used to the type of people you surround yourself with."

I was never a fighting type of girl, but I wanted to pull out her hair and make her scream.

He laughed. "First off, you're not my type. Not in the least."

She placed her hands on her hips. "Carter wouldn't allow you to date me anyway."

"Uh..." Jack rubbed his mouth. "This is going to be awkward as fuck, but let me level it out for you. Carter doesn't like you. He doesn't even want you existing near him, let alone have any plans to indulge your delusion that the two of you will get back together. So let's not pretend otherwise. Besides, there are only two reasons you want him."

Even though I was angry, I wanted to disappear. People were looking over here. Grayson and I caught each other's eye, and we were clearly thinking the same thing. He could make a run for it, but I was blocked by Jack.

However, I had to admit I wanted to hear Jack's thoughts on the matter.

"One. At first, you wanted the two Tennessee senators' kids to be together to put you more in the spotlight." Jack lifted two fingers. "And two, now that Carter doesn't want you, it makes you desperate to get him back."

"That's not true," Katherine insisted, but her voice fell flat. "We're friends."

When I'd first met Jack, I'd thought he was just a shit talker...and he was. But he was also observant and smart. Two things he was good at hiding.

Jack snickered. "You may be a good actress with your facial expressions and poses, but the lack of warmth in your eyes tells the real story. So don't try your hand at that with me."

Katherine straightened as Jack took a sip of his drink.

He placed the bottle back on the table. "At the end of the day, Carter's my boy. We have a code—misters before sisters." He glanced at me and then Grayson. "That is the saying, right?"

Scratching the back of his neck, Grayson nodded. "Yeah, but I don't think any of us actually say that."

It would be best if they never did. I think that saying was something like a hundred years old.

"Still works." He waved a hand and turned back to Katherine. "But let's be real. If Carter was going to trust someone, it sure as hell would never be you."

Katherine laughed awkwardly then glared at me as if this confrontation was somehow all my fault even though she was the one who'd come over here to start shit.

"What is it with you and them?" She tilted her head. "I don't get it." She flicked her attention to Grayson and asked, "Do you?"

He lifted both hands. "She's nice, and you're"—he grimaced and then coughed—"not."

Jack laughed so hard that I startled.

"For fuck's sake." Jack dropped his arm from me, his whole body convulsing. "I needed that."

Katherine straightened her shoulders. "You three have a great day. I gotta get ready for my *date*."

There it was again. A reminder that the man I cared for

would be out with another woman later. I understood he couldn't stand her, but that didn't make it easier on me.

"Stop being a bitch." Jack's neck corded. "And stop trying to rub it in Evie's face. If you keep this shit up, Carter and I will enjoy breaking you." The relaxed, jovial Jack was no more. Right now, he was just as calculating as Katherine. Maybe even more so.

Katherine faltered and took a step back. "Whatever." She turned, whipping her ponytail around, and pranced off.

When she exited the double doors, I let out a breath I hadn't realized I was holding.

"Don't worry about it, E," Jack said. "He truly hates her."

Grayson rolled his eyes. "I'm still confused as to why they're even pretending to date if he hates her so much?"

I winced, unsure what to say.

Shaking his head, Jack leaned back. "It's for Carter's dad and his political career. Nothing more." He bumped his shoulder into mine. "It's not a big deal. Katherine disgusts him. There is no risk of them getting back together." Then Jack launched into all the gory details of his latest sexual conquest, and the conversation returned to normal.

My phone vibrated, and a message rolled across.

Carter: I'm out. Ready to head home?

I smiled as I typed out my response.

Me: I'm on my way.

Snapping his fingers, Jack stopped midsentence and raised an eyebrow.

"Let me out." I pushed on his side.

Jack patted his chest. "I'm midstory. That's just rude."

I hadn't been part of the conversation since Katherine, so I had no idea what he'd been rambling about. He and Grayson had gotten absorbed in some kind of football thing.

"Remember, some of us have to work." I arched a brow.

"Fine, but I expect a drink on the house when I come visit." Jack waggled a finger as he slid out of the seat.

"Expect all you want." I stuck my tongue out at him.

Jack reached out to grab it, and I barely got my tongue back into my mouth in time. He waggled his eyebrows. "Next time, I won't miss."

Grayson cleared his throat and swallowed. "Evie, be careful."

I turned toward him. He wasn't talking about being careful at work around all the drunk people. He was referring to Carter. "I will. I'll see you two later."

As I headed off, I heard Jack growl, "That's none of your concern, man."

"Yeah, it is," Grayson countered. "She's my friend."

I'd heard enough. I jogged out the door, ready to get away from the drama.

However, with every step closer I got to Carter's Escalade, my stomach churned more. I wished it was from the heat of October, which was still pretty much on par with September, but it was dread about what Katherine might have planned next.

When I reached his car, Carter was already in the driver's seat. I slid into the vehicle, and the cool air hit me, giving me some relief.

He smiled. "Hey, you. How was your day?"

Jack had told me to let Carter handle it, but I felt like I was keeping something from him if I didn't bring it up. "It was good until lunch."

One eyebrow arched, and I spilled everything. My voice broke when I told him what time to pick Katherine up.

He scowled and hit the steering wheel. "Of course she would do that to you. I want to put her in her place, but if I do, she'll know why, which will only cause more problems." He pinched the bridge of his nose. "That's her *entire* goal. She's trying to make sure I've cut ties with you."

My life had become a bizarre chess game. Each move was calculated, trying to force the other person's hand. I couldn't live in the moment but, instead, had to try to determine the other person's motives.

I hated it.

However, if I wanted to be with Carter and finish out the year here, I'd have to embrace it...or at least make some kind of peace with it.

Huffing, Carter put the car in drive and pulled out of the parking lot. For the next few minutes, we sat in silence. Every time I stole a glance at him, his forehead was creased, confirming he was still thinking about *her* and her games.

Ever since I'd met him, Carter oozed power. But in this moment, he seemed powerless. He didn't want to paint even more of a target on my back, and that was exactly what he'd do if he stood Katherine up...again.

I cleared my throat and took his hand as we pulled up to the school's gated entrance. "Thank you," I whispered.

His brows furrowed. "For what? Putting you on Katherine's bitch radar?"

I laughed. "I was already on it, remember?" I squeezed his hand. "Her father was the one who pushed for me to come here and got your dad to back it." Now, I wanted to get away from the conversation about her. It seemed like she always haunted our relationship. "I meant thank you for asking Jack to train me today. I know you were the one who put him up to it."

He shrugged. "He would have done it anyway. He actually likes us together, which is strange. He hardly likes anyone.

Getting on his good side takes talent. But I was an asshole for not letting it happen before, and I'm sorry."

"Carter—"

"No. That hellish day haunts you, and you're trying to do something positive... To make a difference if you're ever in a fucked-up situation like that again. And *I* hindered you." His grip on the steering wheel made his knuckles turn white.

"Baby, I was figuring it out and doing it on my own." At the end of the day, I needed to be able to rely on myself. I didn't have any family left. My heart panged once again. "But you doing that today, I just wanted to say—"

"Don't thank me again. *Please.*" He paused for a beat. "I'm sorry I was a jackass to you for so long." His hold on me tightened as he vowed, "But not anymore."

I believed him wholeheartedly. "I know."

"If getting stronger helps you in any way, then we'll make you a world-class champ, to the point you can even kick my ass." He nodded, everything settled in his mind. "And, one day, I'll be the one helping you, not Jackass."

My heart expanded so hard it ached. I was already too far gone, and I just knew he had the power to break me. If things didn't change, he would eventually because of the constant threat hanging over us—Katherine. She'd keep coming until she found a way to destroy us.

I tried to push the thought away and trust that Carter and Jack knew what they were doing.

Soon, we pulled into his garage and headed inside. As soon as he placed our things on the floor in the living room, I couldn't wait any longer. I hadn't been able to touch him all damn day.

I hugged him, and he kissed me deeply, as if the time apart had been as awful for him as it was for me.

His hand snaked under my shirt and around my waist, and

desire knotted in my stomach. I *had* to have him. The ache was so sharp and desperate, and I wanted him in me before he left on a date with her.

I slipped my tongue into his mouth and maneuvered him so his legs hit the back of the couch, then pushed him down, straddling him.

He groaned in approval as his lips devoured me, pulling away from my mouth and lowering to my neck. As his hands glided under my shirt and bra, my mind fogged, making me forget all our problems.

In this moment, it was just him and me.

We removed each other's clothes, and he touched me between my legs. I kissed and licked every inch of him, dying to taste him more. With emotions building on top of sensations, I feared I might say too much too soon, and when he slid on a condom, I rode him fast and hard, losing myself in the physical. He nipped my breasts gently as I ground against him, taking both of us over the top. For a while, we didn't move, just stared into each other's eyes.

But his date with Katherine hung over me. If she was as devious as he said, I was certain she'd have a plan. And I feared she could take him away from me.

THE WORST PART about his date night was that it wasn't with me. The second worst was that I didn't have work to distract me. Instead, I was stuck in Carter's house alone with nothing to do, knowing he was with *her*.

He'd left five minutes ago and probably hadn't even reached her dorm yet to pick her up, and I was already climbing the walls. I trusted him, but I didn't trust *her*. He wouldn't do anything, but that didn't mean she wouldn't try, and I hated that we were in this fucking situation.

I paced in front of the couch, trying not to lose my damn mind. I could call Joe and ask if they needed me to cover a shift tonight, but Mondays weren't usually busy.

I heard a knock on the door, and my heart leapt. A part of me hoped it was Carter...but he wouldn't knock on his own front door. It might be someone who didn't need to know I was staying here. Carter had already changed the cleaning lady's schedule so that she came while we were both in class so she wouldn't have anything to report back to Senator Grisham.

While I tried to decide on what to do, another knock sounded, followed by a male voice. "Evie, it's your favorite person! Let me in."

Jack.

I exhaled, some of the stress leaving my shoulders as I jogged to the door and opened it.

In usual Jack form, he leaned against the wall, looking very casual.

"Hey. What's up?" I asked, tapping my hands against my pants.

"Just thought you might want some company." He waggled his brows as he sauntered into the duplex. "I thought we could play together."

The sexual innuendo was clear, but when it came to me, he was all talk, and I knew it. "Checkers?"

"Strip Twister?" He waggled his brows.

I snorted. "Hard pass."

"Fine." He strolled to the PlayStation and flipped it on along with the TV. "I'll teach you how to play Carter's favorite video game—*Grand Theft Auto*. We've stayed up many a night playing this game, so it seems only right that you be initiated." He tossed one of the headphones and controllers toward me.

Somehow, I managed to catch them.

Before I realized what had happened, my cheeks ached from smiling. I knew what Jack was up to. He'd come here to help me get through the night. He hadn't had to do that for Carter—he was doing it for me. I had no doubt, but I wouldn't call him out on it. He was going the extra mile to be friendly.

Wanting to make him happy, I lifted the remote. "Who says I don't know how to play it already?"

"Please." He scoffed, dropping onto the couch. "I kick everyone's ass."

I settled down and put the headphones on, ready to hand him his ass. He'd made a horrible mistake, and I was going to make him bleed.

The two of us got lost in the game, and the first time he groaned, I had to stop myself from pumping my hand in victory, continuing the onslaught, getting lost in the game.

At a pivotal moment when I was about to kick Jack's ass once again, my headphones were removed from my head—and not by Jack. I dropped the remote and spun around to find myself face to face with Carter.

My heart leapt into my throat.

He was home.

My breath caught. "Hey. I didn't hear the garage door."

"Seems not." He gestured to the TV and then at Jack, who was still playing, oblivious to what was happening. "I texted you and got worried when you didn't reply."

Shit. I snatched my phone from the coffee table, saw two messages from Carter, and then noted the time. It was only seven thirty. He'd been gone only an hour and a half, which included his drive time to campus and back. "I'm sorry. I didn't notice the text."

"Fuck yeah!" Jack leapt to his feet and thrust his hips while swinging his hands down toward his crotch. "Suck that, Evie."

He spun around to see Carter and me standing there together. Then he grinned even wider. "Dammit. Next time since Carter's here."

"Yeah, jackass." Carter reached over and punched Jack in the arm. "You're going to get it now." He then removed his jacket and rolled up his sleeves.

Right then and there, I wanted to drag him upstairs. One simple action had me damn near unglued.

He wrapped an arm around my waist, pulling me into him. He nipped my lips and then leaned toward my ear and whispered, "I know exactly what you're thinking, and if Jack wasn't here, I'd have you upstairs now."

My heart leapt.

"That's the first thing I'll rectify when he's gone," he promised and then kissed me, slipping his tongue into my mouth.

He tasted all things Carter, and I clutched his shirt.

"If you're going to talk shit, sit down so I can put you in your place," Jack said, smacking his arm. "You two live together right now, so you have all night to make her moan."

Cheeks burning, I wanted to bury my face in Carter's chest, but all that would do was encourage Jack.

"Don't worry." Carter kissed my nose. "I'll put him in his place."

I opened my mouth to complain, but before I could, he sat down in my spot and pulled me into his lap. When he wrapped his arms around me and nestled me into his chest, I decided I'd rather be here anyway. For the moment, everything felt perfect. He was done dating Katherine, and I was here, in his arms.

My phone buzzed in my hand, and my stomach dropped.

Senator McHale: Hello, Evie. I'm coming to town in two weeks for a meeting with the school

board, and I was hoping you'd have time for coffee. I want to check in on you.

Shit. This wasn't good. The timing twisted a knot in my stomach. But what could I say?

Me: Sounds great. Let me know when and where.

"What the fuck, man?" Jack shouted as Carter kissed the top of my head.

"You can wait a fucking second," he shot back and moved so he could see my face. "What's wrong?"

I glanced at the TV and then back at him. He'd paused the game, and I could feel a smile creep across my face. "Nothing. Nothing at all."

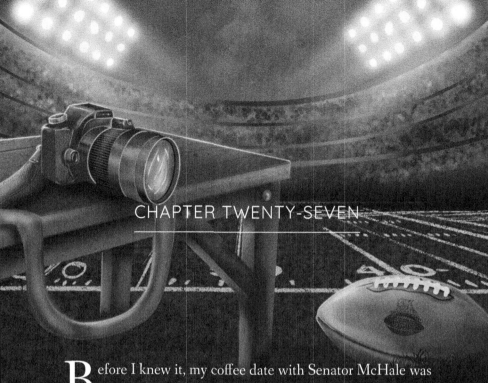

CHAPTER TWENTY-SEVEN

Before I knew it, my coffee date with Senator McHale was here. Unfortunately, his packed schedule had only allowed for a time right after my photography class, which meant my free time between class and work was gone.

When Carter learned of the meeting, he'd been concerned because of Katherine, but what could we do? Senator McHale was the reason I was at HSU.

I'd been confused about why the senator would want to meet with me, but Carter had the explanation. It was all about showing that he was following up with the student he'd sponsored so he could mention me organically and help the public to remember what he'd done for me.

Even though I hated being used as a pawn, the senator had offered me a chance I'd never have been able to afford otherwise, and the least I could do was express my gratitude.

Thankfully, he'd picked a coffee shop that was off campus but near the university, so I was able to walk there with only a slight bit of grief from Carter.

Caffeine Latte was about a half mile down the road from HSU's main entrance. The parking lot in front of the shop was full, and I jogged across the street, hoping like hell that Senator McHale had gotten caught up with political responsibilities and wouldn't show.

When I stepped through the double glass front doors, I saw that the shop had five round tables in front and a bar table with high-top chairs against the glass window. The place smelled of coffee grounds, but my stomach was so tight that if I tried to drink something, I'd probably get sick.

Of course, Senator McHale was already there, seated at the table closest to the mocha-colored wall. He was facing the glass doors and waving at me as if I wouldn't see him. A younger man, I assumed was his assistant, sat at a table beside us. The young man nodded at me then went back to pecking away on an iPad, likely organizing all the senator's commitments.

The place was fairly busy, but somehow, the senator had co-opted the entire table, and one empty chair sat across from him.

Adjusting the backpack on my arm, I went over and plopped into the seat. I tried to smile, but it felt false even to me.

"Hello, Evie. Thank you for coming." Senator McHale nodded and gestured at the cup in front of my chair. "The place was busy, so I got you a skinny vanilla latte. I hope that's all right. Katherine likes them."

"That's great." I forced out the words because I hated sugar-free anything. For some reason, the artificial sweetener always tasted disgustingly sweet, and I feared it would make me even more nauseous. I raised the cup to my lips and pretended to take a sip, not wanting to be rude. "Thank you. It's perfect."

His shoulders relaxed, and he leaned back, taking a drink

from his own cup. "I appreciate you meeting me here. I meant to come and see you sooner, but I haven't had a ton of time despite being a board member. I wanted to touch base and see how things are going. How do you like HSU?"

Hopefully, we could keep this short and sweet. Carter was going to be here in less than an hour, right after his class got out, to pick me up and take me to work.

I placed the cup on the table. "It's been good. Classes are challenging, but I'm doing well. Hallowed Saints is one of the nicest schools I've ever seen, and I'm thankful that you gave me the opportunity to be here. I'm also working on my application to Stanford for their PhD program in psychology." I didn't want to talk about Katherine or anything that might lead to Carter.

"That's what your professors told me as well. You've got straight A's, and I must say, even I'm impressed. Stanford will be lucky to have you."

My stomach dropped. He'd been talking to my professors? I wasn't sure how I felt about that, but what could I say? He'd paid for me to attend HSU. It made sense that he wanted to make sure I was taking my education seriously and not messing around.

"Katherine said you were taking pictures of the football games for your photography class?" He arched a brow.

I dropped my hands in my lap and started picking at my fingernails. I'd hoped her name wouldn't come up, but...she was his daughter. "I was assigned football as my subject of focus for the class." I didn't want him to think I'd asked for it. "We drew our subjects from a hat."

"Well, I'm glad you got football! I'm sure that's what every student hoped for. The team is having an incredible year." He crossed his legs and leaned back. "What made you choose photography as your elective?"

I shrugged. "I've always enjoyed it. From what Mom said,

my aunt was into photography, and Mom gifted me my aunt's old camera when I was younger. I hadn't taken pictures in a while though—not since Mom was diagnosed with cancer—so when I came here and saw the class, it just clicked." As I talked about my mom, that hole in my heart that seemed to make itself known at the worst times opened wider, and I wished Carter was here. I rubbed my chest. "I'm not trying to be rude, but can we not talk about my parents and family? It's...hard."

His face softened. "Of course. I should have realized it would cause you grief. That wasn't my intention."

"No, it's fine. It just still cuts deep." I dropped my hand to my lap, not wanting to continue to make a spectacle of myself.

"I'm sorry." He exhaled and straightened in his seat again. "I didn't intend to make you sad. Well, how is everything else going?"

I said the first words that popped into my head. "Good. Just really busy with schoolwork and not falling behind. Things have been just a little chaotic. I haven't had much time for anything beyond classes." Besides work, but I didn't want to talk about that. I suspected it would cause him to be concerned or lead to more questions. Both scenarios were not ideal for me. "How about you?"

He snorted, catching me off guard. He sounded so *normal*.

"About the same, but substitute work for classes." He shook his head. "It never stops, but I'm glad I found time to come here and talk with you. It's good to see you thriving."

Unsure what to say, I took the opportunity to pretend to take another sip of my coffee. As I set the cup of coffee back on the table, Senator McHale stiffened.

I glanced over my shoulder and saw one of the cheerleaders coming into the shop. When her gaze landed on me and then Senator McHale, her eyebrows lifted. She strolled over, her blonde hair swishing behind her.

"Hello, Suzy." Senator McHale's demeanor relaxed, belying his discomfort just moments before.

"Senator McHale." She turned her icy-blue eyes on me. "Does Katherine know you're here?"

"Indeed, she does." He laughed. "I'm having dinner with her tonight. I came here to get a cup of coffee with Evie and see how she's doing."

This was uncomfortable, and I wanted to get the hell out of here. I cleared my throat and stood. "Well, it was nice talking with you, but I have a lot of studying to get to." I smiled and lifted my cup. "Thank you so much. I hope you enjoy your dinner with Katherine tonight."

I could've sworn the corners of his mouth tipped downward, but that didn't make sense. He'd seen me, and he'd get to tell the media he'd checked up on me.

"Yes, of course." He waved. "Have a good evening."

I spun on my heels and headed to the door. I texted Carter, letting him know that I'd meet him at his vehicle. The last thing I wanted was to be standing here waiting when Senator McHale came out.

I took off, getting the hell out of there.

Two and a half weeks later, I was still staying at Carter's, where we managed to avoid the campus-wide Halloween party and opted for *The Walking Dead* and cuddles. I did hate missing Haven and Leah's party, but with school the next day, it was for the best.

At my house, a remediation team had boarded up the windows to prevent more leaking and drained the basement. Then, they'd set up fans and dehumidifiers for several days to prevent any additional damage or mold. But the remodel was taking forever, and my room still wasn't ready. The landlord had said some supplies were hard to get and that it would be a few more weeks.

Our routine stayed the same. Carter took me everywhere, and when he had an away game, Leah took me to and from work. Carter and I still didn't acknowledge each other at school or home games, and each day, it grew harder and harder. But we kept up the act because Katherine was leaving us alone.

"Babe, we're going," Carter called from the bottom of the stairs.

Today was yet another home game, a big one against Louisiana State University. I headed downstairs to find them waiting for me before heading out to the stadium for warm-ups. One nice thing about the game starting late—I got to miss a shift at work and celebrate with Carter afterward.

"Break a leg, fellas," I said as I reached the bottom and stopped in front of them.

Carter chuckled. "That's my girl. We don't need luck." He pulled me against his chest and kissed me, his tongue slipping into my mouth.

"Dude, I'm right here. If she's gonna do that for you, then she's got to turn around and give me the same kind of luck," Jack retorted.

Pulling away, Carter scowled. "If your lips get anywhere near hers, I'll rip your head off and lose to LSU happily."

I laughed and touched Carter's chest. "Don't worry. That'll never happen."

He booped my nose. "Better not. Be safe, and text me when the Uber drops you off. Then you can ride back with me."

We were going separately because I didn't want to get there too early and deal with Katherine's glares. "Okay, but you'll see me on the football field."

"Not enough. I need to know when you get there." He pecked me again.

"All right." I slapped his hard ass, which made my hand sting. "Now go warm up. You gotta win for me tonight."

"Fuck yeah, we do." Jack pumped his fist.

I watched the two of them head down the stairs, and then I got ready for the game myself.

Though I loved taking pictures of Carter playing, I hated watching Katherine try to hug him after every touchdown. He'd prevent her from getting close or bat her away, but she was relentless.

Between that and the way Sadie was avoiding me like the plague, I wanted to pull my hair out.

The game was tied, and I got lost in the moment of taking pictures in the darkness. I took so many of Carter and had to remind myself to catch the others too. The teams were almost on par. In the last three seconds, we had the ball, and our kicker was going for a field goal.

The energy buzzed around us, and I zoomed in, taking shot after shot. The kicker took aim, and the ball twirled in the air as all the fans waited with bated breath.

Then it sailed barely inside the right side of the goal.

Field goal HSU.

The band played and the crowd went wild. Carter turned toward me, looking jubilant, and took a step in my direction only to stop. His smile faded... We couldn't be there for one another out here.

Katherine ran toward him, but he jogged off the field. Soon, Coach Prichard led them into the locker room.

I watched the team leave, feeling so proud, not only of Carter but of the rest of the team.

I met up with Theo, and we quickly looked over shots. Soon, I was waiting outside the locker room.

I'd barely been there a second before Carter was rushing out, a huge grin on his face. He scanned the area before running to me and pulling me into a hug. For a moment, I forgot where we were and settled into the embrace, wishing we could do more.

The cheerleaders' door creaked open a little ways from us, and I jerked back. I could make out someone standing in the doorway, laughing, sounding babyish.

My joy was replaced with a hardness in my stomach.

My heart dropped as I stumbled farther away from Carter. My gaze darted to the door just in time to see it close once again. Katherine's baby voice simpered, "Oh yeah, thanks. I forgot my phone. How stupid."

Both Carter and I breathed raggedly, our eyes colliding. Even though my pulse started once again, neither one of us could deny that we'd come too damn close to getting caught. However, if she'd seen us, she would be out here now, ending my life.

Somehow, luck was on my side...this time.

Carter's jaw twitched. "Let's go." He took my hand, dragging me to the door.

He didn't have to coax me because, any second, Katherine could come walking out that door once again.

Something bitter settled within me. What Carter and I had was amazing, but we had to hide it because of *her*. Even as we hurried to the door that led to the parking lot, Carter kept glancing over his shoulder, making my blood boil.

I despised hiding. We were treating our relationship as if it was wrong when it was nothing but right.

I was once again reminded of the horrible truth. If I wanted to be with Carter, this was my reality. I needed to treasure the time we had together because who knew what would happen after graduation?

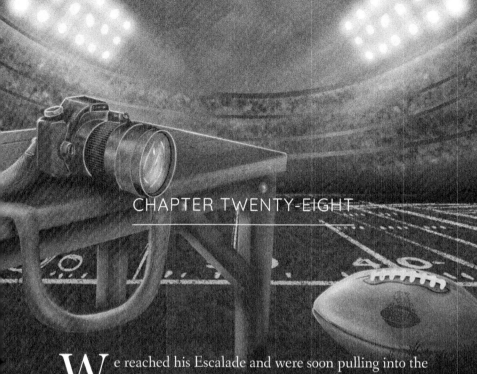

CHAPTER TWENTY-EIGHT

We reached his Escalade and were soon pulling into the heavy stadium traffic.

Now that we were actively moving away from the threat, I removed my camera from my neck and placed it behind my seat. I then smiled, turning my body to Carter. "You guys were *kick ass* tonight. Don't let Katherine take away your high!"

He sighed. "You're right. We were amazing, but you know what would be even better? If I wasn't afraid of kissing my girl in public." He took my hand, squeezing it. "Every damn play we made that I was proud of, I wanted to run to you to celebrate, but I couldn't. Not without making your life a living hell."

It always came back to that. However, I wanted to salvage the night. "There is a solution to that problem."

He arched a brow. "I'm listening."

"Haven and Leah are having a party at the house. We could go." I shrugged my shoulders, trying to pretend it wasn't a big deal. But now that I thought about it, I wanted to go more than anything. "We could even invite your friends."

"And hang out with those Ridge University kids?" He wrinkled his nose. "All they do is toss insults at us."

I laughed and smacked him. "I live with those Ridge University kids, and they were nice to you. And it would be good for you to expand your horizons and see that not all of them are useless. Besides, that way, we'd actually get out of the house instead of being stuck at your place. And we don't have to hide there because none of them go to our school."

He tilted his head as he finally managed to pull onto the main road. "If that's what you want to do, let's go. Better that than having Jack come over and make a fucking mess."

"Tonight especially, there would be a huge chance of Jack breaking something." I beamed, my chest swelling with pride in each and every one of them. "You're all one step closer to the national championship." I kissed his cheek, enjoying the scruff under my lips. "One step closer to your dreams of the NFL."

Chuckling, he turned his head and quickly kissed me. He cupped one side of my face with his hand. "Go ahead and let your friends know we're on our way, and—I *guess*—message Jackass the news and tell him to share that information with only our inner circle."

I snorted. "Does he realize you call him that?"

"Yeah." He shrugged. "It used to be more intermittent, but ever since you came around, he's gotten a lot worse about giving me shit. It's a consequence for making comments about my girl."

My stomach fluttered. I loved it when he called me his girl. I wanted the world to know we were each other's, but that wasn't possible right now.

I shot off the first text to Haven and Leah.

Me: Mind if Carter and I and some friends come to the party?

Leah: 🙄 **Of course you come with your super**

hot smart football friends the night I'm working later than usual.

Haven: Get your ass here. I miss you, bish.

Me: Don't worry, Leah. I'll make sure we stay so we can hang a little when you get home.

Leah: You better.

Then I shot off a text to Jack, Grayson, and Cole.

Me: Party at my house.

Jack: Fuck yeah. Tell Carter not to get his panties twisted in his crack if I drop something.

Me: First off, my old house with my roommates, and second, you dropped a pitcher of sangria that you demanded to make, which could've stained the floor.

Jack: Please. With how anal he is, I'm sure we could torch the place, and he'd find a way to clean it in a few minutes.

Grayson: We'll be there.

Cole: Without Jack.

Jack: Fuck you guys. I'm going to get every single lady and make sure you get no head.

Me: Uh… I'm turning off my phone now. I don't need to be part of this.

Muting the group message, I shook my head. "He really is a jackass."

Carter didn't even ask for an explanation. He just nodded and raised the back of my hand to his lips. "Never doubt my judgment again." He winked.

I stuck my tongue out at him and then glanced out my window. Every person I saw in HSU attire, whether young or old, was smiling, yelling congratulations back and forth at each other, completely thrilled. The LSU fans were hanging their heads.

The game had been so close that I hadn't been sure our team would pull through, but I should have never doubted them. I reached into the back, retrieved my camera, and started to scroll.

Carter glanced over a few times as I slowly flipped through them. There were pictures of Carter throwing a pass to Jack, who ran it in for a touchdown, and a few where Grayson had made a huge tackle just as Carter tilted the ball back for a pass. Each picture had HSU painted as the champions they were sure to become. After all, they were for the school paper.

"You're getting even better." Carter smiled.

I had just started with photography right before Mom died, so I never truly had a hobby other than reading, and it was nice to dig more into that and find something I enjoyed doing. "I see things through a different lens now." I bobbed my head, indicating that I'd been punny on purpose.

He narrowed his eyes. "Really?"

My jaw dropped. "Hey, it was funny."

"It's a good thing you're cute," he countered.

We teased each other until we pulled up by my old house and found the driveway already full. Music blared, and people were hanging outside on the front lawn.

I hadn't been here since the flood, and I was curious to see how the downstairs looked.

Carter parked on the edge of the lawn. "No one better block me in. I don't want to have to hunt down some wasted idiot when I'm ready to go home and make love to my girl."

My chest swelled, and my cheeks hurt from smiling. I never thought I'd feel this way about anyone, and here I was with the sexiest man on campus—hell, the sexiest guy I'd ever seen—and he was talking about taking me back to his house to make love to me.

He smirked. "That is if you behave tonight."

I arched a brow. "And if I'm naughty?"

Leaning over the center console, he kissed me, and I forgot where we were. Then he pulled back, his eyes dark with desire and twinkling with mischief. He murmured, "Then I'll have to figure out some creative punishments."

Waggling my brows, I tapped my chin. "Then I better figure out what kind of sex I want tonight."

"Keep this up, and we might not make it home." He abruptly climbed out of the car.

I froze. What the hell? I watched as he marched past the hood to my side. When he opened the door, I was ready to ask him what was wrong until he gripped my hips and removed me from the seat. He shut the door, pushed my back against it, and pressed his body into mine.

One of his hands cupped my neck while the other slipped under the hem of my shirt. He leaned toward my ear and whispered, "Did I tell you that you look sexy tonight?"

I felt lost in his gaze. "In my shirt and shorts?"

He tilted his head and brushed his lips against mine. "I gotta say, that's a good point. I do know what you look like underneath all those clothes."

I licked his lips, making him groan.

Then he smirked. "And you might just look a little better with clothes on."

I snorted, shoving him, but he didn't move an inch.

"You know I'm full of shit. I wish you were naked right here and now."

His tongue slipped into my mouth, and his minty taste filled my senses once again, along with the faint scent of soap from the shower he'd taken in the locker room.

Opening to him, I lifted his shirt up and traced the curves of his six-pack with both my hands. He quivered as my hands inched lower, and he hardened against me. He sucked on my tongue as my fingertips traced the waistband of his jeans.

"Evie!" Haven shouted from the front porch. I heard a colliding noise, followed by her saying, "I'm sorry. I'm just getting to my roomie."

Carter groaned playfully and pulled back. "We should've gone back to our house. Now I'm going to have blue balls for the rest of the night."

Our house. I liked that way too much.

I rolled my eyes. "You'll be fine. I'll be able to relieve you shortly." Then I smiled at him a little too brightly. "Besides, weren't you the one who said you wanted to make sure we hang out?"

"You fight dirty."

"And you love it." I winced. I hadn't meant to use the *l* word, but now it was out there.

Carter held me tighter, a naughty grin spreading across his face. "Maybe you'll be the one who gets into trouble tonight."

Thank goodness, he didn't make this awkward. I smirked. "We'll see about that."

Haven stumbled toward us, and Carter took a step back a moment before she threw her arms around me. She said way too loudly, "I've *missed* you."

"You just saw me a few days ago at the bar." I returned the hug before pulling away.

She glanced at the house. "It's not the same. But hey, they're going to start on the basement next week!"

Next week. They'd said redoing it could take a month. My room downstairs would be ready to move back into soon.

"So we'll be able to watch our shows together again! Ever since you moved in with Sexy Broody Man, I never get to hang with you." She pouted and reached out to shove Carter in the chest but missed. She tried again and nearly fell down.

He caught her, steadying her.

I took over as guilt settled in my stomach. "I'm sorry. I can come over more."

Carter didn't say anything, but that look he got when he wasn't happy about something slid over his face.

"We'd like that," Haven said and nodded so much that I was beginning to think she was more bobblehead than person. "Leah even complains that you two don't get to talk at work much because it's so busy."

That was true.

"So, now you get to drink with us." She lifted her glass to toast. But when she looked at it to take a sip, she paused and frowned. "Damn. Where did my drink go?"

"On me," a guy yelled from the porch.

"Well then, I guess we better solve that," she said, looping her arm through mine.

I reached back and intertwined my fingers with Carter's, and the three of us headed inside.

Halfway through the packed living room, Haven yelled, "I thought you said you were bringing hot football guys." She paused and glanced at Carter. "I mean, you definitely brought one, but you already locked that shit down. I need guys who are single."

Carter wrapped an arm around me. "Hell yeah. I'm off the market." He then turned to the group of guys in the corner of the room and glared. "And *she* is too."

Standing on my tiptoes, I kissed his lips, proudly emphasizing both points. He pulled me against his chest once again.

Soon, Haven appeared with two drinks. I hadn't even noticed she'd gone. Then she arched a brow. "Where are the hot guys?"

The same group that Carter just threatened lifted their hands.

She waved them off. "The smart hot ones."

I snorted. "They're on their way."

"Good." She swayed and tried handing Carter one of the cups.

"I'm driving home, so I'm good."

She rolled her eyes but didn't press the issue. Then she handed a cup to me. I almost refused, but Carter placed a hand on my shoulder and whispered, "Have one or two. I'm right here."

For some reason, that made me feel safe, so I took the cup from her.

Haven began filling me in on the latest *Grey's Anatomy* season until someone hollered at her on the other side of the room. When she stumbled away, I tugged on Carter's hand. "I want to check on the downstairs."

The door was unlocked, and when we reached the bottom of the steps, the walls seemed to close in on me. There were still puddles on the floor, but that wasn't the issue. Everything was ruined.

"Hey." Carter kissed my cheek and squeezed my hand. He said, "You can stay with me as long as you want. Hell, you never have to leave."

And the problem was, that sounded very tempting. Staying with him would be so simple, and having him near made all the bad dreams stay away.

My tummy churned. That wasn't the right reason to stay with him. "Thank you, but I'll figure it out. After all, I committed to rooming with them all year."

He frowned but didn't say anything. The two of us just stared at the disaster that was my room.

That was when Jack's loud voice thundered over the music, "The party's here. We won, assholes!"

Carter blew out a breath. "We better go up there. There's no telling what he's gonna do tonight."

I laughed, relieved once again. Somehow, these oddball guys had become my friends and had gotten me out of a serious depression.

We climbed up the stairs to find Jack halfway done with a Jack and Coke. Grayson and Cole were in the living room with girls surrounding them.

Grayson glanced at me and Carter, who'd kept his arm around my waist. Grayson frowned but gave me a slight nod before turning his attention back to the girls.

Soon, Carter and I moved to one end of the couch. I sat on his lap, and he wound his arms around me, stealing kisses as we talked to one another like there were only the two of us in the entire place.

Grayson and Cole leaned against the wall, chatting with a new set of girls, while Jack stood in the middle with girls hanging on his every word. It was almost a comedy routine, seeing how the girls reacted to all of them.

Several even had the audacity to glance at Carter, but he never took his eyes off me. He made me truly feel as if I was the center of his world.

Soon, Leah came home, and I had several more drinks, laughing with her and Haven in the kitchen. Before I even realized what was happening, the room was spinning, and Carter's arms magically appeared around me, holding me up.

"Where'd you come from?" I asked, turning toward him.

He grinned. "I've been chatting with the guys, watching you like a hawk. I had to fend off two guys who were trying to come talk to you."

I flipped my hair. "And how many girls talked to you?" The

strange thing was I wasn't jealous. I had no doubt that he hadn't given them a second glance.

"Jack fended them off while I focused on saving you."

Grabbing his shirt, I pulled him close. My body suddenly became very aware of his muscles. I leaned forward, nipped at his earlobe, and whispered, "I'm ready for my punishment."

His eyes heated, and he bent down to pick me up. The walls blurred by as he marched to the front door.

"Hey!" Leah yelled. "Where are you taking her?"

He stepped out, nodding at Jack, Cole, and Grayson. "Home."

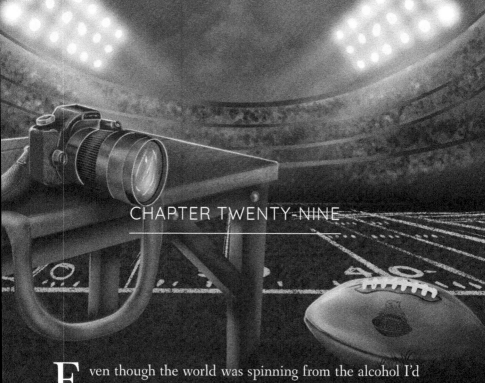

CHAPTER TWENTY-NINE

Even though the world was spinning from the alcohol I'd drunk, I had no doubt I was safe with Carter. When he opened the car door, I hurriedly climbed in, wanting to rush back and ride Carter in my bed.

I cringed. I was so drunk that I sounded like Jack.

"You going to puke?" Carter asked as he leaned over, placing a hand on my forehead.

And somehow, I fell for him harder. My chest squeezed, informing even drunk Evie that she was in trouble. "I'm fine. I just thought of something that Jack would say, and I was a little disgusted."

He laughed, the gold flecks warming. "Please, don't channel Jack. Things could get weird between us."

I wrapped my arms around his neck, pulling him nearer. I murmured, "I definitely don't want that to happen." Then I kissed him.

His hands slipped down my waist, his fingers digging into my sides. I loved when he did that. He made me feel powerful, like he needed me to anchor him.

Wanting to feel every curve of his muscles, I slid my hand under his shirt and traced the lines slowly and eagerly.

He pulled away. "Evie."

"Mm-hmm." I lowered my hand and started messing with his belt. Currently, it was preventing me from getting the very thing I wanted.

"We're still in front of the house," he rasped, trying to bat my hands away.

I leaned forward, eliminating the distance, kissing down his neck. "Your windows are tinted. We can get in the back seat." I rubbed a palm over the bulge in his jeans.

He crumbled against me, thrusting. "Fuck." His fingers dug into my skin more. "You don't know how bad I want to take you up on that."

Unzipping his jeans, I snaked my hand through the opening in both his jeans and boxers and squeezed his tip gently. "Then don't say no."

"Do you know how bad I want you right now?" he murmured, nipping my earlobe.

I giggled. "I sort of have an idea." And I squeezed him again.

"You're dangerous when you're drunk." He kissed down my neck, grazing his teeth against my skin. "But we can't do this. Not here. Not like this. You deserve better than that." He groaned as he snagged my hand and removed it.

I tried reaching for him again. He caught my wrist and muttered, "I can't believe I'm doing this." He zipped up and shut my door, then ran around to the driver's side.

As soon as he slid in, I climbed over the center console. Before he could stop me, I straddled his lap, the steering wheel shoved into my back. I didn't give a shit as long as he was touching me all over.

"Dammit, Evie," he groaned, his hand cupping my breast. "You're making this so damn hard."

"Not hard enough." I rocked against him, causing him to lean his head back.

"Shit." He hissed as I rolled against him again. "What are you doing to me?"

I bit his bottom lip. "I haven't even started."

He grasped my hips, hoisting me up somehow and putting me back in my seat. He growled. "Buckle up."

"But–"

"Now." He started the car, putting it in drive. "Because when we get home, you're going to regret getting me going. I'm going to spread you across my bed and devour you inch by inch."

His words thrilled me instead of scaring me *if that was his intent*. And I obeyed, just wanting him to drive somewhere that he'd be willing to do *all* the things with me.

Once I snapped my seat belt, I leaned over the console and started touching him again.

"Baby, I've got to drive." His breathing quickened. "Which means I need to concentrate so we're both safe."

Safe.

Drive.

My parents.

That was enough to sober me up. I straightened, glancing out the windshield.

He must have noticed the change because he took my hand. "Are you okay?"

"Yeah, I'm fine." I could give him until we pulled into his garage. I could wait that long. I'd gone without amazing sex for twenty-one years. I could wait another five minutes until he parked his car. "Just hurry."

"Don't worry. I'm *not* going the speed limit."

The five minutes felt like an eternity, but eventually, he pulled into his garage. As soon as he put the car in Park, I leaned over the console and unzipped his jeans.

His irises darkened, but he didn't stop me as I freed him. He pressed the button to shut the garage door and moved to kiss me, but I dodged his mouth. There was something else I wanted instead of his tongue right now, and I lowered my head, determined to show him exactly how badly I wanted him.

He groaned and panted, and after a few minutes, he lifted me off him and pulled me into a hug.

"What's wrong?" My chest constricted as I worried that he didn't like what I was doing.

"I don't want to finish that way." He released me, hitting the button so his chair scooted backward, and removed his wallet from his back pocket. Pulling out a condom, he slipped it on.

"You're not going to try to talk me into going inside?" I arched a brow, knowing that there was no way I would get out of this car without orgasming.

He shook his head. "You clearly want car sex, and I'm down for it with you."

I removed my shoes and took off my jeans and panties; then I crawled back over to him, his eyes watching me the entire way. As I straddled him, one of his hands slid between my legs while the other lifted my shirt and unfastened my bra. Within seconds, his mouth was on my nipples as his fingers filled me and his thumb hit the right spot. The onslaught of sensations sent ripples of pleasure through my body immediately. I leaned against him, almost limp, as he continued to work me.

I probably should have been embarrassed, but I was too desperate to care.

Again, he took me over the edge, but it still wasn't enough. I wanted more.

I removed his hands, needing him. As I slid down and he filled me, his mouth found mine. Arms raised, I used the ceiling as leverage, pushing down and riding him harder than ever before.

"Oh fuck, Evie." He thrust up, somehow increasing our pace even faster. "I'm almost there."

He grasped my waist, pushed me down, and rolled his hips one last time, which sent me over the edge yet again. I moaned as the edges of my vision blackened while the strongest orgasm pulsed through me. His body quivered from his own release.

Soon, our sweaty foreheads leaned against one another's.

"Every time with you has been amazing, but that…" He cupped my face. "If I'd known car sex could be that hot, I'd have gotten you drunk weeks ago."

I laughed, enjoying the way his hands were running up and down my sides. My heart was pounding, but I still hadn't gotten enough. I was becoming addicted to his body.

He must have been able to read my expression because he nodded to the house. "Now, let's have shower sex."

"You can already?" I arched a brow. He'd never had a problem with stamina before, but we'd just had mind-blowing orgasms.

"With you, I can get hard from just your touch." He cupped my face. "It's not typical. What we have isn't normal, but damn, I hope it never changes."

My stomach fluttered, and I tried not to focus on the way not only my body, but my heart responded. We had *this*, but it couldn't be more than this because we couldn't be open about our relationship. Falling for someone you had to sneak around with wasn't smart.

The Thanksgiving holiday was quickly approaching, and the basement would be fixed before Carter headed back home. Between the rain that kept falling, the amount of damage, and everything in between—mostly insurance—it had taken a long time to get the downstairs fixed. However, the even bigger problem was that I needed to replace so many things, and my graduate application was due.

On Thursday, the last day of photography class before Thanksgiving break, I packed up my camera, ready to head to the student center to eat lunch with Grayson and Jack.

Sadie had her back to me, talking to her new bestie. No matter how many times I'd texted her or tried to explain, she hadn't listened to anything I had to say, and worse, she pretended like my staying over at Grayson's wasn't even the problem.

At this point, I'd given up, which sucked. She was the type of person I could've been good friends with—she and I had more in common than I did with Leah and Haven—but my roommates didn't hold grudges, and they accepted me as I was.

Not bothering to talk to her, I removed my cell phone from my back pocket and found a new message.

Carter: Why am I friends with Jack?

I laughed, and Sadie shot me a hateful look.

I pushed the tightness in my chest away.

Focusing on the one person who made me truly happy, I read the message again. Though Carter and Jack purposely gave each other shit, they were as close as any people I'd ever met.

Me: According to him, it's because he's good at oral.

Carter: Seriously? You better be glad you started that sentence according to him.

My shoulders shook, but I tried to be quiet. I didn't want to irritate Sadie further.

Me: What did he do now?

Carter: Two girls have passed me notes to give to him. Are we in fucking fourth grade?

Me: Did you take them?

Carter: Fuck no. I told them to piss off. I needed to focus on class.

Me: I'll let him know to keep his dick in his pants.

Carter: No, I'll tell him. I just wanted to message you. I'll meet you at the car soon.

My cheeks hurt, and I realized that I was smiling. I did that a lot now, whenever I talked with him. Somehow, we'd managed to keep our relationship a secret on campus, so there was that. Off campus, we couldn't keep our hands to ourselves.

As I walked outside, turning toward the student center, Sadie caught up to me. She adjusted her backpack on her back and murmured, "Hey."

For a moment, I was at a loss for words after her nasty look. "Hey?"

She licked her bottom lip and focused anywhere but on my face. She cleared her throat. "So, what are you doing over Thanksgiving break?"

I paused, wondering if I'd heard her correctly. "Is this some sort of mean joke?" I'd been dreading next week. I didn't have any family to spend the holiday with, and though Carter had offered to stay on campus with me, I'd refused. He needed to spend time with his parents, and if he didn't go home, it would only cause questions.

"No, I—" Her eyes widened, and then she huffed. "I was

just wondering if you were heading somewhere. You know... with someone."

And here we were, back to Grayson. "Nope, I won't be hanging out with anyone, so don't fear. I'll be alone. Thanks for your concern."

I was usually a decent judge of character, which was good as it was part of being a psychologist and social worker, but I'd clearly misjudged Sadie. Maybe social work wasn't the right calling for me after all.

She flinched. "I'm sorry. I didn't mean—"

"Don't worry, Sadie," Katherine's baby voice came from behind us. "I was actually just looking for Evie here to talk to her about next week."

Great. She must want me to mop her floors, clean her bathroom, maybe even have me use my toothbrush on her toilet to ensure I got every millimeter of grime. A.k.a., nothing she'd ask of me would be kind. I bit my tongue, not wanting to poke the beast more. The school year was *almost* half over.

She jogged to my other side, her hair and makeup perfect as usual.

"Don't you want to know why?" she pressed.

I wanted to grab her by the hair and scratch her face. I'd never disliked anyone as much as her. "Nope, but I'm sure you're going to tell me either way."

"Oh, you're so funny." She laughed way too loudly, causing some of the students next to us to glance our way.

Even Sadie's nose wrinkled, and for once, her disgust wasn't directed at me.

"I just wanted to let you know that, on Saturday, you should be at the airport at noon." Katherine looped her arm through mine and continued, "We'll take the family's private jet home."

My legs stopped moving. "What are you talking about?"

"Well, silly." She rolled her eyes, but her expression was hard. Whatever she was doing was such an act, but she was determined to seem friendly. "Like *Sadie*, I knew you'd be alone since your adopted parents died and you have no family. So I figure you needed a place to go... Unless you have other plans with *someone*?"

That intense sense of loss streaked through my heart, which I was quite certain was the point. I'd give anything to be able to return to my childhood home and have turkey and dressing with my parents. "I planned on staying in town. I'd hate to impose on your family."

"Please. You're sort of family too, right? Daddy is paying for your school. It makes sense for you to spend the holidays with us." She tugged me closer, her fingers digging into my arm, but not enough that I could be certain she was doing it on purpose. She *tsk*ed and continued, "Besides, it would be good press for him and Senator Grisham, who supported your admission. We always have Thanksgiving with Carter and his family. You want to return the favor, right?"

There was no way I'd be able to get out of it without sounding like a user. So I forced a smile and nodded. "Wouldn't miss it," I deadpanned. Though I'd tried like hell to put some excitement behind it, the words fell dead in my throat. "Thank you for the...kind invitation."

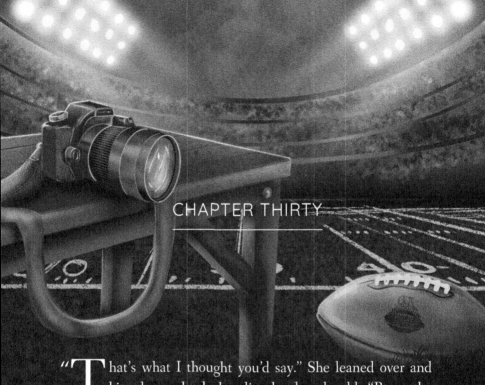

CHAPTER THIRTY

"That's what I thought you'd say." She leaned over and kissed my cheek, her lips hard and cold. "Be at the private airport at noon on Saturday and don't be late." She sauntered off.

I watched her the entire way, hoping like hell that her motive would suddenly be revealed to me.

"So you get Grayson, and now you're hanging out with the cheerleaders." Sadie scowled, her gaze pinning me in place. "Not surprising. I should've known you were just like the others." She exhaled and took several steps away. "Figures having an in with the football players was the only reason you befriended me. I hope you have a *great* Thanksgiving."

For a second, I wanted to flip her off. I didn't know how many times I'd told her that Grayson and I weren't dating, and each time, she'd pretended that she didn't care if we were or not. Now she'd thrown it in my face, and worse, Grayson and I had never even held hands. I was being punished for her misunderstanding a situation and thought poorly of because of who her dad was. "Sadie, I wasn't your friend just—"

"Save it." She waved me off and marched away from me. "I've heard it all before."

Not wanting to stand out here and have something else happen, I stomped toward the student center. Carter was in class, and I didn't want to inform Jack and Grayson about Katherine's invitation. Carter needed to hear it first.

I focused on breathing.

I tried to focus on the positives of going home with Katherine for Thanksgiving. I'd get to see Carter, but would I be able to hide how much I'd fallen for him? At least, I could tell both senators thank you again.

When I stepped through the double doors, I put my game face on and got ready to pretend all was right in the world.

EVEN THOUGH IT'D been only an hour, trying to keep up with Jack's ramblings and fool Grayson's all-too-perceptive eye had made the minutes feel like hours.

Finally, I was able to leave to meet Carter. When the Escalade came into view, I was already exhausted, and I had to work tonight. I slid into the passenger seat...and my heart skipped a beat.

Carter smiled at me, and my mind blanked momentarily. He leaned over and kissed my lips quickly and then took my hand. "Hey, you. It feels like forever."

"You have no clue," I sighed, tossing my backpack over the center console.

His forehead creased. "What's wrong?"

"Can you drive while I tell you?" I wanted to get out of here. Ever since Katherine had ambushed me, I'd felt like I was being watched.

Shifting the car into reverse, Carter pulled out.

I inhaled, gathering my thoughts, but his eyes kept flicking toward me.

He huffed. "You're killing me. I'm not known for my patience."

Instead of overthinking the story, I told him everything. The more I spoke, the stonier his face became.

"Listen, I'd *love* to have you there over the holidays." He took my hand and squeezed it before continuing, "But you can't come with her."

"Believe me, I don't want to." I leaned my head back. "But what happens if I tell her no?"

He blew out a breath. "This is a fucking disaster. You're right. She'd ride your ass." He ran a hand down his face. "There's no good answer."

"Do you think it's about her father supporting me going to school here? Some sort of punishment for him? Like, you wanted to pay for her college; then you can spend the holidays with her too?" That was the only explanation I could think of.

"Yeah, that has to be it. She pulls that passive-aggressive shit on him a lot. Besides, there's no reason she'd be targeting you since you've been lying low."

I wrung my hands. "I could tell her I have plans."

He shook his head. "You should've done that when she asked. Besides, Katherine wouldn't accept that answer. She *has* to get her way."

"Lovely." I stared out the window, watching the gates of the school pass by. "Well, I guess we'll be kinda spending the holiday together after all."

"Not the way I wanted." He squeezed my hand again. "I'd rather it be the two of us in the townhouse, but you told me no."

"Good thing because now I'd be telling you we can't do that." I laughed, but it sounded brittle. I hated not having control of my life, and I'd felt that way ever since my parents had died.

He gritted his teeth. "I promise you. I won't let anything bad happen."

The crazy thing was I believed him, despite knowing he couldn't actually be held to that promise. I nodded and stared out my window, dreading the next week.

I'D BOUGHT luggage and some new clothes despite not having the money. I didn't want to head to Thanksgiving dressed as casually as I did at HSU. I'd be with the senator and meeting the rest of Carter's family, and I wanted Carter's parents not to hate me.

Leah and Haven had gone shopping with me, and they'd talked me into getting this obnoxious pink suitcase that rolled. I walked through the small building, and a guard asked for my name. As soon as I said it and showed my license, he gave me directions to the plane. It wasn't hard. It was the only plane outside, waiting to take off.

Not only was I dreading the trip, but Carter had warned me that things between him and his father were tense. He'd confirmed that he had asked his dad to give him one hundred thousand dollars from his trust fund to help start Touchdown 4 Kids, and his dad had promptly said no. They'd argued again on the phone this morning, so the trip was starting out even less promising than we'd hoped.

Carter had gotten to the airport early, wanting to keep an eye on Katherine. The two of us couldn't show up close to the same time, so I'd sprung for an Uber. This trip had already set me back at least three weeks' pay, but I tried not to focus on that.

As I approached the plane, Carter popped out of the cabin and climbed down the ten metal stairs, then hurried to me. He took my luggage from me just as Katherine stuck her head out.

She laughed bitterly. "Carter, please. No one's here. You don't have to pretend to be the doting gentleman. You made me handle my own stuff—she can do the same."

"I'm helping her," Carter said tightly. "Unlike you, she didn't expect it." He took my luggage from me, his hand brushing mine discreetly during the exchange, causing my heart to pick up momentarily.

The stolen moment was exactly what I needed.

"Go on," he whispered in my ear. "Make sure you stay within earshot of me."

In other words, he would interfere if it came to that.

When I entered the plane, I walked to the right into a section that contained two rows of seats with dark-gray chairs facing each other. Katherine sat on the one to the right, her bare feet rubbing the gray carpet, and I chose a spot across the aisle from her.

The middle-aged flight attendant took my bag from Carter and rolled it into another section farther back in the plane that appeared to have a couch and a TV. I wouldn't mind traveling more if I had the same setup. Being rich must be nice.

Katherine gestured to the seat right in front of her. "Cartey, you can sit here and rub my feet." She leaned back and lifted her feet toward him.

"Gonna pass, *Kat*," he said, taking the seat she'd gestured to.

My chest squeezed. I wanted him to sit across from me, but I knew why he hadn't. It would cause questions.

As he sat, he glanced at me, his eyes full of regret.

Throat burning, I forced my attention from him and pulled

out my phone. I needed to do something...anything to distract me from Katherine being this close to Carter.

I had a missed text, so I opened it.

Jack: Has the devil stuck her horns in you yet?

I laughed. I couldn't help it. I hadn't realized how much I needed a smile, and of course, Jack delivered.

Me: Not yet. But we're not in the sky yet. She might wait until she knows she has me cornered.

I meant it as a joke, but it fell flat...at least on my end. What if that was exactly what she was doing?

Jack: Make sure you have holy water.

Me: Where the hell do I find holy water on an airplane?

Jack: She's not smart. Use the power of persuasion. Just tell her it is, and her skin will melt upon contact.

I chuckled once again.

"Who are you all giggly with?" Katherine leaned over in her seat.

Before I could move my screen from her view, she smirked.

"Oh, Evie. It looks like you have a crush," Katherine singsonged. "Carter, do you think Jack would be interested?"

My stomach soured, and I gritted my teeth. "We're friends. It's *nothing* like that."

Carter's jaw twitched, but he glanced at my phone then at me with the bored look he used to give me when we'd first met. The one that said he didn't trust me.

I hated how my stomach dropped, but he'd warned me that he'd have to act differently around me. That Katherine would be watching how we interacted with one another.

The attendant popped her head into the area, a fake smile

in place. "We'll be taking off in a few minutes, so please buckle your seat belts."

"Oh, yeah," Katherine said and stood, dropping herself into Carter's lap.

I waited for his hands to slide around her like they used to before we were together, but they didn't. Instead, his eyes stayed locked on me, that regret still there as he pushed Katherine away. "Not your seat."

"Come on, Carter." She moved to sit again.

But this time, he didn't even let her get close to his lap, pushing her into her seat forcefully, though not enough that she'd get hurt. He rasped, "Not happening. Quit this shit, or I'll head to the back."

She leaned forward so her cleavage bulged out of the top of her red, low-cut top. "That's not a bad idea. There's a bed back there. We could have a lot of fun, and the flight would go by quicker."

My breath caught, and I clenched my hands, which was the worst reaction I could have if we were trying to keep our relationship under wraps.

Carter sneered. "I couldn't get paid enough to touch you again, especially like that." He then pulled out his phone, trying to end the conversation.

"I could touch you," she cooed and twirled a piece of her hair around her finger. "Or lick. Whatever you're in the mood for. We have a lot of time to make up for since you've been foolish, trying to keep your distance from me. But you won't be able to this weekend."

I had to bite my lip to keep the smile off my face. He might be acting indifferent to me, but his hatred of her was genuine.

"If you think that's *actually* going to happen, you're stupid *and* pathetic," he said with disgust.

My phone dinged, and I gazed at it, watching Katherine from the corner of my eye.

Carter: I'm so sorry. Trust me, nothing is going to happen with her. Nothing. I can't stand to see that look on your face.

"You can fight it all you want, but you know our parents want us to get back together." She flopped back onto her seat. "When we get to the house, let's find some time for just the two of us. The past few dates we had were so much fun."

My stomach roiled, and I dropped my phone in my lap, not bothering to respond. I shouldn't have come, should've just dealt with whatever sort of hell she'd have thrown at me upon her return. He'd still be here with her, but at least I wouldn't have to witness it.

Carter: Babe? I can't help this.

I sighed and texted back.

Me: I know, but that doesn't make it easier.

The pilot came over the intercom. "We're cleared for take-off, and our flight will take about thirty minutes. We'll be arriving in Nashville around two p.m. EST. If you aren't buckled up, do so now."

I pulled up Spotify and selected my daylist music, not wanting to listen to Katherine anymore. My eyes grew heavy thanks to the late night of sex with Carter, and my heart followed, knowing that we'd have to keep our distance while we were at their homes.

WATER FILLED THE CAR, and I whimpered, knowing what happened next. Dad was already gone, but Mom wasn't...not yet. But still, I left her.

Cries lodged in my throat, and hands gripped my arms. Carter's voice nudged something deep within.

"Evie, it's just a dream. Wake up." His tone was frantic.

My eyes fluttered open, and the airplane came back into view, as well as Katherine and the flight attendant standing behind Carter, watching me.

Tears poured down my face. I hadn't dreamed of my parents' death in weeks. Not since Carter and I had begun sleeping together every night. But, of course, today, everything was different.

What the fuck had I been thinking? Coming with them was a horrible mistake.

My breathing was rapid, my lungs unable to absorb any oxygen.

"She's having a panic attack," the flight attendant said with concern. "Does she have medicine?"

"Hell if I know." Katherine rolled her eyes. "She's just being dramatic. She'll be fine."

"Put your head between your legs and breathe," Carter said gently, his hands on my back, trying to help guide me that way. He kneeled before me, rubbing his hand along my back. He leaned forward and whispered, "Was it the dream?"

I nodded faintly, unable to speak. I tried to focus on his hand, but all I could see was their faces...dead.

My friends back in Chattanooga told me I should get counseling—it caused a huge rift between us—but I couldn't. I didn't have insurance, so instead, I was having a meltdown on a plane.

"Breathe, Evie." Carter kept rubbing my back.

"She's fine," Katherine snapped. "She just wants attention."

Carter's teeth clenched so hard I heard them creak, but he didn't say a word.

My head leveled some, and my lungs moved a little bit easier. The fear was still there, but not quite as strong. Of course, that was when the pilot came on the intercom. "We're approaching Nashville. Please buckle up. We'll be down in ten minutes."

Carter continued to kneel in front of me. I could feel the daggers Katherine was shooting at me, so I took a deep breath, ready to pretend. "I'm fine." I sat up slowly, trying to ensure that the panic didn't overtake me. "You need to sit down."

I could see him hesitate, but I flicked my eyes in Katherine's direction.

"Okay." He nodded but took the seat across from me this time.

I laid my head back and closed my eyes, focusing on the air whooshing in and out of my lungs. This entire week was going to be awful.

When the plane landed, I wanted to get out. Between Katherine, the small space, and the memories, I felt claustrophobic. Maybe things would be better in the fresh air.

Unlike a commercial flight, we landed and were off the plane within minutes. We exited into a sizable private building with windows that covered the top and the sides.

Of course, Senator McHale, his wife, and Carter's parents were waiting there. When Senator McHale saw Katherine leading the way, he smiled and stepped toward her, but when his gaze landed on me, walking a few feet to the left of Carter, his face fell.

His brows furrowed, and he tugged at the collar of his shirt. "Evie. I'm... What are you doing here?"

CHAPTER THIRTY-ONE

My heart sank, and even Carter paused. Katherine hadn't informed the senator that I was coming.

"Surprise, Daddy," Katherine cooed in that obnoxious babyish voice. "I thought you'd *love* it if Evie joined us for Thanksgiving."

The senator's expression moved into a mask of indifference before a blinding smile filled his face. "Of course. That's...great. Isn't it, dear?" He turned to his wife, who glared at me, unblinking.

She smoothed a hand down her cream dress and wrinkled her nose. "How *lovely*."

Katherine looped her arm through mine and dragged me toward them. "I want her to stay in the room next to mine."

This was going to be worse than hell.

"How can we say no to that?" Senator McHale's smile remained in place, but the corners of his mouth twitched, the only evidence that he was forcing it. He wanted me here about as much as his wife did.

Hell, I was certain that Katherine didn't want me here either, but she had ulterior motives and was willing to deal with my presence to achieve them.

"Having another person here for the holiday season makes sense," Senator McHale said as he placed an arm around his wife. "Especially when they don't have other family to spend it with."

The words were more effective than a gut punch.

Mrs. McHale scowled but didn't contradict him.

"Son." Senator Grisham ran a hand through his graying brown hair, and the corners of his brown eyes crinkled as he strode over to Carter and patted him on the back. "I can't wait until your game next week. You're going to take the place by storm when you beat Alabama."

The blank expression settled back into Carter's face. "Good to see you too, Dad." His jaw clenched, and I knew he was thinking about their call this morning.

Mrs. Grisham nodded at Carter but stayed next to her daughter, whose name, I'd learned from Carter, was Serenity. Both women had light-blonde hair, but Serenity's eyes were a warm brown like her father's instead of the sky blue of her mother's. She wore ripped jeans and a crop top while Mrs. Grisham was dressed in a cobalt pantsuit.

Serenity didn't even look up from her phone to acknowledge her brother.

My heart ached at the greeting he'd just received from all three members of his family. His dad was focused only on football, and his stepmom and half sister didn't seem interested in him at all. I didn't know as much about him as I'd thought.

Clearing his throat, Senator McHale straightened his shoulders. "We thought you all might be hungry. After your luggage gets loaded into the vehicles, we can head out to a late lunch somewhere."

The last thing I wanted to do was go out to eat, but I held my tongue. I was at their mercy.

"That sounds great," Katherine said as she sauntered over to Carter and reached for his hand.

I thought I might puke. She was purposely making a move on Carter in front of everyone.

When he dodged her hand and flicked a glance at me, my heartbeat steadied. For a moment, I'd feared that he'd allow her to take it. The gold in his eyes sparked, which said more than words ever could.

No matter what, he was keeping his promise.

"What's going on here?" Senator McHale's brows furrowed. "Are you two in a fight or something?"

He didn't know, and worse, he appeared upset that Carter had rejected his daughter. Coming here had been a *monumental* mistake. The best thing I could do was to run to the plane and beg them to take me back. At this point, I was willing to pay any price as long as they accepted credit cards.

Katherine said, "Just a little disagreement," just as Carter said, "We broke up."

Pivoting toward Carter, Katherine glared, but it didn't faze him as he took several large steps away from her.

"Wait, you're not together?" Mrs. McHale huffed. "When did that happen?"

Senator McHale glanced back and forth between Katherine and Carter.

"The summer before registration." Carter shrugged. "You all knew that."

"But we've had fun during our last few dates." Katherine winked and giggled. "So don't give up hope yet."

That was the second time she'd talked about how much fun they'd had, and she seemed to mean it. My heart ached, wondering what they'd talked about and what exactly the two of them had done together when others were watching them.

"Yeah, well, that's why I thought you were back together." Senator Grisham cleared his throat and arched a brow at his son.

Huffing, Carter crossed his arms. "We absolutely are not and will not be getting back together. There are some things that people can't come back from."

Even though he didn't care about her, I knew that catching Katherine sleeping with someone else when they were together still bothered him. Cheating was never fun, especially when you were the injured party. But thinking about him laughing with her, even if it was for the cameras, was a little hard to swallow when both their families were practically begging them to get back together.

"You know how young people are." Mrs. McHale laughed a little too loudly. "I'm sure they'll figure it out."

"On that note, I'm not up for lunch." Carter yawned and stretched. "I'm exhausted, and I don't want to get too off my training schedule with another game coming up so soon. I need to work out and rest."

Thank goodness he'd said that. I wasn't up for it either, but at least, if I was forced to go, I wouldn't have to watch Katherine try to rub herself all over him.

Mr. Grisham nodded. "Very true, son. You should keep up with your workout schedule. Do you want me to call a trainer to help this week?"

"I know what I'm doing." Carter put his hands in his jeans, avoiding his father's gaze. "I just want to go home and settle in. It's been a few months."

"Heading home sounds good to me." Serenity didn't bother to look up from her phone, but at least she was listening.

Katherine pouted. "But we always have lunch."

"Things change." Carter tilted his head back. "It'll be good for you to learn that."

"Actually, this probably works out for the best." Senator McHale closed his eyes, looking annoyed. "The office called, and I need to handle something."

"But I just got here." Katherine stuck out her bottom lip even more. "We can still go to lunch without them."

I winced. Between reliving my parents' deaths and watching the show that Katherine just put on, I didn't feel like going anywhere.

"Maybe lunch tomorrow would be better," Carter suggested, glancing in my direction.

That right there told me everything. He knew I wasn't up for it. A part of me wondered if that was the reason he'd said he wanted to head home. A lump lodged in my throat.

Senator McHale followed Carter's gaze and scrutinized me. I wanted to rub my eyes again to ensure the tears were gone. Nonetheless, after my panic attack and as hard as I'd been crying, there was no hiding my turmoil.

I averted my gaze, embarrassed. I hated appearing weak, especially in front of both senators. I didn't want either of them to think I was trying to get more out of them.

Senator McHale touched his daughter's arm. "Why don't you go shopping, and I'll cover the trip? Then we'll have dinner tonight at the house."

She pouted, but then a twinkle gleamed in her eyes. "Shopping?"

Senator McHale laughed. "I thought that might garner your attention."

My eye twitched. Surely, he wasn't going to bribe her. And surely, she wouldn't let a shopping spree win over spending time with her dad. I'd give anything to have more time with my parents...even give up college.

"What would be my spending allowance?" She crossed her arms.

This was a negotiation. My stomach soured.

"Nothing over ten thousand."

I ground my teeth to keep my jaw from dropping. And here I'd thought the one time Mom told me I could buy anything I wanted as long as it was under five hundred dollars was a big deal.

She tossed some of her hair over her shoulder. "I guess that will be okay, though I was hoping for more."

More? She had no clue how fortunate she was.

"You drive a tough bargain." The senator removed a black credit card from his wallet and handed it over. "Fifteen, tops. Got it?"

"Thanks, Daddy." She beamed. Then she sauntered over to me and looped her arm through mine again.

I couldn't stop myself from taking a step away. However, she held me fast to her side.

"Want to join us, Serenity?" She waved her dad's credit card. "I bet your daddy will let you get some stuff too."

"It's been three months since I've seen—" Carter started.

But Serenity dropped her phone, the device suddenly forgotten, and her eyes lit up. "Oh, Dad. *Please.*"

The gold in Carter's eyes vanished, and his face became stoic. He'd wanted to spend time with his sister, but a shopping spree was more important to her than her brother. My heart ached, not only for him but for everyone here. They valued money over everything.

Mr. Grisham frowned. "But Carter just got here."

"It'd be good for her to get off her phone," Mrs. Grisham suggested, rubbing her husband's arm.

"Well." Mr. Grisham bobbed his head, conflicted.

With his normal blank expression, Carter waved a hand. "Let her. I need some rest anyway."

I heard the sadness in his voice. His comment about making sure I enjoyed his company rang through my head, and my stomach turned. Were these the family members who'd made him feel disregarded? From what both he and Jack had said, it had been someone close to him, but what would Serenity gain by using Carter? They had the same father.

"Fine." Mr. Grisham removed his wallet and handed Serenity an eerily similar card. "Same budget, not a dollar more. Got it?"

"Got it." Serenity snatched the card from his hand like she feared he'd change his mind at any second.

"It's girl bonding time!" Katherine giggled.

I'd never felt more out of place than I did at this moment. This was definitely not the girl bonding time I wanted, and there was one person in particular who I wished would break a nail or fall off her stilettos. For some reason, I suspected that would upset her more than most anything.

"Do you mind having your driver give us a ride home too?" Mrs. McHale asked the Grishams. One of her eyebrows twitched a little, like she was trying to arch it but the muscle wouldn't move. "That way, our driver can take the girls."

"That's no problem," Senator Grisham said, patting Carter's arm again. "I'm glad that at least my son wants to head home and spend some time with me."

Katherine turned to her mother, bottom lip sticking out. "You don't want to come with us?"

Mrs. McHale shook her head. "I need to get home and ensure Evie's room is ready."

"Fine." Katherine huffed, but her cobalt eyes darkened to navy. "We'll have more fun with the three of us anyway." She snagged Serenity's hand and dragged the two of us through the all-glass doors of the terminal. Then I was able to free myself and fall a little behind them.

With the high heels clicking behind us and the men's shoes scuffing the floor, there was no doubt that the others followed. The back of my neck tingled, which meant that Carter was staring at me.

One pair of heels clacked faster, and soon, Mrs. McHale appeared at my side. She smiled coldly and leaned close, whispering so that only I could hear. "I don't know what your endgame is, but my husband thinks of you as a wounded animal. Don't think you'll be around long term. I'll make sure of that."

A chill ran down my spine as she paused, waiting for the others to catch up. I kept moving forward, trying to pretend nothing strange had happened.

Outside, two black limos were parked at the curb with two men dressed in black standing at the back door of each. Katherine dragged us to the one on the left as Senator McHale informed the older gray-haired man with a mustache of the change of plans.

Serenity and Katherine climbed into the limo, and I stole a look at Carter. He grimaced and mouthed *I'm sorry* before I climbed into the limo.

As I slid onto the white leather seat in the back, Katherine and Serenity moved to the other side and poured themselves huge glasses of champagne. They giggled as they downed the entire contents. The driver shut the door without saying anything.

There was no question that both Katherine and Serenity were underage, but I, too, kept my mouth shut.

"Seriously?" Katherine said and rolled her eyes, nudging Serenity's shoulder.

Serenity glanced at me, her brows furrowed. "What?"

"She's judging us for drinking." Katherine leaned back and tilted her chin. "Let me guess, you're going to tell your *lover* on me since I brought you here and shoved you in his face?"

My head snapped back. She must have figured out on the plane that Carter and I were together. "What?" I gasped, unsure what else to say.

Lifting a hand, Serenity pursed her lips. "Who's her lover?"

This was *not* the way I wanted Carter's sister to learn I was dating her brother. There were so many better ways than Katherine running her mouth.

I opened my mouth to attempt to salvage things when Katherine said, "My *daddy*. You saw his reaction to her being here, didn't you?"

"What? No!" My chest contracted. I hated that she actually thought it was possible. Now I almost wished she'd said Carter.

Katherine narrowed her eyes. "Come on, Evie. That's the only thing that makes sense. I know how these things work."

"Ew." Serenity's nose scrunched, and she scooted closer to Katherine, farther away from me. "Then why did you bring her here?"

"To keep up appearances." Katherine rolled her eyes. "I may be upset with Daddy, but I don't want anyone to find out. That would ruin him *and* our family politically."

Serenity studied me again and snorted.

My face flamed. I hated that these two were making me feel worthless. I'd never been ashamed of anything before in my life, and I refused to let these two entitled twats make me feel this way—and yet... "I'm not sleeping with your dad. Nor did I ask to come with you."

"Right." Katherine snorted then tugged Serenity closer and started whispering in her ear.

Though it was probably thirty minutes, it felt like hours before we pulled up to several luxe white buildings and the limo stopped.

I blinked, trying to get my bearings.

We entered a boutique called Posh, where I felt severely underdressed. Though Serenity and Katherine were both in tanks and jeans, they were of high-caliber name brands, while I was wearing Walmart.

Everywhere I glanced, gorgeous, put together people lingered. The few I locked eyes with turned up their noses at me.

Katherine marched to the women's section, seeming to know the store better than HSU back home. She started going through racks of clothes with Serenity right beside her. I hung back, afraid to touch a thing for fear that I might stain it.

Suddenly, Katherine pulled out a dark-purple sundress and beamed. "Hey, this is cheap. You should try this on. It would look great on you."

That caught Serenity's attention. "It would. You should get it." She glanced at the price tag. "It's only five hundred dollars!"

I gulped. Only *five hundred*. A laugh bubbled in my throat at even thinking that sentence. "I'm good, but thanks."

"You're no fun." Serenity huffed then turned back to skimming the clothes.

Both she and Katherine pulled outfit after outfit out as I leaned against the wall. I was quite certain a root canal would be more fun than this. At least, then I'd get pain medicine.

After about forty-five minutes of handing off item after item to the salesclerks to put in the dressing room for them, Serenity rubbed her hands. "I'm going to try on some clothes."

"I'll be there soon." Katherine popped her head around the rack. "Don't decide on anything until I see it on you."

When Serenity hurried off, Katherine bounded toward me, the dark-purple sundress in her hands that she'd mentioned to me.

My head screamed *run away*, but I didn't have anywhere to go.

"Remember this," she hissed.

"What?" She was up to something, and I wasn't in the mood to play any games. She already had Serenity thinking the worst of me.

"That you don't fit in here." She pushed a finger into my chest . "I don't know what you're trying to pull, but you won't win."

I laughed. I couldn't help it. "You're the one who invited me. Remember? Or did you actually believe the lie you told Serenity?"

"Please. *Something* is going on with you and Daddy." She lifted her chin. "And now you want Carter. That whole meltdown on the plane, trying to wear him down? Somehow it worked. He noticed you, but when I get proof of whatever you're doing, the world is going to know what you are."

My breath caught, but I refused to let her know that she was getting to me. I hadn't done anything, so there wouldn't be a damn thing to find. "Go ahead."

She sneered. "Oh, I will. You'll see that you will *never* truly be accepted here...*never* be part of this world." She licked her lips. "Enjoy it while you can because I'll show both Daddy and Carter what your true plans are. I will *protect* them even if it hurts because, in the long term, it'll save them from even more pain and more betrayal. And I'll be there, watching you fall."

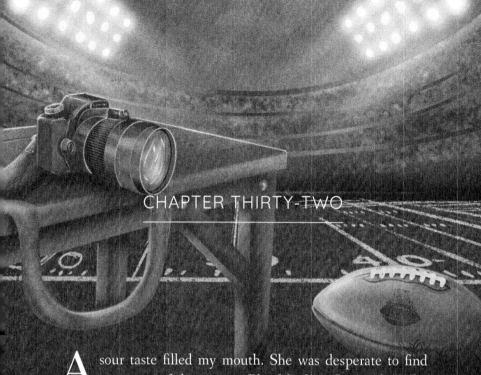

CHAPTER THIRTY-TWO

A sour taste filled my mouth. She was desperate to find some sort of dirt on me. Blood boiling, I gritted, "Why are you always such a *bitch* to me?"

Her face transformed into her gorgeous camera-ready smile. "Oh, honey, I don't hate you. That would mean I care about you." She *tsk*ed. "I don't. You're *nothing* to me. But I do care about my dad and Carter." She got even more in my face, her overly sweet perfume choking me as she continued, "You're a threat I need to expose."

Laughter bubbled out of me. I knew better than to react, but I couldn't help it. "I'm a threat?" I pointed at myself. "You're the one who accused me of being your dad's mistress, yet *you* were the one who asked me to come here." I turned my finger toward her. "What would your mother think if she knew that? And, in regard to Carter, you *cheated* on him. So, *please*, tell me what I'm missing here?"

She scowled, somehow still retaining her beauty. I bet she could make shit look good, which made sense with the putrid personality she had brewing underneath her facade. "That right there proves you don't understand *this* world." She stretched out her arms, indicating the shop. "*You* don't belong here or at HSU." She lifted her chin, staring down her nose at me. "And I don't know what you think you know about Carter, but he'd have cheated on me eventually. They all do. I just beat him to it and bruised his ego." She laughed bitterly.

My stomach clenched because the pain in her eyes indicated she believed what she said.

But I couldn't fathom Carter *ever* doing that, even to her. "You're wrong about him. He's not a cheater."

"Because you know him *so well*?" she spat, examining me. "Yes, the plane ride told you everything you ever needed to know about him."

I wanted to shoot her the bird. In fact, I craved it. I knew him better than she ever had, but she was ready to go to war with me. And it was something I wouldn't divulge unless Carter gave me permission. So I pivoted to a safer topic. "Fine. Then let's focus on your mom."

In fact, knowing that Carter had slept with Katherine in the past made me want to vomit. I understood he'd dated her mainly due to expectations, but knowing she was like *this* and he'd still been with her made my stomach revolt.

I had to remember that she was his past and I was his present…and, hopefully, future.

I froze. I was in deep trouble.

"My mother will be fine." Katherine rolled her eyes. "It's more important that I figure out whatever you're up to." She caressed my face, digging her nails into my skin ever so slightly. Enough to leave a temporary mark, but nothing long lasting.

Refusing to back down, I stayed in place, my eyes locked with hers. I snapped, "There is *nothing* going on between us. Hell, I never met your father before that day in the hospital."

"You're a convincing actress," she cooed, forcing my head to turn side to side. "But I know how this world works, and people like *you* are the best at pretending. I mean, look at what Carter's mom did to him, and you're just like her."

Carter's mom?

That hit close to home. He'd pretty much told me this, but not as directly as Katherine.

"But just know, my daddy's offer to attend *my* school has made you my enemy." Her lips tightened. "I tried playing nice and ignoring you, but when you befriended the football team, you infringed on *my* world." She released me and scrunched her nose in disgust. "Now I'm more determined than ever to uncover your secret."

"I'm not hiding anything," I said a little too loudly, and I flinched internally.

She beamed. She'd picked up on my lie.

I lifted my chin, refusing to cower, which was probably the worst thing I could do. But I was so damn tired of taking her crap. "You won't find anything."

"Sure." She rolled her eyes and giggled. "Believe what you want. Now, I've got to try on dresses with my future sister-in-law." She patted my cheek a little too hard. "Stay here and be a good girl. Don't cause any problems." Then she turned and sauntered away.

Unsure what to do, I stood there. I didn't want to call Carter and tell him what happened. He'd get upset, and he had enough going on at home with his dad and stepmom. And I didn't want to call Jack and confide in him. That felt wrong without talking to Carter first. And Grayson...he was a sore subject for Carter.

All I wanted to do was go back to HSU. I had Haven and Leah there and could work and make some money. A part of me wanted to beg Senator McHale to send me back, but that would make things worse since I'd look guilty.

A deep ache of loneliness sank into me, and my eyes burned. What I wouldn't give to be able to call my parents and tell them everything that had happened. To hear their voices again. To smell their scents, which I was already forgetting.

I blinked, trying to keep my tears at bay and ignore the stares of the people around me. The walls seemed to close in.

I had to get out of here.

Striding out the doors, I decided to wait outside for them. No one would miss me anyway.

A FEW HOURS LATER, I found some solace in my temporary room...if you could call it that. It was gigantic, double the size of the living room in the house I'd lived in with my parents.

I lay on a huge king bed with a headboard made of fuzzy beige material and stared at the off-white walls. Even the sheets on the bed were white and beige as if whoever decorated the room had an aversion to color. The windows were neat though, with arched tops, and they overlooked a large, immaculate green backyard. A huge TV hung on the wall across from me, and I flipped through the channels.

My phone dinged, and I glanced down.

Grayson: Hope everything is going well. If you need to talk to someone, I'm here.

My stomach clenched. I wanted to be friends with Grayson, but sometimes, it was hard trying to keep that friendship without him hoping for more. Still, he knew I was with Carter.

Me: Thanks. Hope you're having a good holiday too.

Grayson: They're not being cruel, right? If they

are, I could come get you. You don't have to be stuck there.

I sighed. I should've never responded. I needed him to get the hint to drop it.

Me: I'm fine. Thank you for offering. See you soon.

When my phone dinged again, I cringed, but then the name that showed on my screen had my heart fluttering.

Carter: How's it going?

My chest expanded. Even with his family issues, he was worried about me.

Me: It's going. Hiding—er—settling into my room. How are things with your dad?

Carter: We fought again over the money I want for Touchdown 4 Kids. He told me he won't release a dime for it. It's pointless to keep arguing.

I frowned. Touchdown 4 Kids meant so much to Carter. I hated that his dad didn't understand how important the organization was to him, but I didn't want to add to the problem by saying so over text.

Carter: I miss you like crazy and it's only been a few hours.

Me: Same. A week here is going to be torture.

My eyes burned with tears. I did miss Carter even though he wasn't far away. And it wasn't because we couldn't have sex. I missed just being with him, laughing, talking, and smiling.

Carter: I'm two doors down if you need me.

Two doors down. Of course, they lived in the same neighborhood, but right now, it felt like we lived in two separate worlds.

Me: That would only cause more questions.

Carter: Meet tonight? I'm going to bail on dinner.

Damn, that sounded so tempting.

Me: Dinner? I didn't even know that was a thing.

Carter: It was just planned, and Katherine's best friend, Lily, and her parents are going to be there too. You could use that as an excuse on top of jet lag.

Me: An evening with just you…hmm…I don't know. Sounds dangerous.

Carter: Never stopped you before.

My breath caught. He was right. The cost of spending time with him was worth the risk, but I couldn't let it go *that* easy.

Me: What do I get out of it?

Carter: Riveting conversation and a chance to touch my body.

Need knotted in my stomach. There was nothing better than touching him.

Me: Touch your body? Please. That's more for you than me.

Carter: I could touch yours too…if you behave.

Me: I'll consider it.

Carter: Please. You're just as much putty for me as I am you. See you in three hours. I'll come to you. Leave the back door unlocked. A part of the fence is broken, I'll sneak in through there.

I dropped the phone on the bed and glanced at the ceiling, praying that the next three hours zoomed by.

"Haven, tell me I'm not crazy for having Carter over?" I paced the gigantic living room in front of the wooden double front doors. The wall that faced the side yard was three massive windows with arches on top, and the wood floor didn't creak anywhere. A beige rug lay between the chocolate-brown couch and love seat with a dark wooden coffee table in the middle.

"You're seriously asking if it's insane for your boyfriend to come visit you?" Haven snorted. "It would be stupid if he didn't."

"But—"

"Oh, I know. You've got to keep your relationship secret from the evil wench, but come on, E, what can she actually *do* to you?" Haven sighed. "You allow her to have that power over you. Screw her, and then screw your hot-ass man—who is expected to be the first draft pick for the NFL, by the way."

She acted as though I didn't already know that last part. I was so damn proud of him, though that fact also caused me issues sleeping some nights. I feared it would be the beginning of the end for us, so I tried to focus on the time we had together now. "She's actually got power though. Even Carter's afraid."

"Carter's afraid of the family drama she'll cause. That's it." Haven huffed. "Which, come on. He needs to grow a pair. His family isn't going to disown him or anything."

After what I'd seen today, I assumed that was exactly what Carter feared. His stepmom and sister were disinterested in him, and his dad seemed to only want to talk football. Now I knew that his mom had caused problems for him, and his life wasn't as picture perfect as I'd assumed.

A scratching sound came from the other end of the house, and I yelped.

"Are you okay?" Haven asked with concern.

"Yeah, he just got here." My heart pounded, and I was certain it wasn't only from being startled. "I gotta go."

"Remember, safe sex, boo." She chuckled. "I get you wanna lock him down, but don't do it—"

"I'm *not*." I hung up, snorting. A baby right now, when I was trying to get my life in order, was the last thing I needed. And I'd never do that to Carter.

Anticipation buzzed through me, and I hurried to the back door as he cracked it open and peeked inside. When he saw me, he opened it wide, body filling the doorframe, his jeans and sage polo shirt deliciously tight.

The gold in his eyes twinkled. "Hey. I knew you wanted to see me."

I wrinkled my nose but stepped back, allowing him in. "Please, I thought you were the pizza guy."

"Uh-huh," he murmured and kissed me.

Grabbing his collar, I pulled him inside, never allowing our mouths to disengage as our tongues collided.

He groaned, pulling me tight against his chest, my hands tangling in his hair. I needed him after the shit day I'd had, and he seemed to need me too.

He lifted me by my ass, my legs wrapping around his waist, and pulled away from my mouth, kissing down my neck as my hands gloried in the muscles of his chest.

His body did so many things to me. Things that no other man had ever made me experience.

He carried me upstairs, and I directed him to the room I was staying in. He shut the door then pressed me into the wall and pulled away to tug my shirt off. My breaths became labored as he kissed down my chest and lifted a breast from one bra cup. His finger rubbed over my nipple, causing a fire to course through me.

We shouldn't be having sex, but my brain grew fuzzy. When he licked and sucked on my breast, my body arched against him, finding the friction I needed.

"I need you," he murmured, his tongue rolling over me again. "But we need to make it fast. I made sure they went to dinner, so we're safe if we make it quick. Unless you don't—"

"Please," I moaned, not even caring that I was begging for this connection with him. I moved my hands to his jeans, unfastening them and pushing them and his boxer briefs down. He sprang out, hard and ready, and desire soared through me.

He chuckled as he hiked up my skirt and murmured, "Was this on purpose for easier access?"

My cheeks flamed. I hadn't expected him to be so willing, but now that he was, I was glad about my wardrobe decision, so I nodded, unable to speak.

Pushing my panties to the side, he set his tip to my entrance. The sensation had me wanting to push against him when I realized something. "Condom."

"Fuck." He pulled away and dug through his pockets, finding one and ripping the package open with his teeth then sliding it on.

Once he was covered, he repositioned himself and thrust into me. We didn't usually do hard and fast, but today we both needed the release, and to feel each other.

Each time he entered me, he hit deeper, and I ground my hips against him. His mouth found mine, and we kissed, not breaking the connection even when we got sloppy and fast.

I'd felt so alone all day, but not now. Not with him here, choosing to spend the evening with me and connecting with me in a way that we reserved only for one another.

It wasn't long before an orgasm ripped through me, and he quickened his pace, riding out my pleasure. As my ecstasy ebbed, his body convulsed with his own release. We stilled, and he peppered kisses all over my face.

"Evie, damn." He pulled away, placing his forehead against mine. "I..."

My heart pounded as I waited to see how he would end this very important sentence.

That was when steps sounded in the hallway. The two of us froze, and then he jerked away from me.

I managed to pull my shirt and skirt down, but just as Carter pulled up his pants, the door swung open.

Katherine's hard gaze landed on the two of us, her mouth gaping open.

CHAPTER THIRTY-THREE

My heart clenched as Katherine closed her mouth. Anger suffused her face, replacing the shock.

There was no way Carter and I could salvage this. Not with my messy hair and Carter fastening his belt.

Carter turned to face me, unzipped his pants, and reached into his boxer briefs to remove the condom.

Lovely.

"Are you fucking serious right now?" Katherine shrieked. "Fucking her is why you didn't come to dinner?" She stalked farther into the room, shaking in rage.

His face twisted in disgust. "No, I didn't come to fuck her. I came to spend time with her, and you being here is getting in the way of that."

"You chose *her* over dinner with our families?" Her chest heaved. "You're falling for her bullshit, and honestly, I'm turned off by it all. I get you wanting to sleep around and get your revenge before you get back together with me. But, damn, Carter. Punishment received, you can stop now. This was a low blow, and if you keep this shit up, I won't want to get back together with you," she spat, gesturing to me.

Carter stepped in front of me, blocking me from her view.

"You *still* think I want to get back together with you?" He snorted. "How much blunter can I be? I've told you that you're nothing to me, that we're over, that we aren't ever going to get back together." He huffed, and his back tensed. "Are you that dense? I only did those outings with you because I committed to them, and our families were aware. It meant *nothing* to me, and every time I dropped you off, I felt relieved. I have no interest in even being friends with you."

She sneered. "You want to move on? To some leech with dead parents?" She lifted her hands. "Fine, but *not* with *her*. She's our dads' charity case!"

I gasped, pain swirling through me.

"Do *not* talk to her or about her in that way." Carter's hands fisted. "She's a way better person than you can ever think of being, and you know what? I like that she's not from *this world*. Maybe that's what we all need. I'm tired of all the fucked-up games and disinterest we all show one another unless we're trying to get something from someone."

Warmth expanded in my chest. This time, he wasn't backing down or saying that I was a one-time thing.

We weren't hiding anymore, and I was both thrilled and petrified.

"I'm sure your dad felt the same way about your *mom* at one time." Katherine crossed her arms, daring him. "But I guess making mistakes like that is in the genes."

"She's *nothing* like my mother," Carter snarled. "Don't compare them. You're just saying shit because you don't know anything about Evie."

I placed a hand on Carter's back, wanting him to know I was there for him. His muscles twitched beneath my fingers. I was fairly certain that if I walked around him in a more visible show of support, it would make things worse.

She scoffed. "And how do you know that? Because she had some manufactured meltdown on the plane? Don't be so stupid. It's your dick talking."

Carter took a step forward, and I moved up beside him. I didn't want him to think he had to fight this battle alone. We were in this together now.

He glanced at me and asked, "Did you know that Evie walks to and from school every day?"

"So?" Katherine stomped her foot.

"Did you know that she was walking home from her place of employment late at night when it wasn't safe?"

She shrugged. "Clearly, nothing ever happened to her."

"So? Why didn't she ask your dad for money?" He arched a brow. "I know for a fact he offered to cover her room and board, and she turned him down."

Katherine threw her hands out to her sides. "It's part of her game." She rolled her eyes. "She can't make it obvious that she's after money."

I laughed bitterly. "I never asked for a cent from your dad."

"Oh, whatever." She placed her hands on her hips, glaring at me. "Senators don't just roll in somewhere and offer some girl almost the same age as their daughter a full ride if there's not *something* going on." She begged Carter, "Don't be so stupid. She's going to wind up pregnant, and you're going to have a child in the exact same situation you were raised in." She pointed at him and then herself. "She's not like us."

Something inside me snapped, and I boiled over. "How many times are you going to repeat that?" I lifted my chin, refusing to cower. "Fine, I'm different. I'm not cruel. I don't take people to a store I know they can't afford and then belittle them in front of everyone. Or make up vicious rumors about them, knowing there's not a shred of evidence. You just wanted to give me a bad name and reputation." I straightened my shoulders. "You're right. I'm not like *you*. And I hope I never am."

Katherine's entire body trembled. "That's how things are done to get what you want. Do you think all politicians are great? Do you think you're the only one my dad has cheated on my mom with?"

"I've *never* slept with your dad," I gritted out. "What is your hang-up about that?"

"Listen here, you bitch." Katherine stalked toward me, but Carter grabbed her arm.

"Katherine, stop this. *Now*," he commanded.

Her bottom lip stuck out. "Are you really falling for her act? After everything?"

"It's not an act. The only person who tried to manipulate and control me was you. I'm done." Carter took my hand and tugged me toward the door. "We have nothing left to say. Now Evie and I are going to take a walk."

"If you think—" she snarled.

"You're going to leave Evie and me alone," Carter cut her off, his irises darkening.

She tilted her head back. "Or what?"

"Both our families will learn *everything* about what you did this last summer and the visit you made to Dr. Gotham."

Blanching, Katherine seemed to turn to stone. "You wouldn't."

Her reaction was startling. Whatever Dr. Gotham represented must be bad.

"I will, unless you leave us alone." Carter's jaw clenched.

She breathed harder. "Is this really how it's going to be between us now?"

Carter nodded. "It is. And if you're going to be catty, I'll do just as much to you as you do to us."

She spat, "Us? Really?"

"*Us.*" He raised the used condom.

My stomach dropped, and I let out a very faint yelp. I couldn't believe he'd done that.

Her nose wrinkled even more, and I cringed.

"Let's get your shit and go." Carter squatted by my bag, which I hadn't unpacked, scanning everything in it.

He knew what I'd put in the bag because he'd teased me the entire time I'd been packing. I rolled my shoulders. "Go?" I'd come here to stay with the McHales, and I couldn't afford a hotel room. I'd spent everything I could spare on clothes just so I didn't look like a slob.

"Yeah, do you think I'm leaving you here with *her?*" He gestured to Katherine, who was now blocking the doorway.

Her nostrils flared, and her cheeks turned a shade of crimson I'd never believed was possible.

This was bad. He went from keeping our relationship a secret to having me desert a furious Katherine. "I'll be fine."

"Yeah, you heard her," Katherine snarled. "She'll be fine."

He zipped up the suitcase. "You didn't unpack anything." Then he placed it on its wheels and rolled it toward the doorway Katherine was blocking.

"What do you think you're doing?" Katherine's voice was sharp. "She came here with me."

"Did she? It sounds like you brought her here to be your punching bag." He leaned back on his heels. "She'll be better off at my house. I don't trust you, especially knowing how selfish and vindictive you are."

My heart pounded. This was all coming to a head now, and of course, I was in Nashville, hundreds of miles away from campus...the only place I could call home now.

"You can't. Daddy will ask..." She trailed off, jaw twitching.

"Why I took her home with me?" Carter asked, taking my hand. "Not my problem. You can figure out an explanation. Lie like you always do. I don't give a damn. Just don't talk shit about Evie."

Though a part of me knew leaving would make things worse in the long run, a larger part was relieved. If I stayed, as soon as Carter left, she'd be on me.

He released my luggage and placed a hand on her shoulder, pushing her back gently but firmly, getting her out of the way.

Once she was far enough back, the two of us hurried past her toward the stairs.

"You're gonna regret this," she shouted at our backs.

"Be careful what you threaten," Carter tossed over his shoulder.

Soon, we were down the hallway and out the front door.

Each stride of Carter's was two of mine, and I huffed, trying to keep up with him. The only thing I could think was that this was going to be a disaster, but I wasn't sure what else to do.

We marched down the sidewalk and up the steep road to the right. When we reached the edge of the McHales' property, where there was a huge line of privacy trees, Carter slowed.

He growled. "I'm so sorry. I should have known better, but I missed you all damn day."

"It's okay. I needed you too." I squeezed his hand back. "Today was rough for me as well, but probably not nearly as bad as yours." The way his dad and stepmom had looked at him in the airport broke my heart. However, I couldn't help but fear how his family was going to react to me being there.

"We should've just stayed at the townhouse," he sighed as we passed a gigantic brick house on the right.

Yesterday, I would've told him he needed to spend time with his family, but now I wasn't so sure.

We continued our trek, anger rolling off him.

I tried to ignore the jealousy that twinged in my heart, but it was hard. His reaction to his and Katherine's altercation bothered me. I didn't like that he was upset, but I had to remind myself that they had grown up together.

We turned and went down the winding front walkway to the next house. It was almost double the size of the McHales', with a gray metal roof and walls made entirely of windows. Despite light emitting through the cracks of the front door, the windows were so dark I couldn't see anything but my reflection. They must be blocked so that no one could see what was going on inside.

Carter slipped his key in the front door and swung it open.

As expected, all the lights inside were on as if they didn't have to pay for electricity. Not only that, but the house was bright since everything inside was basically white. The walls were faint off-white, and the floors were a near-white bamboo wood. A sizable, L-shaped white leather couch sat in the center of the room with a plush, light-beige, expensive-looking rug underneath the white wooden coffee table.

I refused to wear white pants or shirts because I couldn't keep them clean, and his family did *this*. I blinked, trying to comprehend how pristine it all was.

"Welcome to our humble abode," Carter said flippantly as he strolled into the house, not bothering to wipe his shoes on the brown welcome mat.

Stopping, I refused to step inside the living room. I lifted one of my shoes to inspect the bottom.

He turned around to face me. "What's wrong?"

I put my foot down to check the other. "Maybe I should take my shoes off." Knowing me, I'd stepped in mud.

"It's wood. We can clean it." He rolled his eyes and pressed his lips together, trying to hide that blasted smile. "Besides, the cleaning crew mops every day."

"Every *day*?" That seemed a little obsessive.

He shrugged. "My stepmom is a little anal about things like that." He waved me in. "Come on. I still have Evie withdrawals."

How could I say no to *that*? Taking a deep breath, I tiptoed inside. After moving in about five feet, I spun around and almost cried in relief when there wasn't a dirty trail following me.

Carter went left of the living room to a large spiral staircase. I climbed up after him and followed him down the hallway.

He stopped at the first of two doors on the left.

"I'm going to put you in the room beside me." He opened the door and moved inside. "That way, you can sneak into my bed every night."

"Whoa," I panted as I stepped into yet another white-ass room. The king bed was pushed against the wall, the headboard solid white, and the bedding was white too. The lights in here were so damn blinding I wanted to stab my eyes out. "Your parents live here, so I'm not sure if that's wise."

"Fine. I'll come to you. There's no way we're going to stay separated while you're this close." He rolled the suitcase against the wall. "Even though I hate what's probably going to result from this evening, I love you being here. Things aren't the same without you."

Butterflies took flight in my stomach. "Even though you're upset that you and Katherine are fighting?"

He arched a brow. "You think I'm upset because of *her*?"

I shoved my hands into my jeans pockets. "Well, I mean... You wanted to keep us a secret, and then you had to threaten her..." I trailed off, trying to find the words to tell him that it was okay to express his emotions.

Closing the distance between us, he wrapped his arms around my waist. He rasped, "I'm not upset over Katherine, Evie. I'm upset about whatever horrible story she's going to tell her parents about you and everything that's going to happen because of that. She's going to make things so much harder on both of us for the rest of the week." He cupped my cheek, the gold in his eyes warming. "Don't ever worry that I care about her anymore. We were friends growing up, but she changed. She's nothing to me, especially compared to you."

My cheeks hurt from my smile.

"There she is." He kissed my nose and then snagged my arm, dragging me to the door. "Come on," he said, pulling me to the next room down on the left.

Thankfully, his room was completely different than the others. His walls were the color of the ocean, which wasn't surprising given his love of water, and there was a gigantic picture of a river hanging over the headboard of his dark cherrywood king-size bed.

I cringed at the picture, and he followed my gaze.

"Shit," he murmured as he removed his shoes and climbed onto the royal-purple HSU comforter on his bed.

"Don't." This was his childhood space. I didn't want him to change a thing because of my presence. "I'll be okay."

He lifted a brow. "Are you sure?"

I wanted to say no, but I forced a smile and nodded, averting my gaze. In the left corner of his room, a bookcase was filled with football and track trophies, and a PlayStation sat next to his TV. Just further evidence that he set his mind on goals and had the determination to succeed.

He flopped onto the bed and opened his arms. "Get over

here so I can hold you and we can catch up on some *Walking Dead*."

I giggled, feeling a sense of peace for the first time all day. And, of course, I found it in his arms as usual.

He turned on the TV, and I faced him, resting my head on his chest.

When the show came on, I forgot where we were. It almost felt like we were back in his townhouse, safe and sound. And before I realized it, the two of us were engrossed in all things death.

A while later, a loud knock on Carter's door coincided with a zombie taking a bite out of someone on the television. I yelped, sitting up, my gaze averting to the door.

Carter chuckled and yelled, "Come on in."

The door opened to reveal Senator Grisham in his suit. His gaze landed on me, and he narrowed his eyes. "What is she doing in your bed?"

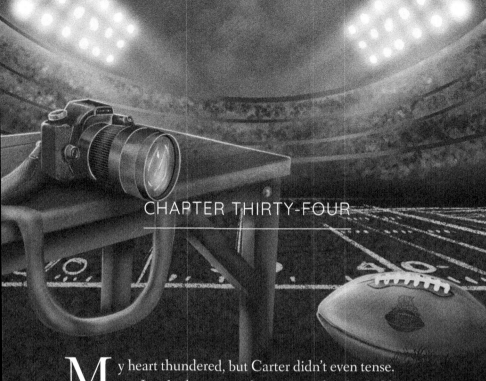

CHAPTER THIRTY-FOUR

My heart thundered, but Carter didn't even tense. I inched away, ready to get up, but his hold on me was tight.

He gestured to the television where our next episode was about to start. "What do you mean what is she doing here?" He tightened his arm around me, tugging me closer as he continued, "We're watching a TV show together, and we'd like to continue if you don't mind."

Senator Grisham's face twisted in anger. "This isn't a joke. Katherine is upset, she called Patrick in tears."

"Uh...I didn't ask you to deal with it." Carter turned around to grab the remote and pause the TV. "So I'm not sure why you're blaming me."

Carter was trying hard to be dismissive, and I wanted to smack him for it. His dad wasn't going to let this go, especially if Katherine had alerted their families about us while upset.

"You're not to blame for Katherine sobbing?" Senator Grisham crossed his arms, causing the sleeves to conform to his muscles.

Carter dropped his remote on the bed and placed his arm back around my waist. "Nope. That was all her. And I didn't make her call him."

"Maybe you didn't make her call him, but she caught you having sex with Evie in her own house," he said, gesturing at me like we wouldn't know who he was referencing. "The girl that Senator McHale paid for and I sponsored to attend Hallowed Saints out of the kindness of our hearts."

My cheeks burned, and I wanted to disappear. I wished he would talk to Carter about me behind my back instead of making me listen to everything, but that must be the point. He wanted me to leave.

"First off, Katherine and I aren't together." Carter's arms turned into a vise around me. "I've made it very clear to her that we aren't getting back together. She's the one who killed that, which I'm thankful for, other than her making me look like an ass. You said you understood that, so I'm confused as to what's going on here."

"Carter." Senator Grisham rubbed his temples. "She's still the senator's daughter. I don't need tension brewing between Patrick and me."

"Yes. Because Katherine was *so* concerned about that when she cheated on your son." The words tumbled out of my mouth before I'd even realized I said them. "He didn't call you crying, asking for you to come home when he knew you were out with *Patrick*."

Carter's chest shook with quiet laughter while his father scowled.

Instead of addressing me, Senator Grisham looked back at his son. "We had to leave dinner early so he could rush home to console her because you couldn't keep your dick in your pants." He looked down his nose as his gaze flicked to me.

The judgment there was so palpable that I felt dirty...like

I'd done something wrong even though I hadn't. Carter and I were two consenting adults, and he didn't get to judge us.

He gestured to Carter's door and announced, "*She* needs to go back to Patrick's house before things get worse."

My blood turned cold. I hadn't considered his dad not letting me stay, which had been foolish.

"Not happening," Carter snapped. "She's staying here with us."

I didn't have to glance at him to know that he was wearing his signature blank expression.

Senator Grisham's eyebrows shot upward to the point that it was almost comical. "She came here to be with Katherine. They are—er, were—friends before she decided sleeping with you was worth more than their friendship."

Carter laughed bitterly. "If you think they were friends, that proves once again how little you know Katherine. She only brought Evie here to torture her father."

"That doesn't matter. I'm more concerned about you." His eyes pinned me in place. "You realize she has no connections."

"What does that have to do with anything?" Carter asked conversationally, but there was a grimness in his tone.

"Everything!" Senator Grisham bellowed. "After everything I've done and gone through, you're determined to make the same damn mistakes *I* did."

"Yes, of course, you. Like I didn't go through shit, right?" Carter removed his arms from my body and sat up.

Now that I could see his face, I saw the heartbreak there. His eyes were dark, and that indifference he tried to put in place wobbled now.

I wanted to be here for him, but I was fairly certain that my being here was making the situation worse. "Maybe I should—"

Carter placed a hand on my arm, his eyes pleading.

"She's right." Mr. Grisham's nostrils flared. "She should *go*."

"If she goes back there, I'll be going with her." Carter lifted his chin. "I won't allow her to be mistreated by Katherine just so you can keep the fucking peace."

My chest constricted. I was causing problems between him and his dad, and I hated it.

Taking a deep breath, Senator Grisham asked, "Is she really worth this?"

"She is. She's *nothing* like Mom. I would know." The intensity on his face made tears burn my eyes.

"Oh, you know her so well after having your dick inside her against a wall?" Senator Grisham laughed bitterly. "Believe me, I had sex with your mother in all kinds of places. It doesn't make her genuine. She conned Patrick into covering her college tuition. Hell, he roped me into this."

Carter lifted his chin, his voice lowering dangerously. "You need to back off. You don't know what you're talking about."

Senator Grisham exhaled and ran a hand through his hair. "I don't like this, Carter. This is going to cause problems."

"I didn't ask you to like it," he shot back. "I told you I didn't like *your wife*, but you married her anyway."

I wanted to hug Carter. The pain in his voice tugged at me. He'd had a shittier life than I realized, and I hated how I'd assumed things about him at first. I wasn't much better than his father.

"You need to focus." Senator Grisham's shoulders sagged. "Football and college will ensure you have a comfortable life. If you break your concentration even for a second, it could come crashing all around you. You don't have time for a high-maintenance relationship, and worse, what if you wind up knocking her up?"

Gritting my teeth, I clenched my hands into fists.

"She's not going to get knocked up," Carter argued. "We're being careful."

"Despite what you think of me, the last thing I want to do is get pregnant." I grimaced at the thought of bringing a child into the world with the sort of life both Carter and I were living. "I just lost my parents—my entire family. My goal is to finish college and go to grad school." Not to mention, I was completely broke, but I didn't add that. It would only validate what he was thinking.

Mr. Grisham narrowed his eyes at me. "Sounds like not having a family would be a pretty solid reason to try to create one. Even better if a rich senator's son is the father."

A shaky breath escaped me. I felt like I'd been kicked in the gut.

Carter climbed to his feet, stepping in front of me, blocking me from his father's view. He spoke way too calmly. "Don't talk to her that way."

"Seriously, Carter." Senator Grisham groaned. "You're going to fight me over a girl after everything I learned from your mother?"

"I'm telling you, Evie is different. I'm not making your mistake."

"But—"

"Don't worry, *Dad*." Carter was as still as a statue. "I'm wearing a condom each time. Katherine can vouch that I wore one tonight."

I flinched. Thank goodness his dad couldn't see me right now.

But luckily, the senator didn't take the bait. Instead, he said, "That's not foolproof."

"I'm on the pill," I added. I'd never told Carter that—we'd always used condoms—but he'd seen me take it. "So it's pretty much impossible."

"You could just be saying that." He tugged at his tie.

"Because every woman who isn't rich is a liar." I rolled my eyes. I hated the way he was treating me just because I hadn't been born to privilege.

Carter glanced over his shoulder at me, a frown on his lips. "Let me make it simple. If she leaves, I go wherever she goes."

"I expected better from you." His dad shook his head. "You've always been driven."

"Oh, believe me. I know how important it is. That's all you've ever drilled into me." Carter lifted a hand. "Don't worry. I won't embarrass you, and my goal is still the same—the NFL."

"Fine." His dad took a few steps back and dropped his hands. "She can stay. But Carter? I really hope you know what you're doing."

Carter chuckled grimly. "I know what I'm doing. Trust me."

"Just, please, don't make things more strained between Patrick and me." Senator Grisham took a few steps back.

"As long as Katherine behaves, so will I," Carter conceded.

His dad lifted his hands, as if he already knew that was asking too much of her, and left us alone in the room once again.

I'd caused even more tension when widening the rift between Carter and his dad was the last thing I'd ever want to do. "Are you sure I should be here?"

Carter climbed back onto the bed and touched my cheek. He smiled tenderly, tucking a piece of my hair behind my ear. "There's nowhere else you should be. I *need* you here."

A lump formed in my throat. "Your dad seems intense, but he's still your family."

"He is." Carter huffed and smiled sadly. "That's the only reason I'm here. Dad got my mom pregnant—she trapped him. They married and divorced when I was two, and she took him for a lot of money. She remarried another sucker, so Dad doesn't have to pay alimony, but her new husband turned out to be a con artist, just like her, so she's back trying to weasel her way into my life. I owe Dad a certain degree of loyalty. He did get me out of a shitty place with Mom, but ever since then, he's been on me about focus and achieving something...like he's afraid that I'll be like her and try to live off him. Each year, it gets worse, and I can't take him controlling me even more, especially now that Mom's been contacting me starting this past summer. I think that's one of the main reasons Dad won't give me the money out of my trust to help Touchdown 4 Kids. He's afraid I'll give some of it to *her* to get her to go away."

"I'm sure that's not it. He's just a human with flaws." I traced his cheek with the tip of my finger and continued, "Have you ever talked to him about her?"

"I've tried, but he always changes the subject back to football or political issues." His eyes darkened. "You're the first person who treats me like a *person*—well, beyond Jack, who's an idiot half the time."

A multitude of emotions coursed through me, and my heart clenched. This whole time, I'd thought he was the one giving me strength, but in this moment, I realized that I helped him too. And for some reason, that petrified me. We had the power to break one another, but maybe...possibly...mend each other too.

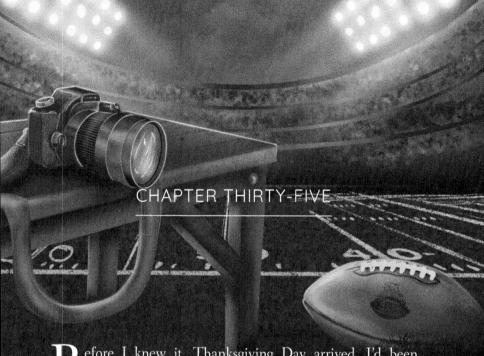

CHAPTER THIRTY-FIVE

Before I knew it, Thanksgiving Day arrived. I'd been dreading it because Senator Grisham had made it clear that Senator McHale and his family would be coming over... including my least favorite person in the world.

Staying with the Grishams had remained awkward too, apart from when I was alone with Carter. Serenity barely acknowledged me, which wasn't saying much since she did the same to Carter, but the looks both Senator and Mrs. Grisham shot me made me very aware that I wasn't welcome.

Between that and Carter sneaking into my room each night, I was beside myself. Though I was fairly certain Senator Grisham thought we were having sex in their house, I knew that we weren't out of some sort of respect for him.

I'd gone downstairs to offer to help cook Thanksgiving dinner with Mrs. Grisham, only to find the kitchen run by a chef and staff. I'd been looking forward to a little bit of normalcy, though I hadn't expected her to take me up on the offer. When I was shooed from the kitchen, it confirmed what I already knew.

Only Carter wanted me here.

Carter had gone downstairs for his morning workout, and I was hiding in my room, waiting for him to get back.

There was a knock on my door.

My heart skipped. Maybe Carter had cut his workout short and was already back?

I swung the door open to find Katherine standing there.

I took a step back as she flitted inside with a clothing bag that said Prada draped over her arm.

"Come in," I deadpanned. I stayed next to the door, ready to bolt if she started anything. I wouldn't fight with her, especially not here in Carter's house.

"Hey, *friend*," she said a little acidly and then flashed her camera-ready smile. "Anne said you tried to help her in the kitchen." She snickered and flipped her hair over her shoulder. "It's kinda sad that you didn't realize we hire people for that."

"I didn't think about it," I answered tightly, not wanting to give her a reaction.

"Right." She waved dismissively. "Well, anyway. I thought that, after that night, I should give you a peace offering." She lifted the bag by its hanger and held it out, revealing the purple dress that had been on sale at Posh that she'd said would be perfect for me. "You can wear this for Thanksgiving dinner. I don't want you to stick out with your clothes and all."

Ah, there was the insult. I'd been wondering when she'd get to it. "Thanks, but I'll be fine with what I have." So what if I wore jeans and a shirt to dinner when they were all dressed up? I'd live.

She pouted. "I told Daddy you wouldn't accept this from me. That you'd shoot me down because you want Carter to stay mad at me."

My hands fisted. Reaching out, I took the dress and forced myself to say, "Thank you."

"Perfect." She beamed. "I'll leave you to get ready. See you soon." She walked out the door, and I shut it a little too hard behind her.

If she was trying to come off like the innocent one, then I couldn't be a bitch and not wear the dress. Maybe blending in tonight wouldn't be a bad thing.

I took a shower, trying to relax. Then, I fixed my hair and took my time with my makeup. By the time Carter knocked on my door, I was slipping into the dress. The silk felt like a caress against my skin, and I could've sworn I was wearing a nightie.

When I opened the door, I found him in black slacks and a pale-yellow button-down shirt. His eyes bulged when he saw me. "Damn, babe. You're gorgeous." He winced. "Not that you aren't always, but this is a different kind of gorgeous."

Stomach dropping, I forced a smile. Of course he liked the dress. It was what he was used to.

I pushed the humbling thought aside and took his outstretched hand. He kissed my forehead and murmured, "The McHales are here. But I'll be by your side the entire time."

Forcing a tight smile, I nodded. "Then let's go get this over with."

We went downstairs and entered the large dining room. An all-glass rectangular table stood at the center with dark cherry-wood seats for eight. In the center was a turkey along with green beans, asparagus, and some sort of weird-looking potato dish. A super-healthy version of what had been one of my favorite holiday meals.

Senator Grisham sat at one end of the table while Senator McHale took the other. Katherine sat on one side of her father and Mrs. McHale sat on the other. Luckily, Mrs. Grisham and Serenity sat together on the same side as Mrs. McHale.

"Oh, Evie." Katherine pulled out the chair beside her. "Sit here, next to me."

Carter and I stopped. He stiffened, but if he tried to intervene, we'd look bad in front of the others, which was Katherine's plan, no doubt.

He moved to the chair on my other side, and we all sat down and began filling our plates. No one spoke, but everyone moved around, keeping busy. Once things were settled and we'd all taken a few bites, Katherine sighed. "You know what, Evie? I'm glad you talked me into getting that dress for you. It does look great."

I froze, and I could feel everyone's eyes on me. "But I—"

"You bought her that dress?" Senator Grisham asked, glaring at me once more.

"I did." Katherine placed a hand on her chest as she finished her bite of turkey. "I told her no, but then she was complaining about how she wouldn't fit in and how she needed it. I mean, if Daddy paid her tuition, I can at least buy her a dress. Right? And apparently, Carter gives her a ride everywhere, and when he can't, he recruits Jack to do it instead. She's our community project."

I stilled, and Carter tensed beside me.

"Also, she drank all the champagne in the limo and talked about how this is what she deserves." Katherine smiled, batting her eyes. "I hope they have a really great life together."

"What?" My mouth dropped, and I turned to face Senator McHale. "I swear, none of that is true. I told her I couldn't afford this dress."

"Please. Serenity." Katherine arched a brow at the younger girl. "You were there."

Serenity nodded. "It's true." She shrugged and took a bite of her asparagus. "But if that's what Carter wants—"

"You've been driving her everywhere?" Senator Grisham

stood. "What about your focus?" He pointed at me. "Son, I know you like her, but this relationship is risking your future."

"My focus is fine. The team hasn't lost a game, and I'm making good grades," Carter growled. "We've already gone through this."

Senator Grisham sneered. "That might be true now, but not in the future with her by your side." He waved both hands at me and continued, "This is what I'm talking about. You're blind to what she's doing here."

Out of the corner of my eye, I saw Katherine smirk. Her plan had worked perfectly. She probably hadn't even talked to her dad about this dress.

"Katherine, you were the one who invited Evie here. Therefore, she's your guest." Senator McHale set both hands on the table. "I don't know what happened, but that doesn't matter right now. It's a holiday, and we don't treat our guests like this, especially at the dinner table. Do you understand?"

Mouth dropping open, Katherine blinked, staring at him. "Are you serious right now? You're going to allow someone to treat me like crap, and I should sit here and take it because I was trying to support you by bringing her here?"

"Both of you need to calm down." Mrs. Grisham slowly released a breath and glanced at me. "Evie, I'm sorry for all this, but I think it'd be best if you leave. Your presence will make the rest of our time here uncomfortable."

"I agree." My eyes burned, but I blinked, refusing to cry. "It's fine," I said to Carter as I moved to go around his seat, but he was already standing.

He leaned over and glared at his stepmom. "If she goes, I do as well." His eyes cut to his father. "She hasn't done a damn thing wrong."

Senator Grisham jumped to his feet. "Now listen here. This is your *family—*"

Carter caught my hand and tugged me away from the table. "I've heard enough. We're out of here."

He led me out of the dining room, the silence deafening.

The magnitude of the situation began to catch up with me, and my legs started to tremble.

Carter had chosen me over his family. Guilt churned in my stomach.

I'd known that I shouldn't have agreed to come here, but I'd done it anyway, trying to take the easy way out. Deal with Katherine for a week instead of catching her wrath for a year.

Looked like, instead, I'd do both.

The two of us had marched to the front door, passing through the all-white living room, when I tugged him to a stop.

He spun, his brows furrowing. "We need to get out of here."

"Well, *I* need to get out of here, but I kinda need my clothes." I took a step toward him, placing my hand on his chest. "But you should stay here."

His head jerked back. "Are you serious right now? We were in the same room, right? Hearing the same things?"

I struggled, trying to not let my fluttering heart get the best of me. "He's your dad. I'd give *anything* to spend one more holiday with my family." Didn't he see that his dad was alive and that was a blessing?

Carter laughed bitterly. "He hasn't acted like my dad, nor have my stepmom or sister acknowledged me as part of the family, for a long fucking time now. They're all about control and how things appear. I'm not staying." He kissed the top of my head. "But thank you for caring. Come on. Let's grab your things. I didn't think about that."

Taking my hand once again, he led me up the stairs and into the room I'd been staying in. I was packing my clothes in my bag when Senator Grisham strode in.

"Son, let's talk this through. I'm deeply concerned about your choices." He crossed his arms and blocked the doorway.

"Not happening." Carter lifted his chin. "I didn't want to come home for the holiday in the first place, and I definitely won't stay around people who treat Evie like trash when she's done *nothing* wrong. I'm done with you trying to control everything I do...every fucking second of my life."

His dad dropped his arms. "I'm only trying to help you."

"*Help me?*" Carter sneered. "You treat me like I don't know what I'm doing." He held out his hands. "I appreciate everything you've done for me. I really do, especially when it comes to Mom. I even understand why you won't give me *my own money* to help Touchdown 4 Kids. But this"—he gestured between himself and his dad—"isn't healthy. All we talk about is football, my training regimen, and my fucking diet. Even when you visit me, it's always about football. You come in for an early game and leave right after. Nothing more."

"Son, I'm busy working with Patrick on the environmental initiative and running our country," the senator scoffed.

"I get that you have important stuff going on, but does every interaction we have need to be centered around football and my future? You've made it clear that you want me to be able to rely on myself and not need you. It's like you expect me to sponge off you. Like you expect me to be like my mother."

My throat constricted, witnessing all the pain Carter was expressing. I hated that he hadn't had a very happy childhood, but at least he was telling his dad how he felt. Maybe their relationship could be salvaged. I kept my head down and finished packing my bag, not wanting to distract them from their conversation.

"You don't get to come home and talk to me like this," Senator Grisham snapped. "That's not how this works. We had an agreement."

Carter nodded. "The agreement. I come home on the holidays, make good grades, and win the fucking national championship, and you pay for my townhouse and expenses." He lifted a finger. "One more game, then we're at Nationals. I'm not sure what more I have to do to prove myself to you."

"Which is why this girl shouldn't be distracting you now," Senator Grisham said, and I didn't need to look at him to know he was pointing at me. The accusation slithered through the air and down my skin.

"Evie and I have been dating since September, and you've been thrilled with my progress." He tensed. "And we've been living together the past few weeks, ever since her room got flooded."

Now, I couldn't help but glance up. Senator Grisham's eyes were wide, his mouth ajar. "You've been dating for over *two and a half months* and living with her, and you kept that from me?" He sounded wounded.

"Because of all this shit right here." Carter exhaled loudly. "I knew you'd give me hell about her, and Katherine would be vile to her. You saw what she just did downstairs."

His dad's face hardened. "Told the truth about how your girlfriend acts when you're not around? That story sounds a little too familiar."

"Evie didn't do that shit." Carter rolled his eyes. He turned toward me. "You packed?"

I licked my lips. I didn't know what to do. The senator clearly still wanted to talk, but Carter wanted to leave. I didn't want Carter to wind up doing something he'd regret, but I nodded because I didn't want to lie.

Carter took my bag in one hand and my hand in the other then headed to the door.

His father inhaled. "You need to stay here, Carter."

"Not happening."

"Evie can stay too." Senator Grisham hung his head.

Carter guided me around his dad and said, "We've already seen how that's going to go. She's not comfortable and has been hiding in her room to avoid everyone. The one time she comes out to spend time with me and my family, you let Katherine pull that shit."

"Your sister backed her up." Senator Grisham's gaze slid to me, his eyes holding so much anger I had no doubt that he believed I was the problem.

"You should believe her since we all know how trustworthy she is," Carter deadpanned.

There was clearly more to that story. I bit my bottom lip, staring at the wall across from us in the hallway. I wanted to go home.

"Carter," his dad warned again.

"I hope you have a wonderful Thanksgiving with your real family and your best friend and his family." Carter led me out once again.

When we reached the bottom of the stairs, Katherine was standing at the threshold of the living room. She lifted her chin. "Look, I'm sorry. Why don't both of you join us at the table again, okay?"

Carter laughed. "You think that I want to put up with you to keep the peace?" He wrapped his arm around my waist and kissed me.

I should have pulled away, but when his lips molded to mine, I couldn't bring myself to. Each kiss with him was like a drug that I'd happily get lost in.

When he pulled back, the gold in his eyes was shining, but it vanished when he glanced at Katherine. "Evie's everything that you're not. And if I have to choose, it's her."

When I followed his gaze, I saw Senator McHale standing

behind his daughter. His eyes softened as he homed in on Carter's and my joined hands.

My head reared back. I would never have expected that reaction from him.

Carter tugged me outside, and when the door shut, I took a deep breath. "Carter, maybe we should go back in."

"No way." He pulled me to his chest. "With you is exactly where I want and need to be. So let's go find a fucking Thanksgiving meal like the one you and your mom used to make."

My chest expanded painfully from the thick emotions burgeoning inside it. I'd been dreading Thanksgiving and any holiday since my parents' deaths. I wanted to cherish the memories I had with them, but I feared that getting through each holiday without them would be excruciating. Somehow, with Carter, I was more confident I'd be able to let the happy memories filter through.

The idea of having a meal that was similar to the one Mom cooked each year had me nodding eagerly. "Is there anywhere around here that will have that?" From what I'd seen, this area celebrated a diet version of Thanksgiving.

Carter chuckled. "Yeah, we'll find something. That in there was just my parents watching their calories."

A car pulled up in front of the house, and Carter nudged me forward. "Come on. Our ride's here. Let's salvage the day."

The trickling of the river had my heart galloping. I couldn't see the water yet; it was blocked by trees as we strolled to the edge of a dock, but the sound and the fishy smell surrounded me.

I'd asked Carter to take me to one of the spots where he liked to kayak when he was in town. We'd rented a car to drive home today, Saturday—a day earlier than when we were supposed to take the jet back with Katherine. We'd agreed that we'd rather travel separately than deal with her.

"We don't have to go here," Carter said, tugging me to a stop. "I've been coming to this river my entire life. Not seeing it one time won't hurt me."

He meant it, but I'd wanted him to visit because he loved it so much. And that wasn't the entire reason. I wanted to come too. I wanted...no, *needed* to face my irrational fear of the water.

I stepped away from the trees and saw the river ripple and meet the ramp where people unloaded their boats.

My skin pebbled as I remembered how cold the water had been when I'd had to swim out of the car and leave my parents behind.

My pulse pounded in my ears.

"Babe, seriously." Carter turned me toward him, his eyes darkening. "We don't have to be here. That you wanted to come for me already means the world."

I cleared my throat, trying to force my face into a smooth expression. "I need to do this." With him by my side, I had no doubt I'd get through it.

He took my hand and squeezed it comfortingly. "If it gets too hard, just tug on my hand, and I'll get us out of there."

I nodded, not trusting myself to speak.

Hand in hand, we slowly headed toward the dock by the boat ramp. Each step became harder than the last, but I focused on my breathing and Carter's touch. Even though part of me wanted to turn and run away, a more sizable chunk didn't want to live with this fear.

Accidents happened.

"Let me know if you need a break," he murmured as he slipped his arm around my waist, anchoring me to him.

We reached the sidewalk that would lead us to the dock. I

gritted my teeth as the air whipped around me, pressing against my chest and lungs. Forcing one foot in front of the other, I inched closer to the water. Carter didn't say anything, just kept his hands on me, holding me tight.

The fishy smell invaded my nostrils, reminding me of the taste of the river in my mouth. The waves crashed and lapped similarly to the way they'd thumped against the car.

Flashes of Dad's injuries and Mom's unconscious face flitted through my mind, and I stilled about fifteen feet from the water, unable to get closer. This would have to be close enough.

Even though there was nothing but open land around us, a wall of blackness seemed to close in on me, panic sinking its sharp claws into my chest and ripping it open.

"Hey, we're here. We don't need to touch the water," Carter murmured, turning me toward him and wrapping both arms around me.

My eyes burned with unshed tears that blurred my vision. "I'm sorry."

"You have absolutely nothing to be sorry for." He kissed my forehead and then placed his against mine.

We locked eyes, and a sensation of safety washed over me, which was almost scarier than anything.

The two of us stood together for a while, the breeze off the river caressing us.

My heart never slowed. Eventually, I'd had enough. "I'm going to head back, but I'll wait for you by the car." I didn't want to pressure him to leave. We weren't in a hurry to get back home.

He laughed. "I don't need more time. This was enough." He tucked a lock of my hair behind my ear. "Being by the river with you in my arms—I'm pretty sure nothing will ever beat that."

Butterflies fluttered in my stomach, and some of the fear

eased as I took in his full lips and sharp cheekbones. "I couldn't have done this with anyone but you," I said, voice raw with my honesty.

He kissed my lips sweetly before pulling back, warm honey in his eyes. "I just hope you know how much I love you," he whispered.

My heartbeat turned rapid, and a tear leaked down my cheek. I wasn't sure if I'd imagined those beautiful words because him saying them to me didn't make sense.

"Hey." He cupped my cheek, staring into my eyes. "You don't have to say it back. It doesn't change anything. I just wanted you to know how I feel."

That was the thing—I'd been hiding the magnitude of what I felt for him, worried it was too soon. I sniffled, smiling. "I'm crying because I'm happy—because, Carter, I love you too. I have for a while."

He beamed and lifted me into his arms like a princess, and carried me away from the riverbank. Then his lips were on mine, and I answered him in earnest.

This trip had started out as a disaster but ended in a way that made everything feel right.

CHAPTER THIRTY-SIX

I was still floating in a love-struck daze when Monday rolled around.

We'd spent the rest of the holiday in the townhouse, watching television, eating, and making love. Then I submitted my application to Stanford, promptly trying to forget I had since I doubted I'd get accepted. I didn't want to leave our little private world, but reality crashed back over us.

At least, Carter and I didn't have to hide at school anymore. We held hands on campus as we headed to class.

When we reached the student center, where we had to go our separate ways, he pulled me flush against him and kissed me thoroughly. When his tongue slipped into my mouth, my legs went limp, forcing him to hold me up.

He groaned and pulled away. "Ugh. I don't want to be away from you."

I kissed his cheek. "You'll be fine. It'll make you miss me and want to be with me more."

"There's no fucking way I could want you more," he said, tickling my sides and making me squeal. "It's already agony."

When I stepped away, he stopped me, a stormy expression sliding into place.

"If Katherine sees you and tries to start something, I want you to text me." Carter lifted a brow.

This was the tenth time he'd told me that. He was more worried about it than I was.

I drew an X across my heart. "I promise."

"Fine." He huffed. "I better get to class before I'm late."

I kissed him again, and when I turned to walk away, he slapped my ass. I yelped, caught off guard, and my body heated unexpectedly. I'd never imagined I might like that.

He chuckled, and I glared at him over my shoulder. "You'll pay for that later."

Beaming, he winked. "I sure hope I do." Then he spun around and walked off, leaving me flustered.

Jerk!

I turned, heading to my class, smiling so big my cheeks hurt. There was no way to dampen my happiness.

Until I walked past a group of girls I'd never seen before, whispering and pointing at me. They broke into laughter, stopping me in my tracks.

What the hell was going on?

I'd just started toward them to ask when something slammed into my side, and I fell, hard.

My palms slammed onto the sidewalk. One elbow gave out, and the cement skinned the rest of that arm.

Something slammed into my backpack from behind, causing the bag to shove forward and flipping my entire front side onto the sidewalk. A guy grunted as I jerked my head back, preventing my face from crashing into the cement but giving me a stiff neck.

"Shit," the guy said, stumbling and trying not to fall himself. He came back and leaned over me. "I'm so sorry. I didn't see you trip..." He grimaced and offered a hand to help me up.

Laughter broke out from the group of girls who'd been pointing at me.

I gritted my teeth, trying to prevent tears from falling. My right arm and palm burned, and I slowly removed my backpack.

The guy tried gripping my left arm to help me, but I shook my head. "I'm fine."

He squatted beside me, his green eyes wide. "You're bleeding." He nodded to my arm.

Of course I was. I glanced in the direction from which I'd been hit and spotted one of Katherine's friends from the cheer squad. Katherine hadn't wasted any time turning people against me.

The cheerleader played with the end of her dark-brown braid. She mashed her lips together, her honey-gold eyes bright with mirth. "Oopsie. I didn't see you." She cringed and covered her mouth. However, when the corners of her eyes creased, I knew what she was hiding.

A smile.

I wanted to roll my eyes but somehow managed to keep them firmly in place. "Accidents happen," I said, managing to keep the malice from my tone.

As I climbed to my feet, my body throbbed. I bet I'd have some good bruises by tonight, but I'd experienced worse pain than this. I swallowed hard, trying to move as if I wasn't hurting. I didn't want to give Katherine's buddy any more pleasure than she already had.

When I went to scoop up the backpack, the guy who'd tripped over me snatched it off the ground. He didn't hold it out at first and asked, "Are you sure you don't want to go to the health center?"

"Yup." I nodded, trying to sound upbeat. "But thank you. It wasn't your fault."

His eyes flicked to the sidewalk, and I followed his gaze and cringed. Blood was dripping from my arm onto the cement. Lovely.

"You should probably get some Band-Aids," the cheerleader cooed, her expression twisted into one of concern. "What if you have an STD? You could spread it to everyone."

"Eww," someone muttered from several feet away.

My face burned. "No diseases here, so everyone's fine." The last thing I wanted was that sort of rumor spreading around campus.

"Yeah, okay." The guy wrinkled his nose at Katherine's friend before turning back to me and saying, "At least, let me get you some bandages."

"Don't worry, man." Grayson's familiar voice sounded from behind me, and he stepped up on my other side, his eyebrows raised and the skin around his eyes tight. "I can take it from here. We're friends."

The nice guy nodded. "Yeah, okay." He exhaled, clearly relieved that a friend of mine had arrived. "Sorry again." He handed my bag to Grayson.

"Hey, Grayson," the cheerleader said, popping the gum in her mouth. "I think I might need some assistance too—my side is kinda bothering me."

Was she trying to pull the sympathy card for something she'd purposely done? Unfortunately, I was learning there were all kinds of manipulators in the world.

Grayson didn't even turn his head in her direction. His attention stayed solely locked on me. "Let's go to the bookstore bathroom and clean you up."

I nodded, knowing that bleeding everywhere wasn't the best idea.

He put my backpack over the shoulder that didn't have his bag on it, and we walked off.

Turning toward the student center, I couldn't help but notice the number of people staring at me. My face burned as I quickened my pace, eager to get out of the spotlight.

"Let's go in the back door," Grayson suggested, heading around the building.

That way was less crowded this time of the morning with people heading in for breakfast.

We entered through the single door in the back between the bookstore and bathrooms.

"I'm going to grab you some bandages. Come out when you're done cleaning up." Grayson didn't wait for me to answer, just strolled into the store.

Not wanting to argue and drip blood all over the floor, I rushed into the women's bathroom and cringed. My arm was skinned from wrist to elbow. That was going to be fun to deal with until it healed.

I turned on the water, holding my arm over the sink as it warmed, and removed my phone from my back pocket. Thankfully I'd had it on my left side, or it could've been destroyed.

Swiping it open, I quickly typed Carter a message. The last thing I wanted was for him to hear about this from Grayson, or worse, on social media if someone had been recording.

Me: No big deal, but my side decided to kiss the ground.

Placing my phone on the edge of the sink, I stuck my arm under the water and hissed at the sting. The water grew pink as it went down the drain. She'd decked me hard, but that wasn't surprising. The cheerleaders worked out almost as much as the football team.

I looked in the mirror. My eyes were glistening, and my hair was a mess. Perfect. At least I didn't have to work this evening.

My phone dinged, and Carter's message flashed across the screen.

Carter: Wtf does that even mean? Where are you?

I blew out a breath. He was way too smart for his own good.

Me: Bathroom at the student center, but don't worry. Grayson is getting me Band-Aids. I'm all right.

Carter: Grayson? Fuck no. You're my girl. I'm on my way now.

Me: No. I'm fine.

I waited, expecting him to text me back, but nothing came. That told me everything I needed to know—Carter was on his way. And I hated that a part of me was relieved.

He *shouldn't* come—he had international business, and the last thing I wanted after the debacle with his dad was for Carter to miss a class because of me.

I squirted soap into my hands and lathered it up before rubbing it over my flesh. If I thought the water was bad, the soap felt like a hundred bee stings. I clenched my teeth, making sure that I got all the scrapes clean before rinsing it off.

I tore off some paper towels and blotted, but I was still bleeding. Putting pressure on the wounds, I was about to head back into the hall, but voices stopped me at the door.

"What the hell happened?" Carter asked, his voice tight. "Was Katherine involved?"

Grayson sighed. "Not Katherine. Susan. From what I gather, she shoved Evie and made her fall."

"That was Katherine." Carter rasped, "It was because of last week in Nashville."

"What happened in Nashville? I told her she shouldn't go."

"Oh, and she should've stayed here alone?" Carter challenged. "Or are you saying she should've gone home with *you*?"

They were about to rip out each other's throats. They'd been getting along better, but it was like my going to Nashville with Carter had gotten under both their skins. Grayson had made it clear that he didn't think I should go, and Carter now agreed but resented him for telling me so.

Grayson texting me the entire time I was there hadn't helped either. He'd texted me off and on last week, and I'd been vague about everything, which had clued him in that something was off. Each time he'd tried to get answers, I'd dodged the questions. At the end of the day, he was my friend, but the details were between Carter and me.

"If she had, maybe she wouldn't have just gotten—"

I couldn't take any more. "Hey," I interjected, flinging open the door of the women's bathroom.

Grayson was leaning against the wall with his and my backpacks on the ground next to the doorway and Carter on his other side. Both their heads snapped in my direction, and Carter pushed past Grayson to me.

His hazel eyes deepened to all brown and somehow darkened even more when he caught sight of my arm. "That's what that *bitch* did to you?"

Once upon a time, his face would've become a mask of indifference, but now it twisted in fury as he took in the state of my arm.

My heart grew warm, but I didn't want him to seek out Susan and confront her. I lifted my left hand. "In fairness, she only shoved me." I forced a laugh, which came out more like I'd been strangled. "I lost my balance and fell." I pretended to curtsey. "And did I mention that there might be a reason my middle name isn't Grace?"

Carter snapped, "Evie, that's not funny."

My head jerked back, and the warmth turned cool.

"Hey, man." Grayson pushed off the wall. "You may talk to us out on the field that way, but not her. She deserves respect."

I crossed my arms but then winced when my hand touched my shirt. I glanced down and saw I'd gotten blood on it. I frowned. Maybe I should go back to the house and start the day over.

Carter sneered. "I don't think that I asked for your opinion."

I lifted my chin. This shit ended *now*. "I told you not to come here, and you ignored me, and now you're getting short with me? That's not how this works." I pointed between him and me.

Exhaling loudly, Carter ran a hand down his face. "Fine. I'm sorry, but this was what I was afraid would happen. I should've walked you to your classroom."

Some of the heat running through my veins ebbed, and I touched his arm. "We were running late. There was no way you could've known." The irony of the situation was that we were now missing class because I'd persuaded him to head on in so he wouldn't be late. "You didn't have time, and it's not like you can be with me twenty-four seven."

He ground his teeth. "That doesn't mean I can't try."

"I don't get it." Grayson shook his head. "Katherine was the one who invited her to Nashville. Yeah, I thought it was a bad idea, but why would things be worse now that you all got back? I mean, Katherine's never gotten her friends involved before, right? What the fuck happened?"

Carter scoffed. "While we were there, our relationship came to light."

"Your physical one?" Grayson's nose wrinkled. "That wasn't a real secret."

"It was from Katherine, but it's more than that." Carter

took my hand, rubbing his thumb against my wrist. "Katherine found out not only that we're sleeping together but that we're in a full relationship."

Grayson's head snapped back. "Wait. Like dating?"

My breath caught.

"She's my girlfriend," Carter said possessively as he placed his arm around my waist.

"Girlfriend." Grayson snorted, his normally warm eyes hardening as he looked at me. "You said dating wasn't on the table for you this year. I thought it was strange when it was clear you two were having sex, but now you're actually *dating* him?"

My face flamed. I had hoped this wouldn't come up, but at least this made it clear to him that nothing would ever happen between him and me. "That was the plan, but..." Carter's arm stiffened, and I placed my uninjured hand on his chest, staring into his eyes. "He changed that."

"Yeah, I mean, he treated you *so* respectfully at the beginning." Grayson scowled and glared at me. "Obviously, someone who insults you and pushes you around should be the exception to your no-dating rule."

I flinched, and a lump formed in my throat.

"If you've got a problem, it's with me. Not her," Carter said as he released me and took a menacing step toward Grayson. "We can handle it right now."

"There's clearly no problem," Grayson laughed bitterly. "Right, Captain? You make all the calls on the field and off—for all of us."

The rivalry I'd seen between these two when I'd first arrived on campus flared once more. The two of them were in each other's faces, and I needed to act now before someone stupidly threw a punch. "Did you get the Band-Aids?"

When Carter froze, I cringed.

"Yeah," Grayson huffed and held out the purple plastic bag with *HSU* on it.

I took it and opened it to find a large box of bandages and gauze. I pulled it out and tried to open it, but my hands were still giving me trouble.

"Here, let me do it." Carter took the package and opened it up. He ripped open the first bandage and motioned for me to hold up my arm.

He carefully placed multiple Band-Aids, and Grayson walked around him and reached into the bag. "I got gauze for your palms."

"Thanks, man." Carter placed the last Band-Aid and stepped so he was blocking Grayson from reaching me. "I can take it from here. How much do I owe you for all this?"

"Nothing." Grayson moved to the side so he could see both Carter and me again and continued, "After all, what are *friends for?*"

Hands stilling, Carter glared at Grayson. The two of them locked eyes in some sort of pissing war.

"*I* can take it from here." I took the gauze and wrapped some around my hand. "And now that this is taken care of, we should *all* get to class." Anything to get these two guys away from one another.

I squatted to get my bag, but Carter swiftly snatched it from the ground before I could and threw it over his shoulder.

"You need to go to class." With my uninjured arm, I reached for my bag.

He arched a brow. "Not happening. I'm walking you to yours. Do we need to discuss what *just* happened?"

"My class is the same way. I can walk with her." Grayson shoved his hands into his jeans and shrugged way too casually.

"*Thanks,* man." Carter's jaw twitched. "But I'd rather be

the one to do it. After all, Katherine is someone I know how to handle."

Grayson chuckled. "You got me there." His gaze flicked to my arm.

Standing ramrod straight, Carter stared Grayson down.

"And you two are making us later." I slipped my arm through Carter's and dragged him toward the door. "If you want to walk me to class, that's fine. The longer we argue about it, the later you'll wind up being."

Some of the tension released from Carter's body. "Sounds good."

The two of us walked outside, and Grayson strolled behind us, allowing us to get some distance ahead. I was worried that they'd wind up in some stupid alpha male standoff again.

When we were closing in on my building, Carter sighed. "Are you sure you should go to class?" He glanced at my hands and frowned.

"I'll be fine." The truth was, if I left, Katherine would know why. All that would do was encourage her to continue acting this way, so I needed to at least pretend that I was unfazed. "And you know where to find me."

As we went into the building, he sighed. "You're not going to wait for me so I can walk you to your next class, are you?"

When we reached the classroom, I batted my lashes and kissed his cheek. "Nope, but I love you for trying."

He shook his head. "You're going to be the death of me."

"At least we had fun before the ending." I winked and then sashayed into class, the back of my neck sizzling as he watched me walk in.

The bar was so damn busy, every possible football game on the television. I hated that the last HSU game of the season was out of town—Carter and the team were down in Tuscaloosa, playing Alabama for whichever bowl game the winner would advance to.

He'd wanted me to go, but I had so many upcoming expenses due to the flood that I couldn't. When I'd learned his dad was going to be in town for the game, I was grateful that I couldn't go. The last thing I wanted was to be around him and Katherine.

"So...how is living with Carter? Are you ever coming back to our place?" Leah asked as I waited for a beer from her brother.

I rolled my eyes. "Of course I am. But I'll have to buy new stuff." Even though my heart ached at the thought of not sleeping in his arms. Tonight was going to be hard.

I snatched a beer from the counter, ready to hand a customer a refill. I wanted to get lost in work and not think of all the ways I missed Carter.

As the bar neared closing time, Carter threw the winning pass to Jack for a touchdown with mere seconds on the clock.

They'd won the game.

Everyone in the bar went wild, except for the local Ridge University football players who were hanging out in the corner. They frowned and set their beers down.

HSU had barely beaten Alabama, but that didn't matter because they'd won in the end. They'd be heading to Nationals, and the bowl game was just for show, though it'd be best if they won it.

I snatched my phone and sent Carter a text.

Me: You were amazing. I knew you'd win. I love you.

Setting the phone down, I went back to closing up. He wouldn't see the text until later anyway.

After an hour of shooing out stragglers and cleaning, I strolled out the door, leaving Joe and the others in the kitchen finishing up. Leah had left a few minutes ahead of me, rushing to yet another party at our house. Surprise, surprise.

As I made my way to Carter's Escalade, I noticed the guys from Ridge University hanging around nearby, including the one who'd given me hell multiple times.

I reached inside my purse for my pepper spray and Carter's keys. Luckily, I felt the cold metal in my hand and wrapped my fingers around the can.

"Hey, wait," the prick yelled, running toward me.

I sped up, but he was faster than me.

He caught up a few feet away from the car and yanked me toward him. He sneered, "Where do you think you're going?"

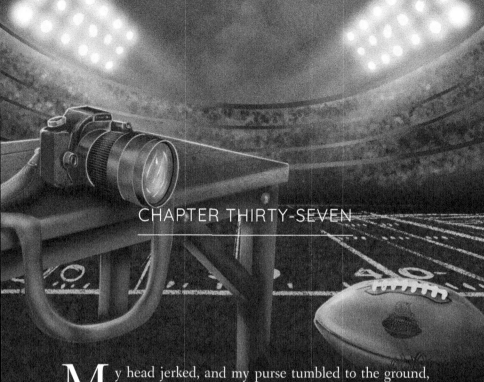

CHAPTER THIRTY-SEVEN

My head jerked, and my purse tumbled to the ground, but I managed to hold on to both the keys and the pepper spray.

I lifted the can, and the guy's jaw dropped. Before he could move, I sprayed his eyes.

"Fuck," he growled, releasing me, and I stumbled back.

Pepper spray had saved me for real now, and I would never denigrate Mom's adamant desire for me to carry it at all times.

I bent down and grabbed my purse as his four buddies raced toward us. I unlocked the car and jumped inside. Before I could shut the door, one of his friends reached into the vehicle and wrapped his hand around my arm.

My lungs seized as I dropped the keys and grabbed the door handle, yanking on the door so that it hit the guy in the arm. He yelped as I did it once more and then opened the door enough to kick him in the face.

That was when I noticed the other two guys running around to the passenger side.

When the guy who'd been blocking the door stumbled

back, I slammed it shut and pressed the lock just as the two reached the other side.

Luckily, Carter's car was new, so I didn't need the key in the ignition to start it. It was on the floorboard and could stay there until I arrived back at Carter's place.

I started the car, put it in reverse, and backed up. Thankfully, the four guys were moving back toward their vehicle, the one guy clutching his arm while the guy I'd sprayed in the eyes rubbed them, no doubt making the burning worse.

Good. The asshole deserved it.

Screeching out of the spot, I jumped the curb, frantic to get back to the condo. Once the bar was in my rearview mirror, my own eyes began to burn. The tightness in my chest kept getting worse as panic set in.

I clutched the steering wheel, too afraid to stop and pull over. What if the guys were following me?

My phone rang, but it was in my purse. My vision darkened, and I could focus on only one thing—the road.

I bit the inside of my cheek, desperate to do something... anything to ground myself. When Carter's townhouse came into view, tears spilled down my cheeks. I hit the garage opener, glancing in the rearview mirror. I didn't know what I'd do if those four showed up here and I was all alone.

Once I pulled the car into the garage, I remained locked inside until the door shut. I turned off the engine as tears raced down my cheeks, but I stayed even longer, in case somehow they managed to get inside.

Once again, my phone rang, but I had no desire to answer it. All I could focus on was what they might have done to me if I hadn't been able to get away. Knowing I needed to go inside before I had a complete breakdown, I snatched my purse and the keys from the floorboard and stumbled into the condo.

My phone went off again, but my vision was darkening.

In the condo, I shut and locked the door to the garage before sinking to my knees. I didn't have the energy to make it upstairs... All I needed was sleep. Sleep would dampen the panic. It had saved me when my parents died, giving me some reprieve.

Crumpled in the fetal position, I succumbed to the one place that felt safe. The darkness.

"Evie!" A frantic voice stirred me from unconsciousness.

The terror of the four guys attacking me flitted into my head. I froze, my eyes popping open. *Are they here?*

I climbed to my feet and searched in the darkness for my pepper spray as footsteps pounded upstairs.

Carter wasn't home, so it had to be them.

My heart galloped as I squatted down and felt around for my purse. I grabbed it and reached inside, but this time, I didn't feel the can—I heard it clank against the tile of the doorway.

I froze, hoping to God they hadn't heard.

"Evie?" Carter called.

A sob racked my body. It wasn't those assholes—Carter was home. I must have slept longer than I'd realized.

His footsteps came to the stairwell, and when he turned the corner, his gaze landed on me. His hair was disheveled; he wore a tank top and shorts and had dark circles under his eyes. He ran down the stairs to me and pulled me into his arms.

Body odor assaulted my nose.

"You stink." Out of everything I could've possibly said, that was what I chose? None of this made sense. He was staying overnight in Tuscaloosa, and he always showered.

"Yeah, that's what happens when you leave right after a

game and rent a car to get your ass back home." He pulled back, his face lined with worry.

I blinked and wiped the tears from my face. "Why did you do that?"

"Are you serious?" He took a step back, his jaw clenching. "When Leah called and told me that she couldn't get a hold of you and you weren't answering the door here, I left the stadium immediately and came back."

My heart stopped. "What?" That must have been who called me. "You didn't have to—"

"Fuck, yeah, I did." Carter's nostrils flared. "Do you know how terrified I was when Leah called me like that? And then you didn't answer your phone. What the hell was I supposed to think?"

I cringed and bit my bottom lip. "I'm sorry. I didn't mean…" I wasn't quite sure what exactly I wanted to say. Nothing would make this any better.

"Why didn't you answer our calls?" His forehead creased as he stared at me. "And what the hell are you doing down here?"

I told him what happened at the bar and that I'd had a panic attack…something I wasn't proud of.

He paused, taking in my hair, my clothes, and my purse and car keys on the ground. "That's why you didn't answer our calls?"

"I'm sorry." I rubbed a hand down my face. "I almost blacked out getting back here, and then I broke down. I didn't know Leah called me. She was going home to party."

"Don't apologize," he said, wrapping his arms around me and pulling me into his chest again. "I should've been here. This is my fault."

"What?" I pulled back. "No, you had a game, which you won." I leaned my head back. "And I ruined it." I swallowed.

"And your dad was there." Great. If his dad had hated me before, it would be nothing like now.

"Fuck my dad." His arms tightened around me. "I was there for the game. End of story. He can't say I lost focus during the game. I needed to get to you...to make sure you were okay. That's more important than some stupid-ass postgame celebration."

"Carter..." I hated that I'd done this and, worse, that I hadn't been with it enough to answer Leah's call. "You should've stayed. I was fine."

He laughed bitterly, startling me, and took a step back. "You were *fine*? That's why you were sleeping on the stairs and didn't have the energy to make it to bed?"

That was the point. He wasn't supposed to know. I thought I was safe devolving here alone. "I should've answered the phone."

"Fuck that, Evie." His jaw clenched, the fire coming back into his eyes. "You went through hell. You did what you had to; don't ever apologize for that." He took my hand, tugging me toward the stairs. "Let's go upstairs so I can take a shower, and then we can cuddle in bed."

I *really* liked the sound of that. "Okay."

He exhaled and took my hand. "Come on."

I didn't argue as he led me upstairs to his bedroom.

While he went into the bathroom, I changed into pajamas and crawled into his bed, completely drained. Sleep found me once again.

THE STENCH of blood filled my nose, and I reached futilely for Mom. The current dragged her away from the car and took me under.

"Evie," someone called out, but I was thrashing, trying to stay above water and get back to Mom.

Something clutched my waist and the same voice said, louder, "Evie."

I pushed away.

"Please wake up," the voice said brokenly.

Carter's voice.

Consciousness crept through my body, and soon my eyes opened. I was in Carter's bed, curled into a ball near the footboard. His olive-green comforter had been pushed onto the floor, and Carter's chest was pressed against my back as he held me.

I slowly uncurled, embarrassed at what he'd just seen. I hadn't had that dream in a while. "I made a mess." I moved to get the comforter from the ground, but he locked my body to him.

"You kept screaming for your mom," he said, sounding broken.

"Yeah." I turned around to face him. "I dreamed about the wreck again. I don't know why. It's been so long."

"Probably because those assholes tried to jump you." His hair was damp, pieces hanging in his eyes. "I'm going to kill every one of them." Anger weighted his voice like he truly meant it.

That wasn't what was scary. It was that I liked the sound of it. "They aren't worth it. I promise."

His jaw clenched. "I'm not so sure."

I caressed his cheek with my hand. "I admit, I like it when you get protective of me."

"Yeah?" He grinned. "Good. Because that's never changing. In fact, I'm thinking it'll get worse each day as I fall more in love with you."

Butterflies took flight in my stomach. "I'm okay with that."

"So you're encouraging me." He chuckled and kissed my nose.

"Maybe." I placed my head on his chest and listened to the steady thud of his heartbeat. The noise calmed me, and I had to be a little crazy because it felt as if mine paced itself with his.

He brushed his fingertips across my shoulders, and his breath hit the top of my head. Despite feeling safe in his arms, a question left my mouth before I could stop it. "What do you think they wanted with me?"

"Fuck if I know," he growled, growing tense despite his fingertips keeping their soft, leisurely strokes. "But it doesn't matter. They'll never touch you like that again."

I believed him.

Carter's phone started ringing nonstop. Eventually, he crawled out of bed and answered it downstairs, away from me.

From his gruff voice, I suspected the call had to do with how he'd left the team last night. They were required to stay together and ride back today.

I sat up in bed, wringing my hands. I had caused him so many problems. If I'd just gotten my shit together enough to answer the phone and tell him I was fine, this could've been avoided.

Finally, Carter came back upstairs and into the room.

When he looked at me, he smiled, but his expression was strained. "Are you doing okay now?"

"Yeah." I ran my hand through my hair. "Listen—"

"Don't." He lifted a hand. "We're not going to have this conversation again. I don't regret what I did for a second. You needed me, but I've got to return the rental and go to the university to talk to Coach Prichard and Dad."

Yep, I wasn't wrong about that phone call. "Okay. I'll just hang around here and clean up before I head to work."

"I will be back in time to take you."

"You—"

"If you say that I don't have to, I may lose my shit." Carter inhaled shakily. "What happened last night, even when I let you take my fucking car, will *not* happen again. You got it?"

My heart expanded to the point of pain, but I couldn't help but feel guilty. "Okay."

"All right, I hate to do this, but I've got to get going." He changed into some slacks and a polo shirt. Then he walked over and kissed me. "Call Leah, let her know you're okay."

I nodded. "Yes, Daddy."

He smirked. "I kinda like that. Maybe you can call me that tonight and we could role-play."

"Eww." I wrinkled my nose despite the traitorous grin spreading across my face. "That sounds like something Jack would say."

"Touché." He chuckled, kissing me once more. "Love you. I'll be back in a few hours."

IT WAS thirty minutes before I needed to leave to get to work, and Carter was still gone. I wrung my hands, unsure what to do. I didn't want to upset him, but I needed this job and the money. So I needed to get there on time. Leah was already at work, so she wasn't an option.

I was pacing the living room when my phone buzzed.

Carter: Jack's on his way to take you. I'll be there for dinner and to bring you home. Love you.

Me: Okay. I'm ready. I love you, too.

I exhaled. Jack wouldn't give me hell over last night...at least, I didn't think he would.

When I heard a car pull into the driveway, I grabbed my purse and keys and rushed out the door. After locking it, I headed down the stairs only to find an Uber sitting there. I paused, heart pounding, until the back seat opened and Senator Grisham stepped out.

"Oh. If you're looking for Carter—"

"I know where my son is." He pointed to the back seat. "Get in the car. I'm taking you to *work*."

I swallowed. "Thanks, but Jack is coming."

"He's not." The senator lifted his chin. "So come with me."

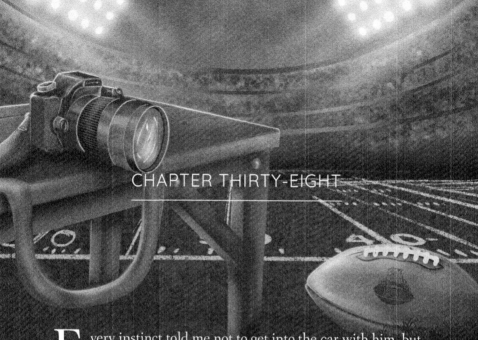

CHAPTER THIRTY-EIGHT

Every instinct told me not to get into the car with him, but that would only make Carter's dad hate me more. And that was the last thing I wanted.

Despite the knot sitting heavy in my stomach, I headed toward the sedan.

Senator Grisham held the back passenger door open for me like a gentleman, but the hardness in his eyes spoke the truth. There wasn't any warmth there.

I slid inside, and he shut the door gently and strode around to his side. He climbed in, and that was when I noticed he wasn't wearing his typical suit. Instead, he wore slacks and a purple button-down shirt with HSU embroidered on the pocket where a black pen was hooked.

He gave the driver directions to the bar and then turned to me. He arched a brow. "Carter's in trouble, especially since a scout was there to meet with him afterward. What did you do to him to make him leave his team and race back to you?"

"What did *I* do?" I snorted, sounding super unladylike. But hell, it didn't matter. He didn't like me anyway.

He arched a brow and remained silent, expecting me to answer.

"Nothing." I placed a hand on my chest. "I did *nothing*."

"Bullshit," he spat, his nostrils flaring. "His mother calls him before the game, fucking with his head, and then he comes racing home to you. That's a *big* coincidence."

My head spun. Carter's mom had called him? He hadn't said a thing. I didn't know what to think of that information, other than to file it away for later. "I was attacked after work, outside the bar, and he couldn't get a hold of me."

He rolled his eyes. "Then how did he find out you were attacked?"

"My roommate called him." I glanced out the window, not wanting to look at the senator. My stomach churned. "She couldn't reach me, so she called him."

"I'm sure that's why she called." He shook his head and pinched the bridge of his nose. "What will it cost to get you to leave him alone?"

I stiffened, acid burning my throat. "*What?*"

"Ahh, I've got your interest now." He removed a checkbook from his back pocket and the pen from his chest pocket. "Name your price, but it's a one-time deal."

"My *price?*" How had this day gone from bad to so, so much worse? After last night, I'd thought there was only one way to go—upward. Now I was sitting with Senator Grisham, who wanted to pay me to break up with his son.

I'd read books and watched movies where this happened, but I'd never expected it in real life.

"Cut the surprised act." He wrote my name out on the top line. "Fifty thousand?"

"No!"

He rolled his eyes. "Fine. One hundred thousand?"

"Absolutely not." I swallowed, determined not to vomit. I'd

already left quite an impression without bodily fluids becoming involved.

The bar came into view, and I was more eager than ever to get to work. I wanted to get away from Senator Grisham and never see him again.

He wrote one hundred and twenty-five thousand on the check, and my eyes bulged. Being able to write a check for that amount was beyond me.

Signing his name, he handed it to me. "There, now go away."

I took the check, staring at it, before bursting out in laughter. This wasn't funny; it was terribly tragically sad, but I didn't know what other reaction to have. I tried to hand it back to him, but he held up his hands.

"I'm not taking this." I straightened my shoulders, staring him in the eyes. "There's nothing you can pay me to keep me away from Carter."

"There's always a price." The senator clenched his jaw.

The poor driver in the front seat was watching, wide-eyed, through the rearview mirror. If I was struggling to come to grips with this, I couldn't imagine how he felt.

"There isn't." I ripped up the check and tossed the pieces onto the car seat. "Your son is amazing, kind, funny, loyal, and hardworking. All he wants to do is make you happy even when he feels like all you care about is him getting into the NFL. I would never sacrifice being with someone like him just for money."

I moved to get out of the car when Senator Grisham caught my arm. "You aren't good enough for him. You don't belong in his world. He deserves better."

"Someone like Katherine?" I snapped and glared at him. "Who cheats on him and manipulates him to get what she wants?"

He winced but didn't deny it.

"You are right about one thing." I removed his hand from my arm and stood, snatching up my purse. "I'm not good enough for him, but lucky for me, he wants me anyway. And I'll be at his side unless *he* tells me that he doesn't love me anymore. Hopefully, you'll wise up and see what you're missing out on by not truly being a part of his life before it's too late and he doesn't want you in it anymore." I slammed the door, spun on my heel, and marched into the bar.

The place was busy, and I kept checking my messages to see if Carter had texted me. It was close to eight, and he was normally here by now.

Jack, Grayson, Samuel, and Cole were already here, and I carried over their usual four draft IPAs. After dropping them off, I turned around to get another margarita pitcher refill for the table next to them when Jack jumped out of his seat and hurried to me.

"Hey, Evie," he called, catching my arm. "Can I talk to you for a second?"

I stopped and frowned. "I really don't have time."

"Just a quick second before Carter gets here." Jack scratched the back of his neck. "Senator Grisham told me not—"

Ah. That was what he wanted to talk about. "It's no big deal. I don't want to talk about it." I didn't even want to think about that car ride. It made me sick, how little Senator Grisham thought of me.

"Really?" Jack's brows arched. "Because if Carter finds out—"

"Then let's not tell him." If Carter's mom called him, he already had enough shit to contend with.

"Yeah, okay, but..." Jack trailed off. "If Senator Grisham said something to upset you—"

"It's fine." I placed a hand on his shoulder and smiled. "It was no big deal. I promise." Other than the senator trying to buy me off, but it would be best if Carter never found that out. They had enough problems between them, and I wanted him to have a better relationship with his dad. "We won't mention it."

Jack rubbed a hand down his face. "I hate lying to him, but between his mom and what happened to you last night, that might be for the best."

Of course *Jack* knew about his mom's call. I didn't know why, but that burned. The senator had said that she'd called before the game, so maybe Carter just hadn't had a chance to talk to me about it. "I agree. And now I gotta work."

He laughed. "You know what? When I first met you, I was unsure about you. But I'm glad you and Carter figured things out. I've never seen him so happy, even today, when he was getting his ass chewed out."

I grimaced. "I feel bad about that."

"You didn't mean to cause problems." Jack patted my shoulder. "I know it. It was a shit situation, but they won't bench him. They're probably adding more time to go over plays for the next game before practice tomorrow. I'm also hoping they make him clean up."

"They do realize he likes to clean, right?" That was one of the things that amazed me about Carter. When I'd first lived with him, I was certain he had a maid, but no. He cleaned up every night while I was at work. I'd come back to the townhouse smelling like lemon and soap.

Jack snorted. "No clue. But I did hear him mumble, 'It's about damn time this got cleaned right.'"

"And it did," a familiar, sexy voice said.

My head snapped in that direction, and I was greeted by warm hazel eyes and full lips tipped upward into a smile. My heart sputtered and my breath hitched. The first time I'd ever seen him, I'd had no doubt he was handsome, but knowing the type of person he was underneath the surface made him drop-dead gorgeous. He was beautiful inside and out.

"Hey." I perked up. "I was getting worried about you."

When he cupped my face and leaned in, I saw the evidence of his hard night. Circles underscored his eyes. "Are you okay?"

"Now I am," he murmured and kissed me. "Sorry for being late. Coach was riding me the entire time, and whenever I even got near my phone, he threatened to call Dad. Then we talked strategy." He rolled his eyes and shook his head at the guys. "Of course they're here, but I'm not complaining." He turned toward the pool table where the guys who'd attacked me normally hung out. "Have the guys who attacked you been here?"

I shook my head.

"If you don't want me coming here, then you gotta get Evie to make food for us every night before she heads to work." Jack lifted his hands.

Carter smacked him in the back of the head and growled, "She's my woman, not yours. Back off."

I laughed. I never thought I'd fit in with anyone at HSU, but these two guys made me feel like I was part of their group. They had no clue what that meant to me. "How long do you have to clean everything?" I wanted to redirect the conversation before Jack tried to aggravate Carter further.

"Just for a week to make a statement that I can't go unpunished." Carter rubbed his temples. "Before practices, I have to run additional laps too, but it's fine. Everything is worth it." He winked.

Biting my lip, I sighed. "I'm sor—"

He kissed me again, cutting off my words, then pulled back. "There is nothing to apologize for, so I don't want to hear that from your lips again." He arched a brow, and his gaze seared my soul.

I wasn't sure I agreed with him, but I didn't want to argue. He wore the intense expression he got when he was ready to disagree with me.

"Evie, get your ass back here," Joe called from behind the bar and lifted the pitcher of margaritas.

I grimaced, not wanting to leave Carter's side. "I gotta get back to work. You want your usual?"

"Please."

I spun around, and his hand grazed my ass. I turned back to find his eyes locked on me. He lowered his lips to my ear and whispered, "Making sure everyone knows you're mine, especially now that we've gone public."

My face heated. "I'm pretty sure they knew that from the way you kissed me when you arrived."

"Better safe than sorry." He chuckled and kissed me again.

"Stop eye-fucking and come work." Leah beamed from her spot next to the counter. "Or we'll have to kick Carter out."

Carter groaned and ran a hand down his face. "Fine, I'll behave."

"Yeah, right," Leah snorted.

Not wanting more attention, I went back to work.

Soon, the guys' IPAs were ready, so I headed over with their drinks and Carter's whiskey neat on a tray. Then I hurried back with their food and set it down.

When I put Cole's club sandwich in front of him, he pouted. "When are you cooking again?"

"What the fuck?" Carter leaned back in his chair at the edge of the table. "First Jack and now *you*. She's my woman, not yours."

Samuel picked at his chicken tenders. "That doesn't mean she can't cook for all of us." He dipped his sandwich in barbeque sauce. "We want her for her food, not her body and the emotional baggage that comes with it."

I placed a hand on my hip. "I sure hope you don't want anything else for the rest of the evening because I'm not sure my emotional baggage will allow me to get it for you."

Jack snorted and lifted his IPA in salute. "Tell him, Evie."

"Hey." Samuel scratched the back of his head. "I just meant—"

Grabbing a fry off his plate, Jack stuck it into Samuel's mouth. He shook his head. "Don't do it, man. Stop while you're ahead. Trust me."

I snorted. "And you guys call Jack the jackass."

Carter placed a hand around my waist and laughed. "You're right. They both are."

"As long as I don't get lumped in with him." Cole lifted half his sandwich. "I'm good."

My laughter froze as my attention settled on Grayson. He'd been quiet, and his focus was locked on Carter's hand at my waist.

Something hard settled in my stomach. I hated how things had changed between us. We'd been good friends, but ever since we got back from Thanksgiving, he'd grown distant. He'd stopped texting me, and it didn't feel right to text him after the way he'd acted toward Carter when I'd gotten hurt. The last thing I wanted was to lead him on.

Running a hand through Carter's hair, I kissed his forehead. "Eat before it gets cold. I'll check on you later." Then I walked off, focusing on work.

Everything would be okay as long as Carter and I loved each other and were together...and he never found out what his dad had done.

CHAPTER THIRTY-NINE

Two weeks after Thanksgiving, I was hurrying toward photography class when I heard that babyish voice outside the student center.

"Don't worry, girls," Katherine said, flipping her hair over her shoulder. "I have a plan. Our families always spend Christmas together, and Senator Grisham has made it clear Evie isn't invited back home with him again. When Carter comes back, he'll forget about the home-wrecker and be right back in my arms where he belongs."

Her gaze landed on me, an evil smirk crossing her lips.

And that was when everything inside me snapped.

My blood boiled. I was done being her pushover. After the shit she'd pulled at Thanksgiving, I'd had more than enough of her making me out to be some sort of monster.

As I stalked up to her and three other cheerleaders, I kept my gaze leveled on her.

Katherine arched a brow, and her smirk widened.

She enjoyed that she'd gotten to me.

"You got something to say to me?" I crossed my arms, making it clear that I had no plans of budging.

"I try not to speak to you." She shrugged. "It's in my best interest."

Her perfectly manicured minions laughed.

If she thought that was going to embarrass me, she'd soon learn otherwise. "Well, it sure sounded like you wanted to speak to me since you were talking about me and Carter." I lifted my arms out wide. "Otherwise, our names shouldn't be coming out of your mouth."

Her smirk collapsed.

"Let me spell this out for you since you clearly haven't gotten the hint. Carter and I are together. You tried to come between us over Thanksgiving and failed."

"His family hates you," she seethed.

I tilted my head. "Maybe. But Carter sure doesn't."

She scoffed. "Don't get cocky, Evie. It doesn't suit you."

Rolling my eyes, I laughed bitterly. "Stop trying to cause problems. It won't work."

"Do you think I've forgotten about my *little* promise to you?" She arched a brow, stepping into my face. Her overly sweet perfume damn near made me gag.

Here we went again. I didn't verbally respond and, instead, rocked back on my feet, wanting to get away from her stench before I got a headache.

I knew exactly what she was referring to.

"Yup, that's what I thought." She snickered despite my silence. "I know I've ignored you and let you and Carter live in some sort of peace. But I'm going to bring you to your knees, and no one will ever want to be around you again."

I rubbed my forehead. Being around her was painful in all ways. "Katherine—"

"I'm not done," she spat, her eyes hardening. "You better

enjoy the little bit of time you have left cozying up to Carter because it's almost up."

Her friends watched with nasty smiles on their faces. They wanted to be here when she followed through.

"Oh, please." She was all talk. "He threatened to tell your father whatever he has over you if you mess with either one of us. I'm quite certain he'd consider this messing with me."

Forehead creasing, she pushed a finger into my chest. "Is that what you want to do? Cause a further divide between Carter and his dad, so he only has you?"

"What?" My mouth dropped. "Of course not. I just don't—"

"Because that's exactly what his mother did, which makes you surprisingly like her." Katherine shuddered.

"I would *never* hurt Carter in any way." The accusation made my stomach churn. I hadn't told him what his dad had done for that reason alone.

Katherine waved a hand. "Well, that's what's going to happen if I don't out *your* little secret. He and I are going to be together, whether he wants to admit it or not, especially since I'm close to revealing it all."

This had to be some lame-ass attempt to play mind games with me. I snorted, unable to keep it in. "There is *no* secret. I'm not sleeping with your father. What is *wrong* with you?"

"Keep saying that. Enjoy it while you can, but I'm so close it's making Daddy scared." She bit her lip, a victorious light shining in her eyes.

The way she looked at me chilled me, like she knew something that I didn't. But that didn't make any sense.

Forcing my shoulders back, I stood as tall as possible. "You're miserable." It clicked. Even though it appeared that she lived a picture-perfect life, she obviously didn't. She was lacking something. "Is that why it's so important to make other people miserable too? You want everyone to be unhappy like you?"

Her face tensed, and she swallowed. "Don't pretend you know me. You don't know anything about me."

"Nor do I want to." I waved a hand in her face. "But I will say this—I'm sorry for whatever happened to make you like this. The fact that you'd rather strip everyone's happiness away 'til they're on your level is heartbreaking."

"You bitch," she snarled and slapped me.

The sound rang through the student center as my head snapped to the side.

Silence descended as the tension permeated everything. Not even the cheerleaders were chuckling.

I rubbed my cheek and stood up straight once more. My vision blurred and my eyes burned, but I refused to allow any tears to fall. Not here and definitely not in front of her.

"Oh my god," a girl whispered somewhere behind me. "Did you see Katherine? Please tell me someone got it on video!"

Hushed voices spread like wildfire, talking about what she'd just done, and Katherine blanched. She spun around. "If anyone did get footage, delete it *now*, or there will be consequences."

There were so many witnesses who'd seen her react in a way that would reflect poorly on her father, but I suspected that wasn't what angered her the most. If I had a guess, it was the fact that I'd gotten under her skin. I hadn't reacted horribly like she'd hoped; *she* had.

She seemed to have already forgotten me as she broke away, flipping her hair over her shoulder and smiling. She had to be preparing for damage control, and the group of bystanders suddenly averted their gazes, becoming nervous.

A shiver ran down my back. A lot of eyes were still on me. I needed to get to class, and I wanted to get away from here. "I hope you have a good day, Katherine."

I strode away, eager to put more distance between us.

She said lightly, "This isn't over," but anger clung to each word while she shot me daggers.

Yeah, I hadn't expected it would be. But at least now, there were witnesses who had seen her for what she really was.

I just hoped that this was yet another thing that Carter didn't find out about.

WHEN I WENT to the student center for lunch, Jack, Grayson, and Cole were already at our usual table. Grayson and Cole sat on one side, and I slid into the other, taking my usual spot next to Jack.

Grayson and Cole stared at me with serious expressions.

Grayson's face lightened. "I'm so glad you're here."

"What's wrong?" I asked as I dropped my bag on the ground. I'd run to the bathroom before heading here and had almost cried in relief when I'd seen that Katherine's handprint was gone. People had stared at me when I'd first gotten to photography, no doubt because of the handprint.

"You're seriously asking *that*?" Jack rubbed his forehead. His usual smile and crass demeanor were lacking, which chilled me to the bone. He shook his head. "Carter is going to flip."

I froze. "What—" I leaned toward him, staring at his screen. There was Katherine, bitch-slapping me like a boss. My head jerked to the side, and the video even included spit flying from my mouth.

It was definitely not flattering for either one of us.

"I saw it a few minutes after it happened." Cole ate a fry. "My ethics class was buzzing about it."

So that was why everyone had been staring at me in class. I'd thought it was the handprint, but it was probably the whole altercation. "But how?"

Grayson chuckled. "You do realize you're the same age as us, right? Because right now, you sound a lot older."

I couldn't help but smile. That was the first time he'd teased me since he'd learned that Carter and I were together. At least, I could count that as a win.

"It's going viral across social media, and a news station broke it." Jack winced.

Vomit burned my throat. "*News station?*"

"Yeah, Evie." Jack blew out a breath. "Tell me you told—" He went silent, staring over my shoulder, and grimaced.

I jerked around to find Carter stalking toward me. His chiseled face was strained, enhancing his cheekbones, and his jaw was clenched so hard I'd bet it would cut stone.

He marched directly up to me, his nostrils flaring. He said through gritted teeth, "Hey, babe. How was your day?"

I'd never seen him this pissed at *me*. However, I refused to act guilty. I hadn't done anything wrong. "It's been better." I pulled out my phone and swiped the screen then winced.

I'd forgotten to turn my phone off silent from class and had twenty missed messages from Carter. The first couple were full of concern, and then they changed to anger when I didn't respond.

Fuck.

He stopped beside me and crossed his arms, tilting his head to examine my face. I'd opened my mouth to say something, but his biceps distracted me, memories of his arms gripping my hips last night consuming me.

"Eye-fucking him isn't going to help," Jack whispered loud

enough that everyone could hear. "If you want to distract him, grab his dick and give us a show."

For the second time today, my face caught fire. Leave it to *him* to call me out.

Carter arched a brow. "Even if she grabbed my dick, I wouldn't budge."

"I'm sure it'd get hard, man." Jack lifted both hands. "If not, there's something wrong with you. If she touched my—"

"Stop *right* there." Carter's glare moved from me to Jack as he continued, "For the sake of our friendship."

Jack poked me in the back where Carter couldn't see. The gesture was clear—I owed him one. He'd helped me out by diverting some of Carter's wrath.

"I'm sorry." I wouldn't let him take the hit, but I did love him for trying. "I didn't hear my phone. A lot happened, and I was out of sorts and rushed to class." I rubbed the cheek she'd hit and caught myself. It was tender to the touch. "And I hadn't realized that *this* had happened." I waved at our phones.

"You should've called me *immediately.*" Carter ran a hand through his hair, his face tightening more. "I shouldn't have needed to reach out to you."

Grayson hit the table. "Why don't you back off a little? She was the one who got slapped, and it was over *you*. If she needs a minute to process it, then she has that right."

I flinched.

"When I want your input, I'll ask for it," Carter snapped. "Right now, I'm trying to have a conversation with *my* girlfriend, so back the fuck off."

Knowing this would only escalate, I stood and placed my hands on Carter's arms. I reached up to cup his face, his faint scruff rubbing against my skin, and I turned his face to me. At first, I thought he was going to fight me, but he obliged.

"I didn't want to upset you. You need to focus on your

classes. The semester ends next week, and we've got finals." I didn't add that I hadn't planned on telling him at all. "The last thing I meant to do was hurt you, but look." I kissed his lips gently. "You're missing your last class to be here and talk to me."

Some of the tension melted from his body, and his arm wrapped around my waist. He gritted, "I was worried, and then you didn't respond. It scared me. I thought…"

He trailed off, features pained, as Jack rambled to Grayson and Cole about something behind me, trying to give us privacy.

My head tilted back. "You thought what?"

"She scared you away from me," he answered. He leaned his forehead against mine, one hand pressing firmly on my back. "Which probably would be best for you, but I'm entirely selfish where you're concerned. I don't want to lose you."

Heart clenching, I laid my head against his chest and listened to his heartbeat. "Us not being together wouldn't be best for me. You make me feel safe, loved, and like I have a home again. Don't ever say you're being selfish."

He chuckled and kissed the top of my head. "I feel the same way about you, so I'm glad it's not one-sided."

"Definitely not." I leaned back and stared into his eyes, which were warming to the color that I loved most.

"Carter," Katherine's cringe-inducing voice called from behind him. "I need to talk to you."

I stiffened, and Carter's arm tightened around me.

Jack laughed *hard*. "You've got to be *fucking* kidding me right now. I used to think she was intelligent and ruthless. Now I think she's a dumbass who doesn't know when to quit."

"For once, Jack and I agree," Carter rasped and turned to the side so both he and I could glare at Katherine.

Her gaze swept over us, and I lifted my chin. I wanted

there to be no doubt that her show this morning hadn't changed my stance on my relationship with him.

Nose wrinkling, she tugged on her purple shirt. "Let's go outside." She flicked her gaze at me. "Alone."

I bit the inside of my cheek so I didn't say something I'd regret.

"Evie and I can talk to you outside," he sneered. "And that's me being generous."

She huffed and stomped a foot. It hurt to keep my eyes from rolling; that's how bad this woman grated on my nerves.

The tables closest to us noticed and went wide-eyed. A few pulled out their cell phones, ready for another confrontation.

"It might be best if she isn't included." Katherine waved, pointing out the increasing number of gawkers.

My jaw clenched, but I didn't say anything. If Carter wanted to talk to her alone, I wouldn't stop him, but I would be annoyed. I suspected she was doing this so he'd leave me to go talk with her and appear like he was taking sides.

He shrugged. "You don't need to talk to me then."

Narrowing her eyes, she focused all her hatred on me like I was the reason for him saying that when I hadn't uttered a word.

"Carter—" She cut herself off, her voice shaking. "We need to discuss how we're going to control the situation. Daddy called me, and he wants the two of us—"

"I'm not doing anything." He moved so that we were standing side by side, one arm wrapped around me. "You ran your mouth and lost your temper. You can deal with the repercussions. Katherine, you've gone too far. I don't give a shit if the media paints you as the villain because you *are*."

If I could kiss him without becoming even more of a spectacle, I would right now. My heart sputtered, not believing how far we'd come in such a short amount of time.

Her chest heaved, and her face flushed. "Between the things she said about my family and the fact that you aren't in class right now, Senator Grisham may think differently of your stance."

I snorted. "I didn't say *anything* to you out there. You were the one saying that, over Christmas break, you and Carter would get back together."

"Like anyone would believe you." Katherine rolled her eyes. "When Carter makes it clear—"

"Tell my dad." Carter waved her off. "Please. I believe Evie, and I know she doesn't instigate shit, unlike you. I won't be making any kind of joint statement with you, and I especially won't paint my girlfriend as the culprit. You need to leave right now because I'm going to be honest—you make me sick."

Recoiling, she blinked as if she finally saw the person standing in front of her. "You're making a big mistake."

"No. I made one when I dated you." Carter took my hand and started walking toward the door. "Come on. Let's get out of here. I can't stand the sight of her."

Laughter came, and Jack shouted, "You got a video of that? 'Cause I wanna see *that* shit again."

I almost expected to hear Katherine's heels clicking behind us. But they never did. Carter and I went to his vehicle, and once the doors were shut with us inside, he shook his head. "Let's go home."

I nodded. Home sounded perfect.

CHAPTER FORTY

Later that day, I was baking in the kitchen when a loud knock sounded on the door.

I pulled two lasagna pans from the oven as Carter strolled into the kitchen, his hair wet from the shower he'd taken when he returned from his cleanup duty at the stadium. He beamed when he saw me standing there. I'd ordered groceries and had them delivered and had just finished making my mom's homemade lasagna with garlic bread and a Caesar salad.

"What's this?" he asked.

I frowned. "If I have to tell you, then I didn't do a good job."

He laughed and slid his hands under my shirt and around my waist. He nuzzled my neck, causing my body to warm.

"I fucking love lasagna," he said with a grin.

Placing the pans on the top of the stove, I turned around, wrapping my arms around his neck, not bothering to remove the oven mitts. "Well, good. But someone's at—"

The knock sounded again.

His arms tensed. "Let me go see who that is." He strolled

across the living room, looked through the peephole, and growled, "Fuck."

He turned around and marched back to me.

My mind raced with possibilities of who might be at the door. Katherine, Senator Grisham, Senator McHale. Those were the three that popped into my mind, especially after the "slap heard 'round the HSU campus" as the news channels were calling it. Carter had called a meeting with the guys, but they weren't due here for at least another hour.

I removed the large brown oven mitts and set them on the counter as Carter reached me.

"Now, where were we?" He quirked a brow and grabbed my hips, tugging me flush against him.

"Who is—" I started to ask, but his lips were on mine before I could finish the question.

When his hands slipped under my shirt again and he pressed his hardness against me, everything but him left my mind.

That was until I heard someone slide a key into the lock.

Carter froze. "You've got to be kidding me."

I opened my mouth to try again to ask who it was when the door swung open.

"You fucker." Jack strolled into the house with a key hanging from his finger. "Why didn't you..." He stopped and sniffed. "Sweet baby Jesus, there is a god."

I snorted, unable to stop myself, just as Samuel, Cole, and Grayson entered behind him.

"Get *out*." Carter released me while he adjusted himself and pointed to the door. "You're early for our meeting."

Of course, Jack's eyes went straight to Carter's crotch. Jack beamed. "Oh my, Carter. Are you happy to see me?"

"Man." Carter covered himself with his hand. "No. That

was all Evie. I was about to talk her into some fun while we waited for the food to cool."

Jack strolled over to me while Samuel, Cole, and Grayson remained close to the door. The three of them glanced at each other uncomfortably.

"Sit your asses down." Jack gestured to the couch. "We aren't leaving. He doesn't get a hot girl, sex any time he wants, and food that smells like heaven all to himself. Nope. He gets to share with his teammates and should be *thrilled* we decided to come early."

Jack opened the silverware drawer and snatched a fork, then went over to a pan and stabbed a corner of the lasagna.

Carter growled, "Evie's mine."

"Fine." Jack shrugged and moaned as he chewed his bite. "I'll happily settle for the food."

I laughed. "There's more than enough for all of us."

Samuel's eyes brightened. "Seriously?"

"Yeah." I nodded toward the pans of food. "Dig in."

Cole and Samuel weren't shy about loading up their plates while Grayson stayed next to the couch, staring at me. His face was lined with either worry or hurt…or hell, most likely a combination of the two.

"Come on. Have some food," I said softly, hoping the awkwardness would dissipate if he had something to focus on other than me.

"Thanks." He smiled sadly. "It smells great."

Carter threw an arm around my shoulders. "Jack, how the hell did you wind up with a key again?"

"A magician never reveals his tricks." Jack piled up his plate. "If I tell you, I might not be able to do it again."

"Bastard."

I shoved Carter in the side and snickered. "Why did you all

stop by early? Carter didn't know I was making dinner, so that excuse won't work."

"We were coming to see if you two wanted to eat with us and start the mission *Keep Evie Safe* discussion early." A huge string of cheese stretched from the side of Jack's plate to the pan as he tried to pile on all the cheese he could. "Samuel decided he could actually hang out with us tonight, so I dragged Grayson and Cole here too."

I glanced at Samuel to find him staring at me. He gave me a smile and nodded.

"Dude, come on," Cole groaned, shoving Jack away. "Your plate is full."

"There's a salad too." I pointed to it sitting at the end of the counter.

Jack traipsed off with a wrinkled nose. "I'm a growing boy. I don't need any of that green shit."

Once Jack was out of the way, the line moved way faster. Soon, Samuel and Cole joined Jack at the table while Carter and Grayson glared at each other.

Not wanting Carter to feel threatened, needing to reinforce that we were together, I wrapped my arms around him. Grayson winced and picked up a plate. Carter relaxed marginally under my touch, which made my stomach flutter.

Pulling me against him, Carter kissed me. He tucked a piece of hair behind my ear and smiled. "I bet you taste better than lasagna anyway."

"I'm sure she does, but she won't be as filling." Jack snorted at his own joke.

"Why did you invite them to stay again?" he grumbled, his breath tickling my ear.

A shiver ran down my spine. "Because they're your friends, and they're here to help us with Katherine."

He arched a brow. "Are you sure about that?"

I giggled. "Yeah. I am." I handed him a plate. "Now eat. You had a tough practice today."

"Yes, ma'am." He winked and loaded up just as much food as Jack had. When I got to the second pan, there was just one large section left and almost all the salad.

I cut a sliver off the lasagna, but before I could move, Carter shook his head. "Nope, you made this." He snatched the spatula back from me and put the remainder on my plate. "Just know this proves I love you since I won't get any leftovers."

"Whoa." Jack's fork dropped, and his head whipped our way. "Did he say *love*?"

Carter kissed my cheek, and I couldn't help my goofy grin.

After I filled my plate with salad, I found an open spot between Carter and Jack. By the time I sat down, Jack had already demolished most of his food.

Smacking his lips, Jack leaned back. "This is so much better than the food at Hallow's Bar."

"Is that where you wanted to go?" I arched a brow.

"Yeah, that's our hangout spot." Jack shoveled in his final bite.

Carter rolled his eyes. "Because she works there."

"So?" Jack shrugged his shoulders. "I like the vibe."

Stabbing some salad with my fork, I glanced at Jack and said, "You do realize that I don't want to eat there on my days off, right?"

"Told you." Cole snorted and took a sip of his Coke. "I wouldn't want to hang out where I worked either."

"Fine." Jack waved us off. "I'll find another place to go when Evie's not working. Problem solved."

The fact that even Jack wanted to include me made that void I carried a little smaller. In a way, the guys had accepted me as part of their group. Something I'd never truly had before.

I settled in as Jack launched into the story of his latest

conquest back in his hometown. Cole and Samuel egged him on, asking for gory details that I'd have rather not heard, but Jack seemed to enjoy answering. Carter tried to hide his laughter, but his shaking shoulders gave him away.

Jack smirked arrogantly, and the story sounded exaggerated for impact, but I couldn't help but notice that his smile was a little flatter than usual. I worried that there was more to the story, but now wasn't the time to ask him about the girl—in front of all his friends.

Then, the conversation changed to Katherine. Each of them agreed to watch out for me when I was on campus. I felt sort of silly since I was a grown-ass woman, but if all four of them were concerned about her, then maybe I needed to take the threat more seriously.

When we finished, Jack threw his napkin onto his plate. "That was fantastic. Even better than Thanksgiving."

My face flamed at the compliment.

"Now that we're done here"—Cole stood, a huge smile on his face—"it's laser tag time."

"You *four* have fun." Carter placed a hand on my thigh under the table.

Jack's face fell. "What? You didn't even ask Evie."

"Not going to." Carter's hand inched higher, brushing my core and making my breath catch. "She's interested in the same activities as I am. The kind where none of you are invited."

"Tell him you're not." Jack pouted at me.

"Sorry." My body had been yearning for Carter ever since he'd wrapped his arms around me when he got home. "He's right."

Jack crossed his arms. "That's not very nice or hospitable."

"Well..." Carter stood.

For a moment, I thought he might have changed his mind.

He walked over to Jack like he was going to pat his arm, but instead, he snatched Jack's keys from his pocket.

"What the fuck?" Jack said and tried to grab them back.

Carter spun and dodged his attempt as he quickly removed the house key from the ring. He slid it down the front of his pants before tossing the key chain back to Jack.

Jack caught the keys and arched a brow. "You don't think I'll go fishing for that key in there?"

I snorted, leaning back in my chair, ready to watch the show.

"You've got to be kidding." Carter stiffened. "You wouldn't—"

That was when Jack attacked, his hand reaching for Carter's belt. Carter retreated a few feet, slamming into the table.

"Get your hands off me," Carter growled, but that didn't prevent Jack from yanking the belt out of his pant loops.

"Then give me my key." He tugged at Carter's waistband.

"What the hell!" Carter's face twisted, and he shoved Jack in the chest, forcing him to stumble back.

Quickly fastening his belt again, Carter grimaced. "Don't ever try to take my pants off again."

"Then don't stuff my key in there," Jack replied, steamrolling into Carter.

My eyes widened as I watched the two of them lunge back and forth. Jack swiped for Carter's belt again, but Carter moved backward, narrowly avoiding Jack's grasp. Jack shoved Carter into the wall and tried to keep him there.

I glanced at Grayson, Cole, and Samuel, who just remained seated. "Aren't you going to help him?" I asked, surprised none of them were jumping in.

"And miss this?" Cole laughed. "No fucking way. My money's on Jack. He's scrappy."

"Never underestimate Carter." Samuel grinned.

Grayson had his arms crossed. He scowled. "Those two are going to get hurt before our game on Saturday."

Uh-oh. I hadn't considered that.

Since the other guys weren't going to do anything, I stood and moved toward the two. Carter punched Jack in the gut, causing Jack to groan and hunch forward.

Now was the perfect opportunity. I slipped between them and stuck my hand down Carter's pants, not bothering with the belt. I let my hand graze him as I fished for the cool metal.

He hardened underneath my fingers, and his hand snagged my waist, pulling me close. He lowered his head to my ear and hissed, "What are you doing?"

"That's right," Jack said behind me. "Get that for me."

My hand touched the key, and I yanked it out then quickly deposited it into my own pants. I turned around to face Jack and arched a brow. "You better not try to get it now."

Jack grinned wickedly. "I hear a challenge."

"Don't you fucking *dare*," Carter warned, stepping around me and placing himself between us. "If you touch my girlfriend inappropriately, I'll really kick your ass."

"Seriously." Jack huffed and looked around Carter to glare at me. "We were having fun, but you had to go put the key out of bounds."

"So you wanted to get in Carter's pants?" I teased.

He shrugged. "I don't discriminate." Mischief glinted in his eyes as he raised his remaining keys and placed them down his pants. He then did a little jig. "Are you going to go searching for these?"

I mashed my lips together, trying to hide my smile. I didn't want to encourage him.

"What is *wrong* with you?" Carter huffed.

Jack pouted. "Hey, it was worth a shot."

"Get out." Carter pointed to the door. "Now. You got fed, we made a plan, now leave."

"But—" Jack whined.

"Come on, man." Samuel rolled his eyes and grinned. "We've harassed those two enough. I want to go beat your ass before it gets too late."

"Beat my ass?" Jack scoffed. "We'll see about that."

Grayson and Cole stood too, and I sensed Grayson's gaze on me. I kept mine averted. I hadn't realized things would be so weird between us once he learned that Carter and I were officially together.

"Thanks for dinner, Evie." Cole winked as the four of them strolled out.

Carter raced over and locked the door behind them, muttering, "Before Jack changes his mind."

I swallowed a chuckle and began cleaning the table. When Carter came up beside me, I expected him to help, but instead, he slid a hand under my waistband.

My heart stopped. "What are you doing?"

"Just need to get that key back before Jack tries to break through the window so he can retrieve it." He nuzzled my neck, his breath fanning my ear.

As his hand went deeper, his fingers slid between my folds, and my back arched against him.

"I don't think it's in there," I whispered as his fingers slipped inside me.

"Better be sure." His mouth lowered, kissing my neck, and his other hand slid under my shirt and bra and caressed a nipple.

His thumb rubbed my most sensitive spot as he pumped his fingers in and out of me. Between that and the wonderful grazing of his teeth and tongue on my neck and how he kept stroking my breasts, I began to come unglued in minutes.

"Carter, I need to touch you," I begged.

"Nope." He chuckled and sucked on my neck. "This is your punishment for getting me hard in front of my teammates."

An orgasm tore through me, and he held me tight, continuing to work my body. When I went limp, he scooped me up and carried me to the couch.

As he stood over me, his eyes were liquid gold with the emotions that brimmed within him. He stripped me down, placed the key on the coffee table, and then removed his clothes. Then he settled between my legs and pressed against my entrance.

My brain fogged, but then something struck me with sudden clarity. "Condom."

"You're on the pill, right?" he asked and propped himself up on his hands.

I nodded. "You see me take it every night."

"That's good enough for me if it is for you. I was tested again last week, and I'm still negative." His eyes locked with mine. "I want you to be the first person I have this experience with."

I held his gaze, feeling a little teary. "Me too," I murmured. My traitorous body answered for me as well, pressing against him...and then he slid inside me.

He hissed. "Fuck. You feel so damn *good*."

It did feel different. It felt amazing. My hands dug into his back, urging him on. And before long, he was moving inside me.

Each thrust felt better than the last, so different than all the times before. But I needed more. "Turn on your back."

He eagerly lifted me and obeyed, and when I straddled him and he slid inside me again, I almost came undone.

I rode him, frenzied, the sensations more intense than ever.

His hands grabbed my hips as he thrust just as desperately into me. His body shuddered, and he rasped, "I can't wait any longer."

The wild need in his voice drove me the rest of the way over, and ecstasy flooded my body. He groaned as he completed his own release.

When we stilled, he pulled me down and into his arms. He kissed my lips as we cuddled together on the couch.

He whispered, "That was unbelievable. You're going to be my undoing."

The words should've brought warmth, but there was almost a sense of foreboding in them. I didn't know why I felt that way...everything was perfect between us. What could possibly go wrong?

CHAPTER FORTY-ONE

C arter turned onto HSU's main road, and I gazed at him and smiled.

Between the tension at school and getting the rest of my graduate school applications out, my uneasy feeling about us had dissipated, and I was both looking forward to and dreading the upcoming Christmas break. After getting the application in to Stanford at the end of November, I'd turned in applications to several safety schools with slightly later deadlines, and today, I would take my first two finals of the semester. The final for photography was a video slide show of our best shots that showed the story of what we'd learned this semester, and I was looking forward to seeing the other students' work. Even Sadie's. My own set of pictures was captured on a hard drive in my bag.

As Carter pulled into the parking lot near my first class, my phone rang. I glanced down to see Haven's name scrolling across the screen. She usually texted, so I picked up the phone.

"Guess whose room is finally ready!" she said loudly.

My stomach lurched. I'd known it could be any day now,

but I still hadn't been prepared. And I still had to purchase new stuff with money I didn't have.

"It is?" I asked, trying to sound excited. Stress weighed on my shoulders. "Okay, I'll get my stuff ordered tonight."

I'd have to apply for a credit card, something I'd been determined not to do.

"I'm so excited for you to come back!" Haven exclaimed. "I've missed you."

I felt bad. I'd been so wrapped up in Carter that I hadn't seen my roommates much beyond Leah at work since before Thanksgiving. I had to do better; they were my friends too. "Me too. I'll text you when I'm bringing things over."

Carter pulled into his spot and turned off the car. When I glanced at him, I was met by a deep scowl.

"What's wrong?" I turned toward him, taking his hand.

"Your room's ready?" He fidgeted.

Heart racing, I tilted my head. "I figured you'd be happy." We spent almost all our time together, and he'd lost his house as a sole refuge—I'd kind of ruined his flow these past few months.

"Definitely not happy. I keep asking you to move in with me permanently." He ran his fingers through my hair, tucking a piece behind my ear. "I mean, you don't have to rush out and buy stuff you don't like. You can take your time, and we could even go shopping together or something."

Relief flooded me, and my lungs worked once again. He wasn't ready to get rid of me, which was nice since I really couldn't afford too many things right now. "I just don't want to overstay my welcome and have things get strained between us. Besides, your parents disapprove of us, and I don't think living together officially is smart...at least, not before you get drafted."

"Babe." Carter leaned over and tipped my chin up so that I was staring into his eyes. "I want to be clear. The nights you're not staying with me, I'll be staying with you. I have no intention of sleeping without you, so we're in *no* hurry. At least, at my place, we don't have roommates who party every weekend. Promise me you won't buy shit just to get out of my hair because I'm not going anywhere."

His words should've scared me because what he'd said was just too perfect. But I pushed that doubt away and kissed him, getting lost in the moment.

A WEEK LATER, I wrung my hands as we drove to the airport. Carter was heading home to see his family over the holiday break, and he'd begged me to go with him, but I'd declined. We'd had enough drama there to last a lifetime.

Luckily, nothing else happened. Katherine had stayed away, and the local university football players hadn't come around. Carter and I managed to finish our finals, work, practice, and spend time together, including sex that just got better and better every night. Things were amazing between us, but now he was heading home, and I'd be alone for Christmas. So I'd finally gotten new furniture for the rental house and planned to stay there with Leah and Haven.

"You can stay at the townhouse," Carter said as he pulled up to the drop-off area in front of the airport. "You know it's your home."

But without him...it wasn't. The place would feel empty. "Nah, Haven and Leah have been asking me to come back, and it'll give me some time to hang out with them one on one."

He got out and headed to the trunk of the vehicle. My heart ached at the knowledge he was going, but this was something he needed to do—be with his family while he still could. How I wished I was able to do that.

I climbed out, trying not to cry, as he walked back to me with his bag.

Smiling sadly, he tucked a piece of my hair behind my ear. He murmured, "You can still change your mind and come."

We'd had this conversation over and over again. "I don't think that would be smart."

"Then I could stay here." He stepped toward me.

"You need to be with your family." I cupped his cheek. "Besides, it's only five days. You'll be back soon to prepare for the bowl game on New Year's Eve."

He kissed me, his tongue sliding into my mouth. I responded eagerly, wishing with everything in me that he didn't have to go.

When he pulled back, he brushed his fingers along my cheek. "I love you."

"I love you, too." My eyes burned as I swallowed the lump in my throat. He was going to be flying to Nashville with Katherine again, and I wanted to lash out in jealousy, but that wasn't right. None of this was his fault, and I trusted him.

"I'll call you when I get there." He slid his keys into my hand.

I nodded, unable to speak without breaking down.

He groaned, kissed me one last time, then headed toward the building as I leaned against the car.

As he disappeared inside, Katherine's words echoed in my ears. *He and I are going to be together.*

I DROVE BACK, letting a few tears slip down my cheeks, and parked on the curb in front of the rental, not wanting to block Leah and Haven in the driveway. It was Friday, so I had to work tonight. Christmas was in five days, and with all the students off for break, the bar shouldn't be that busy.

Nonetheless, Carter made me promise that Joe would walk me to the car each night—not that he even had to be asked after what had happened. Even when Carter showed up to pick me up, Joe had seen us off, afraid that something else might happen outside.

It was nearing noon, so I had about four hours before I had to leave. That gave me enough time to wallow and pout and think about all the things Katherine might be saying and doing while hitting on my boyfriend.

Lovely.

Last night, Carter had helped me get everything set up downstairs. He'd also added another lock on the door in case Leah and Haven decided to have any parties while he couldn't be there to watch out for me.

When I walked through the front door, I found Leah and Haven eating pizza on the couch. Haven beamed as she patted the empty seat between them.

"Hey, you," she exclaimed, placing her plate on the table and launching into my arms. "I'm so glad you're home! We've missed you."

I returned the hug. Haven's optimism and warmth was one of the things I loved most about her. "I missed you too."

"Not enough to come around and hang with us though, right?" She leaned back and arched a brow.

I hung my head. "I'm sorry. Between classes, work, and..." I trailed off, realizing how bad it would sound. "Carter." In other words, I was a piss-poor friend. I hung my head. "I'm so sorry."

"Girl, please." Haven tugged me down so that I sat between them. "If I had a man like that, I wouldn't want to leave his side either. And it wasn't like you had space here to truly be. It's fine. Leah works all the damn time too, so we wouldn't have had much time to hang out. We barely see each other more than in passing most days."

"Hey, she was feeling guilty." Leah threw a piece of crust at Haven. "She deserves to, for having a fine-ass man like that."

I pointed at her. "Yes, he is. And mine, so please refrain from referencing him like that again."

"Aaand she's clearly possessive of him." Leah snorted. "Which, if I had a man—"

I reached over and shoved her, laughing. "Not nice."

"Come on." Haven grabbed the remote. "We thought you might need some company with him gone, so I figured it's time to start something fresh and new. Let's watch some stand-up comedy!"

Even though it wasn't really my thing, I sat back and nestled in, wanting to give my friends the time they deserved. I found myself laughing with them until it was time for work.

CARTER HAD BEEN GONE for two days. It felt like a lifetime. We texted constantly and talked for a couple of hours in the morning and at night, but it wasn't enough. I missed him desperately and needed him here with me.

The nightmares had come back. The past two nights without Carter, I'd relived the accident over and over, waking up soaked with sweat.

Luckily, it was a Sunday night, so the bar was quieter than normal, but we still had a few customers there. I was taking the order of a few local college students when a woman entered the bar and sat near the door, in front of the windows.

Leah was in the back, working the kitchens since we were short-staffed, so I had the whole restaurant to serve.

I strolled over to her and smiled. "Hi. What can I start you off with today?"

Her long chestnut-brown hair waved down her back, and her hazel eyes seemed familiar. She tapped a long purple-and-gold fingernail against the menu she'd pulled from the table holder and tugged at the lapel of her knockoff pantsuit. "Do you have chardonnay?"

"Yes, ma'am."

"Oh." She placed a hand against her chest. "You have manners. That's lovely."

"Thank you." That was an odd thing to say.

"My boy deserves someone like that." She pressed her crimson lips together and batted thick fake lashes. "He deserves someone who treats him kindly."

My pen froze as a frisson of warning coursed down my spine. "I'm sorry?"

"Carter Grisham." She smiled dreamily. "My son. You're his girlfriend, right? The news station said you are."

Fuck me. She must have seen the slap heard 'round campus when the news stations had identified me as the senators' charity case and Carter Grisham's girlfriend.

"I'm sorry. I didn't realize..." I trailed off, not knowing what to say. This encounter felt off, and I wanted it to be over.

"Don't worry." She waved a hand. "Things between his dad and me are tense, but now Carter is almost out of college and going into the NFL on top of that. Plus his trust fund will be released when he's twenty-five. I figure I don't need to stay away anymore since he'll be his own man. I'm Karen, by the way."

Acid burned my throat. She could be coming around because Carter would soon come into a lot of money, especially if he was first draft pick like everyone was assuming. However, I pushed the thought away, hoping like hell I was wrong.

And here I thought I couldn't dislike someone more than his father. Oh, how wrong I was. "Evie. And I'm sure you're very proud of him." I tried to keep the disdain from my voice. "I'm sorry, but I need to check on my other tables. I'll be back soon with your drink."

"Please make it two. I'm expecting someone."

"You've got it," I said and scurried off, wanting to get my thoughts together. Out of every possible situation I could face with Carter's family, I hadn't imagined this one. I didn't understand the woman at all. How could she not want to be in her son's life and be okay with receiving money in lieu of that?

I picked up the drinks for her and another table just as a woman in her midtwenties entered. Her gaze was glued to her phone, and when she looked up, it landed on Karen. She hurried over just as I reached my first table and handed off the drinks. Then I made my way to them.

As I placed the second wineglass on the table, Karen's hand covered mine and she smiled at me. Her companion had her phone raised, seeming completely preoccupied.

"Thank you, darling." Karen batted her eyes. "When you're ready, please bring the check. We won't be here that long."

That was more than fine with me. I smiled, releasing my hold on the glass. "I'll be back soon with it."

This whole situation was strange.

After turning in a third table's order, I generated Karen's check. As I glanced up, I noticed the younger girl sliding an envelope across the table to Karen, who took it and placed it in her large purse.

Something weird was definitely going on, but based on the stuff Carter had said about his mom, that wasn't surprising.

I handed her the check, and the younger woman handed me a twenty while draining her glass.

"Keep the change." She smiled tightly then slid out and left.

"Well, dear. I hope you have a good night." Karen had drunk only half the glass, but she followed her friend out the door.

I was just relieved that they were both gone. I'd tell Carter about it when he got back into town. I didn't want to worsen his time at home by informing him that his mom was in town. He'd want to come back and ensure she didn't bother me.

Pushing the thoughts away, I got back to work, eager for the days to fly by till his return.

CHAPTER FORTY-TWO

Christmas Eve was hard. This had been Mom's favorite holiday, and she'd covered the house both inside and out with lights galore. I stood in the living room of the small rental house, noting that we hadn't done shit to decorate for the holiday.

My roommates were with their families tonight, and they'd both described their families' penchants for decorating. They hadn't wanted to decorate here too, and I didn't want the ghosts of my own holiday memories hanging over me.

So here I sat in the growing darkness, alone.

My hand itched to call Carter, but I knew he was with his family. I hadn't heard from him in a few hours, and he hadn't responded to my last two texts. He and his dad had gotten into it earlier, but Carter refused to talk about why. His silence had me ruminating on the strange encounter with his mother.

Between not hearing from him, the loss of my parents, and my stupid decision to spend Christmas by myself, the deep hole in my chest pulsed with pain, grief, and memories that hurt.

I wrapped my arms around my legs and let out a short sob. Unable to do anything else, I let the pain eddy around me, feeling like I might drown. I shifted to lie down on the couch and was considering putting on a movie when a loud banging sounded on the door.

My breath caught as I startled.

Who the hell would be here tonight?

I jumped to my feet and made my way to the door. When I pulled it open, my jaw dropped.

I blinked, thinking this had to be a mirage or some sort of dream.

Carter's brows rose, and the sequined red nose of his ugly reindeer sweater glistened in the porch light. "This isn't the welcome I was expecting."

Even his voice sounded real, and his scent flooded my nose. I pinched myself, needing to wake up pronto. "Ouch," I exclaimed.

He tilted his head. "Why are you pinching yourself, babe?"

And then my heart took off, and I lunged into his arms. "Carter!" I didn't even give a shit that the sweater's sequins pressed into my cheek uncomfortably.

"Now this is more like it." He wrapped his arms around me, holding me close. "For a second, I thought I'd made a huge mistake by coming back."

I shook my head, pulling back so I could look at his face again to make sure he was really here, but my damn vision blurred. My voice broke as I said, "I'm so damn glad you're here."

"Hey," he said softly, his fingers wiping the tears from my face. "It's okay. I never should've left in the first place."

That was enough to jolt me back to the present. "Wait. Your family. You left them?" My voice rose as if I was asking a question, though I hadn't actually asked one. "Why? You should go back."

"No." He leaned down and kissed me sweetly. "I'm not leaving. Dad and I fought every time we talked—it turns out my mom's been bugging him too, and I was right. He's afraid if he releases any of my trust fund, she'll get ahold of it somehow. Katherine kept showing up, and I had to keep throwing her out of the house. There wasn't any peace there, and the entire time, I wanted to be with you. And then I realized I could. That there was absolutely nothing there that made me want to stay."

"But—"

He kissed me again, cutting off my words. Then he cupped my face, the golden flecks of his eyes, almost the entire iris. "Babe, you had amazing parents, and damn, I wish I would've gotten to meet them to thank them for raising such an incredible woman. But my parents... They aren't like that. They don't make me feel loved or have fun traditions like you did with yours. My mom wants to use me for money. My dad wants to make sure I don't need anything else from him once I graduate. My stepmom doesn't like me, and my sister doesn't even acknowledge I'm alive. There's only one person who feels like family, and I choose to be with her this holiday."

"Carter..." My throat thickened as I stared at the man who owned my heart before me. "I love you so damn much."

"Yeah?" He winked. "That's a good thing because I'm crazy about you."

My cheeks hurt from how wide I was smiling. "But Carter?"

His brows furrowed. "Yeah."

"Why in the hell are you wearing that awful sweater?" I glanced down at poor Rudolph, who had seen way better days.

"You like it?" He took a step back and tugged at the material on his chest. "I thought it screamed holiday spirit."

"It sure does scream *something*." I snorted.

He pouted and then waggled his brows. "So you want to get me out of it?"

Warmth flooded me. "Maybe." I placed my hands on his chest and flexed my fingers, staring at him.

"So that's why people really wear ugly Christmas sweaters." He winked. "I get it now." He took my hand and paused. "Two questions. One, were you really sitting in the dark? And two, where are my keys?"

My stomach sank. "Wait. How did you get here?" I had his car. "You should've had me pick you up at the airport."

"Uber, and then it would've ruined the surprise." He turned on the lights and stepped into the house. "So where are the keys? We need to go home."

I laughed. "We can go downstairs and take your awful sweater off. Leah and Haven aren't here. They're with their families for the night. Both of them tried to drag me with them, but it didn't feel right."

He paused. "And you stayed here by yourself? Were you planning to spend the holiday totally alone?"

I bit my bottom lip. "It's not a big deal. I was—"

I shut up when his eyes narrowed on my face. He rasped, "Don't bullshit me, Evie. I know how much you and your parents loved the holidays. Were you sitting here in the dark alone because you were missing them?"

I shrugged.

"And you were determined for me to stay with my family, knowing that you'd be devastated?"

"It's...just a day." I would've made it through the night even if I fell apart.

His jaw clenched. "It's a damn good thing I came home." He scanned the living room. "Where *are* the keys? I'm ready to take you back to our place."

Our place. I liked the sound of that way too much. "On the kitchen table."

He strode into the kitchen, and I heard the keys slide across the table. Then he was back to me within seconds, a grin on his face.

I tilted my head. "What's up?"

"You'll see. Get whatever you need to stay with me." He winked, so I quickly gathered a bag as well as his gift.

We were on the road in minutes, holiday music playing for the short drive back. We pulled into the garage of his condominium, and the two of us headed up the stairs. When we reached the main floor, I stopped, my heart lunging into my throat.

He'd decorated the entire living room. Colorful lights hung around the fireplace, and a huge decorated tree stood in the corner of the room with presents wrapped in bright, shiny paper underneath.

"How?" I swallowed around the large lump in my throat.

"Well, I got the idea the other day when I noticed how boring my stepmom's white decorations were. I thought to myself, I bet Evie and her parents did things in color, and that was when I decided it was time to come back. I booked a flight the next day and organized all this stuff yesterday so I could put it all up when I got back this afternoon before I came to you."

"*That's* why you weren't answering my texts." I was stunned. He was busy doing all this for me.

He hung his head. "I'm sorry. I should have, but I didn't have much time. I wanted to come get you and drag you here, but I also wanted to make this special. I should've been there for you. I didn't think about you being depressed, but after seeing you—"

I ran to him, cutting him off with my lips on his. No one had ever done anything like this for me before. My hands slid under his sweater, caressing the curves of his abs. He shuddered under my touch, driving my need for him higher.

He pulled away and laughed. "Does this mean you like it?"

"Love it." I cradled his face, enjoying his scruff under my palms. "You are too good to me. I don't deserve it."

His hands clutched my waist. "You deserve all this and more. I never want to spend another holiday without you ever again."

I crushed my lips to his, devouring him. I'd known I loved him before, but right now, I cared for him so much that my chest threatened to burst. I walked him backward until his calves hit the edge of the couch. There was one thing I wanted to do for him, and it was to make him feel as much love as I did right now.

Not bothering to turn the lights on, I unbuttoned his jeans and pushed them down along with his briefs. He was hard, and his eyes darkened as I dropped to my knees. And when my mouth was on him, he moaned, fisting his hands in my hair.

"Hey you," Carter murmured, nuzzling his face into my neck. "If you don't get up soon, we're going to miss Christmas morning."

My face was plastered to his bare chest, and his hands ran up and down my sides. This was like heaven, and I didn't want to move, especially with the way his body warmed mine.

"Keep doing that, and there'll only be one thing I want to unwrap." I reached down, cupping him in my hand.

He chuckled. "I'm naked...it's already unwrapped."

"That's the best kind of present." I lifted my face from his chest so I could kiss him, making my intentions known.

We'd had sex twice last night after my initial thank-you gift, but for some reason, that wasn't enough.

His eyes darkened as he thrust in my hand. "This attraction between us—it's not normal. No matter how many hours we spend together or how much sex we have, I always want more of both."

"I know. I feel the same way," I murmured. The strength of my feelings for him scared the hell out of me.

"Good." He smirked and then kissed me.

His tongue darted inside my mouth, and I eagerly met each of his strokes, wanting more. He rolled onto his back, pulling me on top of him. We were both naked, so our skin touched everywhere, and his hand slid between us. He eased his fingers inside me as he placed his thumb between my lips. My body hummed with anticipation.

My hips moved against his hand as he moved his fingers in and out of me, inching deeper inside. The friction knotted in my stomach.

"God, you're so damn beautiful," he gritted out, his eyes locked on my face. "I love watching you fall apart for me."

Those words urged me closer to the quickest orgasm I'd ever experienced in my life.

"Good girl," he growled as he moved faster, the ecstasy catching me by surprise.

My body quivered as I rode the high, and when I stilled, he removed his hands and nudged his head against my entrance.

If I'd thought the orgasm would sate me, I was wrong. I needed more of him, so I sank onto him, rolling my hips immediately.

His head arched back as his eyelids fluttered. Seeing him at my mercy only made me want to torture him more. I slowed my pace and felt him fill and leave me with each movement.

"You're going to kill me," he said hoarsely, digging his

fingers into my hips, trying to make me move faster, but I kept my languid pace.

His fingers bit into my skin, igniting something wild inside me. With each flick of my hips, he thrust eagerly to match my pace. I spread my knees wider, allowing him to go deeper, and he hissed.

"Babe, you better hurry." His eyes opened, locking on my face. "I won't last much longer." To prove it, he pressed my hips down hard against him as he drove deeper than ever before. He paused, forcing me to grind against him, and I cried out as another orgasm ripped through me.

He quickened his pace, and soon, his own body shuddered with his release. We worked each other's bodies until the bliss faded to a warm contentment.

He grinned. "That was so intense."

I flopped against his chest, and he rolled over, holding me. I smiled, taking in his handsome face. "It was perfect."

"Just like you," he murmured.

Just as I was ready to nuzzle into his chest once again, he removed his hands and stood up. Then he reached over and smacked my ass. "Now, let's get up. I got presents for you."

"Fine." I stuck out my tongue and rolled out of bed. I picked up my pajamas and put them on, and the two of us headed downstairs.

He picked out five of the presents under the tree and brought them to me. My mouth dropped open. "Carter, this is too much. I thought most of these were for other people."

"I wanted to do this." He gestured to the presents. "So deal with it. Open them."

I swallowed my discomfort and nodded. I picked up the biggest box, tore off the shiny silver paper...and saw a top-of-the-line camera staring back at me. I froze and then glanced at him as he beamed.

"You're so talented, I wanted you to have a camera of your own so you can take pictures even when you have to turn the school camera back in." He smiled tenderly, watching me stroke the package.

My hands shook as I opened the next presents. All of them were high-end accessories that went with the camera. When it was all said and done, I couldn't breathe. I hadn't spent a tenth of what he'd spent on me. "We need to return this." The last thing I wanted him to think was that I might be like his mom. That fear burned in my chest like a fire in a dry forest. "I can't accept—"

"You can, and you will." Carter reached over and brushed his fingers along my chin. "I wanted to do something nice for you, so please let me."

I nodded, still unable to believe that I owned something this nice.

"There's still one more. The most important." He took a present from under the tree, one I'd assumed was for someone else.

I grinned, taking note of the rectangular box. "You bought me clothes?"

"Not exactly." He shrugged, biting his bottom lip. "It's more..." he tilted his head "...*gently* used."

My brows furrowed, but I took the box and quickly unwrapped it. After his hesitant response, I wanted to know what it was more than ever.

When I lifted the lid, my breath caught. I ran my hands over the material and lifted it up.

I was holding a jersey with the number twelve. And it smelled faintly of sweat.

"It was my jersey freshman year. I kept it." He bit his bottom lip. "I was hoping you'd wear it to games now that we've gone public with our relationship. I'd love to see you wearing my name and number. I tried to get the sweat stench out, but..."

My heart pounded and my eyes burned. The magnitude of the gift caused my stomach to flutter. He wanted the whole world to know we were together. "That makes it even more perfect. This is the best gift ever."

I cleared my throat and went to pick up the two presents I had for him. Somehow, I'd fallen a little more in love, and now it was my turn to give him something.

Something that wouldn't measure up.

He arched a brow and opened the first one, then paused when the image came into view. It was a framed photo of him throwing a pass to Jack. I'd caught the second the ball sailed out of his hands and arched down the field, and his strong body was twisted in a beautiful running pose.

Without a word, he moved to open the next one. It was an image of him laughing with a group of the football players. His head was tossed back, a huge smile on his face, and Jack had his hands lifted as he told some story. It was so them.

Carter's expression was unreadable, and something heavy sank in my stomach. Did he hate them? "I know they're not much, and I'm sorry. But I wanted you to see two sides of you that I have the privilege of seeing every day." I tucked a piece of hair behind my ear, nerves churning in my stomach. "The focused, determined man on the field, and the loyal, happy man who loves his friends."

"I love them." His voice was a low timbre. "No one has ever done something like this for me." He turned his head and smiled. "But the next gift I want is a picture of you and me."

I bit my lip. "I can do that now that you gave me a fancy camera."

We both laughed, and he pulled me into his arms...and for the first time in a long time, everything just felt right.

THE LAST FIVE days of break were amazing, though Carter had to go back to football practice to prepare for the championship game. The rest of the team had come back from break early too, and now Carter was meeting everyone on campus to board the bus that would take them to Atlanta while I'd returned to the house I shared with Leah and Haven.

There was a knock on the front door, but I ignored it. Anyone who would come to visit me was already getting ready to board the bus, meaning it had to be for either Haven or Leah.

I heard the front door open, and then a few seconds later, a frantic knock banged on my door, followed by Leah yelling, "Uh...Evie, you've got visitors."

My blood ran cold. If it was Carter, he would've just come into my room, knowing he didn't need to knock, so I had no clue who it could be.

I jogged up the stairs, and when I opened the door to the kitchen, Leah's face was stiff. Her gaze flicked toward the small kitchen table where Katherine and Mrs. McHale sat.

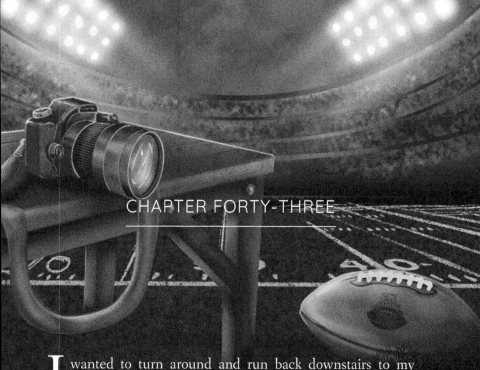

CHAPTER FORTY-THREE

I wanted to turn around and run back downstairs to my room, but I refused to cower. I had no clue why those two were here, but I had no doubt this wasn't going to be pleasant.

Tugging down the sleeves of my fuchsia top, I cleared my throat as fear seized my limbs. "Is Senator McHale okay? Did something happen to him?"

Mrs. McHale wrinkled her nose, and Katherine just laughed.

Katherine tossed her hair over her long-sleeved HSU shirt. "Oh, nothing is wrong with good, sweet *Daddy*. Don't worry. Right now, you need to worry about you and Carter."

I swallowed. "Why would I be worried about us?"

Katherine's lips flattened. "There won't be an *us* for much longer."

"And here I thought you and Carter exaggerated how bitchy she is." Leah's mouth twisted. "I think you actually downplayed it. She's a fucking wench."

Katherine's eyes homed in on her, and she sneered. "I don't

know who you are, but it doesn't matter. I'll crush you like everyone else."

Mrs. McHale rolled her eyes. "Katherine, now isn't the time." She rubbed a hand down her cream top and smiled at my roommate, fakeness oozing from every pore. "Do you mind if we speak with Evie alone?"

"Actually, yeah." Leah placed her hands on her hips.

At this moment, if I wasn't completely head over heels in love with Carter, I was quite certain I would've fallen for Leah. She was gorgeous, loyal, and ready to fight dirty for me. "It's fine." Whatever they had to say, I'd eventually have to hear it. This bunch had their ways.

"E—" Leah started again.

I held up a hand. I wanted Katherine and Mrs. McHale gone, which meant the sooner I heard whatever insults they had to toss my way, the quicker they'd leave. I was all about the latter option.

"Fine." Leah huffed. "Just yell if you need me."

Katherine snorted. "Would she even need to yell? Look how dumpy this house is. I bet we could hear the neighbors if this bitch would stop running her mouth."

"We aren't here for insults, Katherine." Mrs. McHale straightened. "Of course, she'll yell if she needs you. We aren't here to physically harm her."

I didn't miss the fact that she added *physically* in that sentence. They must be here to play more mind games, a price I was willing to pay if it meant I was with Carter.

Blowing out a breath, Leah arched a brow. "Haven and I will be in our rooms, so just yell."

I smiled. "Thanks." I'd kick both women out as soon as I could.

When Leah slowly walked out, I couldn't help but notice

the way Katherine smirked...as if she was in on some sort of private joke. I suspected I was about to learn about it.

Both she and Mrs. McHale remained quiet until we heard Leah's door shut down the hall.

Mrs. McHale cleared her throat and clutched her large purse close to her side. "Sorry to intrude, but we're limited on time since we're heading down to watch Katherine cheer and Carter play in Atlanta."

I arched a brow. "You mean, if you tried to meet me too soon and gave me any warning, you knew Carter would refuse to get on the bus with his teammates and stay here to see why you two are determined to talk to me alone?"

Mrs. McHale pressed her lips into a firm line.

"That's what you don't seem to get." They were so blinded by how they perceived me and the threat they made shit up in their heads, they were clueless about what Carter and I shared. "Even if you did make it clear you wanted to talk to me alone, I wouldn't tell Carter and risk him missing something so important to his future."

Katherine snorted. "You mean *your* future, right? After all, you want him drafted so you can spend his money."

No matter what, I was the bad guy. Either I wanted to control him and make sure he failed at what was important to him so I could drain him now, or I would push him to achieve his every goal so I could spend his money later. I wanted to yank my hair out, but they wanted to get a reaction from me, so I schooled my expression into a mask of indifference.

"What do you want?" I sighed, wanting to cut through the games and insults to simply get to the point. "I'm assuming you aren't here for a visit."

"In this place?" Katherine waved a hand in front of her nose like the kitchen stunk. "No. Pass."

Mrs. McHale ignored Katherine, keeping her gaze fixed on

me. "You want direct? I'll give it to you. If you don't break up with Carter after the bowl game, there will be serious consequences. One of which is the secret that you and my husband have been trying so hard to keep between the two of you."

My head jerked back, and I clenched my hands. "I don't *have* any secrets. I don't know how many times I have to tell you that."

"Oh, *sis*." Katherine twirled a piece of hair around her finger. "Don't keep playing that game."

Sis?

The word sounded weighted, though it truly had no meaning for me, especially if it involved *her*.

She sashayed over to me and rubbed a finger along my cheek. "I told you I would find out what you had over *Daddy*. And believe me, I wish I hadn't, yet here we are. You only have yourself to blame."

My heart thundered with the evil look in her eye. "I don't know what you're talking about."

"Honestly, I'd prefer it if you were fucking my dad to *this*." She grimaced as her fingernail prodded my skin. "To think that we actually share blood is disgusting."

I stared at her, trying to sort through what she'd said.

The reality of the situation slammed into me, making me feel as if I were back in the car with my parents the day of the crash. My knees trembled. "No. That can't be. If Senator McHale was my father, I'm sure I'd know."

Mrs. McHale scoffed. "Don't act like you didn't. Patrick received a call the day of the accident, and he rushed down to Chattanooga. Between that and then him pushing for the scholarship, I knew there was something you two were hiding. The private investigator was able to piece it together. All this time, I thought you were just a fling messing with both Patrick and Carter, but I refuse to allow you to become a permanent fixture."

"But I didn't know." I took a step back, needing space from both of them, but mainly Katherine. "And I don't want to be a permanent fixture. *Believe me.*"

My *half sister.*

Acid churned my stomach and burned my throat. "But if that's true, why didn't he tell me?" I'd never been interested in learning who my biological parents were, and hearing this confirmed why I hadn't wanted to in the first place. All it led to was disappointment and betrayal.

"He must not have wanted you to know. Probably knew you would try to bleed him for every penny we have." Katherine took a few steps back. "At least he was smart. Hell, *I* didn't want to know, but now I understand why he paid for your school." She barked out a laugh. "He should've just let you rot and be alone instead of forcing me to deal with you."

Right. This was all about her. Nothing to do with me.

My stomach tensed. "Does Carter know?"

Mrs. McHale took a step forward now, her gaze turning stony. "None of us did, thank God. It's bad enough that we had to learn of your existence. And you aren't going to tell him, or anyone else, for that matter."

I laughed, relieved that Carter hadn't been keeping this from me. "Uh...I know you're married to a senator and all, but you can't legally force me not to tell my *boyfriend* information I've learned."

"If you don't want him to hate you, that's exactly what you'll do." Mrs. McHale lifted her chin, the challenge in her eyes apparent.

"Hate me?" I touched my chest. "I haven't done anything—"

She opened her purse and removed a manila folder from inside. She opened it to reveal an image of Carter's mother, drinking a glass of wine and hugging me. It was taken from the angle of the person who'd met her there for a quick drink.

I pointed at it. "She came to my work and hugged me. Why would that—"

"She's willing to state that you two have been talking since before the wreck and that you blackmailed Senator McHale into paying for you to come here with the intent of getting a good education to further your career and to trick Carter into falling in love with you."

I shook my head. "You're insinuating that you're going to tell him that I somehow caused my parents' wreck? He won't believe that." Even saying those words made me want to vomit. I loved my parents more than anything. Despite how I felt about Carter, if there was a way I could go back in time and keep them alive, I'd do it in a heartbeat.

"Of course not." Mrs. McHale's nose lifted. "I would never insinuate anything like that. That would make the money we paid for you to attend here reflect poorly on us. But that could explain why Patrick showed up in your hospital room so quickly after the accident. You'd already reached out to him, blackmailing him for money."

Rubbing my hand over my stomach, I tried to hold myself together. "If I was going to blackmail him, it wouldn't be to attend this school with *her*." I pointed at Katherine.

"No, it was for money and this school." Katherine sneered. "It's not like you've shown him your bank account or anything. You played the poor act to lure him in at his mother's suggestion."

These people were awful. So much worse than I'd ever imagined. "If *Senator McHale* knows what you learned, why isn't he the one asking me to keep my mouth shut since clearly I'm a dirty secret?"

"Because Daddy isn't aware of our newfound knowledge."

Katherine fluffed her hair. "It's better that way. The two of you can continue not communicating, and you can start staying the fuck away from Carter."

"And why would I do that?" The thought of losing Carter had what he'd started mending of my heart ready to crumble worse than ever before.

"Because we'd hate for an unfortunate accident to happen to him." Mrs. McHale shrugged indifferently. "You know accidents happen all the time. I mean, look at you and your parents. He could easily get into a wreck and be so severely injured that he couldn't play in the NFL."

My vision blurred, but I swallowed past the large lump that formed in my throat. "Why do you care if Carter and I are together? He's not even your son. He hates Katherine."

"There's a thin line between hate and love, and with you out of the picture, Katherine can get him to look her way again. After all, Carter won't risk disappointing the one person who hasn't abandoned him—and believe me when I say Senator Grisham wants him to be with my daughter. So you're going to get out of the way. I refuse to sit by and watch you coerce him into marrying you and then have to see you all the damn time. I want you out of our lives the day you graduate."

"I think you underestimate him. And believe me…I don't want to be around any of you more than I have to be."

"Then you'll soon see how wrong *you* are." Mrs. McHale held her arms out wide. "I'm not going to risk you hanging around and Patrick's bleeding, weak heart getting the best of him. You will *not* be part of our family or hover around us, so help me. I don't mind dampening Carter's future if that gets you out of the picture." Her eyes flashed with anger and hatred.

She was serious. She would hurt Carter. She was that eager for me to disappear. A kick in the gut would hurt less than this.

In just five minutes, the one amazing thing I had going in my life, that steady rock that I leaned on, was being taken from me.

"Aww." Katherine pouted exaggeratedly. "I think she just realized she can't win."

Mrs. McHale glared at her daughter before turning back toward me. "Break up with him, and keep your distance from him, Katherine, Patrick, and me. You'll still get an education and a chance to make something of your life. I even got you a spot in the psychology program internship in Spain over the summer so you can start—"

I snorted, but it came out choked. "I don't want *anything* from you."

She paused, tilting her head. "Look, I'm giving you a gift for cooperating."

"Cooperating." I took a step toward her, my composure gone. "You come in here and tell me that Senator McHale is my father and that you worked with Carter's own mother to frame me so I look like I'm some sort of manipulative genius, and then threaten to physically injure the man I love, and you think I'm *cooperating?*"

"See?" Katherine flicked her wrist. "Foolish. I knew she wasn't good for him."

I swiveled in her direction and gritted out, "Yes, actually being blunt about your feelings is *so* unhinged, and trying to control someone and threatening them to get them to do whatever you want is normal."

Her mouth dropped open.

Before she could spew more threats, I crossed my arms and glared. "All I want is for you to get out of my house."

Lifting both hands, Mrs. McHale rolled her eyes. "Believe me, we don't want to be here, but we need to make sure you understand the gravity of your situation."

I wasn't going to sit here and listen anymore. They were

forcing my hand, making me break up with the man I loved... the man I could see myself spending the rest of my life with. "You're willing to injure the man your daughter is so desperate to be with and force me to disappear. I understand the situation entirely, but let me make one thing clear." I homed in on Katherine, knowing that, of the two of them, she was the one who would do whatever she needed to get Carter to hate me. "If I even *suspect* that you hinted to Carter that I did any of these false accusations, I will run to *Daddy* and tell him that I know everything. If you don't want to be forced to acknowledge me as your half sister, keep your fucking mouth closed. Got it?"

She placed her hands on her hips. "Now listen here. You don't get to threaten me."

Mrs. McHale lifted a hand. "Katherine, do you understand or not? She has a point. We can't come in here and promise that if she breaks up with Carter, we won't release this and then renege."

Blowing out a breath, Katherine straightened her shoulders. "Fine. I got it."

"Good." Mrs. McHale held out the pictures to me. "Here, you can take these."

I lifted a brow and glanced at the horrible pictures I didn't want to see again. "Why? I thought you were holding these over me."

"Oh, these are just copies. I have the originals at home."

"I'm good." The last thing I wanted was to have reminders around. Seeing Carter and not being with him would be hard enough without this little reminder. "Get the fuck out." I gestured to the back door, not wanting them to spend the extra time it would take to walk through the house to the front door.

"Gladly." Katherine shuddered. "I feel like I need a bath again already." She strolled over to the side door and opened it. "We gotta get back so I can ride on the team bus to the game."

Mrs. McHale walked past the table and laid the pictures there. "Keep these. They'll serve as a reminder. Remember not to break up with him until after the game."

Of course not. We couldn't have him dealing with a breakup hours before the bowl game.

The two of them left, and I raced to the door, slammed it shut, and locked it. I leaned my back against it and slid down to the floor, tears streaming from my eyes. My chest tightened as a loud sob racked my body.

The bedroom doors from the hallway banged open, and I heard both Leah and Haven racing into the kitchen, but I couldn't see them. Not with tears blurring my vision.

"Girl, we tried not to eavesdrop," Haven said as she hurried over and took a spot beside me. "But they were loud; we heard everything."

Leah huffed as her footsteps stopped at the table. "Speak for yourself. I was totally eavesdropping in case Evie needed us. And these pictures are over the top."

I wiped the tears from my face and used my sleeve to wipe the snot from my nose. I knew for a fact that I didn't want to look in the mirror, and I was thankful that I didn't have to tell them everything that was going on. I wasn't sure I'd be able to repeat it.

"Those *bitches*." Leah shook her head. "And you're Senator McHale's fucking *secret* daughter? Holy shit."

Yet another thing that had been dropped on me tonight. "It can't be true." But even as I said it, this entire situation began to make sense. I'd lost my family. If I were his kid, maybe this offer was his way of feeling less guilty for deserting me. And now I wished I'd said no because I was going to lose Carter too. It was going to hurt like hell. "I don't want to talk about it."

"You're not going to agree to this, are you?" Leah tilted her head.

"What choice do I have?" I hit the back of my head against the door. "I either allow Carter to dislike me because I broke up with him, or he could get injured, if not *die*." The image of my dead parents flashed through my mind. "I can't risk anything happening to him."

"Oh, honey." Haven laid her head on my shoulder. "This is so not fair."

"You can't be serious." Leah gestured at these pictures. "They wouldn't actually hurt him. Would they?"

"I think they would." Now, a part of me couldn't get out of my head that maybe my parents' accident hadn't been one at all, not after what she'd insinuated.

My phone dinged in my pocket, and I removed it, tensing at the name scrolling across the screen.

CHAPTER FORTY-FOUR

My heart both leapt and shattered at the message.

Carter: We're heading to Atlanta. I love you. I wish you were here with me. Wear my jersey for luck will ya?

He had no clue how much I wanted the same thing, especially knowing that we wouldn't have another night together now. More tears slid down my face. Between that and not being able to share with him who my biological father was, I'd never felt so alone. But those were things Mrs. McHale had forced me to promise. So I texted back.

Me: Already planned to wear it. I love you too, and I can't wait to see you kick their asses. Just know that, no matter what happens, you've made me the happiest I've ever been.

Carter: Don't worry. I'm not going anywhere. I gotta run before Jack starts singing to force me to pay attention to him.

I laughed and sobbed at the same time. I was going to miss

Jack's horrible antics and the way he gave Carter hell. In that moment, I realized I wasn't losing just Carter but *all* of them.

"You can't let them win, Evie." Leah snatched my phone away and pointed at me. "Seriously. You and Carter have what everyone dreams of. You can't let that go."

I hung my head. Carter's dad was right about one thing; Carter deserved better than me. He'd had a pretty shitty life himself, which I'd only recently been made aware of. He needed someone who didn't have baggage, and more, he needed the NFL. "For now, I'll have to. Katherine and Mrs. McHale...they're heartless. I can't risk Carter's safety. His dream is to play in the NFL. I truly believe that Katherine wouldn't hesitate to hurt him." I had to at least do this for him. He needed someone to care about what happened to him.

Haven rubbed my shoulders, a sympathetic smile on her face. "This is so damn tragic."

"I almost wish Senator McHale had never visited me." My entire future hinged on the idea that I'd get something better out of this. "And, guys, I just learned that Senator McHale is my fucking *father*. That's a lot to take in. I need to know that you two won't say anything to anyone." The one merciful piece was that he'd never know that I knew as long as I followed through on their ultimatum.

Nose wrinkling, Leah shook her head. "You should take the bastard for everything he has, but yeah. You can trust us."

"I can't do that." Not that I would even if I could. "I was adopted, so he owes me nothing."

I was drained and wanted to take a nap. "I'm going to rest before heading to work."

Haven bit her bottom lip. "I'm not sure you should be alone."

"I'm fine. I promise." I needed sleep and solitude. From

here on out, I'd have to figure out a way through things alone. "I just need a nap."

"Okay. We're here if you need us." Her smile was tight.

"Noted." I turned and stopped at the door. "And thank you two for everything. You're truly the only friends that I've got."

Leah's scowl softened. "We'll always be here for you, Evie."

And for some reason, I believed them, so I headed downstairs and crawled into bed. I was asleep before my head hit the pillow.

THEY WON THE BOWL GAME. I wasn't surprised.

It was Tuesday morning, and the team was about to leave the hotel and head home. Carter had been ecstatic and texted me good night right after the game. He hadn't called because it was so loud, and he didn't call later because school had restarted, and I had class.

I wasn't sure if I could handle hearing his voice.

After taking the last bite of my yogurt, I tossed the container into the trash and headed out the door. As I walked to Carter's Escalade, which I still had and would have to return to him when I broke up with him, an unfamiliar black BMW pulled into my driveway. When I glanced through the windshield, I froze.

Senator Grisham.

My heart hammered against my ribs. Katherine and Mrs. McHale yesterday, and now Senator Grisham today.

What was he doing here? He'd been at the bowl game, so he must have left early to already be here.

He turned off the car and climbed out, his focus entirely on me. "I see Carter is letting you drive his vehicle."

Even though the words sounded friendly enough, I could

hear the ice underneath. Wiping my hands on my jeans, I adjusted my backpack on my shoulder. Every reply I came up with sounded wrong. I didn't ask Carter to loan it to me—he'd insisted I borrow it.

I cleared my throat. "Is everything all right?"

"Yes, and I want it to remain that way." He held a checkbook in his hand.

Shit. Were we going to have the same conversation all over again? "I wasn't at the game, and Carter won. So I'm at a loss as to why you're here."

"I'm here to make sure my son doesn't lose focus so close to attaining his goals." He lifted his checkbook. "I have a new offer. One that I won't allow you to refuse."

"Senator Grisham, I appreciate you looking out for your son, but I've already made it very clear that I'm not interested in your offer." I did believe he had Carter's best interests at heart, though he was clearly misguided. But if my child had a parent who'd pulled that shit on them, I'd probably think the worst of people too.

"Once again. This is a different offer, so you need to hear me out."

He was the father of the man I loved, even if I was going to break up with him.

I sighed. "What amount are you offering me now?"

"It's a lower amount. One hundred thousand." He ripped the check from his checkbook and handed it to me.

I crossed my arms, not taking it, but I noted the name of the account owner.

Carter Grisham Trust.

My heart froze. "Carter can't access that money yet."

"He can't, but I can. So here's the thing." He kept his hand extended. "You either take this money and deposit it into your account, or I remove it and give it to Serenity or someone else.

It depends on who I talk to next. Either way, the money comes out of his account, and he never gets to touch it."

Any respect I had for the man vanished. "You'd steal from your own son just to paint me as a villain or punish him for being with me?" I knew exactly why he wanted me to cash it—to prove to Carter that I could be bought.

He nodded. "Because at the end of the day, he will learn a valuable lesson. And let me be clear, if you give him the money, I'll immediately cut another check and give it to someone else, so don't test me. There would be no point not to if he learned of our arrangement through those means."

I hated this. First, Mrs. McHale threatened Carter if I didn't break up with him, and now his dad was trying to force me to take a payoff.

I stared at him as another thought hit me. I had to break up with Carter anyway. At least, this was a way for the charity he wanted to sponsor to get the money he'd wanted to give to them. I could take it and write a check to them, and if his dad showed him this, then Carter would let me go far more easily.

Hell, if I was going to get screwed, I might as well do something Carter would want with the money in his stead. The very thing he'd wanted this amount for originally.

I sighed, hating the next words that came out of my mouth, but I didn't have any other choice. "Fine. I accept your terms."

His dad smiled as if I'd just proved everything he needed. And though he and Carter would both believe it, I'd make sure that I was *never* like Carter's mom.

I PACED MY BEDROOM, knowing that Carter would be back any second. He'd wanted me to meet him at his house, and I'd told him I couldn't. That I'd promised Leah and Haven I'd help them with something.

I'd gone to his house earlier to get my things, leaving behind the camera he gave me for Christmas. I didn't deserve to keep it, not since I'd be betraying him, and I wouldn't be able to use it without falling apart. I was a complete blubbering mess. I couldn't break up with him in person; it would have to be over the phone. When he got home, he'd call me as soon as he noticed that all my things were missing.

A loud knock sounded on the front door, making my lungs seize. Surely not. He wouldn't just come over here when I'd told him I was busy.

But that was exactly something he'd do. We usually did everything together; why would he expect anything different?

"Uh...Carter." Haven's usually chirpy voice was tense. "What are you doing here?"

"Hey, I know you three are having girl time, but I just won the bowl game, and we're going to the national championships next week." He sounded so happy. "I just need a hug and a kiss from my girl, and I'll be on my way."

A huge lump blocked my throat, and I couldn't swallow.

I heard his heavy footsteps enter the house and pause. "Uh... Aren't you having a girls' day?"

"Well..." she hedged. "Uh..."

That was when his footsteps headed through the kitchen, and I realized that I was trapped. He was coming down here, and I'd have to do this in person.

I rubbed my chest, unsure if I could handle it. I glanced at the pictures of his mom and me on my desk and realized I couldn't let him come down here.

Running up the stairs, I reached the door just as he swung it open.

His brows rose, and a faint frown appeared on his face. He was suspicious, and he had every reason to be.

Every cell in my body wanted to propel me into his arms and kiss him like crazy. I'd watched the game, and he and his teammates had been on fire. Grayson blocked like crazy, Carter completed almost every damn pass, and Samuel, Jack, and Cole had made several touchdowns.

I clamped my hands to my sides, and he took a step back.

"What's wrong?" he asked as he examined my expression. "Did something happen?"

I felt stupid standing here, blocking him from entering, but he couldn't go downstairs. The longer he stood in front of me, the more my resolve to break up with him crumbled. "Carter, I didn't want to do this here."

His forehead creased. "Do what where?"

I swallowed, and I heard Haven scramble back into the living room. She knew what was coming.

"Look, this thing between us"—I pointed at him and then me—"it's been great, but—"

He lifted a hand. "Is this some sort of joke?" He looked around the room. "Because it sounds like you're breaking up with me, and I *know* that can't be true."

My chest constricted. "This isn't a joke. I am." My eyes burned, and I blinked, trying to hold back the tears.

"*What?*" His mouth dropped open and he shook his head. "Why?"

"You're going to the national championship, and then you'll be drafted."

"And?" He held out a hand. "If that's the problem, then it's an easy fix. You can go wherever with me. You'll graduate the same time as me, so it's not like you'll have to leave school. Besides, it's not like you have any family to keep you here."

I flinched, and my heart ripped open. Right. Because my

family was dead, and my real dad was the senator who'd made me a charity case for publicity.

And if I didn't break up with Carter, he might die. This time, my vision blurred.

"Oh, baby." Carter's shoulders sagged. "I'm sorry. I didn't mean it like that. God, I'm an asshole. You just caught me off guard, and I was trying to prove it's not a problem. That I got you, and I want to take care of you. Fuck my dad and what he thinks."

The very dad from whom I took a check because he was coercing me. I blinked, desperately trying to keep the tears back. Once they started falling, I wasn't sure when they would stop, and I needed to get this conversation done before it got there.

"Look, let's go home, and we can talk there," he said, reaching for my hand. "And you can tell me what started all this."

"I can't." I refused to lie to him. I wouldn't play the same game as Senator Grisham, Mrs. McHale, Katherine, and *my biological father*. "I'm sorry. All I can tell you is that it's in your best interests if we aren't together."

"My best *interests*?" His brows rose. "I'm telling you, being with you *is* in my best interest. You're the first person—"

I had to stop him. If he said anything else, I'd crumble, and there was no telling what his dad and the McHales would do if I didn't push him away. "Carter, I can't do this. I'm sorry. I need to focus on my degree and make it on my own. It has nothing to do with your dad."

His mouth dropped open. "What? You'll never be a burden."

"You feel that way now." I was searching for the truth, and those words came out. I couldn't disregard them; there seemed to be some merit there. Something that I needed to dig through.

Not only that, but I'd learned that Senator McHale was my biological father. I had a lot of shit to work through, and I didn't need to drag Carter down and distract him. Not when his future was so bright and promising. "But in five years, I don't want you to hate me like your father does your mom." When his dad showed him the check I was going to deposit, it would reinforce everything I said, and it made me sick.

"Fuck, Evie. That would *never* happen. You're *nothing* like her." He ran a hand through his hair, and his eyes filled with hurt. "You know what? You want space. Fine. Have space. But there's something else going on, and I'm going to get to the bottom of it."

My heart shattered, and a traitorous tear rolled down my cheek. "Carter, please—"

"This isn't you." He shook his head. "I know it." He took a few steps toward me. "You can't have what we have and decide to throw it away."

He had to go before I made both of us regret something. My breath caught, and before I knew it, his lips were on mine.

I froze for a moment, but as soon as his tongue parted my lips, I responded. I couldn't let him kiss me like this again, and the agony of knowing this was our last made me wish it would never end.

Because of that, I pulled away. If I didn't, he'd take my whole heart with him. I needed a piece to at least function. "I'm sorry." I turned around, shut the door in his face, locked it, and ran down the stairs.

I could still taste him on my lips.

He hit the door and said, "Evie, don't do this. Please."

His words were like a kick to my gut. I didn't *want* to do this, but I had to. For him, and hell, maybe even for me.

So, I walked into the bathroom and turned on the shower, needing to drown out his voice and wash away my tears.

I wasn't sure how long I stayed in the shower, but the water turned cold, and my fingers were all pruney.

Stepping out, I snatched my cell phone off the counter and texted Leah and Haven.

Me: Tell me he's gone.

Haven: Yeah, he left about ten minutes ago after interrogating us about why you broke up with him.

My heart froze. Leah had been against me doing this.

Me: And?

Leah: Don't worry. I didn't tell him, but I wanted to. He also made us promise not to have any more parties during the school week. Jerk.

My chest constricted. He'd done that because he knew I struggled with sleeping and focusing in class the next day after they pulled that.

Me: Thank you.

I quickly got dressed. The last thing I wanted to do was hang where memories of him were everywhere, so I decided to go to the library.

When I grabbed my bag, a cold realization settled over me. I was so used to someone picking me up that I'd forgotten I'd have to walk to campus.

Good. It would give me time to work through everything.

Upstairs, I found Leah and Haven on the couch. Haven raised a brow. "Where do you think you're going?"

I gestured to my bag. "School."

"Nope, you're with us." Leah patted the spot in the middle of the couch. "We already ordered pizza."

And without protesting too much, I sat down, comforted not to be alone.

The next week went by excruciatingly slowly. I cried every time I was alone, and I struggled to sleep each night. I needed an action plan, especially if I truly wanted to pursue counseling, like getting some volunteer experience. But first, I needed to heal my own trauma and learn to face water once more. Maybe by doing that and helping kids out, I could channel my pain into making a difference for someone else.

HSU won the national championship. I'd worked that night but could barely take my eyes off the game. Carter had played amazingly well, as had the other players, and there was no doubt he'd be drafted.

A part of me had waited for him to text me or try to call me, but he hadn't. It was hard to swallow, but I had asked him to let me go. I'd just sort of hoped that he wouldn't listen. Now, I'd become just as bad as his dad and Katherine.

Monday morning, I woke up earlier than usual, needing time to hide the dark circles under my eyes.

When I walked upstairs to get breakfast, I found Leah in the kitchen. She tossed me her keys and yawned. "I meant to give them to you last night."

I shook my head. "I can't take your car."

"Please, Haven and I don't have class until ten. She said she'd wait on me an hour and bring me home." She waved a hand. "I'm going back to bed. Be careful with her."

"Thank you," I whispered as I walked out the door. I felt strange taking her car, but I'd rather do that than risk Carter driving by and seeing me walking.

It wasn't long before I pulled onto campus, and I hurried to my calculus class for the first time this semester.

When I reached the room, my eyes landed on the one empty seat. Then, my attention flickered to the person sitting beside it, and I froze.

This had to be some sort of nightmare.

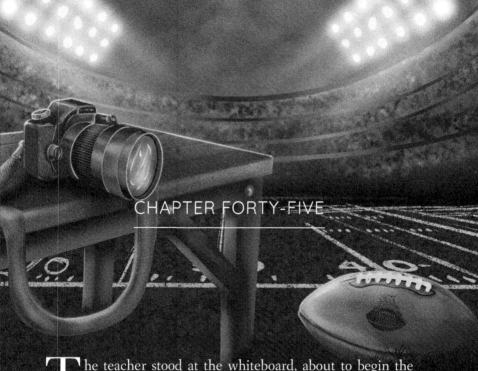

CHAPTER FORTY-FIVE

The teacher stood at the whiteboard, about to begin the lesson, and I was faltering at the doorway.

Jack winked at me, grinning. He pointed to the chair beside him, and it surprised me that it hadn't been taken. Women flocked around him like moths to a flame—like now. The whole group around him was all female, except for that *vacant* seat.

When he reached over and lifted his bag from it, I finally understood why.

The bastard had saved it for me.

But how did he even know...

A spiky lump pierced my throat. Carter and I had signed up for our final semester of classes together, and he'd teased me about taking calculus first thing in the morning. This wasn't a coincidence at all.

For a second, I considered dropping the class. But the teacher turned toward me and arched a gray eyebrow that matched the little bit of hair he had left around the bottom of his head. "Will you be joining us or taking notes from your spot at the door?"

A few hushed giggles had my cheeks burning, and I drew in a shaky breath.

"Come on, E," Jack said loudly, patting the top of the desk. "I saved you a seat here. Not in the back where the smart kids' large heads block the entire view, but not in the front where we can see the professor's pit stains."

Now louder chucklers could be heard, and the professor turned his stony gaze on Jack. "I won't tolerate that sort of disrespect here."

"I'm so sorry, sir." Jack bowed his head. "I meant no disrespect. I get pit stains every game. In fact, all football players do. It's one of the downsides for the people responsible for our laundry. Grass, sweat, blood, we get all kinds of stains on our uniforms. Let's not even talk about the cup situation—"

I mashed my lips together and moved toward the desk. Jack was doing this to keep the attention off me, which surprised me. I figured he'd be angry with me for breaking up with his best friend, yet here he was, trying to take the heat. He had a weird way of helping out his friends, and there was something about his loyalty that moved me, especially now when I didn't deserve it.

The professor laughed. "Let's end it there, Mr. Pearson. We don't need to hear about the stains that surround your cup."

When I slid into my seat, I raised my brows. I hadn't expected the teacher to find Jack funny, but there *was* something about his charisma that was catching.

"Of course not, sir." Jack placed his hand on his chest. "My apologies."

The woman sitting in front of him glanced over her shoulder and smiled. He winked back at her, causing her to blush and quickly look forward once more.

"Now, let's learn calculus." The professor uncapped his pen.

I'd been dreading the moment class was over. For Jack to save me a seat, I had no doubt there was a reason beyond wanting to sit next to me.

As soon as the professor ended his lecture, I quickly shoved my binder and my pencil into my backpack, zipped it up, and threw it over my shoulder. When I straightened, I found Jack standing in front of me with his notebook in hand and his backpack already on.

Dammit. I shouldn't have wasted time packing mine.

"You ready to go, E?" he asked, his blue eyes locked on me.

"Sorry, I can't talk." I took a hurried step toward the door, which he matched, keeping up with me. I continued, "I gotta get to psychology."

He smiled so wide I could see both rows of his teeth. "Don't worry. I can walk with you partway, especially since I learned you did something naughty."

I stumbled.

Carter knew.

I should've known Senator Grisham was watching his trust fund like a hawk, waiting to call his son and alert him about the floozy who was just like his mother.

My stomach roiled, and I knew there was no getting out of this. That was one thing about Jack. When he set his mind on something, he usually got his way. He was persistent, which was both a strength and an annoyance.

When we walked out of the building, he kept pace with me.

"So…I went over to Carter's last night," he said as he watched me.

I couldn't help but flinch, and my heart ached more.

"I'm sure you know what he said." He tilted his head. "But

I'm just as confused as he is, so I'm hoping you can explain to me why a large chunk of his trust fund has gone missing."

My head snapped in his direction. If he thought I was going to break up with Carter again through him, he'd soon learn otherwise. "If you went over there, I'm sure you heard the whole story. I'm just like his mother—I can be bought."

"*Bullshit.* I know you. I've watched you; there's no way you'd take cash over him, so there has to be more to it." Jack pointed at my face and continued, "You're both crazy about one another to the point I'm fucking jealous."

My eyebrows rose. "Jealous? You? The guy who doesn't want to settle down?"

He waved a hand. "We aren't talking about me right now. We're talking about you, my friend, and my fucking *best* friend. So, why are you putting both of you through this torture and making him think the one girl he could trust betrayed him like that?"

I blew out a breath, trying to keep tears from filling my eyes. "Jack, I can't talk about this. Not here."

"Not here?" He spread his arms out. "Fine. You want me to come by later? Carter tried to pick you up this morning only to learn that Leah let you have her car, which made him think you did it because of the missing money."

My heart galloped. Even after I'd broken up with him, he was trying to take care of me. He was one of the most caring people I'd ever met.

A tear trickled down my cheek.

"*See?* That right there." Jack pointed to the tear. "That's what I'm talking about. You don't break up with someone and look like you do right now unless you still love them."

I wiped the tear away and picked up my pace. "I'm sorry. I gotta go. I'm late for class."

He let me walk away despite both of us knowing I'd lied

through my teeth. Walking away was cowardly, but if I'd stayed, I would've broken down. This was the lesser of two evils.

By the time I reached the brick building that housed my psychology class, my vision was blurred with unshed tears, and I collided with a massive frame.

"Whoa," Grayson's familiar voice said. "Where's the fire..." He trailed off, most likely taking in my state. "Evie, what's wrong?"

Well, damn. I *was* going to have a nervous breakdown. I paused, blinking the tears from my eyes and wiping the rest of them away. "Sorry, just a bad morning."

Grayson's jaw tensed. "Did Carter—"

"No." He didn't have to finish that sentence. "He didn't do anything. Uh..." I bit my lip, knowing I had to add more, or he'd just assume the worst. "I actually broke up with him."

His eyebrows rose. "*What?*"

"Yeah..." I pulled on my straps, adjusting the backpack on my back. "But I really don't want to talk about it. Sorry for running into you, but I need to get to class."

"We have seven more minutes." Grayson laughed, but then his expression fell flat. "Let me walk you."

I shook my head. Grayson had been sensitive about us dating, and now he knew that Carter and I were broken up. I didn't want him to get any ideas because my heart belonged to Carter. "I just need a minute. I'll see you later."

I pivoted around him and felt a spark down my spine. I looked around and found Carter standing a mere ten feet away.

My pulse raced.

His hair was messy, and his gaze was on me. He wore a wrinkled polo shirt, which wasn't the norm, and he had dark circles under his eyes. He was struggling just as much as I was.

As he shoved his hands into his khakis, he didn't seem like

the confident man I knew. He cleared his throat. "Can I talk to you for a second?"

The smart thing to do was say no, but my legs moved, taking me toward him. I stopped a few feet away, clenching my hands on my backpack straps, afraid that I'd reach out and touch him. "Hey." My voice was so soft I didn't recognize it.

His gaze flicked to where Grayson must still be standing. "Was I interrupting something?"

My lungs seized. "God, no. I literally ran into him on my way to class. I was sorta running away from Jack." And because of that, here I was with Carter. The only man I wanted to be with...and the one that I needed to stay far away from. But I didn't want him to think there was something going on with Grayson.

Carter exhaled. "I'd run away from Jack too, if given the chance."

For the first time since we'd truly clicked, awkward silence loomed between us. I stared at the ground, biting my bottom lip as he remained quiet. After a few more seconds, I couldn't take it any longer. "Hey, sorry, but I need to go." I spun around, eager to get some distance but wanting to kiss him even more. The two emotions were at significant odds.

His warm, rough hand caught mine, tugging me gently back toward him.

"Can we talk after your class?" He took a step toward me and didn't let go of my hand.

Butterflies took flight in my stomach. "I said everything I needed to." Talking to him would not be good. I already wanted to throw myself at him and beg his forgiveness, but I had to remember why I was doing this.

"But *I* have more to say, and I also have an important question." The golden flecks in his eyes warmed as he reached out with his other free hand and ran his fingers along my cheeks. "Please."

I closed my eyes, enjoying his touch way too much. "Okay."

"Good. That's good," he said, his minty breath hitting my face.

My eyes popped open to find his mouth just inches from mine. My heart skipped a beat as I licked my lips, wanting to feel his mouth on mine.

He smiled, taking in my reaction, and brushed his lips across mine. I almost melted into his body, but he backed away.

My gaze landed on Katherine, who was at the other end of the building, scowling at me.

Shit.

The damage was already done.

"I'll meet you here after class." Carter winked, a little bit of his innate confidence sliding back into place. "Don't disappear on me; otherwise, I'll be forced to find you. I think Dad is trying to make you look bad, and I wanted to give you a heads-up." He took off toward the building next to us, and I stood there for a moment, my eyes on Katherine.

She shook her head and strolled away.

My heart dropped through my stomach.

"Uh...I'm pretty sure he's thinking you two aren't really broken up," Grayson said from behind me.

That was enough to bring me back to the present. "I don't know what you're talking about." I turned, heading to the building as Grayson easily caught up beside me.

"It doesn't matter." He smiled sadly.

That was when I realized we were walking in the same direction. I scoffed. "I told you that you don't need to walk me to class."

"What?" Grayson placed a hand on his chest. "I'm not. I thought you were walking *me* to class."

I snorted, catching myself off guard. That was one reason I'd clicked with Grayson so easily before; he had a way of keeping things lighthearted. "I'm being serious."

"Me too." He laughed. "Let me guess, you have legal psychology?"

"Yup." *Oh.* "I'm assuming you do too?"

"Guilty." He lifted both hands. "I guess we'll suffer through this one together."

"Well then, we better hurry." I walked faster. "Or we'll be late."

The two of us managed to get there, taking two seats next to each other in the back row just a few seconds before class began.

I shouldn't be meeting with Carter, especially not after Katherine saw us. It was asking for trouble, but Carter would show up at the house if I left campus.

Students milled past me and continued to scatter from the building as I paced in the grass just off the main sidewalk, waiting for Carter to appear. Grayson hadn't wanted to leave me alone, but I'd insisted that he go.

I bounced on my heels, and then Carter came into view. He'd already noticed me, and he was marching toward me.

Slowly inhaling, I tried to calm my nerves. However, with every step closer he got, my heart urged me to mend things between us.

When he reached me, he gave me a tight nod. "Thanks for waiting."

"Of course." The nerves coursed through my body once more. "I told you I'd be here."

"And you're a person of your word." He smiled, but it was strained. "I hope."

My heart skipped a beat. I had to rein this in fast. "What do you want to talk about?" We needed to get straight to business so I could go.

"Let's talk in my car." He nodded to the space behind the building, which was a community lot, instead of the reserved one he normally parked in.

"You parked back there?" I was surprised because the lot filled quickly, and normally, we had to park far away from the buildings.

He shrugged and kicked the ground. "Let's just say I wanted to park close to here in case you agreed to talk with me."

I lifted my head. "So you planned this?" I didn't know why that little fact thrilled me.

"Maybe." He took my hand. "Thankfully, it worked out."

His touch was so comforting. I should have pulled my hand away from him, but I couldn't make myself. "Fine, but I need to not be long. I need to get Leah's car back."

He nodded, and we headed toward his car in silence.

However, this time, it didn't feel awkward, not with our hands intertwined.

His SUV was parked about half a mile away in one of the last spots. "You got here late, didn't you?" I laughed.

"I showed up at a woman's house, hoping to bring her to school for the day." He smiled. "It's sort of our thing, but after waiting outside for ten minutes, I went to the door and learned that she'd already left for the day."

My face burned. "I'm sorry. I didn't think you'd come pick me up, and Leah told me to borrow her car..." I shrugged, unsure what else to say.

"Babe, I'll always be there to pick you up as long as you let me." He tucked a piece of my hair behind my ear. "You should know that I have every intention of waiting on you. You're too damn special to give up, and that's what I want to talk to you about." He leaned over, opening the passenger door. "So, can you give me five minutes? That's all it'll take."

I nodded—there was no way in hell I could say no to that—and removed my backpack before sliding into the passenger seat. I put my bag on the floorboard.

Carter got in the driver's seat and tossed his backpack into the back seat.

He started the car and turned his body toward me. He said, "Look, my dad sent me a text last night that seemed pretty damning. A hundred-thousand-dollar check cleared from my trust fund, and it was written to you."

I swallowed. He'd gone straight to the problem, and I couldn't blame him. His mom had hung over his and Senator Grisham's relationship for his entire life.

"At first, I was gutted. I couldn't believe that you would do something like that, and I thought I'd misread you." He leaned over and took my hand again. "I'm sorry I even thought that. I know my dad is trying to make it appear like you took the money, so I'll stay away from you."

I frowned. "Carter, I need to get Leah's car to her."

His mouth tightened. "Listen, just confirm what I think. That my dad's a complete jackass." He put the car in reverse and backed out.

As Carter pulled onto the two-lane road, a car coming in the opposite direction swerved into our lane.

"Watch out!" I exclaimed.

"On it," he gritted out as he tried to swerve onto the sidewalk.

The car hit us, and our heads jerked as we came to a sudden stop.

For a moment, silence filled the car. Then Carter bellowed, "What the fuck?"

Bile burned my throat, and the memory of failing to save my mother reared in my head. I thought I might vomit, and I yanked open the passenger door and jumped out with my bag.

"Evie?" Carter paused, glancing at me. "What's wrong?"

"Your car. The money. The accident." I wasn't sure which one I was talking about, the car that just hit us or my parents. It was all bleeding together. I hadn't been able to save my mother, and if I kept hanging around Carter, I wouldn't be able to save him either. Something horrible had or would happen to them because of *me*.

"Baby, it's no big deal." He gestured to the car in front of us where a guy about our age was climbing out. "It was a ten-mile-an-hour road. There's probably not much damage."

But I suspected this was a warning. The timing was too convenient. I glanced toward the nearest building, and...yes. There was Katherine, talking to some of the cheerleaders. Her head turned my way and her eyes locked on mine just as my phone dinged.

My heart pounded as I glanced at the message that flashed across my screen. I didn't have her number stored in my phone, but from what the text said, there was no doubt who it was from.

This is your final warning. Next time I won't be as gracious.

Ears ringing, I took a deep breath to try and remain somewhat rational. If I ran, Carter wouldn't let me go. I had to get through to him. Make him understand that I was serious about the two of us not being together.

Being apart from him would hurt like hell, but him hurt or even dead would be unbearable.

"Carter, I'm sorry..." My voice broke, but I tried to hold it together. "I love you, but I have to *go*." A tear trailed down my cheek, and I could feel hysteria clawing deep into my chest. "I have to get away from here." I wasn't lying. Being with him, waiting for him to get hurt again, would mean reliving my nightmare over and over.

His face twisted in pain, but he nodded as the guy who'd hit us came over.

A cheerleader from Katherine's team.

"You okay?" he asked, and I forced my gaze from Carter to this guy.

He drove a Lexus and wore name-brand everything. No doubt he was one of her loyal minions.

"Be better if you hadn't hit us," I snapped, unable to shut it down. I wanted to ask how much he'd gotten paid for doing this, but that would lead to Carter asking questions. Then there would be no way he'd let me go.

I was also beginning to realize that the nightmares and reactions I was experiencing due to my parents' deaths were not normal.

The guy winked, his teeth way too white as if he'd bleached for too long. "Sorry. I wasn't paying attention."

"Clearly." The world became loud to the point of being overwhelming.

I had to go.

I glanced at Carter, who was watching me. His forehead creased, and his eyes glistened from what appeared to be unshed tears. He was hurting just like I was.

My phone dinged again. I didn't need to look down to know who it was.

Katherine.

However, I needed to see what her threat was this time.

Ticktock

I swallowed, but the lump prevented my saliva from going

down. I glanced at Carter again and murmured, "I'm sorry. I've got to go. I'll see you around."

"Evie, wait—" But the other guy was handing Carter his contact information.

While he was distracted, I walked away, feeling like pieces of me were falling to the ground and leaving a broken trail behind me. There was no doubt that Carter was the owner of all those pieces.

I had to remember why I was doing this. It was for him *and for myself*. I had to save us both...even if I was a lost cause.

THIRTY MINUTES AFTER THE WRECK, I was holed up in my room, my hands still shaking. I couldn't believe Katherine would set something up like that. She'd proven she would follow through on their threat, which petrified me. To think she could so easily hurt someone she'd grown up with made me queasy.

And we had the same biological father.

I shivered, hating this little-known fact even more.

There was a knock on the front door, and I froze. *Please don't let it be Carter.*

The door opened, and the next thing I heard was Haven yelping, "Hey! What the fuck do you think you're doing?"

"Getting answers," Carter yelled as his feet pounded against the living room floor, and before I could react, heavy footsteps thudded down the stairs to me.

I wrapped my arms around my waist and then glanced at my desk, where the picture of his mom and I sat in plain sight.

Shit.

I raced to the desk just as he rounded the corner of the stairway, his eyes locked on mine.

"Are you okay?" His face softened as he scanned me. "I had to wait for the campus police to come, and then I came straight here. I could tell you were petrified."

Even when I wasn't kind to him, he was treating me like I was the only thing that mattered. "I...I had a flashback of the wreck with my parents." At least, that was one truth I could give him. "Sorry to run off like that."

"Hey, I get it." He walked over to me, pulling me into his arms.

I wanted to resist—I *needed* to—but being in his arms was like coming home.

That was until he stiffened and rasped, "What the actual *fuck?*"

The picture. I was standing right in front of it.

"So it's true." He backed away, his expression changing from anger to hurt to disgust. "And here I was, thinking my dad was a complete jackass." He grimaced, and the warm golden flecks I loved so much vanished. Then he laughed bitterly. "You had me fooled. Good job, Evie. You had me following you around like a hurt puppy. You want me gone? Well, you got it." He spun and walked up the stairs.

My heart ripped out, going with him. My chest constricted so tight I crumpled.

I wanted to go after him. To explain everything.

I got what I wanted...but damn. That look of betrayal hurt worse than anything I experienced before.

CHAPTER FORTY-SIX

Two weeks later, I rushed to work a little late.

After a ten-business-day hold on the huge amount of money I'd deposited, I finally was able to go to the foundation Carter wanted to support and drop off the donation to the charity's manager, Kyle.

At first, he was suspicious. I couldn't blame him, but after I explained that Carter didn't want word of his generosity interfering with the draft and wanted to ensure that the donation was anonymous and unable to be tracked back to him, he bought it. I figured a check for everything Kyle needed to move forward with Touchdown 4 Kids helped too, but the important thing was he promised not to acknowledge Carter as the donor.

Though living without Carter made the smallest thing seem hard, doing this for him brought me a little happiness. Whether he knew it or not, he was about to make a huge difference in kids' lives, which would mean so much to him.

Brushing off the thought, I tied on my apron just as Grayson came strolling through the pub door without his buddies.

When he took a seat at the closest high-top table to me, I went over to him.

"Hey." I smiled, hoping this interaction wouldn't be awkward. I missed our friendship and banter, but things had remained strained between us. "Where are your shadows?" Carter hadn't been here since we broke up, but Jack still came occasionally with Grayson, Samuel, and Cole.

He smiled, reminding me of the Grayson I'd met on the first day, who'd helped me despite the way Katherine and Carter were treating me. "With football season over, we don't hang out as much."

I tilted my head. "You were in with Cole and Jack last weekend."

"I said *as much*, meaning we do get to breathe on our own sometimes." He winked and gently touched my hand. "And I didn't want them here because I want to see how you're really doing since you and Carter...you know..."

I looked down. "I really don't want to talk about it." I thought about it way too much already. Besides, I might not be able to talk about Carter without breaking down, and no one needed to be here for that. I lifted my arm, causing his hand to drop. "What would you like?"

"My usual."

"Got it." I jotted down his cheeseburger, fries, and beer.

When I turned, he caught my arm again. "I know we had a rocky start, but I'm here for you, Evie." He shrugged. "And he's a fool for letting you get away."

I grimaced but then forced a smile, hoping he hadn't noticed. I didn't want to lead him on, but my heart completely belonged to Carter. "I'll be right back with your beer."

Before I could turn around, Grayson sighed and groaned, "I'm sorry, Evie. I'm not trying to make you uncomfortable."

The thing was that I believed him. "Just because Carter

and I aren't together doesn't mean I want to jump into another relationship or date someone else."

"Oh, I know." He pinched the bridge of his nose. "I can tell you're still hung up on him, and I won't lie. I'm jealous. I've been into you since the day we met, and you friend-zoned me." He scrunched his nose. "That should've been my first clue."

"Look, you're handsome and nice. Any girl would be lucky to have you." I patted his shoulder, making sure it came off clearly platonic. "Like Sadie." Even though Sadie and I weren't friends anymore, I'd seen how smitten she'd been with him. She would jump at the chance to date him.

"Coach Prichard's daughter." He looked pointedly at me. "Not happening. That's asking to be kicked off the team."

He had a point there.

"Look, I gotta get to work before Joe yells at me." I took a few steps back. "But I'll be back with your beer in a second."

A little later, I delivered his burger and fries

Before I walked away, Grayson asked, "Wanna hang out soon?"

I bit my lip. I wasn't sure that was smart.

"As *friends?*" he emphasized, reading the hesitation in my eyes.

"Yeah, okay." I welcomed any sort of activity that would get my mind off Carter. "That'd be nice." I did enjoy our friendship.

He beamed. "Perfect. It's a date."

And just like that, I worried that I'd made yet another mistake.

A THUMPING CAME from the top of the stairs to my room, startling me awake. I sat up in my bed, panting as the vision of water crashing against the car slowly faded.

I glanced at my phone. It was almost eleven o'clock in the morning. There was no text from Carter, which wasn't surprising. However, that didn't stop me from hoping one would be there.

I threw off the gray sheets and hid Carter's jersey under my pillow. I should've given it back to him, but I couldn't do it. Pathetically, I slept with it every night, because it smelled like him.

My feet touched the cool, smooth cement floor. Even though the downstairs was fixed, it was still pretty much the same as before, just patched up and newer.

Another knock sounded upstairs, followed by Leah groaning, "She's probably still asleep."

"Oh, well. I thought she'd be up by now," Grayson replied.

I stilled on the stairs, unsure what to do next. It was Saturday morning, and he knew I worked later tonight.

"She might not have a boyfriend, but her heart is taken. You do realize that, right?" Leah yawned. "And I don't think Carter would like you being here."

"Evie and I talked last night. We're just friends."

My shoulders relaxed. That was what I'd wanted to get across all along. The fact that he was saying it gave me hope that our friendship was back on track.

"You never had a chance with her." Leah snorted. "She was already in love with him the first time he came here."

Okay, time for this conversation to be over. Grayson and I were just getting to be friends again; I didn't need her imploding that within seconds.

I jogged up the stairs and opened the door, only to come face to face with him.

His eyes widened as he looked me over.

Shit. I wrapped my arms around my chest, realizing that I was wearing a thin cotton shirt and pajama shorts. "Hey. Everything okay?" My voice was groggy.

"Uh. Yeah." He laughed awkwardly, taking a step back. "I didn't think you'd still be asleep. Clearly, I should've called."

"Yeah, that would've been the smart thing to do," Leah snapped from her spot at the small kitchen table. "We worked late and then came home and watched some shows together. This is early for us."

He scratched his neck. "Sorry. I just thought maybe you'd want to go do something today. Maybe a hike or something."

A hike. That...actually sounded nice. Get away from the stress and get lost in nature. I could bring my camera and snap some pictures. "Sure. Sounds great. Leah, you and Haven wanna come?"

"Ugh," she groaned. "No, but I think I should, to make sure Grayson here doesn't get any stupid ideas in his head."

Some of my tension left. Though I wanted to hang out with him, I hadn't realized I was desperate for my friends to tag along. Things might be a little weird out there in solitude with him. "Great!" I said enthusiastically.

To his credit, Grayson didn't frown or flinch, which gave me hope that the two of us were finally okay after all.

I smiled. "Let me go change. I don't think I want to go hiking like this."

He laughed. "Sounds good. You might catch a cold."

I opted for a thin, long-sleeved lavender shirt, jeans, and a light blue jacket. I jogged down the steps, getting ready for a relaxing start to the day. And maybe I wouldn't constantly be thinking of Carter.

CHAPTER FORTY-SEVEN

Time seemed to stand still yet speed by since Carter and I broke up. It was an awful cycle where my dreams were haunted, either by my parents or by Carter; some nights, Carter was the one in the passenger seat instead of my mom. And on those rare nights where the dreams were amazing, I'd wake up to realize that Carter and I weren't together anymore and everything I'd dreamed hadn't even happened.

And then my heart would break all over again.

At least I was making progress on my own life goals. I'd joined a clinical psychology internship program and shadowed doctors at the hospital on Mondays.

"Hey, you." Haven sat down at a table in the middle of the bar, right at opening. It was Thursday night, and we weren't busy. "How are you doing?"

I was running on less than two hours' sleep and had been losing weight. I was far from okay, but I didn't want to worry anyone. "I'm fine." I pulled out my pad, tucking a stray piece of hair behind my ear, wanting to get away from the conversation I felt coming. "What are you having?"

"Just get me a cheap draft beer and some chili cheese fries." She winked. "It's truly an amazing combination."

Before I could head to the bar and kitchen, Haven caught my arm.

"You want something else?" I asked.

Haven bit her bottom lip. "Well...I heard you crying this morning. I didn't want to bring it up then, so I decided to stop by and check on you."

That. I blew out a breath and leaned against the table. "I just miss my parents and Carter. It's not a big deal." I couldn't believe it had been four weeks since Carter and I broke up. "I'll be fine." I forced a smile.

Leah strolled out of the kitchen. Her gaze landed on me, and she grimaced. "Are you constipated or gassy, Evie? I think I have some Gas-X in my purse."

Great. Clearly, I hadn't managed a smile. "Nope, I'm fine. Just thinking about all the things." I stuck my pen to my pad and headed to the kitchen. "Now, let me go get this order put in for Haven. We know how she is if she gets hangry."

"Wait." Haven grabbed my arm again. "You're studying to become a psychologist for kids, right?"

I nodded. I wasn't sure what she was getting at.

"I'm not trying to be mean," she started.

She didn't even need to say that. Haven didn't have a mean bone in her body.

"But how can you expect to counsel someone through their grief and problems if you aren't willing to do it yourself?"

My head snapped back, and the oxygen zapped from my lungs. Realization curled in my stomach.

Haven patted my arm and continued, "What I'm getting at is—maybe you should get some counseling yourself and begin to heal."

I cleared my throat, disliking how exposed I suddenly felt.

"Yeah, okay. Thanks." I scurried away, needing some distance. "Now let me get your order in."

ONE WEEK LATER, early on a Saturday morning, I walked into the swimming center a few miles off campus. My new therapist had encouraged me to begin facing my fear of water, and she recommended I come here. I was to start in a shallow pool in a controlled environment to handle this fear progressively, in baby steps.

I'd picked an early time slot, wanting to get it over with for the day so I could get home and study before heading to work that evening. I wanted to get my mind off Valentine's Day and all the romantic crap that inundated campus.

It was technically an open swim time because I wasn't brave enough to join a class, but my therapist had lined up an instructor who was close to my age to help guide me into the water. I didn't want to freak out kids younger than me due to my irrational fear.

I was wearing a one-piece black bathing suit, standing at the door that led to the pool with my hand on the knob. Though it was a pool with no current, scenes of my parents in the car were running through my head. I grew dizzy as the chlorine scent overwhelmed my senses, and I started hunching over.

This was a bad idea. I had to get out of here.

As I turned to leave, someone came up behind me.

"Evie?" Sadie's soft, familiar voice murmured. "Is that you?"

I tried to straighten, but I couldn't get my thoughts under control. I wished I had an anchor to the present, but I'd had to push away the one person who was.

Carter.

Oh god, how I missed him.

The ache in my heart nearly brought me to my knees, adding to the grief of losing my parents. I wasn't strong, not anymore. Something had broken inside me.

"Hey." Her voice sounded full of concern, and before I knew what was happening, she moved to my side. "What's wrong?"

She'd been rude to me and ditched me as a friend, and all of a sudden, she was standing in front of me as if she cared. I couldn't help but laugh bitterly. "Um... Nothing you need to worry about." Between my panic attack, heartbreak over Carter, and Sadie being here, I realized that I wasn't ready for this. Maybe I never would be. My therapist was wrong. "I'm gonna go."

When I released the handle to the door and turned around, Sadie's eyebrows rose. "Whoa, you're sweaty and pale. You're most definitely not okay. Are you—"

"Let's not, okay?" I must have looked horrific because her face was now even more twisted with concern. "You got mad at me for no reason, treated me like shit, and were rude when I tried to make things better between us. We don't need to pretend to be friends."

Her shoulders fell as she recoiled. "That's fair. I haven't been a good person to you, and I'm sorry."

"You do realize we're still in photography class together, right?" We'd both signed up for the intermediate class this semester. Apparently, Sadie enjoyed photography as much as I did. I hadn't done much of that since Carter and I broke up. So, there's no point in pretending now and then going back to our routine of ignoring one another on campus." I stepped away, ready to flee this horrible place and never come back, but then a hand caught my wrist.

"Look, I got jealous, okay?" She shook her head ruefully.

I removed my wrist from her hand and turned around, placing them on my hips. She was *jealous* of me? The irony hit me just as the hot waves of anger rolled through me, and I embraced them. Anger was way better than hurt. "You continued treating me like crap even after you realized Grayson and I weren't together. And for the record—not that it should matter—I never did *anything* with him."

"At first, yes, it was Grayson, but it was more than that too." She ran her hands through her hair and shrugged. "It was all of them."

"All of who?" I had no clue what she was even talking about anymore.

She hugged her towel to her chest. "The football team—Carter, Jack, Grayson, Cole, and hell, even Samuel at the end. And all the other guys noticed you even if they weren't in the in-crowd."

"You hang around them too." I spread out my hands. "You're the coach's daughter. You help out with practices half the time!"

She rolled her eyes. "Yes, I do, but that's all they see. The coach's daughter, which equates to 'definitely keep our distance from her so Coach doesn't cut off our balls.' I'm always around them, but they don't *see* me. Not like they do you."

I stared at her. "Do you think I've been dating others besides Carter?" She was acting like they were my harem. In stories, a group of men sounds nice, but here in the real world, I couldn't walk into any room that Jack regularly inhabited. It smelled of feet and cologne.

"No, I don't think you're dating them all." She laughed, her smile toward me genuine for the first time in months. "It's just… They all want to hang out with you. It's stupid, I know. Yes, I thought you and Grayson slept together at first and was hurt when I thought you went back on the girl code. But then, when I saw how they all accepted you, it turned into more than just that, and I'm sorry."

Sorry.

Sometimes that word didn't cut it, but damn. How could I ever try to forgive myself for my mom's death if I couldn't forgive Sadie for being young and foolish?

And the fact that I just posed that question to myself scared me even more.

How could I forgive myself for not saving my mom?

"Hey," Sadie said softly, placing her hands on my arms. "I get it if you don't want to forgive me. I was an idiot, and I can find someone else to help you get into the water."

I stopped breathing. "Wait. Are you the person my therapist arranged to have help me?" I hadn't even considered it would be someone I knew, considering how large the campus was.

"Yeah." She bit her bottom lip. "But if you don't want to work with me, I totally get it."

Of course, that's why she was here. "So that's the real reason you want to mend things between us?"

She shook her head. "No, I planned to talk to you next week. I heard that you and Carter broke up, and I noticed that you've lost weight and don't seem like the same person. I felt awful for not being there for you. I mean, I know we weren't super close or anything, but I felt like we could've been if I didn't get all in my own head." She wrinkled her nose in disgust at herself.

"Yeah, me too." I shrugged. "That was why I tried making up with you all those times."

She nodded. "I really am sorry. But I'm willing to help you if you want me to."

Haven had been right the other day. If I wanted to be a

psychologist, I had to practice what I preached, which meant doing the one thing I *really* didn't want to. "Are you sure you don't mind?"

"Yup." She winked. "And you already know me and know that, even when I'm mad at you, I won't try to kill you, or you'd already be..." She trailed off and contorted her face. "That probably wasn't smart to say to someone who fears the water."

I snorted, already feeling more at ease with her. I didn't know what it was, but having her joke with me like I was a normal person was refreshing. "No, that sounds good to me."

"All right." She opened the door and waved me toward the pool. "The first step in overcoming your fear is getting near the water."

Sweat sprouted over my body, and the carefreeness I'd felt moments before fled. I couldn't do this. Not now.

I spun around to escape once more and slammed into a brick wall.

Large hands steadied me, and I took a step back. I looked up into gorgeous hazel eyes that I'd only ever seen on one man.

Carter.

What was he doing here?

CHAPTER FORTY-EIGHT

Every cell in my body sizzled. I wanted to leap into his arms and revel in his scent. It'd been so long since we'd been this close and the deep ache that hadn't healed at all ripped through me once more. My home was here.

And he thought I'd accepted money over being with him.

His forehead creased as he studied me. He glanced at Sadie and then toward the pool before refocusing on me. His jaw tensed as he glared at Sadie and asked, "What the hell do you think you're doing?"

"What?" Sadie gasped. "I didn't—"

He wrapped an arm around my waist, pulling me close to his body. "She's pale and shaking."

For a second, I leaned into his side. It felt so right to be back in his arms, and I wanted to curl into his chest and never let him go. But that was enough to wake me up.

Katherine's threat was still real, and I had to protect him. I pulled back a little. "Carter, Sadie's going to help me face my fear of the water."

"She didn't trick you into coming here?" He gestured at Sadie.

I laughed. "No. You know that no one has that sort of power over me. Besides, look." I pointed at my bathing suit. "I'm even dressed for the occasion. Do you think she snuck this on me as well?"

He winced. "Point taken. But you looked so afraid, and I was just trying..."

My heart squeezed uncomfortably, and that all-too-familiar ache stole my breath. "I know. You were trying to protect me." I snorted. "Believe it or not, this is me trying to face my grief. My therapist has been pushing me to do this."

His brows rose. "Therapist?"

I wrung my hands. "The nightmares haven't gotten better." They'd gotten worse, but I didn't want to tell him that. I bit my bottom lip. "I mean, how can I expect to help others with their fears and issues when I've been avoiding addressing my own? It's hypocritical, isn't it?"

Worse, my therapist had suggested that I should think about reaching out to Senator McHale to talk to him about what I'd learned. It would be disastrous for everyone involved, but I couldn't tell her that. She'd report it since someone had threatened someone physically, and Mrs. McHale and Katherine wouldn't stand for that.

"Evie, you don't—"

"Son?" Senator Grisham entered the hallway. When he saw me, his brows furrowed. "Evie, what a surprise." He arched an eyebrow. "The owner is waiting for us to talk about additional resources at HSU." His dad frowned at me and continued, "We shouldn't keep him waiting."

"Uh. Yeah." Carter exhaled and turned toward me. "Are you sure you're okay? I could help—"

"Your dad's waiting." If he finished that sentence, I might

very well take him up on his offer. "Besides, this is something I need to do on my own." Even though it was *nice* to have him here beside me. Even after all this time, just his touch made me feel safe and loved.

He nodded. "Yeah, you should get over that fear so it doesn't prevent your next adventure."

I raised a brow. I had no clue what he meant, but the longer we talked, the more my heart hurt, and I already had too much turmoil I needed to face. "Thanks for being here."

"I still care about you despite everything," he murmured and ran a hand along my arm. "I'll see you around." Then he glanced over my shoulder. "Sorry for being rude."

"No, it's fair." Sadie laughed awkwardly. "I've been a bitch to her."

"Yeah, you have." Carter nodded, his face turning into a mask of indifference. "Don't let it happen again. I don't care that you're Coach's daughter." He squeezed my arm before dropping it and strolling after his dad.

Everything inside me screamed to go after him. But then the memory of Mom flashed into my head, along with the wreck Katherine had her cheerleader friend cause. I *had* to do this. I had to focus on healing myself.

I spun around, facing Sadie again.

"Are you sure about this?" She arched a brow.

I nodded. "It'll get harder the longer I put it off."

She smiled and held out her hand. "Then let's do this together."

Unable to swallow around the large lump in my throat, I forced myself to take her hand and hoped this didn't come back to haunt me.

It'd been twelve weeks, sixteen therapy sessions, some medication balancing, and eight swim lessons since Carter and I had broken up, and I was finally feeling somewhat normal. Close to my old self again.

Not only that, but I'd gotten my acceptance letter from Stanford this morning. I'd immediately grabbed my phone to call Carter and then remembered that I couldn't. The joy I'd felt at my accomplishment suddenly seemed less bright.

And that was my biggest problem. I still missed and loved Carter the same as the day that we'd broken up.

It was the beginning of April, and signs of spring were bursting out all around us. School would end in five weeks, a fact that I both dreaded and looked forward to. Not seeing Carter even in passing would be both a blessing and a curse, but at least then, maybe I could finally get over him.

"Evie," Sadie whispered from ten feet away. She ducked below a bush and pointed her camera up at the cloudy sky.

Grayson, Leah, Haven, and I had continued our hikes sporadically, and I'd mentioned them to Sadie and invited her to join us. Since we'd reconnected at the swim center, she'd become a regular part of our outings.

Today, although Leah and Haven had other commitments and it was going to rain, Sadie had still managed to talk Grayson and me into this hike with promises of nature and pictures. She'd had Grayson at nature, whereas I was merely here to take pictures. Our assignments this semester were focused on techniques and apparatus rather than a particular subject, and without my specific focus on football, I hadn't been taking as many photos as before.

Grayson chuckled. "You better hurry, or she'll complain the rest of the way back."

I rolled my eyes but hurried over, holding my camera up to find a beautiful bald eagle. My fingers tensed as I snapped a few shots of my own. The bird was majestic and so damn beautiful.

Soon, it flew out of sight, and Sadie beamed. "I told you this would be amazing."

"You were right." I stuck out my tongue at her. "I bow to your awesomeness."

Thunder rumbled from far away.

"And that would be a sign it's time for us to head back to the Jeep." Grayson stared into the distance where the noise came from.

"You do realize you can't see thunder, right?" I scrunched my nose at him as I turned my camera off and settled it across my chest. "But I agree we need to leave. Let's go before we get electrocuted."

Sadie rolled her eyes. "Please, you have a better chance of winning the lottery than getting struck by lightning."

"Maybe." I shrugged. "But with my luck, if I was going to have something rare happen, it would be the latter, not the former."

She laughed. "Fair. Let's go. No need to tempt fate."

The three of us strolled along the hiking trail as the cool breeze picked up. Hanging out casually had brought all three of us closer again, and even though I was quite certain Sadie still had a thing for Grayson, she handled it way better. They were able to interact as friends.

Halfway to the car, it started to sprinkle. I wrapped my camera in my jacket to keep it from getting wet. It was still the loaner from the school since I didn't keep the one Carter gave me.

The three of us ran, laughing, and the rain came down harder just as we reached the Jeep. As we climbed in and took off, I realized that I'd gone a whole morning without dwelling on my parents or Carter, and I held out hope that maybe the rest of my life wouldn't be awful.

ONLY A FEW DAYS AGO, I had hoped that things wouldn't get worse. Now, I was quite certain there was a sort of higher power and that it *hated* me.

I stood in my room, staring at myself in the mirror. I'd lost fifteen pounds, and my appetite hadn't come back. Haven, Leah, Grayson, and Sadie were constantly worried, and my therapist said it was a combination of getting used to medication and everything that I was working on dealing with. My eyes were sunken to the point that even my makeup couldn't hide it, which was a *huge* problem since I'd be around *him* tonight.

The last time we'd truly spoken had been at the pool.

For the past few weeks, Grayson had been picking me up and dropping me off from school. I'd half hoped Carter would intervene, but he hadn't, making me wonder if he was over me. That thought caused what little remained of my appetite to vanish.

Tonight, I was going to have to go to the office at the football stadium and then, early tomorrow, head to Nashville to photograph Carter for the NFL signing day. Worse, his family, Coach Prichard, and no doubt Katherine and the McHales would all be there for both occasions.

I tried putting on makeup, desperate to hide the circles in case Carter was paying attention, but all I did was cake on a little too much. I got a washcloth and wiped it all off. With a shaky hand, I tried again and made sure I didn't put too much on. Better to have a little than make it obvious I was hiding something.

Every attempt I'd made to get out of taking the photos, Professor Garcia had squashed. Football season was over, but she wanted me to follow through with this last thing since I'd covered the games last semester. I also hadn't delivered quite enough material for the class, thanks to my depression and lack of inspiration lately, so this was sort of extra credit to help me this semester.

When I finished, I glanced in the mirror. The dark spots were still there, though not as noticeable with the makeup, and my HSU purple shirt with gold writing would make me blend in with the crowd. That was the point—I wanted to be invisible.

I glanced at my phone and saw that it was six, and I had a message from Sadie.

I'm out here, waiting for your sexy ass.

I'd never been more thankful that we'd restarted our friendship. I needed her tonight and tomorrow. Thankfully, with her dad being the coach, she had the authority to be there and act as my shield.

I grabbed my camera and jogged up the stairs. Haven and Leah were both out, so at least I didn't get peppered with questions and concerns as I hurried out the front door. I jogged to Sadie's Honda Civic and slid into the passenger seat.

She smiled. "You look nice."

"I don't feel it." I chuckled as I buckled up. "But thanks."

"It's just your nerves." She put the car in drive and headed toward campus.

Feeling this unsteady was strange, and it had everything to do with Carter. All the panic of having to be close to him after all our time apart ate at me. What if he didn't have any feelings for me anymore? Worse, what if he'd moved on? Finding out for sure might destroy me.

Sadie reached over and squeezed my hand. "I'll be right

there with you. Nothing bad is going to happen. Just remember the breathing techniques your therapist taught you, and focus on your photography."

At this point, Sadie had those techniques just as down pat as I did since I routinely had to use them when we were in the water. "I know, but this is a different kind of panic." I bit my bottom lip as my leg bounced. "It has everything to do with Carter."

"If you're worried about Carter dating someone else—"

"Stop." I lifted a hand. I'd firmly told her and Grayson that I didn't want to know his relationship status.

She shook her head. "Fine. Have it your way."

All too soon, we were pulling up at the stadium and into a front parking spot. It was odd being able to find parking so close to the side door, but there wasn't a game today. This was just Carter, his friends and family, the coaching staff, and reporters for pre-signing-day interviews. The other players that were being recruited here at HSU were juniors and didn't want to graduate early. So, probably no more than one hundred people total, just a little national news coverage.

No big deal.

Forcing my lungs to fill completely, I opened the door. Sometimes, anticipation was worse than the actual event itself...at least, that was what I was going to keep telling myself.

The two of us entered through the side door and went down the long hallway. Soon, we were inside the main stadium where we could see the field, and we turned left and went past the cheerleaders' dressing room to the men's locker room. There was an office and a large conference room inside for times like this.

We entered the locker room, and I took in the royal-purple lockers and gold benches where the guys changed. To the right was a huge room with people hanging out in the doorway.

That had to be it.

Loud, excited voices came from inside, so many that I couldn't make out any particular conversation. Sadie looped her arm through mine, and the two of us pushed between two older men at the door.

I didn't expect walking through the doorway to put us right in front of Carter, his dad, Senator McHale, Mrs. McHale, and Katherine. She stood next to Carter, smiling at him, and my heart twisted.

Did he get back together with her?

Our entrance drew Carter's attention, and he stilled as his eyes met mine.

I couldn't breathe. All I could do was gaze back, completely at his mercy.

He winced and bit his lower lip, but his eyes remained on me. There was no warmth there—more like sharp disappointment.

Katherine glanced my way, and anger flashed in her eyes. "Don't worry, Car. I'll take care of this."

Shit. I should've pushed harder with Professor Garcia and told her that I couldn't do this because I had to work. Or I was ill. I hadn't wanted to disappoint her, but *this* was beyond what I could handle.

"No, *I'll* talk to her," Carter rasped, his eyes never leaving mine. And then he headed toward me.

My heart pounded. This was dangerous. I shouldn't have come here. He clearly didn't want me here.

A hand landed on my shoulder, and I startled. Kyle appeared next to me.

I blinked a few times.

"Hey, Evie." He beamed. "I thought I might see you here."

What was *he* doing here? He wasn't friends or family of Carter. "Oh...hey?"

That was when Carter reached us, his brows pulled together.

"Hey, since you found some friends, I'm going to talk to Dad for a second." Sadie slipped away, leaving us alone.

My heart started racing. I drew a deep breath in, counted to five, and breathed out. I had to believe that everything was okay. I'd told Kyle that Carter wanted to remain anonymous. He wouldn't say anything about the donation to Touchdown 4 Kids. I had to believe that.

"You two know each other?" Carter asked, glancing from Kyle to me and then to where Kyle's hand rested on my shoulder.

Shit. This looked *bad*.

Kyle threw his head back and laughed. "Good one, man." He nodded at Carter like we were all in on a secret joke.

Sweat pooled in my armpits.

Carter's head jerked back as if he'd been slapped. "Are you two dating?"

"What?" Kyle's mouth dropped open, and he removed his hand.

Some weight fell from my shoulders.

"We met because of...you *know*," Kyle said as he elbowed Carter. "And if *that* wasn't enough, you invited me and the first five kids we recruited to come here and meet you and see the action. Man, you've done too much."

My heart was pounding so loud that I could barely hear over it. This was bad, and I needed Kyle to shut up *now*. "You brought kids! I'd love to meet them." Anything to get Kyle away from Carter.

"Of course." Kyle beamed and then clapped Carter on the arm. "And thanks, man." He winked. "And I mean *for everything*. Even the thing you asked me to never discuss."

"Kyle—" I started.

"Don't worry." Kyle placed a hand on his heart. "Like I promised you, I will never say a word to anyone else, much as I'd love to shout to the world what you did. I just wanted a chance to say thanks... You know. For everything. My dream would've never been possible if it weren't for you." He patted his chest as he looked at Carter.

Carter's gaze flicked toward me, and something unreadable passed through his expression. "You know what, Kyle? Forget I asked you never to discuss it. You can tell *everyone*. I've reconsidered."

"Really?" His eyes widened.

"No," I exclaimed, tugging on Kyle's hand, trying to get him away from Carter. "We should really move over here so Carter can get back to—"

"Nah, you heard him." Kyle pulled away from me and took Carter's hand, shaking it hard. "And I want to capitalize on that generosity because I think so many more kids will hear about the opportunity and want to sign up, knowing that the number one NFL draft pick funded my entire startup. But you had Evie write the check from her account to ensure that the donation stayed anonymous—are you sure you're okay with me talking about it now?"

I started seeing black spots. Butterflies took flight in my stomach, and I wanted to run before I threw up.

"No reason to keep it a secret." Carter's eyes narrowed, still locked on me. "But thanks for respecting my wishes. I just didn't want my name going around and people thinking I was trying to buy goodwill or some shit for draft day."

"You're a class act." Kyle punched him in the arm and sighed. "Well, when you have a second, the kids would love to meet you. I should get back to them."

"Yeah, of course. I'll be there in a minute." Carter smiled, but he continued to stare at me.

I *almost* begged Kyle to stay, but I knew Carter well, and if he had something to say to me, he'd find a way.

He stepped closer, the gold and warmth that I loved returning to his eyes. "You've been busy."

"Yeah, you know, the semester is wrapping up." I licked my lips, unsure what to say or do.

"It's funny." He tilted his head and smiled tenderly. "The *exact* amount of money he needed for the startup was the amount you accepted from my trust fund."

I barked a laugh, the sound so forced I cringed. "Well, that is strange. I should be setting up to take your pictures." I started to walk away, but his hand caught my wrist.

The touch felt so warm, rough, and familiar that my heart broke all over again.

"This conversation isn't over." He tugged me back and into his chest. "And I have a lot of questions that I *really* need answers to."

"What's going on here?" Katherine asked loudly. She glared at me. I hadn't noticed the McHales and Grishams moving toward us.

I froze, and Carter's brows furrowed.

"You know Carter and Evie are friends." Senator McHale cleared his throat. "She must be here to support him."

"No, they broke up." Mrs. McHale glowered. "There is no reason for her to be here."

"Hey," Carter growled as he threw an arm over my shoulder.

I had to clear the air before something horrible happened to him. "I'm here to take pictures. For the school—for a class." I lifted my camera. "The football team was assigned to me last semester, and my professor asked me to be here today and tomorrow to take pictures for HSU."

Carter straightened, his jaw clenching. I was fairly certain he was beginning to put some of this clusterfuck together.

That didn't stop Katherine from wrinkling her nose. "I'm sure someone could take your place."

"She tried." Sadie had returned and now flanked my other side. "Believe me. Especially since I was already going to be here. But Professor Garcia said it should be her. The school's been *so* impressed with her work."

"Interesting." Katherine flipped her hair over her shoulder. "Well, I need a potty break before we get started." She smiled at me, her lips tight. "And Evie should join me. You know how we girls go in groups and all." She strode over to me, nudging Carter out of the way and grabbing my arm. She started dragging me toward the door, and Carter stepped after us.

But then his father called out, "Son, the coach and I need you here," halting him in his tracks.

Sadie's father joined them and got her attention as Katherine marched into the covered area outside the locker rooms where the underside of the bleachers rose over our heads. She led me into the exit tunnel where the team and cheerleaders always ran out onto the field. I glanced over my shoulder and saw a reporter and camera crew on the field, walking slowly toward us, along with a guy carrying a video camera in his hands. They seemed to be gathering footage of the stadium. The reporter was talking into a microphone. They must be live.

Katherine's focus was entirely on me, her back to the camera guys. She gritted her teeth. "Find a replacement for tomorrow. You being here tonight is bad enough."

"I *can't*." Had she already forgotten the conversation we just had? "The campus news asked me to be here, and Professor Garcia insisted. I agreed, so I have to finish this. It's too late for a change now."

The men were now maybe fifteen feet away.

"It's not for a grade, and you need to stay away from Carter and *Daddy*. Or did you forget what we promised would happen?" she snarled.

The reporter turned our way, and my heart nearly stopped. "Katherine, we should talk about this later."

The guy with a microphone gestured at us just as the camera swung in our direction. The middle-aged reporter with the microphone strolled toward us, lifting the microphone to his mouth as he opened it to talk. I shook my head at him, trying to make a "go away" gesture. "H—"

Instead of listening, Katherine said loudly, "Don't tell me what to do!" She shoved her finger into my chest, the nail stabbing me. She continued, "*I* tell *you* what to do. Mom and I told you to stay the fuck away from Carter, or there would be consequences. And yet, here you are at the prep meeting, and now Daddy has yet another chance to see his long-lost daughter." She got into my face. "So leave right fucking *now* before I make you."

My face paled, and she smirked, thinking that my reaction was about her.

But it wasn't.

That was when the reporter gasped. "Did you get all that, Phil?"

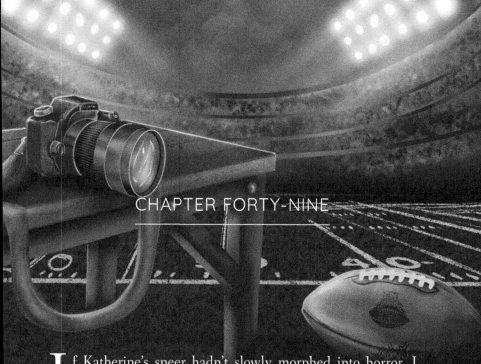

CHAPTER FORTY-NINE

If Katherine's sneer hadn't slowly morphed into horror, I would've thought she was frozen.

I wasn't in much better shape than her, seeing as she'd just outed who my biological father was to the entire *world*.

Her eyes narrowed. "You set me up."

As if this situation wasn't horrible enough, she was now going to blame me for this. I shook my head. "I was *trying* to stop you."

"Bullshit." She spun toward the camera and pointed at the reporter. "Delete that footage now, or I'll slap a libel suit on you so fast you won't know what hit you. I'll end your career."

The reporter's eyes bulged, and he scratched his neck under his white collar. "I *would* if I could, but—"

"But *nothing*." Katherine stomped her foot and turned her frosty glare to the man holding the video recorder. "Put that down now and stop recording."

"Ms. McHale..." The sports reporter lifted his free hand. "That's not possible."

I zoned in on the red light on the video recorder.

No.

Please no.

This couldn't be happening.

I stumbled to the cameraman and whispered, "Turn it off now."

Katherine zoned in on her new target. "And why the fuck not?" Her hands shook with rage. "Do you know who my father *is*?"

The cameraman obeyed, and I watched to ensure the red light vanished, and then he lowered it to his side.

This was unbelievable.

The sports reporter nodded at Katherine. "We do, but the problem is that was a *live* feed from ESPN, taking a quick tour of the football field. We were finishing up here when you got loud, and we live streamed the entire conversation."

Katherine's mouth gaped. "But all the reporters are in *there*." She gestured toward the locker room.

"Yes, but part of our broadcast is including footage in the stadium from a perspective fans don't usually see."

I swallowed and tried to do the breathing techniques my therapist had taught me because, boy, I needed them now. This was a fucking disaster.

"Ha, we knew that." Katherine's easy smile slid into place as she stepped closer and wrapped an arm around my neck. "It was just for show. Wasn't it, Evie?"

But I couldn't form words. Carter would see this. Senator McHale would see this, and everything I'd been protected from having to directly deal with would crash down all around me. My therapist had said I needed to deal with everything, but over time—it was up to me when I wanted to focus on something.

"Evie!" Katherine snapped, her gaze cold.

I blinked a few times, snapping out of my haze. "Yeah, of

course." I laughed a little too loudly, unable to pull off the act as well as Katherine. My heart pounded as the urge to get away from Katherine, the reporters, and this entire town swelled in my chest.

Katherine spun around, seeing the camera recorder at the man's side. She snapped her fingers. "Turn it back on so we can tell the world about our trick."

The sports reporter touched his earpiece. "I'm sorry. That's not possible right now."

"*What?*" Katherine screeched. "You were just recording not even two minutes ago."

"But we've moved on to another school." The cameraman shrugged, and his forehead creased in disgust. "We can't just cut off another school because you had a meltdown. It was clear that it wasn't an act. No damage control is going to fix that. Just look at her now." He gestured to me.

The sweaty, panting mess. My vision was going dim at the edges.

Great.

Katherine pivoted to me, fury on her face. "It was an *act*, and now you've forced my hand. I'm getting my father."

I couldn't stay here.

I couldn't handle Katherine, her threats, Kyle giving me away, and the impact of the footage that had just been released to the world. The only salvation was that it was ESPN. Most of the viewers wouldn't care about my non-sports-related confrontation with Katherine. Why should they?

Stumbling away, I snatched my phone from my back pocket and shot off a text to Sadie.

Me: Hey, not feeling well. Can you take pictures for me? I saw your camera in the car. I have to go home.

The sports reporter touched my arm and asked, "Are you okay?" His brown eyes were kind, but his touch just felt wrong.

It didn't feel comforting, and it didn't make me feel safe. I wanted Carter.

"Yeah." I took a few steps back and grasped the handle of the door that would lead me outside. "Sorry, I just realized I forgot something." Eyes burning, I spun around and threw open the door, leaving the two men behind. I was making a scene, but it didn't matter at this point. Katherine's verbal assault couldn't be beaten.

My phone vibrated, and I glanced down to see a text from Sadie.

Sadie: Go. I'll stay here and make sure I get what you need. Just be careful. I'm sorry I let her talk to you.

Once I was in the long corridor to the door that led to my freedom, I sprinted. I didn't want to chance anyone chasing me down.

When I broke through the back door, I saw there was no one in the parking lot, and the tightness in my chest loosened, allowing me to take a big gasp of air.

With each step I took away from the stadium and toward home, I tried to calm myself. Thanks to the NFL draft pick tomorrow, this would be overlooked. Everything would be okay. I'd be able to go to Nashville, take the pictures from a safe distance away, and then leave.

Stanford couldn't get here quickly enough.

By the time I marched into the house, I'd finally calmed myself down. I shut the door, turned on the lights, and jogged to the couch, glancing at my phone.

There were five missed calls and eleven texts.

My lungs seized.

I noted three missed calls from Carter and two from

Senator McHale. They must have wanted to talk to me about what Katherine shared.

Then I checked my messages.

Five were from my group chat with Haven and Leah.

Leah: Girl, what the fuck? Are you okay? That bitch has got to go.

Haven: That was really bad. I don't even work at a bar, and everyone is talking about it here.

Leah: Do you need us to come home?

Haven: We have your back.

Leah: If you don't answer soon, my ass is coming home.

Then I had messages from Grayson, Sadie, and Jack.

Grayson: Do you need me?

Sadie: Uh…this is a whole lot more than feeling bad.

Jack: I'm going to hurt that bitch.

One from my…father.

Senator McHale: I didn't know anyone knew. This isn't how I wanted the information to come out. I'm so sorry. Can we please talk?

And then there were two from Carter.

Carter: Where are you? I'll come get you.

Carter: Sadie told me you were going home. We need to talk tonight.

I sat up, the world spinning, and pulled up the internet.

Breaking news on all the major news stations had me ready to throw up. There was an image of Katherine pressing her finger into my chest, my eyes wide and pale, with the headline "Senator McHale's Charity Case or Secret Daughter?"

I couldn't breathe. I placed my head between my legs, trying to prevent myself from passing out. There was no way to get ahead of this. Everyone knew my dirty secret, one I hadn't fully come to terms with myself. Just when I'd thought I might have a chance at being normal, this blew up in my face, reminding me that I wasn't destined for happiness.

A fist pounded loudly on the front door, and my head jerked up. I held my breath—as if that would prevent the person on the other side from knowing I was at home.

"Evie, it's Carter." He knocked again, another series of bangs. "Open up. I know you're in there. I saw you walk into the house when I turned onto the road."

My heart leapt with happiness, and I warned it to calm down. He must be furious with me.

Shit. I didn't want to see the look on his face. I was fairly certain he'd seen the news and now knew just how much I'd kept from him.

He groaned. "Seriously? This is how you're going to play this?"

I was being a coward, but I couldn't bring myself to walk to the door. His disliking me was one thing, but if he were disgusted... I trembled.

"Fine." He huffed, and the doorknob jangled. "I'm going to talk to you one way or another."

Damn persistent man.

I jumped to my feet and hurried to the door. "Carter, please stop. You must have seen the news, and Kyle told you everything. I just—"

"Fuck yeah to all that," he grumbled. "Evie, *damn it*. First off, how long have you known about Senator McHale? And were the threats the real reason you ended things with me?"

"What?" The question caught me off guard.

Something thumped like he'd dropped his forehead to the wooden door. "Baby, I don't give a shit who your dad is, and I'm so damn sorry that I jumped to conclusions about you working with my mom and taking my money. I don't deserve you. But, babe, I still *love you* despite it all."

He still loves me. My heart galloped at the seemingly simple confession. "You had no reason to think well of me after the check and seeing the picture." I shook my head, knowing that I couldn't have this conversation through a door, not after what he'd said to me.

I opened the door and met his gaze. Carter's hair was messy and hanging in his eyes, just the way I loved it. He took several steps toward me, cupping my face. "I should've never doubted you. I should've known that you wouldn't take money for your own gain, and I fucked up. I'm so sorry. I even left without giving you a chance to explain your side. Is there anything I can do to get you back? Or have you already moved on?"

"Moved *on*?" I gasped. The words didn't make sense. "Why would you think that?"

"Grayson's been taking you to school, and you two have been hanging out a lot." He shrugged, but his face was worried. "He's been chasing you since the first day of school, and I hate to admit it, but he's a nice guy. I thought—"

I shook my head. "Grayson and I are friends. That's all. I haven't moved on...I never wanted to."

"I want you." He stepped closer, his chest touching mine. "I'll take you however you'll let me, and I want to be there for you when you face your fears and help you deal with Senator McHale being your dad."

Each time he spoke, it was harder to remember why we couldn't be together. "I..."

"Look, I'm not going to hold you back." He rubbed his thumb over my bottom lip. "Dealing with your grief, your pain, even when you need to go your own way. I'm here for you as a friend if that's all you'll give me. I can't stand living a life separate from you any longer. And if you don't want me, then I deserve it. Because I should've never doubted you. Not even for a fucking second."

His tender confession violently ripped my heart wide open. Standing here like this with him was going to destroy me all over again. I took a step back, spun out of his arms, and hurried downstairs. I needed to get away from him and clear my head before I did something foolish.

Before I could shut the door to my room, he caught it and barged inside.

"You shouldn't be alone right now." He didn't reach for me, just stayed at the threshold.

"Maybe, but being with you is a problem." I turned, desperate to get away from his warmth and smell. "I can't think straight when you're near." I couldn't lose focus. I had to save him. I hadn't been able to save Mom, but *him* I could.

He tromped after me, his steps steady and strong.

I paced in front of my bed. It had been foolish to come down here, but I'd thought I'd be able to shut the door and lock him out. I knew, without a doubt, he wouldn't risk messing up that door.

"You not thinking straight around me doesn't sound like a problem." He hovered in the doorway, staring at me. "It actually gives me hope because I feel the same way when I'm around you."

I exhaled. This was going opposite to the direction I needed. "Carter, we *can't* be together."

His features filled with pain. "Why? Just fucking tell me what's going on and why you took the money in the first place. And how the fuck do you know my mom? I trust *you* and no one else. Don't be like the others. Please. Just be honest with me."

I nodded. "Okay." He deserved that much, and I didn't want to damage him like everyone else had. "Your mom came into the bar over Christmas break—that's when the picture was taken. That was the only time I've ever met her, I swear."

He eyed me and glanced at the picture again. "She's hugging you like you're friends."

"Katherine paid her to come in so a friend of hers could take that picture." My voice cracked as my hands shook at my sides. "Katherine and Mrs. McHale came here the day you left for the bowl game and revealed the truth about Senator McHale, then told me I had to end things with you."

His jaw twitched, his nostrils flaring. "And the check?"

"Your dad came the next morning while you were packing up to head home. He told me that if I didn't accept the check, he'd make it out to someone else. Either way, the money was gone. I figured if I had to break up with you, I could at least take the money and use it the way you wanted."

Here it was. After all the nasty things I'd just said, he'd call me a liar. It all sounded unfathomable, even for them.

His nostrils flared, and he yanked on the ends of his hair. "Unbelievable!"

And my heart was annihilated, the pain worse than anything I'd ever experienced. I'd lost him.

CHAPTER FIFTY

I sobbed, and his head turned toward me, his face twisted in anger. He rasped, "He threatened to give my money away after saying no to the charity I wanted to give it to, and the McHales threatened you so you'd break up with me? What the fuck is wrong with all these people?"

My heart skipped a beat, and I inhaled and held it for a five count. Did he actually believe me?

He laughed bitterly. "The timing adds up. That was why the cheerleaders were running late. Katherine stopped here with her mom to have a little chat. Figures. And Dad rushed off earlier than I expected him to." He dragged a hand down his face. "So that's why you broke up with me?" His face changed from anger to hurt. "You didn't think I'd believe you were set up? I mean, I get it. I didn't give you a chance after seeing those pictures, but I wanted to hear you out at school. I thought you knew me better than that. I thought we *saw* each other." He shook his head. "Obviously, it was one-sided." He put his hands into his pockets and shrugged. "I've got to go."

No. I couldn't let him believe I thought he wasn't worth

fighting for. "Wait. Stop." I hurried over, taking his hand in mine. The familiar warmth of his hand spread tingles through me.

"It wasn't that." I licked my lips. "I knew you'd believe me."

His brows furrowed, but when he interlaced his fingers with mine, some of the pain receded. "Good."

I hadn't completely lost him...at least, not yet.

"Then why?"

I shook my head, tears streaming down my cheeks. "I...I can't tell you." I took a step back, forcing myself to release his hand. My chest tightened, and the walls seemed to close in.

"Wait." He came back over to me, scrutinizing me. "You're scared." His jaw clenched and his nostrils flared. "What did they threaten you with, Evie?"

He *knew*. It both freed and petrified me. At least he knew there was a reason we couldn't be together that wasn't my doing. "I can't—"

"Fine." He lifted both hands. "I'll go figure it out myself. I'm so over Katherine and her shit—"

No. If he confronted them, he might as well be kissing his career goodbye. "You."

He froze, his confusion plain. "Me? What are you talking about?"

"They threatened to injure *you* if I didn't break up with you." My hand clutched my chest. "They said accidents happen—after all, look what happened to my parents."

Carter blanched. "Those sick, manipulative assholes." His hands clenched at his side. "They used your parents' death to solidify their threat? Baby, they'd never do it."

"But Katherine *did*." Now, tears were streaming down my face. I took a step forward, needing him to understand that I wasn't paranoid. "She had that guy run into us that day when you pulled out of the parking lot." I grabbed my phone and pulled up her text. "See?" I handed it to him.

He read it and growled. He tossed my phone on the bed and ran his hands through his hair. "This is beyond too far." He laughed bitterly and glanced at me. "Did you get offered that summer psychology internship in Spain?"

My brows rose. "Well, Mrs. McHale got it for me, but I told her no. There's no way in hell I'd want anything the McHale family tried to hand me. Why?"

"That's why I stayed away from you." He bit his finger. "Even when I thought you took my dad's money, I started thinking, so what? I knew you were in debt, and I wanted to help you anyway, but Katherine told me you were offered the internship and the coordinator thought you were turning it down because of me. I didn't want you to miss an opportunity because you were afraid to leave me."

I laughed—I couldn't help it. "So you're telling me I stayed away from you to protect your dream, and you stayed away from me to make sure I pursued mine?"

"That's what I'm saying." He smiled sadly. "If that doesn't prove we love each other, I don't know what will." He strode to me and wrapped his arms around me.

I melded into his body before I could stop myself, but then I stiffened. "This doesn't change anything." I attempted to step back, trying to gain distance.

He tightened his hold, anchoring me to him. He murmured, "This changes *everything*. I'm not letting you go again. I can't." He cupped my face and vowed, "I won't."

Hope soared inside me, making my chest expand, and I tried to tamp it down. "If you get hurt because you're with me, I can't live with that."

"Oh, don't worry. That's not going to happen." His body tensed. "Because your text will confirm everything for Dad, and he won't stand for threats against me, Senator McHale's family or not."

"But your dad is always busy, and we're here. I can't risk you being h-hurt." Another tear trailed down my cheek. "I couldn't live with myself if I was the cause of someone else being injured or dying."

He lowered his forehead to mine and whispered, "I know why you did it. I understand. I'm just so damn pissed that you were put in that situation. If I—"

"It didn't have anything to do with you. Not really." That was one thing the therapist had gotten me to see. "It was Senator McHale. They're afraid that if I hang around, he'll want a relationship with me. And if I'm with you, well, that makes it more likely that I'll be hanging around."

His gaze landed on my lips. "Like I said, we're done being apart. I'll listen to your concerns, but I now know without a doubt that you love me as much as I love you. We're going to work this out, and I am *not* letting you go."

The possessiveness should've scared me, but truthfully, it thrilled me. My pulse raced, and I was so happy I thought I might implode. "Okay, but I've gotta tell you something else."

"What?" Wariness darkened his eyes.

I licked my lips. "I'm not going to Spain, but I did get accepted into a PhD program. Stanford."

"Stanford?" He beamed. "That's amazing. I've got something to share with you too, because this moment is too damn perfect."

My cheeks hurt from smiling, and I tilted my head. "And what's that?"

"I've worked out a deal with a team ahead of time. I will be the number one draft pick in the morning. Everything is signed and dotted."

My mouth dropped open, though my stomach ached.

There was no telling how far apart we'd be, but I'd make sure he came and visited, and I'd work like a dog to go to him every chance I could. "That's great." I threw my arms around him, but he jerked back.

"Wait." He waggled his brows. "It gets even better. The team is the San Francisco 49ers."

I swallowed. Was I dreaming? It was as if everything was working out perfectly for us to be together. "Both of us are moving to almost the same city in California?"

"Fuck yeah." He chuckled. "I spent the last four months without you, and I won't be separated from you like that again. Hell, don't even try to rent a shitty basement because I'm hoping you'll say yes to moving in with me. We can find a place halfway between us. I want you with me every day and night. I can't stand being away from you anymore."

I kissed him, hoping I never woke up. "I don't want to be anywhere without you anymore."

"You don't know how badly I needed to hear you say that." His lips were on mine, his tongue demanding entrance.

I opened my mouth, and when our tongues met, I moaned. I couldn't help it; I'd missed him so damn much.

His fingers dug into my sides in that way that drove me wild. My heart pounded as I responded to each stroke. He lifted me against him, and I wrapped my legs around his waist. When I felt him harden underneath me, the world seemed to spin. Need knotted inside me and drove me to near madness.

Stumbling to my bed, he lowered me onto the mattress, pressing his body on top of mine. His minty taste and smell enveloped me, and I badly wanted him inside me. We'd been apart so long, and I needed to connect with him again.

I yanked his shirt up, and he moved so I could remove it from his body. As I tossed it to the floor, he pulled mine off as well. One hand went around my back and unfastened my bra. His eyes darkened as he ogled my breasts.

"Damn, I didn't think I'd ever get to see these again." His head lowered, and he suckled one nipple, his tongue flicking against the sensitive skin, causing my back to arch. He chuckled. "Or taste you like this again. Dammit, Evie, I've never stopped loving you, and I've craved your body like crazy."

"Same," I gasped as his fingers rolled over the other peak. "I love you, too. I never stopped," I panted. "But dammit, Carter. I need you *now*. We can go slow later."

"Hell yeah, we will. *Tonight*." He stood and unfastened my jeans, then pulled them and my panties off. "Back at my place, so when your roommates get home, they can't bother us."

I nodded, my vision unfocused from my insatiable need. I couldn't even talk...not right now.

With him standing, I tugged on his slacks and almost whined over how long it was taking him to toss them and his boxer briefs aside.

He paused. "Your door isn't shut."

"They won't be home for an hour." I wasn't above begging if that was what it took to get him inside me. "Now, *please*."

He grinned, placing his fingers between my legs, but I smacked them away and scooted to the edge of the bed, rubbing myself against him, making it clear what I wanted.

"But I need to get you ready—"

"Believe me, I am." I leaned back, taking in his curves and six-pack.

Smirking, he pressed against my entrance, his eyes on me. Right when I thought he'd press inside, he paused.

I blinked. "I'm still on birth control. It's okay."

"No, that's not the problem." He leaned down, stroking my cheek.

His touch was warm and safe, but there was something

off in his eyes. I asked, "What's wrong?" My chest constricted. Maybe he was having second thoughts about everything.

"If we do this..." he said, slipping a little farther inside me, only his tip. He moaned, his body shuddering. "I'm not letting you go ever again. You're mine. Forever. Got it? I don't care what anyone threatens you with or what baggage we still have to work through. We figure this shit out together from here on out."

My stomach fluttered, and I nodded. "I promise. You and me, *forever.*" That should've scared me, but it felt right. I didn't want to spend my life with anyone but him.

"That's *fucking* right." He thrust inside, filling me.

And I couldn't help but watch him as he stood at the edge of the bed, hovering over me. He slid his hands under my legs, lifting them so he could hit deeper. At first, his pace was slow, but after a few thrusts, we quickened the pace, both hungry for release and for each other.

He dropped a hand, caressing my breast as he slid in and out of me. Friction heightened into exquisite pressure, and before I even realized it, ecstasy slammed through me.

All through my pleasure, he kept up steady and fast movements, watching me as I succumbed to the sensations.

"Damn, baby." He groaned, pumping faster. "You're so fucking hot." He removed his hand from my breast and settled it between my legs, circling as he continued his pace without breaking.

I wasn't sure how it was possible, but my body was already tensing again. The wild need for another release pulsed through my core.

I'd been deprived of his body for too long, and having him again was like a drug. I could now officially be labeled a sex addict.

His fingers pressed a little harder, not enough to hurt but enough to cause tingles to explode.

"Are you close again?" he asked through gritted teeth.

I nodded, at a loss for words.

"Thank God." He grunted, and then his body jerked.

Moments after his orgasm happened, a second one crashed through me. I moaned even louder than before as we rode it out together, our bodies completely in sync.

When both of us calmed, he slid out of me and climbed into bed beside me, pulling me into his arms. He kissed my forehead as I turned and nestled into his chest. It didn't take long for me to drift off to sleep, and I could've sworn I heard him mumble, "I'm never letting you go again. You'll see. You're stuck with me forever."

I GLANCED at the television screen for the last time, checking my hair and outfit. I stared at Carter's jersey. The one he'd given me before we'd broken up. I wanted him to know I was committed to us, and this was the best way I knew how to show him.

"It's about damn time you two got back together." Leah lay on the couch and yawned. "If you two couldn't make it, then I had no hope for love."

I laughed. "Yeah, well, crisis resolved. I'd hate for you to lose hope." My heart pounded, and I played with the camera around my neck. I'd spent the night back at Carter's place, and he'd dropped me off here this morning, saying he needed to get to Nashville a little earlier than he'd thought to take care of something.

At first, it had taken me aback. We'd just reunited. But I had pushed him away, and I had to accept that maybe our relationship had changed because of it. I needed to work on myself for the two of us to get back to where we were before.

"Why aren't you riding with Carter?" Haven strolled into the living room with a cup of coffee.

"He needed to go early." I shrugged. "And besides, it's probably best we don't walk in together until he talks with his dad."

My phone dinged. Sadie was here.

I tried to push the nerves away and smiled. "I gotta go, but I'll be back later."

"You better be." Leah rolled her eyes. "Don't let him take you away without a goodbye."

I jogged out the door and slid into the passenger seat of Sadie's car.

She lifted a brow. "I was worried you might not come today after the drama yesterday."

"It'd be nice to hide." I shrugged. "But they've controlled me for far too long. I need to face them."

My phone went off again, and I glanced at the message.

Jack: Carter wants you to text me when you get here so I can meet you and Sadie outside. Don't stress, friend. I got you.

I rolled my eyes as Sadie pulled out and glanced at me again, lips pursed as she scanned me. "You seem chipper and look like you did your makeup. With that jersey you're wearing, I'm assuming you and Carter at back together? Did something happen with Carter? He stormed off not long after you left and everything went viral. If you aren't together, it's going to be awkward, showing up in that jersey."

I messed with my camera. "Yeah, we got back together."

Sadie chuckled. "Not surprising."

My brows furrowed. "That's what everyone keeps saying." Clearly, they'd seen things that I hadn't.

"Well, I'm just glad you two are back together." She smiled. "You deserve happiness, and he gives you that. It's like you two can't stand to be away from each other."

"That's not healthy though." I frowned.

She waved a hand. "Not true. You two can function apart. Look at the last few months. It's just a kind of love that doesn't exist for many. You two are lucky."

However, those four words didn't resonate as we reached Nashville. We parked, and I put on a jacket to fight the chill, but also so I didn't cause any problems for Carter and his dad while I was here. I'd show him I was wearing his jersey when we had a moment alone.

We started walking to the Bridgestone Arena, where a sizable group of reporters loitered in front of the dome. When one of the men saw us, he pointed at me and yelled, "The senator's secret daughter is here!"

I stopped in my tracks and texted Jack.

Me: SOS.

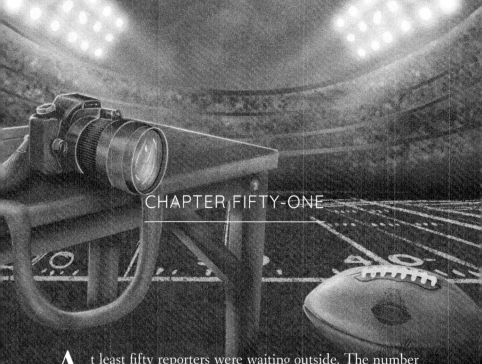

CHAPTER FIFTY-ONE

At least fifty reporters were waiting outside. The number didn't surprise me—signing day was a huge deal, especially in the South—but them pointing at me was a *huge* deal.

A light flashed, and someone else yelled, "Hey. The one person bigger than the draft is here!"

Then they raced toward me.

More lights flashed, and a woman reporter on the leading edge of the pack shoved a mic in my face. She asked, "Can you tell us how it feels to learn that you're not only the daughter of a *senator* but part of one of the richest families in the US?"

I froze, blinking. The last time I'd stood in front of reporters had been shortly after my parents' deaths, and they'd asked how it felt to have Senator McHale covering my tuition. My chest tightened. The first sign of a panic attack taking hold. I didn't know what to say or do, but one thing was true, I most definitely didn't want to be *here*.

"Hey!" Jack shoved his way through the crowd. "What the hell is wrong with you people?" He marched over to me and wrapped an arm around my shoulders. "She just learned about this last night and hasn't even had twenty-four hours to process. Go talk to the sister who truly loves the limelight—Katherine McHale."

A part of me wanted to step closer to Jack, but I suspected that might create more rumors. The last thing I wanted was for Carter and me to have to face another rumor about our relationship, even if it was false.

"Are you two dating?" the woman asked, her dark eyes widening.

"*Please.*" Jack rolled his eyes. "I'm not good enough for her, but you even thinking I am is the biggest compliment." He winked, which made her giggle.

I leaned close to his ear and murmured, "How about you help me get inside, and then you come out here to flirt with her?"

He smirked. "Why, Evie! Are you jealous?"

Now, *I* was the one rolling my eyes. "God, no. I just don't want them to keep taking pictures."

His eyes softened. "You got it." He dropped his arm and stepped forward, taking my hand behind him. "Stay close." And he began shoving through the people.

As we passed, more reporters shouted questions, but I kept my gaze firmly on Jack's back. I could see the muscles twitch, indicating that he wasn't as comfortable as he'd seemed earlier.

What felt like hours but was truly just a few minutes later, we stepped inside the doors that led to the arena. When Sadie slipped in behind us and the door shut, I stopped and took a deep breath.

"I thought they'd follow us inside." I was afraid that I wouldn't get a break the whole time.

Jack wrinkled his nose. "Only sports press is allowed inside. They're stuck out there."

I leaned against the cement wall. "So I'm safe until we leave." That was better than nothing.

"I'm not sure about that." Sadie frowned. "The sports reporters won't be as bad, but I wouldn't be surprised if they try to ask a few questions when they're able."

"Ugh." I thumped my head against the wall. "Seriously."

"Don't worry, E." Jack nodded toward the side where some stairs came into view. "That's why Carter asked me to get you."

"Thank you."

He booped my nose and replied, "That's what friends are for. Now come on. Carter's been worried about you."

The three of us headed up the stairs, and I gasped to see the seats filled in the arena as we headed to the more exclusive location. Jack didn't pause as we entered the Lexus Lounge. People began whispering when they saw me.

"We're over here." Jack led us past a bar to a section of the room where there were numerous wooden tables. He took the one closest to the door where Sadie's dad and Coach Bing, the team's offensive coach, sat in front of the pom-poms and banner that said HSU.

I'd taken off the lens and was preparing my camera, trying to focus on my task, when Carter and Senator Grisham strolled into the room and went to a black couch across from the coaches.

Carter's gaze landed on me, and he smiled. I understood the message without words; he was happy that I was here, even if it wasn't on the couch beside him.

I nodded and raised the camera, ready to get to work. I was surprised that no one else was with him besides his dad, but I was *hugely* relieved.

As I took pictures, a tall figure moved in my direction. I shifted a little bit so they could get by as someone else turned on the television in the corner. The draft had officially started.

"Evie," a way-too-familiar voice said.

I jerked my head toward him, confirming my worst fears.

Senator McHale, my biological father, stood beside me.

Unsure what to say, I cleared my throat.

It was almost as if Carter could feel my distress because he focused on me and stood.

Senator Grisham tugged on his son's arm.

My father cleared his throat. "Look, I know now isn't the time, but—"

"You're right." I needed to end this conversation before Carter did something he'd regret. The draft had started, and if he was first pick, then he needed to remain on camera. I cut my eyes toward Senator McHale, my voice sharp. "It's not. I need to work."

The senator's eyes widened, but then he nodded, taking a few steps back.

Carter arched a brow at me.

I nodded, and he sat back down. His dad glanced at me and frowned.

Having his family dislike me made the whole ordeal *so* much fun.

Murmurs grew louder around me, and I suspected it was because of the senator trying to talk to me. I tried to focus forward, and Jack and Sadie flanked me, blocking me from nearly everyone's view.

I didn't know what I'd do without them.

Getting back to taking photos, I lost myself in my work, taking shot after shot as the announcement went live.

The sportscaster on the television shouted, "Carter Grisham is the first draft choice, going to the San Francisco 49ers."

Everyone in the room clapped, and Carter's dad patted his

arm. However, Carter's eyes were locked on me. He mouthed, *I told you so.*

My stomach fluttered.

His coach and offensive coordinator both leapt to their feet, hugging and clapping Carter on the shoulder as sports reporters were finally able to descend on him.

Carter winked as he stepped out of the room and headed to the stage set in the main auditorium. I stayed put and watched on the large screen television as they showed clip after clip of his plays over the year. And then it showed him standing on stage with a 49ers jersey, shaking the head coach's hand.

Once that was settled, he headed off stage with the 49ers coaches, and then he made his way back to us. When he entered the room, one woman reporter, who had to be only a few years older than me, flipped her hair and glanced at the camera and then Carter. She said, "Carter, how does it feel to be the number one draft pick of the year?"

I snapped pictures, honored to be able to capture this moment for the school and for Carter.

Carter smiled. "A little surreal. I mean, I've worked my ass off, but if it hadn't been for my coach, teammates, family, and my girl, I would've never made it this far."

My hand froze. My heartbeat quickened, but I refocused on taking pictures.

"Your girl?" Another news reporter glanced my way. "You mean Senator McHale's illegitimate daughter?"

Beside me, Jack stiffened and snarled, "You mean the badass woman who doesn't put up with any of our shit? Yeah, this would be her." He wrapped an arm around my shoulders, making it difficult for me to take pictures.

"Any other questions?" Carter cleared his throat, bringing the attention back to him.

"Oh, yes!" A middle-aged man lifted a hand. "Are you excited to head to the Golden State of California?"

With the focus off me, I was able to snap pictures once again. Carter answered each question thoroughly, and I wouldn't be surprised if politics was in his future, considering how well he carried himself and spoke.

After a few minutes, the coach came up to him and patted his shoulder. "One last question, and we're done here."

The woman who had asked the first question asked another one. "Are you going to do something special to celebrate this occasion?"

"I'm going to do something even more special. The one thing that feels most right after everything we've gone through." He walked between the reporters, heading toward me.

I lowered my camera, and when he stood right in front of me, a lump formed in my throat. I had no clue what was going on, but I didn't like being the center of attention.

"Evie, the time we've spent together has been amazing. You make me stronger and a better person, and even when I tried to keep my distance from you, I couldn't. Something about you pulled at me, stripping me down to who I really am and revealing the incredible person you truly are." He licked his lips and took my hand in his. He continued, "The last three months without you have been hell, and learning why we were apart made me fall in love with you all over again. Made me realize that, no matter what, I need us to be together. I can't do this without you, and I don't want to. Not anymore."

"Damn straight you can't." Jack nodded. "She makes kick-ass lasagna. We can't risk losing that."

Normally, Carter would respond with his own snark, but instead, he reached into his pocket, removed a jewelry case... and bent down on one knee.

My breath caught, and the world spun. "What are you *doing?*" I squeaked.

"I'm making it clear that you're the one for me." He opened the case, revealing a three-carat round diamond with smaller diamonds circling the large stone. "We've hidden our relationship and allowed too many people to influence it, and I'm sick and tired of it all. I want the world to know that, no matter what, they can't separate us. I love you so much, and I can't live without you. I will fight each and every one of them to stay by your side."

"Son?" Senator Grisham sounded like he was choking.

I couldn't take my eyes off Carter.

"I want to wake up to you every single morning and hold you every night until we fall asleep." His eyes warmed to gold. "You're the person I need by my side for the rest of my life and the person I want to have children with. What I'm saying is, Evie Stone, will you marry me?"

Tears filled my eyes, and my hands shook. I would've never believed this would happen, yet the man I was head over heels in love with was in front of me on one knee. I nodded, unzipping my jacket. There was only one way to answer his question.

His brows rose.

Unzipped, I removed the jacket, and a cocky grin spread across his face as he took in what I was wearing.

Pictures flashed as I dropped the jacket to the ground, wearing his jersey proudly as a sob strangled me. "Yes."

He laughed, and Jack whooped loudly in my ear while Sadie exclaimed congratulations. Carter slipped the ring onto my finger and said, "Best fucking way for you to say yes."

When he kissed me, the world around us disappeared.

Then he led me into the smaller room he'd come out of just before the pick, away from the crowd. As we sat down on a small couch, I kept staring at the ring on my finger. I couldn't believe how it looked and what it must have cost him.

"What's going on in that pretty head of yours?" he asked, tucking a piece of my hair behind my ear.

I looked at him and said, "You just caught me by surprise. I never would've expected…"

"If you aren't ready—" he started, his brows furrowing.

"It's not that." I didn't want him to think that I was the problem. "Honestly, I hadn't thought about it, but when you asked, there was no doubt in my mind. I just hope you realize you didn't have to propose on draft day."

He smiled. "Babe, I didn't feel like I had to. After we got back together last night, seeing how our futures lined up perfectly without us even knowing, I realized that I never wanted to spend another second apart from you. Nothing felt more right than proposing to you. To have my dream complete with you promising to be my wife. I want the world to know that you and football are the two things that mean the most to me."

"Me *and* football." I arched an eyebrow. "You got lucky, naming me first."

"Oh, you definitely come first." He kissed my nose. "It'd hurt like hell to lose football, but being apart from you these past three months was worse than hell. It was unrelenting and unyielding."

"Well, you kinda can't get rid of me now." I leaned into him. "I take this ring very seriously."

"Then, dammit, I should've given it to you on Christmas before the whole thing exploded." He touched the ring. "That had been my original plan, but I thought that maybe I should wait so I could prove to my dad that you weren't a distraction instead of him blaming you more if I'd somehow messed up."

My head tilted back. "You were going to propose at *Christmas*?"

"Yeah, I realized you were the one over Thanksgiving." He nipped my bottom lip. "That's why I left this morning and didn't take you with me. I didn't want to risk you seeing me with it before this moment."

I arched a brow. "And Katherine and Mrs. McHale didn't have anything to do with the timing? You proving that you aren't scared of their threats?"

"It was an added benefit, but I would've done it either way." He wrapped an arm around my waist. "Now everyone knows you're mine and I'm off the market."

Carter suddenly stiffened, and he got up and moved so that I was hidden behind him.

Something was wrong.

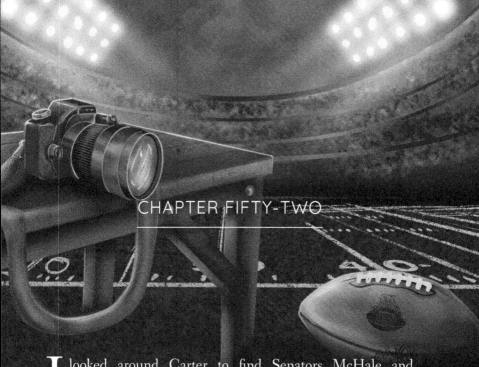

CHAPTER FIFTY-TWO

I looked around Carter to find Senators McHale and Grisham standing in the room. Slowly, I stood and moved to Carter's side.

My father had the decency to avoid my gaze while stuffing his hands into the pockets of his black slacks, but Senator Grisham wore a scowl.

He marched over and glared at me as he muttered, "We had an *agreement,* and you"—he pointed at his son and continued—"get your future handed to you, and then you propose to *her* within one minute? After knowing that she took a bribe to leave you?"

Carter tensed and tried to tuck me behind him, but I was tired of feeling broken. Tired of feeling like Carter needed to handle and protect me. Fuck that. I now knew that I could stand on my own two feet and that Carter wanted to be with *me.*

"I took the money you *forced* on me and gave it to the charity that Carter wanted it to go to. I didn't keep a dime." I lifted my chin, refusing to be intimidated. "I love your son. I want the best for him, and I'm willing to sign any prenup you get drafted by your lawyer to prove it."

Senator McHale stepped close to me and turned to Carter's father. "You're out of line. I struggled to even get Evie to accept the tuition for HSU. She didn't want to take my money, and every damn time I tried to pay for something extra, she shot me down. If you had come to me with your concerns, I would have set you straight from the beginning."

Senator Grisham's jaw dropped open before he shut it and nodded. "Regardless, Patrick, a prenup is an excellent idea. I'll get—"

"No, you won't." Carter shook his head, wrapping an arm around my waist. "She might be okay with it, but *I'm* not."

"Son, this is what she wants. She brought it up." He waved a hand in my direction.

Carter's harsh laugh startled me. However, his hand on my waist kept me grounded.

He took a step toward his dad and released my waist to take my hand instead. "Yes, Senator McHale paid for her school, but did you know that she rented a house with two local university girls and lived in the basement despite Patrick offering to cover her lodging? That she works five nights a week at a bar to cover rent and her school expenses while walking to and from the university and her job because she can't afford a car?"

My father turned to me. "Evie, why? I offered to help you."

"Don't get upset, Patrick. She's playing you too—Carter drove her everywhere." Senator Grisham rolled his eyes.

"Because I saw her walking in the dark, and I couldn't have her getting hurt on my conscience." Carter glanced at me, a tender smile spreading. "And I wouldn't trade those rides for the world because that's how we got to know one another."

"I don't understand." Senator McHale's eyes bulged. "When you said that you didn't want me to pay for your lodging, I was shocked, but I thought it was because you had enough money from selling Janet and Larry's house in Chattanooga to cover it. That place was easily worth two hundred thousand."

I tightened my hold on Carter's hand and took a ragged breath. "How do you know that?" I understood he was my biological father and had somehow figured out that I'd been in an accident. But for him to know my parents' names and how much their house was worth...it caught me off guard. It seemed ...*familiar*.

His brows furrowed. "Because when I was dating your mother, I came and visited them a few times while Janet still lived there with her parents. Janet and Larry kept the family home after your grandparents passed away. And for twenty-two years, Janet sent me monthly updates on how you were doing."

My head spun. "Wait. Mom kept you up to date on my activities, and she knew my biological mother?"

"Of course she did." Senator McHale chuckled a little too loudly as if he were uncomfortable. "They were closer than any two sisters I'd ever seen before."

Flashes of memories ran through my head. The way Mom would tell me about her sister and how she missed her and their parents. How her sister died far too young of natural causes, and my grandfather died of a heart attack a little while before my grandmother died of cancer. She'd always go on to say that I reminded her of Lizzy so much that it hurt—that even the way I wore my hair was similar. Now, those comments didn't seem so random. But why wouldn't she tell me that my biological mother was her *sister*?

"She didn't tell you?" Senator McHale's jaw dropped.

I shook my head. "I...I don't know why, but no." The world shifted under my feet, and the only thing keeping me steady was Carter beside me. "Why wouldn't she say something?"

"Because if she had, you might have gone digging and figured out who your biological father was." Carter's nose wrinkled. "What did you do to make them fear Evie finding out?"

"Nothing." Senator McHale held out both hands. "I told Lizzy that we had to take a break because my parents were upset about her getting pregnant. They told me if I married her, I'd have to kiss my trust fund goodbye. I told her that I needed time to figure out a way to provide for her and Evie. She was due any day." His eyes glistened as he rubbed his hands together. "The next day, I got the news that Lizzy had died giving birth. I thought you were both dead, and it destroyed me."

Acid burned my throat. I didn't want to hear more, but at the same time, things weren't adding up. "So you thought I died along with her? But you said you got updates."

He shook his head. "I thought I'd lost both of you, but then Janet called to tell me that they'd saved you, and I couldn't handle it. I couldn't handle losing Lizzy and then seeing you, knowing that you were half of her, so..."

I snorted bitterly. "You signed away your rights."

"I was young and naive, and the media was all over me. I realized Janet and your grandparents could give you a more stable life and keep you out of the spotlight. You'd have an actual childhood." Senator McHale ran a hand through his hair. "So I married Lisa since that's who my parents always wanted me to be with, and the rest is history. But Evie, I know you took your first steps at eleven months, loved taking pictures of the woods and animals, and that you graduated valedictorian from high school. Even if I wasn't in your life, I always knew you were okay."

Senator Grisham sighed. "Son, see, their story is the same

as mine. Her mother was broke and didn't fit in. I'm trying to save you from making a bad decision. I don't want you to suffer the same way I did."

"Lizzy didn't want me for my money." Senator McHale rubbed his temples. "She kept trying to talk me into leaving my family behind and starting a new life with her, even if we were broke, but I wanted to provide everything that she deserved. I wanted her to take over the world with me. Had I known the cost, I would've chosen differently."

Reality crashed over me. He'd truly loved my biological mother…and me. He even knew random facts that only Janet would know.

"Carter?" Coach Prichard called from the doorway. "Do you need anything?"

He shook his head and glanced at me. "No, Coach. I'm good. I just want to head home."

Coach Prichard raised his eyebrows, but Carter wrapped his arm around me. And once again, I realized I was home already because I was standing by his side.

I glanced at my ring, and for the first time, despite what I'd just learned, I truly believed that everything might actually turn out all right.

EPILOGUE

Four months later

Life flew by in a blur. Carter and I moved to San Francisco, and his father begrudgingly came to accept me. It helped that Carter and I eloped, getting married on a beach in Hawaii. Far enough from the water that it didn't remind me of my parents, and in a way, coming full circle, embracing my fears with Carter by my side.

I hated that we'd spent all that time apart since we loved one another, but I'd realized that I needed that time to face my fears. I'd been using him as a crutch. Now, I was healed enough to understand I could lean on him without worrying I wouldn't be able to control my panic and terror when he wasn't here beside me. His presence became part of my happiness and comfort instead of something I needed to survive. The difference might not have seemed huge to many, but it made my love for him all the more genuine.

After my first day of class, I strolled into our home on the outskirts of San Mateo, California. Unlike Tennessee, summer here wasn't unbearably hot.

The cream-colored, newly built house screamed *California*, and I pulled into our double garage and parked my white BMW sedan, which Carter had bought me as soon as we moved in, next to his SUV.

When I entered the house, my sneakers squeaked on the maple floors. The smell of garlic and tomato sauce hit my nose, making my stomach grumble.

I walked down the hallway and stepped into the kitchen.

Standing there in all his sexy glory was my husband.

Damn, that was still so hard to believe.

His hair was wet, bangs hanging over his forehead the way I liked, and his muscles flexed, bulging from his shirtsleeves. When his eyes met mine, they smoldered as he smirked.

I sniffed. "That smells good."

He lifted a hand. "Don't get too excited. This is my first attempt at making lasagna, but it seemed fitting with Jack visiting for a few days before his senior year at HSU and Patrick joining all of us for dinner."

Patrick.

I'd moved away from calling him Senator McHale and was now on a first-name basis. *Dad* didn't seem to fit...at least, not yet. I'd had one father who loved me, and he'd died. That didn't mean I couldn't have a relationship with Patrick. Or so my new therapist told me.

Between the felony charge against Lisa, who was now serving time in prison, and placing Katherine in a psych ward to get help, Patrick was trying to form a relationship with me—one that was surprisingly supportive—which was another reason Senator Grisham had come around. After all the stuff that Carter's mom had done, Carter had slapped a restraining order on her, not wanting her around either of us.

I sashayed over to my husband and wrapped my arms around his neck. He kissed me, pressing me against his body.

Though we were married and rarely apart, my need for him hadn't diminished. If anything, it'd gotten stronger.

He nipped my lips, confirming he was thinking the same thing.

"How was your first day?" he asked, pulling back but keeping me flush against his body.

"Good." I smiled, enjoying the moment between the two of us. "How was practice?"

"Awful." He snorted. "Jack harassed me from the stands. I think he's having girl trouble."

I arched a brow. "Girl? As in singular?"

"Yeah, that's what I've gathered from his grumbles and texts." He shrugged. "When he's not busy giving me hell."

"Well, we have about ten minutes before Patrick gets here, and Jack is nowhere in sight." I winked. "I say, while the food finishes cooking, we take a quick tour of our bedroom."

He chuckled, his hand sliding up my shirt. "Now I really like the sound of that." He leaned down and hoisted me into his arms, then darted toward our bedroom.

There was no doubt in my mind this was how Carter and I would be for the rest of our lives. We'd gone through difficult times and come out stronger. Now, we'd not only built a place for both of us, but we were each other's home and comfort. And nothing would ever change that.

We'd both make sure that we were in this together. Forever.

ABOUT THE AUTHOR

Brandy Silver is the sports romance pen name for *USA Today* Bestselling Author, Jen L. Grey, who writes Paranormal Romance, Urban Fantasy, and Fantasy genres.

The author lives in Tennessee with her husband, two daughters, and two miniature Australian Shepherds. Before she began writing, she was an avid reader and enjoyed being involved in the indie community. Her love for books eventually led her to writing. For more information, please visit her website and sign up for her newsletter.

Check out her future projects and book signing events at her website.
www.brandysilver.com

ALSO BY BRANDY SILVER

Hallowed Saints University (All Standalone)

Hidden Games

Fake Play

Printed in Great Britain
by Amazon